ONE NIGHT TO CHANGE THEIR LIVES

TINA BECKETT

FRIEND, FLING, FOREVER?

JANICE LYNN

MILLS & BOON

First Published in Great Britain 2019
by Mills & Boon, an imprint of HarperCollins*Publishers*
1 London Bridge Street, London, SE1 9GF

One Night to Change Their Lives © 2019 by Tina Beckett

Friend, Fling, Forever? © 2019 by Janice Lynn

ISBN: 978-0-263-26961-1

MIX
Paper from
responsible sources
FSC™ C007454

This book is produced from independently certified FSC™ paper
to ensure responsible forest management.
For more information visit www.harpercollins.co.uk/green.

Printed and bound in Spain
by CPI, Barcelona

ONE NIGHT TO CHANGE THEIR LIVES

TINA BECKETT

MILLS & BOON

To my family: here's to twists.

CHAPTER ONE

PEARLS WERE NOT her thing. Not anymore.

Adelina Santini dropped the necklace into its velvet lined jeweler's box, snapped the lid shut and put it in the growing stack of things to donate to the hospital's charity auction. Five years of marriage and the necklace and her wounded pride were the only things she had to show for it.

The bed had been stripped of sheets, pillows and the comforter—she'd jammed everything into the trash along with her wedding pictures. But even with brand-new bedclothes, she couldn't face sleeping in that room. So she'd spent the last six weeks sleeping on the couch, and that was where she'd stay until she could decide what to do about the bed, about the house…about everything. Divorce papers were filed and her soon-to-be ex had moved in with the woman she'd caught him cheating with—the same day she'd walked in on them. Getting rid of those pearls—his wedding gift to her—was the first step toward leaving an ugly part of her past behind. At least she hoped so.

All she wanted was to wash her hands of him and never see him again. But he was an EMT who regularly brought patients to her hospital. Unless she moved to another city, she would see him. Daily at times. So far, those encounters had been far from fun. There was no way she was going to let her distaste at seeing him drive her out of her job, though.

Abandoning her task for the hundredth time that week, she went to shower and get dressed for work. Right now, her job was her only salvation. The fact that she arrived before her shift started and left long after it was over was no one's business but her own. With that thought, she stepped under the stinging flow of hot water and waited for it to wash away all her troubles.

A half hour later, juggling five boxes of items for the auction, she walked through the doors of the emergency room of Miami's Grace Hospital and headed for the staff lounge to drop off what she'd brought. Five feet from the door, a familiar voice stopped her in her tracks.

"Dr. Santini, could I see you in my office for a minute?"

Peering over the stack, her eyes widened as she saw she was right. Garret Stapleton, the hospital administrator, stood with one shoulder propped against a nearby wall, arms crossed over his chest. A hint of biceps made a rare flush of warmth go through her.

Lord, Addy, what is wrong with you?

Then he moved toward her, and she took a quick step back, the parcels teetering for a second. The heat in her face turned red hot.

"Let me help you with those."

"It's okay. I've got them. Just a few things for the auction."

Why did he want to talk to her? Had she done something wrong? She'd been at this hospital for several years—longer than he had, in fact. And ever since her husband had walked out, her view of the world had shifted, opened up. That view now encompassed the sexy administrator in a way that made her cringe.

In her growing panic, the boxes tilted sideways, the jeweler's container sliding off and falling to the floor. The lid popped off and the pearl necklace spilled onto the tile.

Yikes!

Dr. Stapleton reached down and scooped up the necklace with his right hand, letting it dangle from his fingertips. He peered at it, a frown puckering his brow. "These are real."

She swallowed. "I—I know."

"This is for donation?"

"It is. Just clearing out five years of debris." The words tumbled out faster than she meant for them to, and the frown swung her way.

He nodded at the rest of the boxes. "Any other valuable 'debris' in there?"

"No."

"I think I'll put this in my office safe for security's sake." He paused. "And in case you change your mind, you should probably have them appraised, if you haven't already."

"I won't change my mind." She didn't tell him why, but hopefully he could read the conviction in her voice.

He opened the door to the staff lounge and waited while she put the rest of her items onto the table with the others. By now her legs were shaking. She'd hoped to leave everything there without anyone seeing her. But he was right. It was probably better to safeguard the pearls than to leave them lying around, not that she thought anyone on staff would take them. At least the hospital would benefit from her mistake.

Speaking of mistakes, did she really want to sit in his

office on a day her eyes had trailed over the muscles in his arms?

Turning to face him, she asked, "What was it you needed to talk to me about?"

"Let's go into my office."

Ugh. There was no getting out of it. And it sounded serious. The last thing she needed right now was "serious."

Garret Stapleton stretched the fingers of his left hand and winced as the act pulled tendons and ligaments that were tight from disuse. He knew better than to try to grip the lock to his safe with the twisted digits. Or a scalpel.

Why were his thoughts heading in that direction today?

He knew. And he'd be damned if he'd sit back and let someone else make the same mistake he did. He'd heard what had happened with Addy, even though he did his best not to listen to the rumors that floated around. He was sure there were plenty out there about him and his hand.

The "five years of debris" comment made him think that those donations had something to do with her marriage. He shifted the long flat box so that it was under his left forearm as he quickly turned the tumbler right and then left, opening the safe. Then he took the box and slid it on top of a set of files. His files. Files that mapped out what his own errors had cost him.

"Have a seat."

She skirted one of the leather chairs and folded herself into it.

Was she thinner than when he'd first arrived in South Beach three years ago? Or maybe he was imagining things.

"I'm not sure what this is about."

"Aren't you?"

She tipped her head, sending several locks of dark hair cascading over one shoulder.

Maybe calling her into his office to have this conversation wasn't such a good idea after all. But where else could he do it? Certainly not in the staff lounge.

The thumb of his damaged hand scrubbed over his pinkie finger; he wasn't quite sure how to approach this. But if he didn't drop the ax and something happened… "Whenever a doctor's name appears on a chart, it's entered into the system. If the computer finds a disparity between assigned hours and actual hours worked, it sends up a red flag. Do you want to guess how many flags you've generated in the last several weeks?"

"I've had a lot of free time and so I—"

"Try again." He softened the words with a smile. He didn't want to come across as a game warden.

Her chin went up and green eyes flashed. "Why are you asking those questions? If you have a problem with my work, surely that's a matter for Human Resources."

"Normally I'd say you were right and shoot it up to them. But the Emergency Department is the heart of Miami's Grace Hospital. So it's important to me. To the entire hospital."

"My working a few extra hours would help that cause, I would think."

"Yes. One would think. But that's not always the case." He dropped his hand behind the desk, unwilling to use it as an example of what could happen unless he absolutely needed to. "I need you to be at your best."

"I haven't been?"

"You've been a huge asset to this hospital. I'm sure you know that. I don't want one of our best doctors burning out or going elsewhere."

"I have no plans of going anywhere. At the moment, anyway." Her eyes dipped to the edge of his desk before coming back up to meet his.

She *was* thinking about leaving.

"Are you having a problem on the floor? Is someone making life difficult?"

"You mean other than you?" She flashed a grin that traveled all the way to her eyes, crinkling the corners in a way that made his insides clench. But when he didn't smile back, her mouth went back to neutral. "No. Of course not."

"Why the sudden jump in hours, then?" He forced himself to concentrate on the subject at hand. There was no way she could deny that her habits had changed. He might be treading into forbidden territory, but it was his job to make sure this hospital maintained its reputation for providing stellar care.

She hesitated. "I'm going through a personal crisis right now. I just need to work through it, and this is the best way I can think of to do that."

The familiar ring of those words made him tense. He'd gone through a personal crisis of his own a few years back. "Anything you care to share?"

Her head came up, neck turning a dark shade of red. "No. Yes…" There was a long pause, as if she was struggling to figure out a way to tell him something. "I'm divorcing my husband, and things have been difficult."

He sat back in his chair, relief washing through him that her crisis had nothing to do with him. Not that he was happy she was getting a divorce, but the way she'd backed away from him when he'd tried to help her with those boxes had set an alarm off in his head. He'd racked his brain thinking of something he might have done to make her uneasy around him, but had come up empty.

"A divorce."

Okay, so the matter-of-fact way he'd said that had probably sounded crass and unfeeling. He hadn't meant it to. After all, he'd been through a divorce himself and had lived to tell the tale.

"I'm not sure how my hours are a problem as long as I'm not endangering anyone."

He leaned forward. "Sometimes you don't realize you are until it's too late."

"Are we talking about me? Or are we talking about your hand?"

"Excuse me?" Only then did he realize that his injured hand was resting on his desk, the almost useless fingers curled into a ball.

"I'm sorry. I shouldn't have said that."

She was right. She shouldn't have. Except the reason he'd asked her to step into his office had more to do with him than it did with her, and she'd just called him on it. He lifted his hand, turning it over and studying it for a few seconds. "Actually you're right. I did call you in because of this. You've heard about what happened?"

"You know the grapevines. Not much escapes them."

"Ah. I imagine not. And calling you in here isn't personal. It's professional. I don't want to see anyone else ruin their career by working themselves to exhaustion."

"I know my limits."

He smiled to cover the churning in his gut caused by those words. He'd thought he'd known his limits too. How wrong he'd been. "Sometimes we only think we do."

"Believe me, I have no desire to jeopardize something I love more than anything."

He hadn't wanted to either. But once Leticia died…

Swallowing, he stood. "I just wanted to bring it to your attention and ask you to stick to a more sensible schedule."

She laughed and climbed to her feet as well, tossing those wild errant locks back over her shoulder. "I think 'doctor' and 'sensible schedule' are incompatible terms, don't you? Are you going to write me up?"

"Do I need to?"

"I hope not, but that's your prerogative. You can even fire me, if you want. I can always practice somewhere else."

And now he could bring up an earlier thought. "You're already thinking of doing just that, though, aren't you? Leaving?"

There was a long pause. "I hope it won't come to that. My—ex—works for the EMT company that services this area. If he makes things difficult, I might choose to move."

He took a step closer, gratified when she stood her ground this time. "How can I help? The hospital, that is."

"You can't. It's something I have to work through myself. I'll either be able to face him and move on, or I won't. Our parting was not the most amicable in the world."

That made him frown. "Let me know if he causes trouble."

"I think he's caused all the trouble he can. The sooner the divorce goes through, the better." Fingers fiddled with a small gold ball that clung to the delicate lobe of her right ear. Something contracted in his chest.

She allowed her hand to drop back to her side, standing straight and tall. "I'm sure the last thing you want to hear today is someone moaning about their impending divorce."

He glanced back at the safe.

Before he could even give voice to the question, she nodded. "Yes. He gave it to me. And all of those other items as well."

"Ah, understandable. I still think it should be appraised. I can have that done if you'd like."

"It's up to you. I won't want the necklace back no matter what its value."

He glanced at her hand. No rings anymore, but the indentation was still there. "I'm sorry. About your breakup."

"Thank you." She shoved her hands in the pockets of her pants. "Now, if there's nothing else…"

"No. Nothing. Just keep an eye on those hours, okay?"

"I will. Thanks for bringing it to my attention."

Walking over to the door, he held it open and waited as she walked through it. "Oh, and, Dr. Santini."

"Call me Addy."

He nodded. "Addy, then. Thank you for the donations. The hospital appreciates them."

How was that for impersonal? Maybe he'd sounded canned and overly formal, but he didn't like the way he was suddenly noticing little things about her.

"I'm glad someone will be able to use them."

Because she wouldn't. He shut the door and went back around his desk. Giving his damaged hand one last glance, he sat in his chair and tried to lose himself in his work. But Addy's face—and that damned gold earring— kept circling through his thoughts. He hoped she came through her crisis unscathed. And that it wouldn't cost her something a lot more valuable than a set of pearls.

* * *

Two days later a piece of mail caught her attention. It was from the hospital. Her breath stalled in her chest. She'd done her best to cut back on her hours, but knew she'd still stayed on the floor longer than she should have.

Sliding her finger under the tab, she was surprised when a single sheet of paper fell out—a handwritten note containing only seven words:

Two thousand dollars appraised—are you sure?

The signature was Garret Stapleton's. A shiver went over her as she sat and stared at his handwriting for a few seconds. Bold strokes crossed those Ts. She touched a finger to one of them, then gritted her teeth.

She knew exactly what he was referring to. The necklace. She wasn't shocked by the price tag. What she was surprised at was that he'd written to her personally. And at the funny twist to her stomach when she'd opened the envelope and realized who it was from.

But at least he hadn't called her back into his office to break the news to her. Their last meeting had made her squirm. Maybe because she'd called attention to his hand, when she hadn't meant to. She'd gone all defensive, trying to deflect his attention to something other than her.

He'd been right to chew her out. But he hadn't needed to. She did know her limits. And she loved her job too much to risk driving while exhausted. Which was why she'd been known to leave her car in the parking lot and take a taxi.

Did he call every single doctor who worked overtime into his office? She didn't think so. Which meant he had seen some kind of warning sign.

She'd heard that the fiery crash that damaged his hand

had almost cost his life as well. That thought made her heart ache. He'd been one of the best neurosurgeons in the country. And it had all been snatched away in a split second. He'd then gone from New York City to the shores of South Beach.

Why so far away?

Maybe, like her, he'd felt he needed a change of scenery. A new start. Maybe she needed to do the same—like go from South Beach to New York.

Except she was a Florida girl. Born to a family of Italian immigrants, but a true surfer girl at heart. With her dark hair, she didn't exactly look the part, but she didn't care. Those waves had coaxed her back to the water time and time again.

In fact, she'd met Leo Santini during a surfing contest five years earlier, when she'd been undergoing another crisis—with her mom, this time—and had fallen in love. Looking back, she realized their quick romance had been a desperate attempt on her part to claw her way out of a dark hole, but the effort had backfired. As her mom's condition had continued to deteriorate, their marriage had begun to change gears too. Their surfing trips had dwindled to nothing over the space of a year. She still caught an occasional wave, but Leo had turned in his board for the party scene, something she had no interest in at all. She should have seen the breakup coming. Talk about warning signs. She'd missed them all.

But no more.

Maybe she needed to take her board and head to the beach on Wednesday, her next day off. Then her boss wouldn't be able to say a word about her working too many hours. And maybe it would clear her head and help her find her equilibrium again. Just the thought made her pulse pick up its pace. How long had it been since she'd paddled through the surf, looking for that one great wave?

Too long. That was what she'd do.

Taking a pen, she sat down and crafted her reply to Garret. And she could do it in fewer words than he had: "Very sure." Rather than mail it, she would drop it on his desk. In person. Probably not a good idea, but it was the best way she knew to make the break from Leo definitive, not that it wasn't already.

Shoving the note back into its envelope, she hurried to get ready for the day. Then tonight she would drag her surfboard out of the spare bedroom and check the weather in hopes that conditions—in more ways than one—were perfect.

CHAPTER TWO

THE EMERGENCY ROOM wasn't as busy as it normally was. Sometimes the room was full, medical personnel running back and forth. But it was still early, and the hospital was exceptionally good at triage. His hospital in New York had also had a great quick-response team that could handle multiple trauma cases at the drop of a hat. That attention to skill and speed had probably saved his life after his accident, even though he could only remember bits and pieces of what happened.

Winding his way through the space as he often did on Monday mornings, he mentally kept track of what he saw. He'd made it a habit to visit a different department at the beginning of every workday. Not so much to check up on everyone as to make sure people felt comfortable approaching him. That they felt as if they were being heard.

The last thing he wanted was to be one of those aloof bosses that sat in his office issuing edicts and making sure everyone followed them to the letter. He wanted people to stay at the hospital because they wanted to, because it had an atmosphere that was conducive to sticking around.

Which was why when he'd sensed Addy might want to move on, he'd reacted so strongly. Right?

The emergency-room doctor had caught his attention,

and not just because of her hours. Her colleagues talked as if she were some kind of superhero.

Was he sure that wasn't why he was here now? To make sure the hospital's star player wasn't going to burn herself out?

Or was it more personal than that?

Nope. It was Monday. He was simply sticking to routine.

And the envelope he'd found on his desk this morning? She'd arrived even before he had. Had she not heard a single word he'd said?

Nodding to a staff member who made eye contact, he suddenly wondered if he should have skipped coming down here. He didn't want Addy to think he was seeking her out.

Because he wasn't.

Pivoting on his heel, he almost ran over the very person he was now hoping to avoid.

"Dr. Stapleton." Her wide eyes and breathless tone made him smile. Okay. So maybe it wasn't just him feeling awkward.

"Garret, remember? Everyone else calls me by my given name."

"Oh. Of course." She glanced at the electronic file-storage device still in her hands. "Did you get my note?"

"You mean the one that was lying on my desk when I arrived?"

"I always get here at six." Her quick response was defensive, and her eyes came up to meet his. "I'm off on Wednesday, though. I'm actually planning on surfing."

"Surfing as in the internet?"

Her head cocked sideways. "No. Surfing as in at the beach." Her hand twirled through the air. "In the ocean. Catching waves."

"You—surf?" A quick image of Addy flashed through his skull. A wetsuit? Or, worse, a bikini? He suddenly wished he hadn't asked her to clarify her response.

Up went her brows. "This is South Beach. Doesn't everyone?"

"I haven't taken a survey recently."

She laughed. "Sorry. I just thought that most Floridians... Oh, wait. You're from New York. Sorry. Coming here must have been a big change for you."

His imaginings died a painful death.

"Not as big as other changes." His hand curled next to his side. Why had he just said that? "Both places have a lot of people. And a need for good medical care."

"Of course." She hesitated. "Do you still do consulting at all?"

"Sorry?"

"On cases. I had a head trauma come in the other day and the neurologist on duty was tied up in surgery. It took a little longer to get the patient evaluated than I would have liked."

"Did it change the outcome?"

"The patient didn't make it. But no, the outcome probably would have been the same. But it would be nice to know there's someone else I can call if the need arises."

His jaw tightened. No one at Miami's Grace had asked him that question before. Which was another reason he'd relocated. If people didn't think of him as a neurosurgeon, they wouldn't treat him like one. Did he really want to open that door? Then again, did he want to risk a patient's life by refusing?

"I don't do surgery anymore." Said as if he still could. So why hadn't he said "can't"? Maybe because he hadn't quite faced the fact that he would never again use a scalpel to excise a brain tumor.

Addy frowned. "I realize that. So you're not willing to consult? I just want to be clear so that I don't keep that as an option."

"I'm available if you need me." And just like that, it was out there. Not exactly the way he'd envisioned this conversation going. He'd been all set to chastise her for flouting his request that she moderate her hours, and she'd ended up subtly chastising him for putting himself above their patients.

And she was right. His embarrassment over his hand did drive some of his decisions. Including being the motivating factor behind calling her into his office a few days ago. It had nothing to do with her patients—or even her well-being—and everything to do with him.

That had to change. Starting now.

"Thank you, Dr.—I mean Garret. You won't regret it."

He already did, but he wasn't going to tell her that. Instead, he nodded at the tablet in her hand. "Nothing neurological this morning?"

"Not so far. Just a gator hunter who shot a hole in his boat. But not before the bullet went through his buddy's foot."

His brows shot up. "Well, I can't remember seeing anything like that at my last hospital."

"You didn't have hunters in New York?"

He thought of the gangland shootings and senseless loss of life. "We did. But they tended to hunt a different kind of prey, and when they shot someone, it wasn't an accident."

"We have that here too." She sighed. "I wish people were different. Kinder."

"There are still some good ones out there." Addy was one of those good ones. He could see it in her work ethic, in the fact that she cared enough about her patients to risk a firm refusal when she'd asked him to consult on cases.

Sometimes, with hospital politics in play, it was easier to just go with the flow and try not to make waves. But that wasn't always what was best for the patient. Here was someone who was not only willing to make waves, but more than willing to swim against the current. Well, surfers had to do that each time they took their boards into the water, didn't they? She was just doing what came naturally.

"Yes, there are. Some of those good ones even come from New York City." She gave a smile that lit up her dark green eyes. Eyes that met and held his for long seconds.

He swallowed. She didn't know him very well. Because if she did, she'd know he wasn't good. Not by a long shot.

But even as he thought it, a warmth seeped into his chest that had nothing to do with a defect in the hospital's climate control system. It had been a while since someone had handed him a compliment that didn't originate with his position at the hospital. He wasn't quite sure what to do with it.

Better just to ignore it. And the way that her smile messed with something inside him.

"So what happened to the man in the boat? The one who was shot?" he asked.

"What didn't happen to him? He fell overboard right after the bullet hit him, dousing his foot with swamp water. Then once back in the boat, he had to bail more water, while his friend drove them back to shore, giving his foot another good dunking." Her smile widened, and it kicked straight to areas best left alone. "So we soaked it with the good stuff, shot him full of antibiotics and updated his tetanus booster."

"Poor guy. And it wasn't even his fault."

"No, it wasn't. I don't think he and his friend are on speaking terms at the moment."

Eyes that had seemed tired and defeated during the meeting in his office now sparkled with life and laughter. He liked the transformation. He tried imagining her with a surfboard under one arm, water streaming down her back, her dark hair wet and tangled from riding in to shore. That was another transformation he'd like to see. And one he wasn't likely to.

"I imagine they're not." He tried to turn the conversation around before he ended up showing the cards in his hand. Cards he had no business holding at all. "Anyway, about the appraisal. I'll let the person in charge of the auction know about the necklace."

"Good. I was hoping to drop it off without making a big production out of it."

That wouldn't have happened. "We would have put a notice in the staff newsletter asking for information, just in case the donor had no idea as to its value."

Her eyes widened. "I'm glad that's not how things went, then."

"I can understand that. Now. Its presence at the auction isn't going to complicate things for you, is it?"

"I doubt my ex will even attend, so no. It was a wedding gift from him to me, so it's mine to give away. Just like our marriage was his to give away." She wrinkled her nose. "Sorry. I don't know why I said that."

He waited for a nurse to go past, lowering his voice. "He cheated?"

A single nod. "How else do you throw a marriage away?"

He could think of lots of ways. One of which he'd done. Or maybe it had been inevitable, once they'd lost their daughter to a disease that was as relentless as it was deadly.

"Did you try counseling?" He often wondered if he could have saved his marriage if he'd suggested that earlier, before it had been too late. Instead, he'd become unreachable, staying away from home as much as possible.

"Counseling. Right. Would that have been before or after he slept with a mutual friend? Or moved in with her once I discovered what they were doing—had been doing for almost a year."

"Ouch. Sorry." The one thing he'd never done during the whole grieving process was turn to someone else. He'd been so destroyed, so emotionally empty that he'd had nothing to give to anyone else, not even his wife.

None of that had changed with time, and he wasn't sure he wanted it to. The divorce had been his fault—he could acknowledge that now. Some people just didn't deserve second chances.

"It's okay. I knew on some level something was wrong. He was unexpectedly called into work a lot of nights—which now I see probably wasn't the case. Even when he came home, he wasn't really 'there,' if that makes sense. I was dealing with some issues of my own, but if I'd suspected he was that unhappy, I would have done something. Before it got to the point it did."

Garret, on the other hand, had been able to see the slow slide of his marriage and had chosen to do nothing… except put in grueling hours at work. His wife had left him after the accident, while he'd still been in the hospital, saying she wasn't going to watch him throw his life away. She was right. He had been. He'd gotten counseling afterward, had tried to convince her to go with him, but she'd refused. And that had been that. Papers had been waiting for him at the house where they'd raised their daughter. Within weeks he'd sold the place, resigned from his practice, and, after a year of surgery on his hand and physical therapy, the offer from Miami's Grace Hospital had come up and he'd decided to make the move to Florida. But at least his divorce hadn't been as a result of either of them cheating.

"I'm sorry he put you through that."

"It's over. I'm kind of relieved, actually. I'm my own person again."

"A person who surfs in her spare time."

She glanced at him. "You've really never tried it?"

"Nope. Not ever. Is it like snow skiing?"

"Um, no." A quick laugh. Although the falling part might be similar. "Why don't you come with me on Wednesday and see?"

"Excuse me?"

She blinked as if not quite sure what had just happened. "My bad. You're probably not even interested in surfing. Forget I said anything."

Addy was asking him to go to the beach with her? The previous image he'd had began tickling at the edges of his consciousness again. Wetsuit? Or bathing suit? He was a jerk for even letting those kinds of thoughts bounce around his head. "I'm interested in a lot of things."

And that was better?

"So you *want* to go?"

Better that than admit it wasn't surfing that was on his mind.

"Possibly. What time, so I can see if I can juggle my schedule?"

She pursed her lips and studied him, maybe sensing he wasn't being entirely honest with her, then tucked the tablet under her arm and pulled out her phone. She scrolled for a second.

He wasn't sure what she was doing. "Do you want to text me the time?"

"I'm looking right now. Okay, we want low tide, just as it's coming in. Looks like the wind direction will be good as well."

She could have been speaking a different language. "And can you find an actual time somewhere in there?"

"You don't have a board, I take it."

"Not of the surfing variety, no." A flicker of enthusiasm colored her voice and it lit a matching one in him. How long had it been since he'd actually gone anywhere with a woman? It wasn't a date. But it could be fun. He was allowed to have fun, wasn't he?

"It's okay. We can rent a board."

"Whoa." He held up a hand. "I'm not planning on climbing on a surfboard. I was just going to watch."

Like a voyeur.

"You don't even want to paddle out? You don't have to stand up, if you don't want to. You'll be bored if you just sit on the beach."

Doubtful. He turned his scarred hand so she could see it. "I'm not exactly able to use this the way most people can."

"It'll be fine. Believe me. There are surfers who are missing limbs and still get out there and catch plenty of waves."

He was pretty sure he wasn't going to be one of them, but he didn't feel like arguing the point with hospital staff passing them in the hallway. "So what time would we need to leave?"

"Do you want to meet at the beach or here at the hospital?"

"Beach." The word came out without hesitation. He had no idea if she'd be wearing a bathing suit under her clothes, but he certainly didn't want to meet out front if she was only wearing some kind of cover-up. The gossip chain would have a field day with it. And there was no way he was showing up in board shorts.

"Okay. Well, the tide should be right and the shops open at around ten a.m. Can you swing it if we meet a half hour before that? We'll want to go over some basics. Or you could take a class."

"No. No classes. I don't plan on making a career out of surfing. But yes, I should be able to make time to come out."

"I think you'll like it." She grinned. "Even if you don't plan on making a career out of it."

She tucked her phone back in her pocket and held up her electronic file. "Well, I'd better get back to something that actually is my career. I'll see you Wednesday at nine thirty?" She suggested the name of a local surf shop as their meeting place.

"I'll be there." He wasn't sure why or how this had happened, but it had. And there was no way he was going to back out and be stuck explaining that his reasons involved a mental tug-of-war over her choice of beach attire. "Anything special I need to bring?"

"Nope. Just yourself and some swim trunks."

Swim trunks. She'd just cemented every reservation he'd ever had about Wednesday's trip.

Instead of swim trunks, maybe he should settle for bringing along what was left of his sanity. Because going to the beach with her was not on his list of smart ideas. In fact, it might just be the dumbest thing he'd ever agreed to. But it was too late to do anything but own his decision… and hope for the best.

* * *

Addy pulled her surfboard out of the walk-in closet and ran her hand over the smooth, glossy surface. What had she been thinking asking Garret to go with her? Being with him was hardly going to fill the ticket of taking some time for herself.

She was on edge around him. Had been ever since he'd come to the hospital three years ago. She'd just been careful, because, unlike her husband, her marriage had been important to her.

And look where that had gotten her. Maybe she should have been the first to have an affair.

Her nose crinkled. Not that Garret would have agreed to be her partner in crime. Besides, it wasn't in her to cheat. She was loyal to a fault. It showed in her friendships, and she'd thought in her marriage.

Except that had all been an illusion. Like the perfect wave. It teased and beckoned you to paddle out and see what it was all about. Only it was rarely as glorious as it looked from the shallows. Up close you saw the imperfections and the flaws hidden within the turbulent whitewater.

And a surfboard was incomplete without a wave, just as a marriage was incomplete without trust. That was something she'd never get back again, even if she'd allowed Leo to stay and they'd gone to counseling as Garret had suggested.

And there was the fact that, once discovered, he'd moved right in with his lover.

Oh, well. That part of her life was over. At least it would be once the divorce was final. The sooner the better.

Picking the board up, she set it on the forbidden bed. She gritted her teeth and forced that thought from her mind. Tomorrow if she had time, she'd wax the board up and get it ready for its first outing since her ex had moved out. Garret was right. She had been working too hard. But the alternative was nights like tonight when she had nothing to do but think. And that wasn't good.

All she had to do was get through this evening, and then tomorrow morning she could work her shift, come home again and on Wednesday she'd be out on the water. Not alone, but out there just the same.

She wasn't sure why she'd asked Garret to go with her, but now that she had, she was relieved. Having him there would keep her from backing out and sitting at home brooding the day away. Because she didn't dare show up at work. He would have her head.

It was up to her to show him that she knew how to cut loose and have fun.

Or at least pretend to. Because deep down inside, with everything that was currently going on in her life, she was pretty sure she was going to be anything but a fun date.

No. Not a date. This was an outing. To prove a point.

How did that saying go? Fake it until you make it? Well, she'd better start faking being a fun-time girl, and soon. Or Garret was going to figure out the little secret that she'd been hiding.

What secret was that? That she had eyes for her boss?

She gulped. No, she didn't. And it was up to her to prove that once and for all. If not to him, to herself.

CHAPTER THREE

ADDY SNATCHED THE brochure from the information desk at the front of the hospital in dismay. Oh, Lord, she hoped Leo didn't somehow see this.

And if he did, would it matter?

No, not at all. But she hadn't wanted a lot of attention placed on her. Maybe she'd better make sure she emphasized to Garret that she wanted that donation kept as anonymous as possible. Marching to the elevators, she got in and pressed the button for the fourth floor. She had no idea what she expected him to do about this, but she'd at least like an assurance that her name wouldn't be attached to the pearls.

Going to the door, she knocked and waited for him to respond. When he called for her to come in, she saw that he was with another doctor. Jake Parson, the pediatrician from the first floor.

"Dr. Santini, what can I do for you?"

Oh, so they were back to titles again. She gritted her teeth. Of course they were. It wasn't as if Garret were going to greet her like a long-lost friend. They weren't friends. They were colleagues.

Actually, they weren't. He was her boss, even though it didn't quite work like that in this type of setting.

And she was taking her so-called boss surfing. Another possibly messy situation, if not handled the right way.

Unfortunately, she had no idea what the right way was.

"I didn't know you were with someone. It can wait." Realizing the auction brochure was still in her hand, she tried to shift it so it was hidden behind her leg. She certainly didn't want to talk about this in front of anyone else.

"Jake and I were just finishing up."

Hmmm, okay, so he used Dr. Parson's first name, but not hers?

Maybe realizing he'd been dismissed, the other man stood, throwing her a quick smile as he shook Garret's hand and slid past her with a murmured goodbye.

Once the door closed, Garret came around the side of his desk, nodding in the direction of her hand. "What didn't you want him to see?"

So he *had* noticed.

Now that she was here, she felt kind of idiotic. He more than likely had nothing to do with the marketing division of the hospital's fund-raising events.

"It's the pamphlet for the auction."

"May I see it?"

She gulped. It was obvious he didn't have a stack of them lying around his office. He probably hadn't even seen one yet. Hesitating, she finally pulled the brochure from behind her and held it out for him to take.

A soft whistle sounded as he glanced at the cover. Then he looked up. "I didn't know they were going to put this on the front."

"Neither did I." He'd put the pearls in his safe, so he had to have helped set up the picture, but from his reaction he'd had nothing to do with the photo's placement.

"Is there any way you can make sure my name is not attached to them?"

"Is this because of your ex?" He frowned. "I can have the pamphlets recalled, ask them to be redone, if you want. I'm not even sure how they came up with these so quickly."

"No, it has nothing to do with Leo. I'm feeling a little ridiculous even bringing this up here actually. It was just a shock to see the necklace front and center."

"Don't worry. I'll make sure your name isn't listed anywhere. I think the pearls were easier to capture in a simple photo than some of the other donations." He flipped the top page open. "Although they did put some of the cruises on the inside."

He glanced up. "They're not family heirlooms or anything whose ownership can be contested, are they?"

"No. He bought them at a jewelry store." She held up a hand. "And don't ask me if I'm sure again. Once I make up my mind you'll find I don't change it easily."

He made a pained sound in the back of his throat. Before she could ask what it meant, though, he said, "Can I keep this copy?"

"Of course." She gave a wry smile. "There are plenty of them around the hospital, I imagine."

Garret indicated the chair the other doctor had vacated moments earlier. "Have a seat."

"Don't tell me I'm in trouble again. I've tried to keep my hours to pretty much what I've been assigned."

"No, I actually wanted to talk about tomorrow."

Tomorrow?

Oh, the surfing trip. Suddenly she just knew he'd changed his mind about going. A wave of disappointment crashed over her before she could stop it.

You should be glad!

She lowered herself into her chair and braced herself for the news.

"You do realize I'm almost forty, don't you?"

She blinked, not sure where he was going with this. Oh, Lord, he hadn't guessed about that weird little crush she was developing, had he? She was in the middle of a divorce, for heaven's sake. The last thing she should be doing was scoping out his broad shoulders and the way his waist gave way to narrow hips. Except she found herself doing just that. And more.

Even his damaged hand held an odd attractiveness. Maybe because it belonged to him. And this particular "him" had a lot of physical attributes going for him. Attributes she'd noticed against her will.

It was because she was almost single again and Garret was the first hunky man she'd interacted with since her breakup. It had to be that. She *prayed* it was that.

Yes, she'd been looking forward to seeing him on a board and no amount of self-recriminations were going to change that.

Time to ask where he was headed with that particular question before her thoughts went even more haywire. "What does almost being forty have to do with tomorrow?"

If he warned her off him, she was going to slink away, never to be seen again.

"Let's just say I'm a little less sturdy than I used to be." Sturdy? *Sturdy?*

That was where the crack about his age had come from?

She laughed out loud. Partly in relief. Partly in disbelief.

Up went his brows. "I didn't expect that news to be quite so funny."

"It's not that." She struggled to catch her breath before it betrayed her in another fit of giggles. "You do realize that I'm only five years away from being forty, don't you? So I could take your words as an insult to all of us who are over thirty."

"You don't look thirty-five."

Oh, God. Did he think she looked older? But how to ask…?

"Do I look *more* sturdy? Or less?"

This time, he was the one to laugh, his chuckle rushing across her like a warm sea current, curling around her toes and almost pulling her feet out from under her. She put her arms on her chair as if the tug might be real.

"Do you really want to know?" he asked.

"I *thought* I did. Surely you have access to the hospital staff members' personnel records."

"I do. And you look much younger, although I realize very few doctors make it out of medical school before their late twenties and then with specializing and residency…"

"Well, I'd like to think I'm pretty sturdy for my age, and I bet you are too. At least if a surfer falls, he lands on a more forgiving surface than, say, a frozen mountain."

"I guess we'll see, won't we?"

The phone in her pocket buzzed. She pulled it out, glanced at the readout and frowned. "It's the nurses' station." She pressed Talk and put it on speaker. "Santini, here."

"Addy, we have a family who's been involved in a house fire. They're en route as we speak. Five people, one adult, four children, one of them an infant."

"How bad?" Addy knew it could be anything from smoke inhalation to third-degree burns.

"Two burn victims, but I don't know the extent of it. ETA ten minutes."

"I'm on my way. Call Dr. Hascup and see if he can come in. And make sure we have some rooms ready." Having a doctor there from the hospital's burn unit was a must.

She ended the call and glanced at Garret, hating to ask since she'd promised she would only request consults on neurological cases.

"I don't know how I can help, but I can at least do triage and direct the nurses."

She sagged with relief. "Thanks. How much use do you have of that hand?" She stood, then realized the question might seem insensitive. But she needed to know before things got hectic.

"I can pick things up with it, but it's more like those claw games that drop, grasp and lift. I can't do anything with it that requires fine motor skills."

Her heart ached at what that admission must have cost him, but there wasn't time to do much more than digest the information. "You can still wield a stethoscope, do visuals and call out treatment orders, so you'll do." It was better not to make a big deal over it.

"I can do that." He stood. "Now, let's go wait for our patients."

He wished he had full use of his hand.

Everyone else was in place outside and knew their jobs. Everyone, except for him.

His screaming nerves almost drowned out the scream of a siren as an ambulance rounded the corner and pulled into the bay of the ER.

He could do this. All he had to do was use his brain. Not his hand.

A blast of hot summer air met him as the sliding doors opened to let him and Addy outside. Despite his feeling like a fish out of water, adrenaline pumped through his system in a steady stream. At least *that* was familiar.

The gurney from the first squad hit the ground with a bump. He went to it as Addy met a second vehicle.

A toddler, who couldn't be more than three years old—and unconscious—came into view, her face streaked with soot. She was clad only in a T-shirt and pull-up diaper, which was understandable since they were at home and the heat index today was closing in on one hundred degrees. The EMT held an oxygen mask over her face. Good. At least she was breathing on her own. "Vitals?"

"BP ninety over sixty, pulse ninety, respiration forty-five. No burns, but she was found in a smoke-filled room."

Right on cue, the girl's diaphragm spasmed in a series of harsh, dry coughs.

Her vitals weren't bad, all things considered.

"Take her inside while I check on everyone else. Anyone critical that you know of?"

The technician nodded. "An infant is pretty bad, and the mom has burns from a pan of grease that caught fire. She tried dousing it with a bucket of water and—"

The flames would have gone everywhere. It played out in his head, and he winced.

The EMT went on, "She has burns mostly on her hands and arms, but luckily the actual fire didn't reach her. A neighbor saw smoke coming out of the window and called 911."

"The other kids?"

"She was holding the baby while cooking. When she threw the water, some of the hot oil hit her, and she must have dropped him. I've heard he's bad, but I had my own patient to take care of, so I'm not sure the extent of it."

The sound of raised voices came from somewhere behind them.

"This is not the time, Leo! Let me treat my patient."

Garret frowned at the EMT, who'd glanced back to where the voices were growing in volume. "Go ahead and take her in. I'll deal with the other patients." Then he headed to where Addy stood, a tech not quite blocking her way, but close enough that it would be awkward for her to try to move around him. Another man who must have been his partner was near the back doors, shifting from foot to foot, obviously not comfortable with the situation. Garret looked the EMT near Addy in the eye, already surmising who he was.

"Is there a problem here?"

The tech—who Garret remembered seeing before—drew himself to full height, but took a step back as if realizing he now had an audience. "No. No problem." He then looked at Addy. "I'll talk to you later."

"I don't think so. And right now I have a job to do. So do you."

Garret's brows lifted. So this was her ex-husband. The man was cocky and confident and obviously hadn't expected Addy's negative reaction to whatever he'd said.

The man glanced at him one last time and then moved around to get behind the wheel of the vehicle. The other EMT, who'd been tending to the patient—a boy this time—rattled off the child's vitals. This one was around ten years of age. Once he was done, he murmured, "Sorry about that."

Addy smiled, although it was strained. "Not your fault. Do you mind taking him inside and asking someone to find him an exam room?"

"Not a problem."

She started to walk off as another rescue squad arrived. Garret's fingers encircled her wrist and gave a reassuring squeeze before releasing his grip. "Hey, you okay?"

"I'm fine. Leo's just a jerk sometimes."

It sounded as if it was more than just sometimes. But there was no way he was going to say that. Plus, Addy was already heading toward the back of the vehicle, stethoscope swinging around her neck, her steps sure and determined.

He caught one more glance at Leo, who threw a scowl his way, but wouldn't hold his gaze.

A fourth ambulance came in, and Garret headed straight for it just as another doctor burst through the emergency-room doors. Lyle Hascup, known for his work in the burn unit, had made it to the hospital more quickly than he expected.

He let Lyle take the lead on what turned out to be an adult female, the one with grease burns to her arms and torso. The woman was in obvious pain, writhing on the gurney, but still asking about her baby in loud tones. Lyle tried to get her to calm down, but she wasn't having it. He glanced at the rescue worker. "Do you know where the baby is?"

"He's following. It took longer to get him stabilized." The man's voice was low. "Head and neck trauma from a fall."

Lyle nodded. "Dr. Stapleton, that is up your alley—do you want to take that one?"

His gut tightened in dread. "Yes. But make sure there's another neurosurgeon in the building, just in case."

"Got it." Then the other doctor was busy with his own patient, barking out orders and running alongside the gurney as they rushed the children's mother inside.

Addy came over. "Have you got the next one? I'm

going to go start treatment on the other children. Lyle will do great with the mother."

"I'm good. Go."

The first ambulance pulled out as did the second, which contained Addy's ex. Questions burned in his head, but, as Addy had said, now was not the time. Besides, Addy's relationships were none of his business. Unless it affected her work.

His hand burned with a phantom pain that reminded him that sometimes your private life did bleed into your professional life. He ignored the thought and waited for what seemed like an eternity before finally hearing the telltale wail of the fifth and final siren. The rescue vehicle pulled in and there was a rush of activity in the back as the other squads pulled out to make space for the newcomer.

The back doors swung open and a young EMT jumped down. "We've got a critical patient here. You a doctor?"

Only then did Garret realize he wasn't wearing his lanyard. He'd taken it off in his office so it didn't continually bump the edge of his desk—a constant annoyance.

He also realized the man was staring at his hand, a quizzical look on his face as his eyes swung up again.

"Yes, I'm a neurosurgeon. You can ask anyone inside that building." He didn't go into the fact that he was now basically a desk jockey—a bean counter—who, while retaining his medical license, rarely treated patients nowadays.

"That's good enough for me."

His partner jumped out of the vehicle and came to help lower the gurney as vitals were read. They weren't great. Skull fracture or a brain bleed were at the top of his list. He wouldn't know until he could get a CT scan.

He quickly peeled back the baby's eyelids, looking for pupillary reflex.

Neither pupil was blown, which was good, but the right was a little more reactive than the left. He didn't carry a penlight with him anymore as a matter of course. He'd have to borrow one inside, although it would be next to impossible to hold a light while using his good hand to peel apart the baby's eyelids.

He gave a quick listen to his patient's heart, instead, which thankfully sounded strong even if the baby's blood pressure was lower than he'd like it to be. He glanced at the baby's head. No bleeding that he could see in front and the backboard and neck brace prevented him from looking at the back of his skull at the moment.

"Let's get him inside. I want a CT of his head and neck to get a visual on what's going on in there."

They rushed the baby into the emergency room and transferred him from the ambulance gurney to one of the hospital's. He read off orders to the nurse who, in turn, called up to Radiology to let them know they were on their way. "Any idea if there's another parent in the picture besides the mom?"

The EMT shook his head. "I don't know. Another squad was treating her. Maybe check with them."

They were already long gone, but it didn't matter at the moment. He called another nurse over. "Can you see if mom is able to sign a consent form? I'm taking him upstairs."

"I'll get on it and call you when it's done." It was gratifying not to have anyone question his requests, not that he'd thought they would. But he had expected more sideways looks or raised brows. He'd gotten none.

By the time they arrived in the imaging department,

the consent form had been signed and scanned into the system. "The mother's pretty upset," the nurse said.

"Understandable. I'll let you know as soon as we have an idea on…" he glanced at the form on the electronic pad "…Matthew's condition. How are the other kids?"

"Mostly smoke inhalation. One broken finger from the melee right after the fire broke out. It's already been splinted. They'll be admitted overnight to watch for anything else."

Another nurse came over. "ER just called up. The mother is single and says the dad is out of the picture. She's having someone call her mom, who's in Michigan."

Michigan. Hell, that might as well be the other side of the world. If they couldn't find a relative or friend who could watch the kids as they were discharged, what would happen to them while their mother was in the hospital recovering?

That really wasn't his call. And right now, he had a little boy to worry about.

The imaging technician made quick work of getting the baby into the machine. Since he was still unconscious there were no issues with keeping him still, a very small blessing. All in all, the procedure took less than five minutes.

While a nurse waited with the baby, Garret looked at the scans, noting immediately there was indeed a basilar fracture, which would make sense since the mother had reportedly dropped the baby when the grease had flared toward her. The force of his head striking the hard tile floor could have caused a linear fracture like the one he saw on the film. He didn't see any areas of brain compression that might indicate an active bleed. Another good sign.

The fact that he hadn't gotten burned as well was a

testament to the way his mother had reacted to the fire
by turning away. It could have been worse. Much worse.
It didn't look as if he'd need to call in an actual surgeon.
They could treat conservatively and get a good result,
hopefully. The baby's eyes were darkening underneath,
meaning he would have two good-sized shiners by morning, but that was also normal with this particular type
of fracture.

No neck injuries that he could see on the scans, so they
could take the collar off and find a bed in the pediatric
ICU area so he could be watched.

He quickly wrote up orders for Matthew's care and
made sure there was a room available. The baby's vitals
were stabilizing, and he was starting to stir. And fuss.
No wonder. He had to have a massive headache. Garret
touched a finger to the back of the baby's hand. "Don't
worry, little guy. We're going to take good care of you and
hopefully get you reunited with your mom very soon."
He made a note to hand off the case to another of the
hospital's neurologists. He would see who was due to
come through to do rounds in the morning, since it was
already getting late, judging from the sky. But for tonight,
he would check on the baby before he left the hospital.

Speaking of which, he wanted to peek in on the mom
as well. Glancing down at his curled fingers, he hoped
her hands would fare better than his had.

By the time he made it back to the emergency room,
the rooms had been cleared out and there was no sign
of Addy. Maybe she'd left for the day. He glanced at his
watch, surprised to find it was almost nine in the evening. He was supposed to meet her in the morning for
the whole surfing thing. He'd done his best to think of a
way to weasel out of it, but had come up with nothing.

Just as that thought hit, she rounded a corner and

stopped dead as if shocked to see him. Had she thought of turning in the other direction only to realize it was too late? It was what he might have done, given the opportunity.

He decided to speak up first. "How are they?"

"I was just about to ask you the same question. I was on my way to the elevator to check on the baby."

"Matthew."

"Sorry?"

Why had he said that? "The baby's name. I saw it on the consent form."

"Ah. How is he?"

He nodded toward the chairs at a nearby waiting area, noting the way her eyes widened.

"He made it, didn't he? Grace will be devastated, if something happened."

"He has a skull fracture, but nothing that time can't heal."

Addy sagged into one of the chairs. "Thank God. Grace kept saying she would never forgive herself for letting go of him."

"If she'd held on, he might have shielded her from the flames, but would have gotten the worst of it himself." Garret sat beside her. "I take it you've heard about how the others are?"

"They're all in rooms for the night. We juggled some patients so we could keep the family as close together as we could. Two of them will be on oxygen for the duration of the night. One of them could probably be discharged, but—"

"There's nowhere for them to go. Yeah, I heard that from one of the EMTs. I take it the grandmother is making arrangements to come down?"

"Yes. Grace said she found a flight. She should be here later this evening."

"How is she, by the way? The burns?"

"Believe it or not, she's fairly lucky. She has several partial thickness burns. Most of the ones on her arm and neck, though, are superficial. But there are two areas on her hands that are deep."

Also known as second-degree burns, partial thickness burns affected the first two layers of the dermis.

He swallowed. "Her hands. Nerve damage?"

"Possibly, but they'll keep an eye on them and watch for infection. It could have been a whole lot worse."

He leaned back, expelling the air in his lungs. "I just got done saying that after looking at Matthew's CT scans. Did they lose their house?"

"No. One of the EMTs told me the fire was contained quickly. One wall in the kitchen has some fire and water damage, and smoke, obviously, but it could have been—"

"Much worse." He laughed.

She smiled and twisted in the seat to look at him. "So how does it feel to play doctor again?"

Play doctor? He glanced sharply at her.

"It feels strange. And kind of nice." He was going to avoid thinking about any other connotation behind her words. "I've missed it."

"You're still a doctor, Garret. You realize that, don't you?" She touched his injured hand, sending a burst of heat through it. The friction from her fingers was almost unbearably intimate. "This…" she brushed her skin against his once again "…doesn't affect who you are or what's in your head. In your heart."

He gritted his teeth, fighting the tension growing inside his belly and sweeping to other areas.

"It affects what I can hold in my hand, though, doesn't

it?" Even he could hear the bitterness in his words. "My whole life changed in the space of a few seconds."

When he looked in her face he saw a wide range of emotions: concern, dismay and, finally, compassion. What he didn't see was what he dreaded the most: pity. But even without that, he could guess what the next words out of her mouth would be before she'd even given voice to them.

"What happened, Garret? To your hand?"

CHAPTER FOUR

THE WAITING ROOM was still empty; the day-to-day visitors in this area had gone home for the most part. Addy loved it when the hospital was like this. Quiet and almost peaceful. You could almost forget there were life-and-death battles raging inside these halls.

The battle going on in Garret's head right now might not be life or death, but she could tell he was trying to decide how much to tell her. She knew he'd been in an accident that had damaged his hand, but she didn't know how it had happened, although she'd heard some vague rumors about his daughter dying and him going off the deep end.

"I was in a car accident four years ago. I was coming off a fourteen-hour shift, and I was tired." He rubbed a hand across his brows, his mouth twisting. "I fell asleep behind the wheel."

Something in her heart twisted, that meeting in his office taking on a whole new meaning that was impossible to ignore. Hadn't she driven home desperately tired before—found her eyelids sinking and had to jerk herself back to wakefulness?

"I didn't know."

"I'm surprised, actually. I thought hospital grapevines were notorious about digging up the dirt on everyone."

"Hard to do that on someone who's just as notorious about his privacy. I heard you had a daughter who died. I'm sorry."

"We lost Leticia to leukemia at age ten."

His daughter had been ten? He must have married young. But it would be just as devastating to lose a child no matter what the age. "I'm sorry."

She had to ask. "Is this why you wanted me to cut back on my hours?"

"Yes. I wouldn't wish this—" he lifted his hand "—on my worst enemy."

"I can understand that. But there's still so much you can do, Garret. You showed that today as you were treating that baby. You could teach. I've heard stories about how talented a surgeon you were—still are."

"I can't do surgery at all."

Her head tilted. "Yes, you can."

Reaching over, he used his damaged hand to grasp hers, tried to raise it off the arm of the chair. He made it up a few inches before losing his grip. The laugh he gave was humorless. "See? Nothing more than a claw game. So do you want to rethink that?"

She leaned forward, forcing him to meet her eyes. "You can still do surgery. In here, Garret." Her fingers lifted to touch his temple. His skin was warm, his dark hair tickling the back of her hand. She swallowed back a rush of emotion. "And then you can share that knowledge with medical students. You have so much to offer them."

"No. Absolutely not." His eyes darkened, pupils swallowing his brown irises.

"But why?"

He got to his feet as if he couldn't stand her touching him. Why had she even done that? And how stupid was she for discussing this with him? She barely knew the man. He worked in the same hospital, but that didn't mean they were automatically friends or confidants.

In fact, it appeared he resented her personal questions, as well he should. She owed him an apology.

"I'm sorry. I had no business asking you about your private life."

He didn't answer for a minute, a muscle in his cheek pulsing in the sudden silence. He finally blew out a breath. "I'm the one who should apologize. I overreacted. It tends to be a touchy subject."

And yet he said he missed practicing medicine. Why wouldn't he want to share his love of it with others? She would probably never know.

"I pried where I shouldn't have. It won't happen again."

He brushed off her words with a wave of his hand. "No harm done. I think I'll go up and check on my young patient and make sure he's okay before I head out for the night."

"Okay. Good night."

She wasn't sure how to ask if they were still on for tomorrow. They probably weren't. She wouldn't blame him if he'd changed his mind about going after that tense exchange.

Well, she'd simply show up at the beach at the specified time and place. If he came, great. If he didn't, she would still catch some waves on her own. In fact, it might even be better that way. No distractions. And no opportunities to put her foot back in her mouth.

Heaving a sigh that felt heavier than an elephant, she waited until he was out of sight and then got out of her chair and made her way through the exit doors. The image of Garret driving home late one evening and waking up in the hospital was not going to be easy to erase. But she'd better at least try. Because he'd made it very clear that he did not want to talk about his personal life with anyone.

And most definitely not with her.

It was a typical balmy South Beach morning. Addy propped her board against the rail of the surf shop and glanced at her waterproof watch—one of the few times she actually wore one nowadays, since she couldn't carry her phone into the surf. Nine twenty-nine. He wasn't coming. Why that sent a wave of disappointment sloshing over her, she had no idea. But it did. She'd told herself she didn't want him to come and watch her surf, but it was a lie. Because unlike him, she did like to help people explore new things.

She'd never officially taught anyone to surf, and she had no idea if Garret would even want to try, but she had helped colleagues who'd had an interest in learning get the basics.

Oh, well. It didn't look as if that—or anything else—was going to happen. He was a no-show.

Picking up her board, she started to move toward the sand of the nearby beach when she heard her name. Her feet quit moving.

Garret!

She shut her eyes and tried to stop the sudden gallop of her heart. This was ridiculous. She was not going to go all starry-eyed.

Ha! Too late.

Well, then, she wasn't going to let him know how glad she was that he'd decided to come.

She turned and there he was, tanned legs emerging from solid black board shorts. The white drawstrings at the top of his waistband teased her eyes for a split second before she jerked her gaze upward. She decided then and there she wasn't going to try squirming into the light wetsuit she'd stuffed in her beach bag. That would be a fiasco. She'd just wear her bikini, as plenty of other surfers in Florida did.

The racerback top was snug enough to stay in place no matter how big the wave. Besides, it was pretty obvious that Garret hadn't brought much with him, other than himself.

And that was plenty.

Her mouth gave a slight twist of exasperation. She needed to get her thoughts under control.

Sporting a black nylon exercise shirt, he had a gray beach towel draped over his left arm. His injured hand was hidden in the folds. On purpose? And there was not a surfboard in sight.

Then again, she hadn't expected him to buy a board just for this excursion, but the idea of him sitting on the beach watching her ride the waves made her swallow.

Oh, no. If she was surfing, he was surfing. Or at least he was going to paddle out there with her.

"They have board rentals at the kiosk."

"I'm not sure—"

"I am. Sure, that is. You need to try."

"Has anyone ever told you that you have a one-track mind?" He smiled, and the transformation from the grim reaper figure of last night snatched the breath from her lungs.

Ugh! She needed to be careful. It would be a long time before she let another pretty face charm her into giving a piece of her heart away. Leo might be over and done with, but the repercussions of their relationship were not.

Only Garret's face wasn't pretty. It was rugged. With touches of danger around the edges. She'd seen a little bit of that last night when she'd probed too close to a painful area.

"Maybe a time or two." She smiled back.

Keep it light and friendly, Addy. Steer clear of any flashing caution lights.

Like that drawstring? Oh, yes, exactly like that. She didn't let herself blink for a few seconds, afraid if she did, her pupils would head straight for—

"I have no idea what size," he said.

Addy froze.

Size? Don't even think it!

She took a deep breath. "It's fine. I'll help you choose."

Telling the man at the desk what they were looking for in a voice that wasn't quite steady, she waited while he pulled a teal board from a walled-off storage area.

"Are you sure this is a good idea?"

She wasn't sure at all anymore, but hadn't she said she was going to fake it until she could make it? That flip advice suddenly didn't sound so smart after all. "Don't worry. It'll be fun. You'll see."

Fun. She had no idea how she had ever thought coming here with him would be anything short of a disaster.

"The last time I heard that, my dau—" Any hint of a smile disappeared. His throat moved a time or two, then went still. "It was a teacup ride. And it was not a good idea."

It would have been funny, except for the obvious pain on Garret's face.

All the sexy thoughts she'd had moments ago vanished, replaced by a terrible ache in her chest. She couldn't imagine what he'd gone through losing his daughter, even though she'd experienced her share of loss in the emergency room. Every single child she was unable to save was imprinted on her brain. The names were long forgotten, but the faces weren't. Nor were the tears shed by those who'd loved them.

And then there was her mom.

And this was not what she wanted to think about right now. "Well, this is nothing like a teacup ride. It's more like Mr. Toad's Wild Ride."

"Mr. Toad's what?"

"It's a ride the theme park in Florida is famous for." She glanced at him for a second. "It doesn't go in circles, but it does go up and then plummets, and has plenty of stops and starts to keep you busy. That's what I'd compare surfing to."

"That's what I was afraid of."

She laughed, and the atmosphere changed in an instant. Once he'd paid his rental fee, he hefted his board onto his shoulder, his bicep flexing in a way that made her tummy tighten. Just like that day at the hospital.

It wasn't the way people normally carried their boards, and it broke the unwritten etiquette about how to transport them, but it worked. And it looked good. Very good.

Or maybe it was just him. Several women's heads had already swiveled in their direction.

Only then did she realize that he was using his bad hand to hold the board in place. So he could use it, when he had to. He tended to try to keep that hand out of sight. At least she'd noticed him doing that in his office and when they were caring for the house-fire victims.

She wondered if he was even aware of it. But the hand, riddled with red and white scars from his burns, was able to curl perfectly around the rim of the board.

A claw game.

If he didn't have to flex and extend his fingers, then they were useful.

To avoid staring more than she already had, she hiked her beach bag onto her shoulder and tucked her own board under her arm. She then led the way to the beach where some other surfers were already riding the waves. It looked like the perfect day to learn. The waves weren't all that high. Normally that would be a disappointment, but in this case she was glad of that fact. He'd talked about his hand being a detriment, but she didn't know how true that would be when it came to surfing. If he was self-conscious and worried about how it might appear to others, then it might make him clumsy about manipulating his board in the water. She stopped halfway to the ocean, set her board and beach bag down and spread her towel on the sand.

"We're a long way out, aren't we?"

"It's low tide. We don't want to come back and find out the water stole our clothes, do we?"

A muscle twitched in Garret's cheek as he set his own things down next to hers. "No. We wouldn't want to find our clothes gone."

Oh, Lord. She hadn't exactly worded that very well, had she?

Too late. She was picturing them—a very naked them—standing on the shore, muttering about their missing garments. Garret's shorts were floating, those pesky drawstrings waving goodbye as they traveled away on ocean currents.

Trying to quickly change the subject, she sat on the towel and kicked off her sandals. "Are you ready for a crash course on riding the waves?"

"I didn't think I had a choice back at the kiosk."

"You don't. I'm only here because you wouldn't let me stay at work." She shook her head to keep him from making a comment. "And you were right. I have been working too many hours. I'll try to do better."

"Your ex. Is he causing trouble?"

She rolled her eyes. She'd been hoping he wouldn't

bring up the scene outside the ER. "He is, but I can handle him."

"Are you sure? I can intervene, if you want."

"Not necessary, but thank you. He decided he wants to do counseling."

Garret shot her a quick look. "And will you?"

"It's not the kind of counseling you're thinking of. It's divorce counseling called *The Amicable Parting of Ways*. It's his new girlfriend's idea. She and I were once friends, and she's decided she wants to kiss and make up."

"What did you tell him?"

"I told him no. I have no interest in trying to stay friends with either of them. I'm sorry our messy split was put on public display in the hospital loading zone, though."

"Not your fault at all." He dropped his own board onto the sand and put his towel next to hers. Staring out over the ocean, he grimaced. "I'm pretty sure I'm not going to make a good surfing student."

"I bet you'll surprise yourself. Let's go ahead and get started."

Since she'd already slathered herself in sunscreen just so she wouldn't have to do it in front of him, she stood and hesitated for a second. But there was no way she was going into the water with her shorts and T-shirt on. And she wasn't going to turn her back on him like a shy schoolgirl either. This was Florida, and they were both adults. They'd both been married—were both doctors— so they'd seen the human body thousands of times. It was no big deal.

Taking a deep breath, she stripped her shirt off and then shimmied out of her shorts, standing in front of him in just her red bikini.

She thought the color drained out of Garret's face, but

he quickly got up as well and yanked his shirt over his head in one quick motion, using his good hand.

Her lungs seized, and her heart tripped over itself several times before tumbling into a chaotic rhythm she was powerless to control.

And that was when Addy knew she was in trouble. Big, big trouble.

Garret tried to replicate the fancy move Addy had shown him on the beach. But while she was able to scramble to her feet with easy grace and ride the wave in, he'd swallowed so much salt water that he was pretty sure the ocean levels had dropped an inch or two.

Dragging himself in to shore, he carried his board the way he'd seen Addy and others do it—under his arm. It was kind of a necessity, since the tether attached to his ankle didn't stretch far enough to put the board back on his shoulder. When he reached where she stood he groaned. "I am never going to be a surfer. I still can't get it."

"The pop up isn't easy." She dropped her board onto the beach, then pushed aside some sand so her fins were buried. "Let's practice it again."

Practice? He'd watched her, but there was no way he'd been willing to copy her. He'd barely been able to keep his knuckles from dragging on the ground as he'd tried to pay attention. The way her back arched on the board put his senses on alert. Not that they weren't already.

He glanced around the beach, which seemed even more crowded than it had a half hour earlier. "I don't think so."

"Come on, people do it all the time. It's how they teach surfing. Afraid someone will look at you?"

He was sure people were already looking. But not at

him. At her. That fire-engine-red bikini she had on had set a few embers burning, and the longer they were out of the water, the harder that was to conceal. The top was some kind of weird halter-top-looking thing with straps that gathered together in the back. But it fit like a glove and was somehow sexy as hell.

It was absurd and maddening but there was absolutely nothing he could do about his reaction to it. He'd tried.

Hell, he'd done everything he could think of. His libido was going all caveman on him and it was driving him crazy, which was where his knuckle-dragging thoughts from a few minutes earlier came from. All he wanted to do was to stay in the water until it was time for them to get dressed and go home.

And then he was never going surfing with her again.

"Not exactly."

"Okay, I'll show you again. Watch the way my legs move."

Not a problem. He was watching her legs and everything above them. And if she kept phrasing things that way, he was going to have to go stand waist deep in the ocean for his own sanity.

And she never gave him a chance to refuse, lying down on her board in one smooth move. "Okay, so you've already paddled out and have now turned to face the shore. You're in the center of the board and your feet are on the tail." She arched her back, and there it went again. The swallowing of saliva. The inner panic that he was going to lose it.

"There'll be a moment where you feel yourself picking up momentum as the wave catches you. Put your hands under your chest and push hard, and kind of jump onto your feet."

She demonstrated in one fluid move, her hips moving

in time to an imaginary wave. "Now you're riding it, all the way in to shore."

This was bad. Very, very bad.

Before he'd totally recovered, she went back into a prone position on the board and showed him all over again. "And that's the pop up. If that doesn't work for you, you can push off, get your back knee under you, plant your front foot and stand. Whichever method, it's got to be fast. Explosive, even. If you take too long getting to your feet, you'll fall off. Basically, your front foot should end up where your chest was on the board."

The last way looked a little more doable on a moving board. "I can try that kneeling method."

Anything to stop those long limbs from demonstrating again. And keep her from talking about riding anything.

"Great. Let's try it again, then."

Once in the water, he shook his head. Hell, whether he got upright on the board or not, her moves were going to haunt him long into the night.

He paddled beside her, and tried to concentrate on what she'd told him. There! A wave was forming in the distance. Following her lead, he turned around and started paddling, keeping his chin up.

Damn. There it was. That push she'd talked about. In one quick move he shoved himself onto a knee and suddenly found himself standing sideways on his board. For all of a second, before he dived headfirst into the water. Again.

But he'd stood!

"Plant your feet further apart," she yelled when he came up. "You almost had it."

Three tries later, he was on his feet, shaky as hell, but he stayed up, trying to follow the quick movements of his board. This time when he jumped off it was on his terms.

"Great job, Garret! You did it!" Her smile was wide and excited, and she held up her right hand for a high five. He smacked her palm with his, their fingers twining together for a second or two as a feeling of victory stole over him. He'd actually done it. He'd surfed. Something he'd never done in his life—never had a desire to do. But it was exhilarating and his hand hadn't given him much of a problem at all. Flattening it on his board to push himself up was painful, so he'd allowed it to curl in on itself instead, as he did when he did push-ups. It had worked like a charm.

Well, not exactly, but at least it hadn't kept him from doing what he wanted to do. As it had with surgery.

He'd had an ortho guy tell him he could probably help stretch his tendons so he was better able to open his hand, but it would never be the way it once was. He'd opted not to have additional surgery. As long as he could zip his pants and button his shirt, it would have to do. And there was always the possibility that surgery would make things worse, if there were complications.

They released their hold on each other and carried their boards onto shore. Addy released the clip holding her hair back and shook it out as they sat down, finger-combing out the tangles and adjusting the bottom edge of her bikini top. "Do you like it?"

His mind blanked out for a second before he realized she wasn't talking about the curls she'd set free or her swimwear. Lord, he could see the hard press of her nipples.

He shut his eyes for a second.

"Garret?"

Oh. The surfing. Had he liked it?

He actually had. He couldn't remember the last time

he'd high-fived someone. And the way she'd gripped his hand afterward…

Yes. He'd liked it.

"I did. Thank you for asking me to come." He undid the Velcro tether around his ankle and leaned back on his elbows, the heat from the sun jump-starting the drying process. "I may have to look into buying a board."

"Seriously?" Her brows went up and a smile hovered around the corners of her mouth.

"Seriously." He liked making her smile. Liked her jubilation over his successful ride on that last wave.

And that should worry him. Everything about today should worry him. He'd screwed up one woman's life, making her walk a lonely path before she finally threw in the towel. He didn't need to repeat that with anyone else.

But it was one day. One great day, where he could leave his dark past and his mistakes behind. It wasn't likely to last, so why not enjoy it to its fullest?

She turned toward him, face tilted upward to catch the sun. Her hair pooled on the ground behind her. His hand ached to touch it to see what the salt did to those shiny locks.

"How is Grace and her family?" she asked. "Have you heard?"

It took a minute to drag his thoughts from touching things to where they needed to be. "The house-fire victims?"

"Yes."

"I actually went in to the hospital to check on Matthew and his mom before coming to the beach. It's why I was a few minutes late. They're doing really well. The grandmother arrived just as I was leaving, so Grace will have some help with the kids when they go home."

"That's great." She paused. "I actually thought you were standing me up."

"If Matthew hadn't been doing well, I might have. But I would have called to let you know." He frowned. "You really thought I wouldn't come?"

"I wondered. After last night—"

His head tilted sideways. "The argument with your ex?"

"No, your reaction to my suggestion about teaching."

He'd had a pretty strong reaction to that. He'd realized almost as soon as he'd left that he'd been abrupt to the point of rudeness. He'd already apologized, but felt the need to do it again. "Sorry. I've just had several people ask me the same thing. You know the old saying, don't you? 'Those who can, do—those who can't, teach.'"

Her frown was as big as her earlier smile had been. "You can't seriously believe that. How do you think people get through medical school? If there were no teachers, no one would ever become a doctor."

"No, I don't believe that philosophically. But in practice? In my case, it's true. And I just haven't been willing to face that—to accept it as my new reality."

"Is it such an awful reality?"

"No. I guess not." Being the administrator of a teaching hospital had seemed like a good thing when it had been offered to him, but was he really happy doing what he did? He wasn't sure. Three years wasn't really long enough to make a determination on that. "Maybe at some point I'll think about it."

"If you'd had a resident working with you on Matthew's case, he could have learned some valuable tips about skull fractures and how to assess and treat them. Instead, you handed him off to a veteran neurosurgeon and no one learned anything."

"Point taken." She was as blunt as she was beautiful.

She put a hand on his wrist, the clinging grains of sand pale against her tanned skin. "I didn't mean that to come out as harsh as it did. You just have so much talent."

"I could have been a complete hack, for all you know."

"I heard the hospital in New York didn't want to let you go. They don't fight a resignation unless they consider you valuable."

Yes, they had fought it. They'd offered him a huge incentive to stay, even though they knew he would probably never operate again.

"If I hadn't left, I never would have learned how to surf, though."

In her case, those who could also taught. And being at the beach with her had been fun.

"Well, there is that. Are you glad you came?"

He couldn't remember the last time he'd actually enjoyed an outing with a woman. Certainly those last months with his ex-wife had been pretty excruciating. She'd been right to leave him. He knew there was no going back and fixing things. Nor did he want to. He'd been an ass. And now that he knew he had it in him, he didn't trust himself not to repeat some of those mistakes.

So he needed to tread carefully with Addy, because something was brewing that he didn't quite understand. That he didn't quite want to stop.

"I am. I had a good time."

"I'm really glad. I think we both needed to get away for a while."

Her words were low, fingers still on his wrist. He let them stay there, unwilling to pull away as more and more of that uncertainty began swirling inside him.

"I know I did."

Her eyes centered on his. There was a dot of sand on

her chin, and he couldn't stop himself from reaching over to brush it away with his thumb. Her skin was soft and warm, the ocean water having dried to a fine film.

If he kissed her, would she taste of salt?

Was it "if" he kissed? Or was it—when?

"Garret?"

"Sand."

"I'm sure it's on more than just my chin."

Was that an invitation?

His gaze skated down the line of her throat, the indent of her waist, the curve of her hip. And yes, she had sand clinging to her arms. Her legs. Her feet.

And suddenly he knew. He was *going* to taste her skin.

He leaned forward and stopped within an inch of his goal. He waited for her to pull away or make a move that said she didn't want this. She studied him for a few seconds and they hovered. Person to person. Mouth close to mouth.

Before he could finish assessing her reactions, or decide if he would actually go through with it, she did the last thing he expected. Addy closed the gap and kissed him first.

CHAPTER FIVE

GARRET'S MOUTH WAS WARM. No, it wasn't. "Warm" was too ambivalent a word. It was hot, burning hers. He'd stayed still for a split second when her lips touched his, but surely he'd been headed in this direction when he'd moved so close. She'd just jumped in quicker than he had. Mainly because she'd been afraid he was going to back out. She'd been wanting to kiss him ever since she watched him strip off his shirt before they hit the water. Each moment of their lesson had inflamed that need, as had the brief moments she'd caught him looking at her.

God, she really did have a crush on him.

Did it matter, if he felt the same way?

When she'd demonstrated the pop up on her board, she'd watched color creep up his neck and into his face and wondered if it was pooling in any other areas of his body.

It had been driving her crazy.

It was still driving her crazy.

His hand came up and slid beneath her hair, curving around her nape, his thumb stroking the side of her neck in a way that made her shudder. Heat rushed through her, winding around and around until she was encased, held prisoner by her own need.

Her tongue slid along the seam of his lips, and his

thumb ceased its movements. She settled closer, desperate for him to touch her.

They were on a public beach, for God's sake. He couldn't just lay her back and yank off her bikini bottoms. Even if she ached for him to do just that.

Without warning, Garret jerked back, the movement so sudden that she almost fell on top of him.

He shut his eyes, his chest rising and falling with a ragged sound that was nothing like the muted sounds of the ocean around them.

She had no idea what made him pull away, but, God, she was glad he had. She'd been on the verge of making a fool out of herself. A very, very big fool.

What had gotten into her? Hadn't she let herself get involved with Leo after barely knowing him? Had she learned nothing from that experience?

Garret probably thought she was overeager—maybe even desperate. A hot wash of embarrassment poured over her.

She didn't want his eyes to open, because when they did—

"Ah, hell, Addy. I have no idea where that came from."

An apology, right? Dear Lord, she hated that he was sorry. Hated that she was shaking like a leaf, unable to capture any of the words rattling around in her head.

Finally, she sat up, dragging her fingers through her tangled mass of hair. She counted to three in an effort to compose her thoughts then sucked down a deep breath, reaching for the first excuse she could find. "It's the ocean. It gets to you."

"Is that what it was?"

Was she that desperate to explain her behavior? Evidently, because the look he gave her was a mixture of doubt and relief. She was the one who'd planted her lips on his. She could only hope what she'd said was true, that the ocean was actually to blame.

"It was on my part." Said as if she truly believed what she was saying.

He planted his elbows on his knees, sending her a frown. "I didn't come out here hoping something like this would happen. I hope you know that."

Was he worried she'd file a sexual harassment report with the hospital? That made her cringe, more heat piling on top of the previous batch in her face.

"I'm the one who asked you to come, remember."

"I do, but—"

She gulped. This was ridiculous. "Listen, I know you didn't come here with anything in mind. I didn't either. It just—happened. People kiss all the time. It's not a big deal." It was to her, since she didn't actually "kiss all the time." But he didn't need to know that. "There's no reason we can't just put this behind us, is there?"

She wasn't exactly sure she could do that, but she was desperate to get back to the place they'd been before any of this had happened. To kill the growing awkwardness between them.

This was nothing more than a day on the beach where there were skimpy suits, tanned skin and impulses that drove men and women to have sex.

Sex.

That was not going to happen.

As impulsive as kissing him had been, spending the night with him would be a hundred times worse.

She was not going to jump into a relationship again. Especially not in response to a crisis the way she'd done the last time. Her mom's condition had driven her into Leo's arms. She wasn't going to let her marital breakup drive her into someone else's arms. Especially not her boss's.

Not that there was any chance of that happening.

"No, there's not."

At first she thought he'd read her mind and was responding to her thoughts. Then she realized he was simply answering her earlier question.

"Good." She wrapped her arms around her knees and looked out at the ocean. "It was simply the euphoria of perfecting the timing on your pop up."

"Why the hell do they have to call it a pop up, of all things? Couldn't they have come up with a better term?" His voice sounded strained.

She smiled, having a pretty good idea why the description was bothering him. And she could have done a better job with her phrasing.

Perfecting the timing on your pop up?

That could definitely be taken to mean something entirely different.

Right now, she was very glad she was a woman. Her insides might be tied up in knots, but at least there wasn't any outward physical evidence of her thoughts.

Making a conscious effort to edge the conversation back onto neutral territory, she said, "You've never heard of popping up on your board?"

"I barely knew what a surfboard was before, much less tried to use one."

Smiling, despite herself, she said, "Well, now you can put a new skill on your résumé."

"Popping up. New skill. Right."

Maybe she could put that on her résumé as well. Having urges pop up where they weren't welcome. Maybe that was her cue to get out of there before she did anything else stupid. "You never know. And as fun as this has been, it looks like most of the surfers are giving up. The tide has come in too far for the waves to be any good."

Glancing at how the water was lapping several yards further inshore than it had been, she knew it was the truth. But it was more than that. She needed to escape, to have time to process what she hoped was a simple case of the atmosphere getting the best of her. "I guess it's time to turn in my rental board."

"You can stay if you want." A quick glance at her watch showed it was almost twelve fifteen. They'd been out here for almost three hours. And in spite of her doubts about what had happened, she'd had a good time. "I need to go home and catch up on some fun things, like laundry and cleaning."

"You won't go into the hospital today."

"Not unless I'm called in."

He nodded. "Good."

"What about you? Are you taking the rest of the day off?"

"Yes. I do learn from my mistakes."

He could have been referring to his accident. Why, then, did she feel as if that had been directed at what had happened between them a few minutes ago? Well, that was fine. She would learn from her mistakes as well. Like never watching him undress ever again.

That meant no more beach outings. And she was going to have to be okay with that.

Because to do anything else was inviting disaster on a whole new level. And with Leo standing as a bright reminder of what could happen when she let herself off her leash, she needed to watch her step.

So what did she do now?

First thing was there would be no more outings with Garret. She was making a promise to herself. Unless it was related to work, it was off-limits. Everything was to be business as usual. No more kissing. No more surfing. No more anything.

No matter how hard that promise might be to keep.

A week after the kiss, Garret stood with Grace and the rest of her children at the front entrance of the hospital. They were being discharged. Actually three of the kids had gone home with Grace's mom a day after the fire.

Repairs to the house were well under way, so life would soon get back to normal for them. Well, maybe not completely normal. It would take a while for Grace to come to terms with dropping Matthew. Right now, her mom held the baby, even though the burns on Grace's hands and arms were healing. But it was something she would work through, hopefully.

Kind of like he was working through what had happened between him and Addy on the beach.

Addy had asked him to call when the family was released so she could come see them off as well. He'd paged her, but she hadn't responded. Actually he hadn't seen her much, since that day at the beach.

Was she finding it awkward to see him? Since he'd skipped his normal Monday ER visit this week, he would say she wasn't the only one.

As long as they didn't let it damage their working relationship beyond repair.

She suddenly appeared out of nowhere, her hands deep in the pockets of her pants. "Sorry, I had a patient. I was afraid I was going to miss you."

She looked toward him, but not quite at him.

Well, that was fine.

Grace reached up and clasped Addy's hands. "Thank you so much for everything. I can't believe how amazingly lucky we were. Mom says the house is almost as good as new. After only a week."

"That's wonderful. And Matthew is doing okay?" This time she met his eyes as if seeking confirmation for her words.

He gave her a nod. "Yes, he's well on his way to a full recovery."

Kind of like Garret was. As difficult and uncomfortable as the aftermath of that kiss had been, maybe it actually had accomplished something. Maybe it was busy working behind the scenes, sawing through the first link in a chain that bound him to his past. If so, the ocean should carry warning labels for those who didn't really want to be free.

Or maybe he did.

And he could admit—at least to himself—that kissing her had been a memorable experience. She had definitely tasted like salt.

His mouth went up in a half smile. She must have caught it, because her head tilted in question. He gave a quick shake of his head to indicate it was nothing.

Beverly dropped a kiss onto the baby's head and shifted his weight higher on her hip. "He's doing great. He's back to being as ornery as he ever was."

Right now, the baby looked anything but ornery as he smiled and babbled, staring at the lobby as if it was the most fascinating place he'd ever been. The bruising around his eyes was fading, a yellow shadow replacing the red and black he'd been sporting.

And his fracture should heal without any problems.

Something twisted inside Garret, obliterating his pleasant thoughts from a few minutes earlier. At least this family would get their happy ending.

Beverly was actually thinking of relocating to South

Beach. The fire might be just the motivation she'd needed to move closer to her grandchildren and daughter.

Addy went over and picked Matthew's chubby hands and clapped them together several times, smiling when the baby laughed. "He's back to being as cute as ever, if you ask me."

She looked completely at ease with the baby, the furrow between her brows disappearing, her face shining with what looked like joy.

Oh, how he remembered that feeling. Looking down at Leticia had made his heart swell with love. A complete and utter happiness that he'd thought nothing could take away.

How wrong he'd been.

He swallowed, as the moment between Addy and Matthew continued, and for a brief instant something flashed inside his skull, before he blanked it out, taking a step back.

"Oh, I almost forgot," Beverly said. "Is the auction open to the public? I picked up a brochure."

"It's open to anyone who would like to come." He somehow managed to keep his voice smooth and calm, hoping any evidence of the turbulence inside was well hidden. "We should have a complete list of auction items a week before the gala, if you want to come by and pick one up. They'll be here in the lobby."

"I'll do that, thank you." Then Beverly turned to her daughter. "I'm going out to bring the car around."

"It's okay, Mom. I can walk."

"Are you sure, honey?"

"I'm positive." Grace's eyes went to her baby and then skipped away, a quick look of fear crossing her face. "If you could just strap Matthew in his car seat for me. I don't think I can manage yet with my hands."

Although her hands were still red, Garret was pretty sure she could click a baby into his seat without too much difficulty. After all, she'd grabbed Addy's hands and held them without a single wince. He glanced at the other doctor and saw her frown. So, he wasn't the only one who'd noticed.

Grace stood and turned toward him. "Thank you for everything. With Matthew especially."

"That's what we're here for. You have those cards I gave you?"

He'd given her the numbers of the hospital crisis line and chaplain in case she needed to talk to someone about what she was going through. Something he should have done much sooner than he had after his daughter passed away.

"I do. I won't need them, though."

"Hang on to them, okay? Just to make me feel better." The last thing he wanted to do was ask someone from social services to check in on the family, but if push came to shove, he would. Hopefully, with her mother there, things would click back into a normal rhythm.

Kind of like he was hoping would happen with him and Addy. That their little incident would be forgotten or that they would at least stop avoiding each other.

"I will. Thank you again." With that, they walked outside and made their way into the parking lot, one of the younger kids turning to give them a wave. Garret waved back.

"What cards was she talking about?"

"I gave her the number for the hospital counselor in case she needed to talk."

"I'm glad." She pulled her stethoscope from around her neck, coiled it and stuck it in the pocket of her sweater.

"I was a little worried about how she was going to cope once she got home. I'm glad her mom is here."

"I was thinking that very same thing." He paused, then decided to act on his earlier thoughts. It was time to move past the beach, at least for him. "Can I buy you a cup of coffee?"

"Uh-oh. Am I in trouble again?"

This time he allowed himself to fully smile. "No. I think I might be the one who's in trouble, and I want to make things right."

"You're not. In trouble, that is. If you're talking about the day at the beach, don't worry about it. It was fun. Let's just call what happened a minor hiccup."

He'd hardly call that kiss a "hiccup," but better that than turn it into a crisis that caused her to call it quits on the hospital. "It *was* fun. Coffee?"

"I don't actually drink coffee, but a cup of tea might be nice. I'm due a lunch break anyway."

"It's almost three o'clock."

This time she laughed. "That tone says it all. We've had a busy day in the ER. But don't worry—I've only put in one hour more than usual today. But I am ready to get off my feet for a while."

A few minutes later they were in the hospital cafeteria, and she had a steaming cup of Earl Grey tea between her hands. While he had her here, he decided to broach something that had been brought up by one of the auction committee members. It also provided a means to put things back on a solid footing between them. "Part of the reason I wanted to have coffee—or tea—with you is we need a few volunteers to help display the items that are being auctioned off. Are you interested?"

She blinked a time or two. "Helping with the auction? How?"

"Mostly just holding up the donations while the auctioneer describes them. If you can't, I'll certainly understand. I know it's short notice."

"It's not that."

"Worried that your ex might show up?"

"Let's just say I'd rather not hold up the set of pearls while they're being auctioned off."

"Understandable. We'll have a couple of people there rotating in and out, so we'll be able to assign them to someone else." He took a sip of coffee. "Oh, and just so you know, I bought a surfboard."

She set her cup down on the table. "You did what?"

He had no idea why he'd just admitted that. But it seemed important somehow. Maybe he just needed her to know that he wasn't a quitter. With their earlier discussion about his hand, he wondered if he'd come across that way, just resigning himself to life behind a desk. Maybe this was one way to show her. He could even offer to do a little more consulting in the neurology department.

Why was it suddenly so important, when he wouldn't have even thought of doing so two or three months ago? He wasn't sure—didn't even want to question his motives too closely.

"I actually liked surfing. And since there is no snow here on South Beach…"

"Not much, no." She reached across as if she was going to touch him. He even braced himself for contact, but she changed her trajectory at the last second, setting her hand flat on the table instead. "I'm so glad, Garret. It really is kind of addictive."

Like her?

Not where he wanted his thoughts heading right now.

"I can see that it might be. I need to do some more practice on my— What is it called again?"

"Pop up. And you were already getting the hang of it. A few more trips into the surf and you'll be well on your way."

"I guess I should have asked about sharks when we were out there."

It had been hard to think about anything that didn't revolve around her, when they'd been on that beach. And watching her slim limbs as she'd demonstrated how to stand up and ride a wave hadn't left room for worrying about anything but himself.

"There's danger in everything. We just do whatever we can to minimize the risks."

Minimize the risks.

The only way to do that with Addy was to avoid her entirely, and he wasn't willing to do that. Even though he found himself hyperaware of everything she did, from the way her fingers curved around her teacup to the way a tiny dimple zipped in and out of sight on the corner of her mouth as she talked. It was fascinating, and he found himself watching and waiting for its next appearance.

Not good, Garret.

He was supposed to be here scoping things out, hoping that the patches of quicksand had dried up.

And if they hadn't?

"We weren't wearing wetsuits, so there's not much danger of looking like a tasty seal snack to them, right?"

"Even those who wear them don't have much trouble. There's an occasional bite, but very few fatalities. I've been surfing most of my life, and I still have all my limbs. Just pay attention to the surfing conditions. There are several apps you can use."

"Okay, I'll do that."

"Good. Now, as far as holding up the auction items,

please tell me I don't have to dress up like a game-show host and suddenly become graceful and beautiful."

She already was both of those, but to say it would be the same as ignoring those surf conditions she'd just talked about. These were dangerous waters full of riptides and crosscurrents. One wrong move and—

"No, just wear whatever you normally would to the auction."

"Why am I remembering the words 'black tie'?"

"Because it is?"

She groaned. "Ugh. That's not my cup of tea at all. I'm a true tomboy at heart."

A tomboy who surfed and looked totally at home on the water. He liked that. A little too much.

"You've been here longer than I have. Are you telling me you've never gone to one of these events?"

"Um, I'm a tomboy? Remember? I tend to stick to the donating side of things."

He'd assumed she was going to the fund-raiser or he never would have asked her to participate. "I'm sorry. I didn't realize you weren't planning to be there."

"It's okay. It's about time I went to one. It's easy to forget about all the efforts that go into keeping this hospital in operation."

"Are you sure?"

"I am. If you can take up surfing, I can certainly make an appearance at the auction." She smiled and took another sip of her tea. "It seems we're both moving a little bit beyond our comfort zones."

"It appears so. I'm not sure if that's a good thing or a bad thing."

"Oh, it's a good thing, Garret. A very good thing."

CHAPTER SIX

Addy knocked on the door to his office, even though Garret had told her to just go in and lay the auction participation form on his desk.

Knocking one more time to be sure, she opened the door and tiptoed into his office, which was ridiculous. He wasn't here, so there was no need to be quiet. She would just drop the paper on his desk and leave.

Laying the signed sheet in the very center of his desk, she was amazed by how clean it was. Nothing was on it but a three-tray wire rack, a pencil cup, a lamp and three rubber spheres the size of tennis balls. Each one was a different color and had a ring at one end of it. That was odd. She'd never noticed those before. Stress balls?

If so, why three of them? He only had two hands. Maybe they were something for the auction. She touched one, something about them striking a tone in her memory banks. Where had she seen these before?

She froze. She'd seen them down in physical therapy. Something in her throat caught as she realized these were not stress balls at all. They were exercise balls for the hand. The ring went over the middle finger to keep the ball from being dropped by someone with a poor grip.

She was pretty sure these hadn't been on his desk the last time she'd been in here. He must have forgotten to put them away. She picked one up, allowing the rubber to sit in the middle of her palm. It was heavier than she'd expected.

"Having fun?"

Oh, God. Her eyes closed.

What had she been thinking? This was something very private, and for her to have handled them…

She turned to face him.

"Sorry, I actually thought they were something for the auction until I—"

"Until you—?"

He wasn't going to help her wiggle her way out of this. She was supposed to have come into his office, dropped that paper on his desk and then turned around and walked out. Instead, she'd given herself license to explore, something he hadn't invited her to do.

"Until I remembered where I'd seen something similar." Her chin tilted. "I didn't realize you were still working on strengthening your hand. I'm glad."

It was the truth.

"I don't know why I got them out. They've pretty much done all they're going to do."

She set the ball in her hand next to the others, while Garret went around and sat in his chair.

"Is that what you told your patients? 'Well, six months of therapy hasn't helped. You might as well give up.'"

"Try four years."

She swallowed. Somehow she hadn't realized it had been that long since his accident. But, of course, he'd been at the hospital for three years, so the timing sounded right.

She picked up the ball she'd discarded. "Why keep them at all, if you're so sure they can't help?"

An irritable shrug was her answer. "Maybe as a reminder."

"You know what I think?"

"Are you going to tell me either way?" A muscle in his cheek told her to tread carefully, but, unlike him, Addy tended to wear her heart on her sleeve.

She said what she thought. "I think there's still a part of you that wants to help patients. I saw it in your eyes when you looked at Matthew."

"Oh, so you can read my thoughts now, can you?"

"No, but I know how I would feel if I were in your position."

"Do you?" He laid both hands on top of his desk. One of them spread flat; it became one with the surface it was on. The other hand sat awkwardly in a half crouch. Garret pushed down hard with it, the knuckles whitening, lines of pain forming on his face.

"Stop it."

He let the tension out of the damaged fingers and they went back to the way they were. "You're not in my position, though, are you? So you can't know how I do or don't feel."

She'd made him angry. That hadn't been her intent. Actually, she hadn't been going to say anything about the strengthening balls at all, except he'd caught her with one in her hand.

But, dammit, his life wasn't over, and for him to act as if it were was just—

Infuriating.

"You need to get a grip." She tossed the ball at him. He caught it with ease with his good hand. "In more ways

than one. Use those. Maybe they won't make a difference in what you can or can't do, but they can keep you
from losing the gains from whatever therapy you've had."

All the caged emotion seemed to drain out of him in
an instant. "Maybe you do know after all."

"I don't, Garret." She went around the desk and touched
his shoulder. "I truly don't. But don't settle for something
less than what your heart wants."

"And if my heart wants something it can't have?"

She knew all about that. She'd give anything to talk
to her mom one more time. And for her mom to recognize her as her daughter. But that wasn't going to happen.
Garret wasn't faced with that kind of useless wishing.
He could still salvage his situation into something good.

"Then find a compromise," she said. "Something that
gives you purpose and meaning."

He stood and faced her. "You think I don't have that
with my current job?"

"I don't know." She nodded toward the therapy balls.
"I'm not trying to tell you what to do. You have to decide
that for yourself."

He stared down at her for a long moment, a series
of emotions moving across his face. Unexpectedly, he
cupped her cheek, the warmth of his hand sifting into
her system.

Shock held Addy completely still, her lungs filled with
air she didn't dare release. He leaned down and brushed
his lips across her cheek in the lightest of touches. Then
he was gone, moving halfway across the room to where
a leather sofa and two chunky chairs sat. He shoved his
hands in his pockets. "Thank you, Addy. For believing
in the impossible."

"Hey, you didn't think you could surf either." She
smiled, although her system was still a wobbly mess over

that kiss. A kiss that hadn't even touched her lips, but had moved her more deeply than the one on the beach. Because the beach kiss had come from a place of physical attraction. Lust, even. And this one? It had come from the heart.

She'd never had anything like that with Leo. They'd had the lust. They'd had what she'd thought was love. But moments like this had been absent.

And, boy, she'd better be careful about where she allowed this to carry her. Having a harmless crush was one thing. Letting it grow into anything deeper?

Well, that was something entirely different. The next time she got involved with a man, she wanted things to go slow. She wanted to take her time and make sure she got it right. Make sure she knew everything about her partner.

And Garret was still her boss. She had no business getting into a relationship—no, not a relationship, an *infatuation*-ship—with him.

"The jury is still out on the surfing. But I'm going to practice." He opened his palm to show the ball she'd tossed him a few seconds ago. He put it into his damaged hand and contracted his fingers.

He was going to practice more things than surfing. At least, she hoped that was what he meant by his actions.

A smile played on her lips. She was suddenly happy, and she wasn't sure why. But right now she didn't care. All that mattered was he wasn't giving up.

"I would ask for a high five, but I think that's part of what got us in trouble last time."

"Hmm, I disagree. I think it was the bikini."

She laughed. "I think it was the shirt."

"The shirt?"

"Well, let's just say it was the lack of a shirt."

He blinked, then gave a grin that went straight up

her spine and lodged in the part of the brain that housed her emotions.

"Well, unless we want to get ourselves in trouble again, maybe we'd better confine our talk to something besides our clothes."

Her happiness turned into a sense of giddy euphoria. She should stop, just as he'd said, but she couldn't resist one last riposte.

"Ha, Dr. I-can't-take-the-heat-so-I'm-getting-out-of-the-kitchen Stapleton, I'll take that as my cue to leave."

He took a step forward and her eyes widened, but he didn't stop in front of her. He went to the door instead.

"Oh, I can take the heat just fine." Even as he said it, he twisted the knob and opened the door. "It's just not the right place. Or the right time."

She went out throwing him what she hoped was a saucy smile, even though, inside, her heart was shivering with a new kind of heat. Garret wanted her.

And, Lord help her, she wanted him too.

Just as Adelina was getting ready to head out for the night, her purse already slung over her shoulder, an elderly woman hobbled into the emergency room, using a walker. Glancing past her, Addy looked for whoever had brought her in, but there was no one, unless that person was parking the car.

They'd had a few people trickle in this evening, but it hadn't been enough to take her mind off what had happened in Garret's office.

He was going to keep trying? Because of what she'd said?

She was giving herself way too much credit.

"Can I help you?"

"I need a doctor."

Addy prayed Garret was already gone and wouldn't come down here. "I'm a doctor. What seems to be the problem?"

"It's not for me. It's for my husband."

She again glanced toward the door. "Is he in the car?" She didn't see how the woman could have driven a vehicle. She was barely able to keep herself upright. That was when she realized the woman was wearing a stained bathrobe rather than street clothes.

"Can't you see him? He's right here."

She swallowed. "What's your name?"

"He's right here. You're just not looking hard enough. His name is Daniel Lloyd Trentford. And I'm Marilyn Trentford."

A nurse came through the doors. She looked at Addy in open puzzlement.

"Can you look up a chart for me? Marilyn Trentford."

"Right away."

The woman gave her walker a little thump against the floor. "It's not for me, I told you. It's for my husband. He's ill."

Addy nodded and motioned Marilyn to follow her. "Let's take him back to an exam room, then, shall we?"

Waiting patiently as the woman made her way into the back, she intercepted the nurse, who spoke in low tones. "I overheard part of your conversation. I looked up her chart, and she does have a husband. But his name is Ben, not Daniel." There was a moment's hesitation. "Marilyn was diagnosed with Alzheimer's three years ago."

Addy's fingers curled into her palm as a spear of pain arced through her.

"You're sure."

"I am, sorry."

She might actually need Garret's help for this one,

if he was still here. "Can you see if Dr. Stapleton is in his office, while I get Mrs. Trentford into a room? And call the number she has listed and see who answers the phone." She was afraid if she said Ben's name, the woman might grow agitated.

Once she was in a room, she proceeded to get vitals on Marilyn, even though she protested that she wasn't the one who needed a doctor. Everything seemed normal, although her blood pressure was a little low. Addy also wanted to check for a urinary tract infection, since that could cause confusion in some elderly patients. If she had Alzheimer's, though, that was probably the cause of what basically amounted to a hallucination.

Garret came into the room a minute later with a frown directed right at her.

"Before you say anything, I was headed out the door. There's my purse."

"Good to know." He glanced at the patient. "Neuro consult?"

"No, I need some advice. Can I see you outside for a minute?"

Once they were in the hallway, she gave him a quick rundown of what they were dealing with. "In short, Ann is calling the house to see if her husband—her *real* husband—is home."

"And if he's not?"

"That's where I need the advice. Do I call social services?"

"We may have to, if we can't find a caregiver."

Ann came over a minute later. "I got an answer at the house."

"And?" Addy and Garret responded at the same time.

"Mrs. Trentford's son is there, but I'm afraid— Well, he found Mr. Trentford dead of what looks like natural causes. And when he went to look for his mother, he couldn't find her anywhere. He's relieved she's safe."

Tears blurred Addy's eyes for a moment. "She walked all the way to the hospital, and no one noticed?"

It was now pitch black outside and the streets of South Beach were no doubt gearing up for another Friday night of partying. It was a wonder she hadn't been hit by a car at some point.

Ann gave her shoulder a quick squeeze. "She knew enough to try to get help for him, even if she couldn't remember his name."

"How did she even find the hospital?"

"She's been here quite a bit. It could just be imprinted somehow. Who knows? Alzheimer's doesn't always follow a prescribed course."

Garret glanced at the closed door, his jaw tight. "Is her son coming for her?"

"He's waiting on the coroner to get to the house for his dad. But his sister—Mrs. Trentford's daughter—is on her way."

Addy knew this scenario played out time and time again across the nation, but it never failed to break her heart when someone came in with dementia. Her mom had passed away from it in this very hospital a year ago. Ann would remember that, which was why she'd squeezed her shoulder.

And tomorrow was her mom's birthday. She was going to put flowers on her grave—the start of what she hoped would become a yearly tradition. Her mom had loved daisies, her flower beds had been filled with them, until she could no longer remember how to care for them.

Garret didn't know any of that, however. And there was no reason to tell him.

"I'll just go make her comfortable, until they get here."

When she turned to go to the room, though, Garret stopped her. "Are you okay? You seem a little funny."

"I'm fine."

It was a lie, but he wouldn't know that. Unless he could somehow see the hard squeeze of her heart in her chest.

"You don't look fine. Why don't you let me take this one?"

"I want to care for her."

Ann stepped in. "I'll do it, Dr. Santini. Why don't you go ahead on home? Her daughter will be here soon."

She stood there, torn. There was really nothing she could do. And she could still remember her dad's heartbreak over her mom's death as if it were yesterday. Even though her mom hadn't known any of them by the time she passed away, he'd still insisted on caring for her every moment of the day. Then she'd choked on some food and contracted aspiration pneumonia.

Her dad was still living on his own in the house where Addy was raised, and, although she grieved her mother's death, she was glad her father was no longer shouldering that weight by himself.

Would Marilyn even realize her husband was gone?

That wasn't any of her business. "Thanks, Ann. I do appreciate it."

"Sure thing. Go home."

She went back in the room to retrieve her handbag. "Ann, one of our nurses, is going to come in and help you get settled."

"What about Daniel?"

Addy swallowed hard. "She'll help him too."

Then, feeling like the worst form of traitor, she walked out of the room and started down the hallway. Garret fell in step beside her.

"I think I need a drink," she said.

"May I ask why?" He tugged her arm to make her stop walking. "And if you're planning on driving home afterward?"

"I'll catch a cab—don't worry."

"How about if I join you?"

"Why?"

"Let's just say I've had a rough day as well." He rolled his eyes. "Hospital politics. Nothing new."

She hadn't told him about her mom, but he seemed to sense something was wrong.

"Are you going to take a taxi as well?"

"I'll be the designated driver." He smiled. "I don't generally drink anymore. But if you're planning on getting completely wasted, you might want to give me your address before you're too far gone."

"Nope. One drink is my limit. But I would appreciate the ride home. I'll catch a cab to work and pick up my car tomorrow. It'll be safe in the parking lot."

A half hour later, they were in one of the bars that didn't boast thumping music or a party atmosphere, because Addy was definitely not in the mood for a party of any type. Instead it was a small Irish pub that served sandwiches with their liquor. Addy had been planning to get a margarita, but decided on a dark ale instead.

"A surfer with a penchant for dark bitter beer."

The grief that had threatened to overcome her in the hospital dissipated. "I have to keep people on their toes."

"I'd say you do that on a regular basis."

The waiter brought their drinks and took their food order. Garret was getting a burger, medium rare, while she was getting a turkey club. "A doctor who eats partially cooked meat. What would our patients say?"

"I deal with politics, nowadays, not patients, remember? So I'm pretty sure they wouldn't care."

Damn, she'd forgotten that he didn't practice anymore. Garret still had all the mannerisms of a doctor. "You treated Matthew. And I'm sure there are others you've looked after since your accident."

He took a long drink of his water. "Nope. Matthew was the first."

"He's the first patient you've treated in four years?"

"Yes."

She couldn't help but wonder if he was headed down a wrong path. Whether he could operate or not, he should be in there consulting or diagnosing, something where he could still have a hand in medicine, even with a damaged hand. But that was his choice. She'd already tried to meddle once and he'd rebuffed her in no uncertain terms.

"Well, you did a great job. I'm pretty sure his mother thought so as well."

"There was no choice and no one else. It was as simple as that." He leaned forward. "Mind telling me what that little exchange between you and Ann was back at the hospital, and why you suddenly felt the need to come to a bar?"

She toyed with how much to share, but decided to hell with it. Why shouldn't he know? Maybe he already did, in fact.

"My mom died of Alzheimer's a year ago. It was a long hard road. And her birthday is tomorrow."

"I'm sorry. Tonight's situation with Marilyn must have hit hard. Your dad?"

"He's still alive and well, but it was an awful time for him—for all of us. She lived for five and a half years after her diagnosis. But at least she wasn't aware of what was happening at the end."

It hadn't helped that Leo had pretty much withdrawn from the marriage by the time she died. It made the grieving process that much harder. He attended the funeral, but as far as emotional support? There'd been nothing. So it shouldn't have come as much of a shock that he'd cheated. She hadn't exactly been a fun partner for the last couple of years. She wasn't going to tell Garret any of that, though.

"Any siblings to help you through?"

"Nope. I was an only child and my mom was my rock. And that rock slowly rolled further and further away, until it was a mere speck on the horizon. And then one day it blipped out of sight forever."

"It's a pretty terrible disease."

"Yes, it is. And when she was first diagnosed, I kind of went crazy. Made some stupid choices. Got married." She took a deep drink of her beer, welcoming the bitter taste that lingered at the back of her tongue.

"Ouch. But I do understand about making stupid choices."

She swallowed her mouthful of brew. "What about your parents? Still living?"

"Yes. They're in New York. Both retired at this point. My dad was a neurosurgeon like—like I was. My mom was a schoolteacher. She still tutors algebra on the side."

"Algebra. Wow. That's impressive." And his parents were probably the same age as hers. He was blessed to have them both alive and healthy. "Do *you* have any sisters or brothers?"

"I have a younger sister. She's a colonel in the army."

"You have very strong family members."

"Yes. Your dad had to have been pretty strong too, from what you just said."

He was, and that was what had made her life with Leo such a disappointment. He'd presented himself as calm and stable, something she'd really needed at the time, but the reality had been far from that. He'd barely scraped by in his studies to be an EMT. And wanting to get divorce counseling?

She pushed her beer away from her with a suddenness that almost sloshed some of the liquid over the rim of the glass.

"Are you okay?"

"I must be a lighter weight than I thought."

If he suspected she wasn't quite telling the truth he didn't say anything. And then the waiter had their food ready, placing the plates in front of them and asking if there was anything else they wanted.

"I think we're good," Garret said.

"Thanks for coming with me. You were right. That patient hit me a little harder than I realized."

"It saved me from going home to an empty house. It's nice to go places from time to time. Something I haven't done in a while."

"Me either." She and Leo hadn't gone anywhere together since her mother died. There was no way their marriage could have survived, affair or no affair.

They ate their food, the conversation turning to lighter subjects like medical school horror stories. They'd gone to different schools but the trials and tribulations were the same everywhere, it seemed. Every school had "that" instructor. One who seemed to delight in making students' lives miserable.

"You'd never be that guy," she told Garret. She pulled up short, realizing what she'd just said. "Sorry."

"It's okay. I'm not saying I'll never teach, but it's not on my radar at the moment. My current job keeps me pretty busy."

Well, at least he was no longer reciting that stupid quote about teachers not being able to do what they taught.

He went on. "Are you that anxious to get rid of me?"

"What? Of course not."

He smiled. "Maybe you have your eye on my job."

"Huh-uh. No way. You couldn't pay me enough to be a hospital administrator."

"Why not?"

She pulled her glass back toward her, deciding maybe she did need a little more after all. It seemed she was determined to keep stepping into dangerous territory. The beer would either set her on a right path or make it so that she didn't care if she stumbled into a ravine. Too bad Garret wasn't indulging as well. Then maybe he wouldn't remember every stupid word she was busy spitting out.

"It just isn't something I'd be interested in. Your mom is good at algebra. I am not."

"I don't remember using any algebra at all in my job."

Do not use the term "bean counter," Addy, if you know what's good for you.

"Since I don't really know what your job involves, I guess I shouldn't make blanket statements like that. I'm just not an administrator type. I'd rather be out on the floor doing stuff."

Another gulp of the bitter brew to wash her mouth out. She was such an idiot. Maybe she really was a lightweight and the beer was doing the talking. Somehow she didn't think so, though.

This time Garret didn't correct her or tell her she was wrong about his job.

"I'd rather be out on the floor 'doing stuff' too. But since I can't—"

And that was so much worse. Because he'd put her in her place with a plop and there wasn't a damned thing she could do about it. Because he was right. Hospital administrator wasn't his chosen profession. He was a surgeon. Except surgery was now out of his reach.

It was really none of her business what he did, or what field he chose to go into. Sometimes life dealt you a bad hand. And sometimes you dealt yourself a bad hand. He'd had an accident after falling asleep at the wheel. And Addy had married a man who was wrong for her in so many ways. They'd both whipped up disasters and been forced to dine at the table afterward no matter how awful the main course turned out to be.

But, as he'd said at the beach, you could learn from your mistakes and avoid making them again.

She was never going to jump into a relationship without carefully considering the person and the timing. She and Leo had come together and married way too quickly. The fact that disappointment had come just as quickly shouldn't have been a surprise to either of them.

"You're right, Garret. And this is why I shouldn't drink. And why I should have come by myself. I hope you'll forgive anything I've said that might be off the mark."

He smiled. "Was it really the beer talking? I seem to remember having some of these same conversations and you were stone-cold sober at the time."

She laughed. "Okay, you've got me there. My mouth has gotten me in trouble plenty of times—as you can tell. I remember more than one teacher sending home a note to my parents with that same remark. I'll try to do better."

"I like that you say what you think. So many people don't anymore."

The topic changed to treatment options and work-related subjects and Addy was off the hook. Because these were things they could agree or disagree on without being in danger of stepping on each other's toes. She assumed Garret was divorced. He'd never actually mentioned a wife, but had said his daughter died of leukemia. So either he'd been a single dad or he was divorced or separated.

And then they were done with their meal and Garret was asking if she wanted to walk down the sidewalk on this balmy South Beach evening.

She did, and she wasn't sure why, other than she'd enjoyed tonight far more than she should have. Maybe it was just such a change from what she'd had with Leo.

The moon was huge as they strolled down the walkway, its reflection on the ocean turning it into a shimmery curtain. She'd come out here a few times with friends when she was younger, and they'd actually skinny-dipped at midnight without anyone catching them. Another of the times she'd let her impulsiveness take charge.

Not that she was going to skinny-dip with Garret.

So why did she itch to go down to the shore and feel the sand between her toes? Because it was a beautiful night, and she didn't often get down this way anymore after dark.

"Do you think we could walk on the beach before we leave?"

"I'm not exactly dressed for wading."

He wasn't. His polo shirt and chinos were very business-oriented. But that didn't matter. She'd already told herself she wasn't going to do anything wild and crazy. So they'd be fine.

"Neither am I. It's just so gorgeous, and we're right here." She turned to face him, walking backward, the breeze lifting her hair off her neck and making her sigh. "Come on. Just for a few minutes."

"You talked me into it."

"Good."

Kicking off the low heels she'd worn to work, she

twisted the side of her loose gauzy skirt into a knot that held it up without actually revealing anything more than a little sliver of her legs. She bent down to pick up her shoes and then ventured onto the fine grains that made up the beach. The sand was still warm from the afternoon sun and felt so good against her bare toes. She glanced back to make sure Garret was following her lead.

He was. He'd taken off his shoes and socks and had rolled his pants up to midcalf. His legs were still tanned from their outing last week.

Her mouth watered.

The man looked as good in business attire as he did in his board shorts. It wasn't fair. He had everything a woman could possibly want in the looks department. And the more she learned about him, the more she realized he had a lot going for him in the personality department as well. She held her arms out from her sides and closed her eyes, letting the breeze flow across her. Her skirt billowed against her legs, a sensual tickle that nothing could imitate.

"Feels so good out here."

"Yes, it does." The words were a soft murmur. "I don't think I've ever walked on a beach at night."

Her eyes flew open. "You're kidding."

"I didn't grow up in a coastal town, remember? I went for walks in Central Park instead."

"Is it as beautiful as this?" Her arms were still outstretched, and she did a slow spin to encompass everything around them: the sand, the moon, the stars glistening on the water.

"There are a lot of beautiful things in this world."

Something about the slow solemn way he said that made her stop turning, a shiver going over her. He was watching her, hands planted low on his hips, his bad one seeming to perch comfortably for once. His shoes were now on the ground beside him. "Addy…"

"Yes?" Her breath caught in her throat.

He took a step closer. "I think I'm about to do something incredibly stupid."

"I doubt that." And if the look on his face was any indication, she was in complete agreement.

"Just how drunk are you?"

"Am I acting like I am? I didn't even drink the whole beer. I'm just so glad to be out here tonight…" She hesitated, then decided to just say it. "With you."

"I was hoping you'd say that."

In a second, he had closed the gap between them, his right hand encircling her wrist and tugging her to him.

And when his head came down, she knew the kiss was coming. Only this time, it would be different than the previous one. Very, very different.

CHAPTER SEVEN

ADDY'S HOUSE WAS the closest, and the second she unlocked the door, they were through it, the passion that had ignited on the beach still burning just as strong after the ten-minute drive—which had seemed to take forever. The only saving grace were the kisses that punctuated the stoplights along the way.

Somehow he managed to close the front door and then his mouth found hers again. The taste of beer still clung to her lips along with whatever it was that made Addy, Addy.

She was intoxicating. Breathtaking. More heady than any alcohol known to man. And tonight, he planned to drink his fill. It seemed as if the last couple of weeks had been leading to this very place, and, right now, Garret couldn't think of anywhere he'd rather be.

Her arms twined around his neck, body flattening to his, and, heaven help him, his libido was already roaring at him to pick up the pace.

No way. No how.

If they ended up in bed—and he hoped to hell they did—he wanted this to last for as long as possible.

He'd told himself to stay away from her after that surfing lesson, but they were both adults. This didn't have to go any further than one night of wild sex. If she was using him to drown out the pain of losing her mom, even better. Neither one of them needed a permanent relationship. She was in the midst of getting a divorce and he was in the throes of…

He had no idea. All he knew was he wasn't getting married again. Or having kids.

His good hand slid beneath the back of her shirt, the warmth and softness of her skin making something growl to life inside him. No, it wasn't just growling to life. It was already wide awake and howling for attention.

Addy's palms cupped the back of his head, one on either side of his neck. She leaned back slightly as her lips left his.

"Where?"

He knew exactly what she was asking.

"Babe, it's your house. You choose."

The endearment had dropped from his tongue without warning, and he tensed for a second. But if she minded, he couldn't tell. Right now, her thumbs were drawing designs in his hair that were getting to him in all the right places.

She glanced toward the back of the house and her teeth came down on her lower lip as if puzzling through something or other. "How about the couch? It's long and… It's long."

"It can be the floor, for all I care."

She leaned up and whispered in his ear, her warm breath slicing and dicing his control. "The floor would be *much* too uncomfortable."

"The couch it is, then."

Her hands slid down his back, fingers tucking into the waistband of his pants, sending another jolt of need through him.

He took a long, slow drink of her mouth, before murmuring, "Lead the way."

Taking him by the hand, she tugged him through a door that opened to the dining room, a big round table giving him some definite ideas, before she ducked through yet another doorway.

The living room.

And she was right. The couch was long. And it went in two directions, forming an L. It was perfect.

Just as she was.

His index finger touched her bottom lip then glided over her chin and slid over her throat, reaching the rounded neckline of her stretchy top.

God, he wished he had a second hand. Or at least one that worked. He didn't try to unbutton the front; instead he let his palm wander down, bumping over her breast, hearing her hiss of air as he did. "Will this go over your head?"

She didn't ask what he meant, just took the initiative and made short work of the buttons. "They can be tricky."

They weren't, but he blessed her for sparing him the ordeal of having to fumble with them. He could do it, he did up his own shirts daily, but it took a while. Doing it for someone else would embarrass him somehow, even though it was a ridiculous feeling. And nowadays, he tended to wear polos instead of shirts with a long line of buttons unless it was a special occasion.

She let her blouse drop to the ground and stood there in her skirt and a very lacy white bra that played peekaboo with his gaze. For a few seconds he couldn't do anything other than stare.

"You're beautiful, Addy."

She smiled. "You're pretty nice yourself." Moving forward, she kissed the bottom of his throat, her tongue swirling in the spot at the base of it. Then she reached behind him and balled up the bottom of his shirt and tugged it out of his pants and tried to pull it over his head. He bent forward slightly to help her. Then it was on the ground beside hers.

With one arm around her waist, he walked her backward until her legs met the couch. She sat and kicked her shoes off, then lay back. He followed her down, sliding up her body, using his elbows and hands to support his torso. "You're right. Comfortable couch. I approve."

"Yes, it is." She leaned up to lick along his lower lip. "And it's still a virgin."

He blinked for a second before smiling. "You and your—?"

"No. Never."

"Ah…in that case." His good hand slid behind her back and felt for the clasp on her bra. Found it. Snapped it open and then pulled the lacy item off from the front. He tossed it over the side of the couch.

He swallowed, awed and a little uncertain with how this was going to work. He hadn't been with a woman since his divorce.

Oh, he knew the mechanics, and that he could get there, but he wanted more than that. He wanted her to enjoy it. Wanted to take her to heights she'd never reached before.

Only he wasn't sure he could.

As if she sensed his doubts, she ran her hands up his back and tickled behind his ear. "Roll over, Garret."

"What?"

"You heard me."

She half hefted him when he didn't move fast enough, but then he was on his back, with her half sprawled across him. Tucking her skirt up around her upper thighs, she sat up and straddled his hips. And there was no way she could miss his reaction to her. Not quite the way he'd envisioned this going, but he appreciated her removing some of the worry more than she could know.

"So, now that I've lured you into my lair," she whispered, "what should I do with you?"

She had a skirt on. No buttons. No zipper. That was a good start. As were those creamy breasts that jiggled with every move she made.

"You should lean down here so I can kiss you."

Right on cue, she curved her torso forward, only he didn't kiss her mouth. Lowering his head, he sought out the curve of her breast, using his hand to cup it and help him reach. And reach he did. When his tongue stroked across her nipple she whimpered, back arching into him.

He took that as a sign and settled in to enjoy.

She planted her hands on his shoulders and balanced, her hips pressing down and hitting him in just the right spot.

It was ecstasy. And torture.

Time to somehow get that condom he carried out of his wallet. He'd kept one there, but had never used it. And right now he wasn't sure how he was going to get it on. One-handed it would have to be.

Letting go of her, he shoved his hand under himself and found his back pocket and the wallet in it. He grappled it out and flipped it open. Most of the time, he laid it on a counter and pulled whatever he needed from it, but right now, he was upside down and had no flat surface in sight. And there was no way he was going to hold it in his teeth.

Without hesitation, Addy took it from him. "Where?"

"There's a compartment in the side of—"

"Found it." She fiddled with the opening and then

pulled the packet out and got to her feet. "You take care of what you need to, and I'll take care of what I need to." She set the wallet on an end table and laid the condom on his stomach. Then she reached under her skirt and down came her panties.

Garret's heart began pumping out obscenities in his chest. The very best kind.

Right. He was supposed to be doing something. He undid his button and zipper and pushed his pants and briefs down his hips. His shoes were already gone, so Addy tugged his socks free one by one. Then she took hold of his trousers and pulled them the rest of the way off along with his underwear until he was bare before her.

She licked her lips, taking the condom package and ripping it open.

"I can do it."

"Okay." She handed it to him and watched him roll it down his length, her eyes focused on the act.

So much for taking his time. He wanted her. Badly. And he knew himself well enough to realize he wasn't going to last. "Come here."

"I thought you'd never ask." Straddling him once again, she cupped his face and kissed him, the contact sweet and hot and everything in between. "Mmm, hurry."

"Hell, I don't want to—"

"It's okay. It'll be good. I've wanted this."

She had? Well, so had he. More than he cared to admit.

Grasping a hold of himself, he brushed over her, gently, feeling his way. Any ideas he might have had about entering her slowly went to hell. The second he was in position she took his entire length with one hard push.

He swore. And prayed. Broke out in a cold sweat as he willed himself to hold very, very still.

She moved, but when he tried to stop her, she ignored him.

Taking his hand, she pressed it to her. "Go, Garret. Oh, go!"

Finding her, he stroked and squeezed while she rode him, her head thrown back, hair tumbling loose around her shoulders. She moaned, lips parted as she held herself steady with one hand on the back of the couch and continued to rise and fall.

And then he felt it. Boiling up inside him in an uncontrollable tide. He gritted his teeth as it poured over him, aware on some level that she was climaxing as well, her body contracting around his and urging him to lose himself inside her.

Minutes passed. His eyes had closed at some point. And she'd stopped moving. He reached up and curved an arm around her back, hauling her down to him, kissing her bare shoulder.

"That was…"

Her breath came out in a long hum of sound. "Yes, it was."

She settled against him, nuzzling closer to his chest, head turned sideways. Her hair tickled his chin, but he didn't care. A slow contentment began to weave its way through him. He didn't want her to get up. Didn't want to ever move off this couch.

But maybe she wanted him out, now that it was over.

When his hand moved, though, she murmured, "No. Stay. Please."

He was pretty sure that tomorrow he was going to feel differently about spending the night, but right now…? Right now he was perfectly happy to stuff any and all doubts about what they'd done out of sight and worry about them later. Because he was going to do exactly what she asked. He was going to stay with her. All night long.

Addy covered him with the sheet she'd taken from the linen closet. He didn't stir. Waking up and seeing his face all soft with sleep, that injured hand for once out in plain sight… She gulped as a wave of longing swept over her.

When he'd asked where she wanted to make love, she'd frozen for a second or two. She hadn't wanted to go to her bed, didn't sleep in it herself, much less want to spend the night there with another man. She'd been meaning to toss it out and get a new one, but she just hadn't had the time to go and look for one.

The couch had seemed like the perfect spot.

And it had been. It still was. He looked gorgeous parked there, his clothes now neatly folded over one of the arms.

His insecurities over how to proceed had been obvious and had touched her deeply. There had been no need to worry, however. It had been fantastic. Better than she could have imagined.

She shivered, realizing she wanted him all over again.

Lord, it probably shouldn't have happened.

She'd slept with him for all the wrong reasons: the Alzheimer's patient had set off a fresh round of grief about losing her mom. She hadn't wanted to be alone.

She was having a hard time caring about the should-not-haves. They were adults. And it was good sex. Very good sex, since she was standing there contemplating waking him up for some more of the same. People here did things like this all the time and never thought a thing of it.

Easy to think that now. But what she'd do when he actually got up, she had no idea.

For now, she could go cook some breakfast.

She heated the skillet and then cracked some eggs, flipping them with a flick of her wrist a few minutes later. Between that and the smell of the bacon she'd started in another pan, she had to admit, she was famished.

Hopefully when he woke up it wouldn't turn all awkward and complicated.

Why wouldn't it?

She'd been issuing orders right and left last night. "Roll over. Hurry."

Yikes. She'd never realized she had the heart of a drill sergeant. She didn't. She'd simply been trying to ease the way for him, never stopping to think that maybe he would find that uncomfortable.

He would have said something if it was. Wouldn't he?

Her own doubts began crowding in, making her second-guess everything she'd done.

"No fair."

She whirled around and found him with his pants back on his hips, the zipper still undone. And his briefs? Nowhere to be seen that she could tell.

"What do you mean?"

He took several steps into the room. "You're up. And dressed."

She'd had that same thought a few minutes earlier.

"Shouldn't I be? It's six o'clock."

"On Saturday. Do you work one of the shifts today?"

"Not until noon." She grinned, turning off the burner controls. "But I have something I need to do this morning."

He grabbed her around the waist and yanked her to him. "So do I." His head was just lowering to kiss her when a piece of bacon made a loud popping sound.

They laughed. And broke apart so she could turn off the other burner.

"What was it you had to do?" he asked as he stood behind her, watching.

She hesitated. "I want to put flowers on my mom's grave for her birthday. She loved daisies, and I think she would like knowing someone thought about her today." A rush of tears formed, and she struggled to push them back. "I hope she knew how much my dad and I loved her."

"Daisies." Something about his voice made her swipe at her eyes and then whirl around to look at him. What she saw shocked her.

He had his good hand braced on the countertop, holding himself upright, while a muscle worked in his jaw. Tight lines radiated out from his eyes.

He looked like a man in agony.

"What is it? Your hand?" Her glance went down to his side, where his injured fingers were curled in their normal position.

"No. It's not my hand." He stopped, then shook his head. "I should go."

He pulled up his zipper and fumbled with the button on his pants.

And just like that, the mood was gone. No more fuzzy feelings. No more playful words.

Just Garret's face, which looked—blank.

He'd seemed fine a few minutes ago. Maybe the pop of the bacon had jerked him back to his senses.

Ugh. What was she thinking, begging him to stay until morning and then tucking him in and cooking him a cozy breakfast?

They weren't friends. Or really even colleagues.

He probably thought she was a complete idiot. God, how stupid could she be?

It didn't stop her from trying to salvage the situation, though. "Do you want something to eat before you go?"

"No, I'll grab a bite a little later. Thanks, though." He went into the other room and when he came back he was completely dressed, including his socks and shoes.

"I guess I'll see you at work on Monday."

"Yes." He walked to the door, leaving her to follow him. "And, Addy?"

"Yes?" Why did she suddenly feel as if she could burst into tears at any minute?

"I'm sure your mom knew you loved her very much."

And with those quiet words, he let himself out of the door and closed it with a quiet click.

He'd signed the divorce papers. She'd tossed the packet on her console by the door. The day of their argument in front of the ER, he'd said he wanted to do divorce counseling before signing anything. She'd been flabbergasted. He had cheated on her. Was now living with his girlfriend. And he was worried about an amicable split?

He'd evidently changed his mind about the counseling. The thick envelope from his lawyer had been in her mailbox when she'd come home from work last night.

A week had passed since she'd placed flowers on her mom's grave, since Garret had walked away from her house after uttering a line that had made her sink to the ground and cry the second the door had closed behind him.

She'd barely seen him since then, and the regrets she hadn't had the night they had sex had been growing like weeds ever since. Now they were tall and thick and choked out anything that might have disagreed.

What had you pictured, Addy? A kiss on the cheek as he sent you off to work?

Maybe she'd expected a series of cozy little rendez-vous with Garret. Well, that was not going to happen.

Thank God he'd used protection. For both of their sakes. The last thing she needed was to get pregnant by accident. Leo had wanted to wait a while before having kids. That "while" had turned into their entire marriage.

She should have seen it for the sign that it was.

And now she was thirty-five and wondering if it was too late and feeling like a fool. In more ways than one.

Well, she could consider this her free pass, redeem-able for one dumb move.

And which move was that? Marrying Leo? Or hav-ing sex with Garret?

Well, if Garret hadn't taken off like a shot, she might have considered that a casual dalliance. People did it all the time, right?

Just because she wasn't built like that, didn't mean there was anything wrong with it.

How about the fact that Garret seemed to be avoiding her like the plague?

Maybe she needed to confront him and clear the air. He hadn't exactly apologized, but the way he'd left had bothered her.

Whatever it was, they couldn't go on avoiding each other forever. Besides, they were down to a week and a half before the auction. She and the other volunteers were supposed to meet with him and some of the marketing team this morning to discuss everyone's part in it. She was going to see him. Unless she dropped out of helping.

She thought for a second.

No. She'd given her word. He might be uncomfortable about what had happened, but that didn't mean she was going to change her life over it. Besides, he was the one who'd asked her to participate in the fund-raiser, so he could just suck it up and deal with it.

And afterward? She was going to corner him and either figure this out or agree not to figure it out. But she wasn't going to be made to feel she needed to duck for cover any time he was around.

With that decided, she headed off to the bedroom to take a shower and get dressed.

For work.

CHAPTER EIGHT

HE HAD A pretty good idea why Addy wanted to see him after the meeting. But the last thing he wanted to talk about was what had happened between them.

Her mention of putting flowers on her mom's grave had been a punch to the gut, reminding him that he'd avoided going to the cemetery for far too long. He and Patrice had gone together to put flowers on Leticia's grave for the first year after her death. Then he'd somehow had to work, whenever his wife had suggested it, so she'd gone alone. Continued to go alone. Until the accident. And then he'd moved here.

He should have been there. Should have gone to put flowers on his own child's grave, dammit!

His jaw clenched as he tried to rein in the emotions that were threatening to explode.

Addy had reminded him of everything he'd lost. And now she wanted to talk.

What the hell was there to say?

He had no idea, but right now, he needed to concentrate on getting through this meeting in one piece.

They were to the question-and-answer portion, and thank heavens this was Marketing's area. He'd been all too aware of Addy sitting out there in her scrubs, the lanyard around her neck proclaiming her a doctor of Miami's Grace Hospital.

And he was up here with the people who took care of the building and employees—but not patients.

"Last thing. We'd like to have a screen as in previous years that flashes through some of our hospital's success stories, so if you have any suggestions, please see me afterward so we can contact those patients and ask for a picture or two. We don't need details, since we have HIPAA laws to consider." Someone whispered something to the speaker. "Okay, I've just been told we've had some photographers floating around the hospital taking candids these past couple of weeks, so we'll intersperse your suggestions with those shots."

Garret leaned a shoulder against the wall, crossing his arms and scanning the twenty people in the room. When he got to Addy, she averted her eyes.

She'd been looking right at him.

That made him swallow. He'd walked away from her house without an explanation, without even eating the breakfast she'd obviously made for him.

And when he'd awoken, he'd found a sheet over him. That had turned him to warm mush. He'd gone to the kitchen intent on dragging her back to bed, and then she'd mentioned her mom's grave. About wondering if she knew she was loved. It was as if she'd dumped an icy bucket of water over him. All he'd wanted to do was get out of there.

Had Leticia known? Could she somehow see that he couldn't be bothered to go and visit her grave?

The meeting was over, but instead of coming over to talk to him, she went up to the front to talk to one of the presenters, instead. He gave her a piece of paper and she scribbled something on it and then handed it back to him.

What was that all about?

A second later, she headed his way and his whole body tensed. Here it came.

"Can we go to your office, maybe?"

That made it official. Whatever she wanted to talk about was something she didn't want anyone to overhear.

"Sure." He tilted his head to indicate the table where the marketing person was still standing answering questions. "What was that about?"

"They asked for suggestions about the slideshow. I decided to give them Grace Turner's name."

"Grace…" His head cocked as something jogged his memory. "The house-fire family?"

"Yes. I thought they'd be a great choice."

"They would." He'd wondered a couple of times how that family was doing. Hopefully Grace was feeling better and had made her peace with what had happened.

He led the way to his office, which thankfully was just down the hallway from the meeting room. He started toward the desk and then changed his mind when he saw the exercise balls still sitting on top of it. He didn't want to pave the way for any more lectures on her part. Especially since he'd just stood in that meeting and wished he were sitting in one of the chairs instead of standing up at the front.

Motioning her to the sofa, he chose one of the chairs and then waited for whatever it was she had to say.

"So…" She leaned forward and clasped her hands on her knees. "I'm not sure exactly how to say this, but things have been awkward since— Well, you know. I'm not quite sure how to fix it."

"There's nothing to fix." That came out a little bit harsher than he'd meant for it to, so he tried again. "We work together. A relationship of any kind between us would be hard."

Her brows went up. "You think that's what this is about? That I want something more than what happened? Um, no. I'm in the middle of a divorce and I was mourning my mom. The last thing I want is to start something." Her face hardened. "Is that why you left so suddenly, and why you seem to be going out of your way to steer clear of me now? If so, don't worry. What happened was a onetime thing."

Despite her words, a flash of something that could have been hurt appeared in her eyes. He owed it to her to tell her the truth.

"I left like I did because I can't—didn't—put flowers on my daughter's grave."

"What?"

"You heard me."

"I did, but I don't understand. What does that have to do with what happened?"

"You mentioned getting flowers for your mom's grave and it brought back things I thought I'd dealt with. Evidently I haven't." He swallowed. "I didn't put flowers on Leticia's grave, even when I could. Even when I was still in New York. Her death did something to me. It changed me, and not for the better."

"I had no idea. I'm sorry."

"I didn't want to explain that morning. Didn't think I could get through an explanation, actually. So if you think I've been avoiding you, you're probably right. I just didn't stop to think about how it might look."

"Maybe you should go."

He froze, her words cutting like a scalpel. "You want me to leave Miami's Grace?"

"Oh, no! Not at all. But maybe you should take a week and go take flowers to your daughter."

He frowned, not expecting that suggestion. "Maybe someday."

"If you have other children, you might want them to—"

"I won't. I'm not having any more children."

Her head tilted. "Not ever?"

"No. Losing her was too hard." If he couldn't even visit his daughter's grave, how the hell would he be able to look into another baby's eyes without thinking of her—without wondering if that child, too, would be taken from him. Even the thought made a spurt of bile shoot up his throat.

She nodded. "I can't even imagine. But thank you for explaining."

"You're welcome." He heaved out a gust of air, relief washing over him. "So we're good?"

"I thought I did something wrong."

That was the problem. She hadn't. She'd done everything right. A little too right.

"Nope. Not at all." He smiled. "I didn't drive you to working too hard, did I?"

"Possibly."

"What?" Tension began building at the back of his head all over again.

"I was joking, Garret. But it wouldn't be a tragedy even if I did. Working actually helps clear my head—it takes my mind off myself."

"Using it to dull your pain can backfire, though. I know from experience."

"That won't happen to me."

"You know that for a fact?"

Her mouth twisted as she seemed to think about how

to respond. "I won't drive when I'm exhausted. I'll take a cab. And at least I'm helping people in the process. I'm not burying myself in a bottle or drugs."

"You're right." He sat back and crossed an ankle over his knee. "And now I'll get off your case about it."

She laughed. "Thank you. So what are you going to do with your weekend? Take your new surfboard out for a spin?"

"I thought about it, but I don't think I'm proficient enough to go out on my own. Buying it was probably a mistake."

"It wasn't a mistake. Learning a new skill is always good." There was an obvious hesitation before she added, "And it might even help your hand more than those therapy balls."

Her glance went to his desk, making him wish he'd put the balls away. He'd begun using them again, even though he wasn't sure why. "Surfing will? How?"

"It's a natural way to add to what you've already done." Ticking down on her fingers, she named a few ways. "Carrying your board helps with grasping skills. Paddling out to a wave—the water creates drag on your hand and fingers, like resistance bands would, but there's a better range of motion used in the ocean. Planting your hands on the surfboard when you pop up into your stance. You've said you have problems flexing the fingers on that hand. I noticed when we went out that you curled the fingers and used your fist. Why not flatten your hand as much as you can instead and let the weight of your body do the work? I would say do the same with push-ups, if you do them. It might hurt, but as long as your tendons aren't in danger of snapping, it can be a good way to coax them to lengthen."

She took a breath to continue, but he cut her off.

"You'd make a great physical therapist. I hadn't thought about surfing being good for anything but recreation, but maybe you're right. You thought about all of this when we were out on the water?"

"I didn't until you said you'd bought a board. Swimming is always good exercise, and surfing works a lot of muscles in a lot of different ways. Why not use it to your benefit?"

"Why not indeed? I'll give it some thought."

"If you don't want to go by yourself, maybe we can set up one day a week when we spend a few hours out. I'll have to plan my schedule around the tides on weekends, if those are the only days off you get."

He wasn't sure spending more time with her outside work was a good idea, but since they'd gotten any baggage off the table in regard to the night they'd spent together, what could it hurt? They were both aware of the lingering attraction between them, so they'd be on guard now. Right?

"Weekends are my official days off, but I can sneak away for a few hours every now and then."

And that sounded a little suspect. But she knew what he meant.

He certainly wasn't opposed to the idea, even if he wasn't convinced his hand would reap much benefit from it. He could still go and have a good time.

"There are whole surfing communities, so it wouldn't have to be forever. Just until you meet some people. I do understand about not wanting to go out alone. I have the same problem, which is why I don't go out as much as I'd like to. So this will get me back into the groove as well."

He didn't see himself hanging out with the surfer crowd, but he didn't contradict her.

"I don't think you've ever lost your groove, from the way you looked out there."

She smiled. "Well, thanks. I think. But you don't have to be an expert surfer. There are people of all ages and abilities out there."

"Easy to say when you're one of the experts."

"I'm not. I just enjoy the sun and surf." She stood. "Let me check the surf reports and I'll come up with some options for some days next week. How does that sound?"

"Are you sure?"

He didn't want her to feel forced into babysitting him.

"I am. But only if you'll admit that it might actually help your hand."

He got to his feet as well. "I'm willing to admit the 'might' part, while retaining a dose of healthy skepticism."

The skepticism outweighed anything else at the moment. But doing something other than working and sitting at home would be good for him in general.

"That's all I'm asking."

"Sounds good, then."

He saw her to the door and closed it behind her before he could watch her head down the hallway, slim hips swinging as she went.

She was the one who'd offered, he reminded himself as doubts began popping up like surfers on their boards.

It was then that he remembered that images of popping up were the last ones he should be bringing to mind. Because the previous mental pictures of Addy on a surfboard were branded in his skull from here to eternity.

Okay, so Garret hadn't quite expected to be on the water the day after she mentioned juggling her schedule. But he was. And each time he paddled his board out, he was aware of the tension of the water on his bad hand, the way the gentle pressure coaxed his fingers to stretch and release in rhythmic strokes. In fact, where he had always used his right hand to compensate for the weakness in his left, he purposely began to pull harder with his bad hand, making his fingers come together to form a cup that moved more water. Tendons strained, muscles burned, but it wasn't painful.

He selected a wave in the distance and waited for it to arrive, then flopped his midsection onto his board and paddled. As soon as he felt that magical push, he flattened his hands on the board and tried to spring to his feet. Big mistake. Daggers stabbed at his fingers the second his weight fell on them and lights flashed behind his lids. He crashed into the water and came up sputtering, holding his hand to his chest as he trod water and waited for the agony to subside. Too much too fast.

Hell, this was a terrible idea.

Addy paddled over to where he was. "Are you okay?"

"Yes. It just hurt more than I expected it to." He let his hand sink below the surface both to cool the burning and to hide the vague sense of embarrassment. He'd told her he didn't want to come out here alone, but he hadn't really thought through the ramifications of her seeing him in pain. He didn't like the feeling.

"Maybe try cupping your hand. I know I told you to try to keep it flat, but maybe somewhere in the middle of those two extremes would be better."

She was so matter-of-fact about it that it eased some of his misgivings.

The next time, he kept his fingers curled more so that his weight was distributed along the base of his palm rather than the fingers themselves. Then he was up, hands held as he'd seen others do to get his balance.

Addy had caught the wave behind his and dropped off further in to shore than he did, making her way back to where he was. "How was that? Better?"

"It's going to take some work, finding that balance between not protecting it and not hurting it."

"Isn't that the way with almost everything in life?"

He mulled over the words a time or two, then forced a lightness into his voice that he didn't quite feel. "Adding philosopher to your list of medical titles?" What she'd said had hit way too close to home. He was still struggling to find that balance in life. The balance of retreating behind a wall of steel to avoid emotional pain, and exposing too much of himself and getting stung for it.

Kind of like the night he'd spent at her house. He'd allowed himself to become vulnerable only to take off at a sprint at the mere mention of flowers on a grave. She'd implied that she'd been confused and hurt at the abrupt way he'd left.

He wasn't confused. But he was going to be more careful. The last thing he wanted was to accidentally cause Addy pain.

Sex might blur reality for a little while, but it soon showed back up, shining a spotlight on every character flaw he possessed.

And he was finding out his biggest flaw of all was running from his problems. He'd used work after Leticia died to flee from not only the pain of her death, but also the breakdown of his marriage. He swallowed. Maybe he was even using his position as administrator to run from the possibility of practicing medicine again.

"A philosopher? Not hardly. Just throwing out the first thought that came to mind. I seem to be good at that." She propped her chin on her board. "You up to catching a few more waves?"

Anything to keep from dissecting her words any more than he already had.

"I am. And thanks for coming with me today." He might not be sure of the wisdom of spending more time with her, but she was right about surfing being good for his hand. The muscles were aching slightly from the work. He normally used that hand as little as possible. Not only was it faster just to use his dominant hand for most things, it was also a way to keep the damaged hand out of sight. Running from the reality of his situation by hiding it away?

Just as he'd run from her house.

"You're welcome. I'm trying to turn over a new leaf of working less and enjoying life more, but it's going to take some time."

He couldn't argue with that. He'd been forced to go cold turkey when he'd had his accident, since he'd been unable to work at all, much less put in too many hours. But he'd made it through the worst of it. The desire to put in long hours was still there, but it no longer consumed him. Maybe his grief was fading. Or maybe he just never wanted to go through months of grueling physical therapy again.

While the waves were still decent, Garret worked on his hand during the pop up. Eventually, his digits said "enough" in no uncertain terms, and he was forced to call a halt to the day.

"I think I'm done." He carried his board out of the water and walked toward where Addy was already sitting on her towel, her hair in chaotic curls from the salt water.

Unlike their other trip to the beach, Addy's swimsuit was blue. And it was all one piece, this time. She'd even put a white lace cover-up over it as she sat on the sand.

Because of him?

He hoped not.

"You outlasted me, this time," she said, putting her hand over her eyes to look up at him. "How did it feel?"

"Like I've swallowed a couple more gallons of salt water, but I was able to actually stay upright longer than the last trip."

"So I saw. I thought you did great. And how's the hand?"

"Tired and sore. But it's a good kind of sore."

"Surf therapy. Kind of has a nice ring to it. You could start a whole new trend."

Laying his board down, he sat on the towel next to hers and leaned back slightly. The salt water drying on his skin caused a prickly tightening sensation that he combatted by rubbing his palm over his chest. "Thanks for this. I needed it."

"Any time."

He probably wasn't going to take her up on that. Because being with her here today—indulging in small talk and having her take a genuine interest in his hand—was taking its toll on his resolve.

He wanted her. Again. There was no doubt about that.

But to travel back down that road right now would be a mistake. His marriage had been a disaster. Addy's current marriage was a disaster. Neither one of them had the best track record in that area.

The truth was, Garret didn't know how to have a healthy relationship. He'd been so consumed with grief over his daughter's death that he'd added the final boulder, which had collapsed an already teetering marriage. Where shared pain might have drawn them together, his unbending selfishness had hurt both him and Patrice.

He wasn't sure enough of himself to know that he wouldn't do it again, given the right circumstances. He'd like to think he was done running, but until he was sure, he wasn't going to take that chance.

But what he *could* do was sit next to this particular woman and enjoy being with her. No strings. No commitments… No running.

"Garret, are you okay?"

"Sorry, my mind was on something else. Did you say something?"

"Just that Leo signed the divorce papers, so hopefully there will be no more scenes at the hospital."

Meaning she would stick around. Maybe she wasn't so unlike him after all. Hadn't she thought about leaving the hospital if things got too tough? Although that wasn't exactly the same thing as running. Was it?

"That has to be a relief."

"It's not exactly what I'd hoped for when I married him." She sat up and crossed her legs. "But it is what it is. There's no way to change it, and I wouldn't even if I could. I never really knew him. We never gave ourselves a chance to learn about each other before rushing into marriage."

He and Patrice hadn't rushed in, but the marriage had ended just the same. "Relationships are hard under the best of circumstances."

"You sound like you speak from experience."

"Let's just say my marriage didn't survive my stupidity. Not that it was all that strong to begin with. But Leticia's death was the final straw. I started working, had the accident…and the rest is history, as they say."

She frowned. "You were grieving." She pulled her cover up closer around her, and he noticed the shadows were growing longer. How long had he been out there anyway?

He glanced down at his watch. "Hell, I'm sorry, Addy. I had no idea it was almost seven o'clock."

Only a few intrepid surfers were still out there trying to find a wave to make it worth their while.

"It's fine. I had a good time."

"Yeah. So did I." He really had and that bothered him on a level he was afraid to examine. Because it was no secret to either of them that he wanted her physically. But now he was enjoying her company more than ever. And the thing he was afraid of most was that he might even come to want her friendship. Might already be on his way to getting it.

And at this moment, Garret had no idea what to do about it. Or how to stop it from becoming a reality he could no longer ignore.

CHAPTER NINE

HER PERIOD WAS OVERDUE. By almost four days.

Standing at the auction in her new dress, she found herself shivering.

It was so unlike her body that she'd taken a pregnancy test this morning even though she knew it was too early to know.

He'd used a condom.

But, looking back, neither one of them had wanted to break that intimate connection between them. Had it been long enough to cause a leak?

The rehearsal yesterday had gone smoothly, but her life right now was pretty much a blur of which she could remember nothing.

God, what if she was pregnant?

Hadn't she just been thinking about the fact that she and Leo had never had children and that she was getting older? Could she have somehow willed her body to find a way?

And then along came Garret, revving her hormones up to a fever pitch. Had the fates conspired against her?

She swallowed. So far she hadn't seen him tonight, but she was pretty sure he had to be here somewhere in the crush of tuxedos and dark suits.

There was no way she was going to tell him unless

her test revealed a pink plus sign. She actually clasped her hands and sent up a quick prayer that that would not happen.

There were a lot more people than she'd expected there to be, so many that it was standing room only in the conference center of the swanky hotel. After the auction there was a buffet of finger foods and a dessert line. She wanted nothing to do with either of those two things.

"Addy, you all set?"

The low voice behind her was both familiar and strange. She spun around to find Garret standing there in a dazzling white shirt and the requisite tux. Only he did for it what few men here could do: transform it into a sexy, meet-me-at-the-dessert-bar siren call.

One she was going to resist with all her might. But at least it made her feel better about things. She wasn't pregnant. She couldn't be.

He glanced at her dress and his Adam's apple bobbed dangerously.

"Wow. Green suits you. You should wear it more often."

That made her smile, despite the craziness that had gone on in her head. "Well, since I'm an ER doc, white lab coats are kind of the color of the day. But I'll keep it in mind. You look great too."

"I'm serious. We better make sure no one thinks you're up for bid."

"I'll be sure to set them straight." Something inside her shifted, his words giving her a shot of confidence she'd been lacking since Leo's unfaithfulness. She might have backed out, if she hadn't promised him she would be here. And since she'd promised him she wouldn't put in crazy hours at work, here she was. She needed to be somewhere that she didn't have time to think.

At least she hadn't been worried about a possible pregnancy at the beach last week. She was glad. It had been a wonderful day. And talk about confident… Each time he'd paddled out, he was becoming more and more proficient at the mechanics. Watching him from shore had been a treat.

It wasn't beautiful, yet, but that would come with time—the flowing motion of becoming almost one with your board.

She was proud of him. And a little nervous that she cared enough to feel that way.

"How's your hand?" she asked.

He lifted it and made a slow painful fist with it. "It'll never be normal and I might be absolutely crazy, but I think I see a little improvement in flexibility."

"That's great! Now you just need to keep up the good work."

"Do you want something to drink before we get started? We still have a few minutes to go."

"I'd love one, actually. Just something refreshing." She hesitated before adding, "Nonalcoholic."

You are not pregnant, Addy.

"I know just the thing. I'll be right back."

Thank God he hadn't seemed to notice that pause before she'd specified that she didn't want any alcohol.

Addy watched him head toward the cash bar. His back was ramrod straight, eyes on where he was headed. He was a proud man.

Realizing your surgical career was over couldn't have been an easy thing to get to grips with. But he seemed to have made the shift. He was doing a great job at the hospital, but there was a part of her that wondered if he wasn't selling himself short. Taking the easy road, rather than the best one.

Leo had done that. He'd kind of skated along in his job, content just to do the bare minimum required.

Not fair, Addy. Garret is nothing like Leo.

And it wasn't up to her to tell her boss what he should or shouldn't be doing. He had to decide that for himself.

When he came back, he was carrying a margarita-sized glass containing something with orange on top and pink on the bottom. It sported a little umbrella. His own drink of choice was sparkling water.

"I bet that got some looks. What is it?" She took the drink from him, intrigued by what he thought she might like.

"Pomegranate and citrus."

"Sounds delicious." She touched the glass to her lips, expecting the strong taste of orange juice to assail her taste buds. But this was sharper, notes of lemon and maybe grapefruit cutting through the sweet. She took another sip. And yes, there was the pomegranate. "I love it. Thank you."

"I was hoping you would." He took her arm. "Come see the auction items."

Tropical-themed cabanas were set up in a ring, each containing a different genre of items. Whoever had chosen what went where had an eye for design. It was amazing. There were things that ranged from a children's book basket topped with a cheerful teddy bear to spa treatments. In the jewelry cabana, she spotted her pearls laid out among piles of faux oysters. The attention to detail took her breath away.

"Is it always this beautiful?"

"Yes. Last year the theme was an ocean voyage. They set everything up like a cruise ship, complete with a buffet line and fake pools."

"Local businesses pay for all the decorations?" She

remembered the auction brochure listing sponsors and what each had helped with.

"Yes. They get some advertising in, as well as knowing they're helping the hospital expand its services to the community."

He steered her over toward another part of the room, where a large screen flashed images from the hospital, mostly the children's ward since this auction would help fund equipment and needed upgrades.

"Look!" She gestured toward the slideshow. Although she'd put in a request for Grace's family to be included, she could hardly believe the pictures they'd come up with. Grace, her mom, and the children from the house fire were displayed. One picture showed the family in the lobby as they were getting ready to leave. She and Garret were there. Their eyes were focused on each other, and she had a slight smile curving her lips. Heat rose in her chest and suffused her face, but the image winked out as quickly as it appeared. The last picture was the family in what looked like the kitchen of their home. They were smiling, and—a sudden pricking behind her eyes came out of nowhere. Grace was holding baby Matthew, something she'd refused to do when they were at the hospital. Before she could say anything to Garret the picture was gone.

"Did you see that?" Her voice came out as a whisper.

"I did." His hand touched the small of her back and stayed there. "I went to see them and asked if I could take the picture."

"You went to their house? Why didn't you say anything? I would have liked to have known how they were doing."

"I wanted to surprise you."

A lump formed in her throat and stayed there, refusing to go down even when she took a sip of her drink.

She did her best not to imagine herself holding a baby like Matthew in the near future.

She wanted that. So very badly. But not like this. She wanted it with someone who loved her. Someone that she loved in return.

"You did surprise me. In the best possible way." She watched other families come on the screen. Patients she didn't know. "They were okay with these pictures being displayed? I don't even remember anyone taking the pictures at the hospital."

"The photographers were working pro bono. They come when they have holes in their schedules and shoot candids for us. We get permission obviously for any that would end up here at the auction."

"How were they—Grace and her family—when you saw them?"

"They were good. Even Grace. She seems to have worked through whatever she was dealing with when she was here."

She glanced at the screen, hoping the loop would work its way back around so she could see them again. "Their kitchen?"

He shrugged. "It was repaired."

Why had he said it like that? As if it didn't matter at all. It certainly did for that family. "Did they have insurance?"

"No. I don't believe so." The response was quick. He somehow knew they didn't have insurance. But how, unless he'd asked? Unless he'd—

Her heart clenched.

"You paid for the repairs, didn't you? It's why you went over to the house."

"It doesn't matter."

Those familiar faces came scrolling by again. She

watched as from one frame to the next, they transformed from tragic to healed. She swallowed and turned to look at him. "It does matter. It matters very, very much, and I—"

A booming voice interrupted her. "Welcome to the tenth annual Miami's Grace Hospital fund-raising auction. If those who are a part of our volunteer force would take their places, we can get started."

"That's us," he said.

Garret hadn't wanted his deed made public. Why?

Whatever the reason, it made her respect him all the more. Along with that thought came a quick flash of something else that she soon banished.

Right now, there was no time to think about anything other than her job. She had to find her cabana—of beach items, of all things. That had to have been Garret's doing as well. To go along with her surfing. Well, she certainly would feel more at home there than in the fashion cabana.

He'd said he liked her choice of dress, though. She glanced down. The scooped neckline was a little lower than she was normally comfortable with, showing a hint of cleavage at the top. But it didn't go below the tan line from her bathing suit, so that had to be something, right?

The bodice clung all the way down to her upper thighs, where it suddenly swooshed out into a full skirt that swirled with every move she made. It also clung to her derrière in a way that was a little disconcerting, but the salesperson swore it was all the rage right now, that it was supposed to fit snugly.

She'd decided to step outside her comfort zone and buy it. Wow, she remembered when she and Garret had had that conversation about comfort zones and he'd joked about not being as sturdy as he used to be. Looking at him now, she couldn't see anything in him that was anything but sturdy. He was strong and compassionate—even if he didn't really want anyone to know it.

Why hadn't she met him five years ago, instead of Leo?

Well, maybe because he'd been married and had suffered one of the biggest tragedies a person could go through: losing a child.

He'd been a different person back then.

So had she.

The auctioneer introduced Garret and had him go up to the podium to say a few words of welcome as people made their way to their seats, auction paddles in hand. The short speech he gave was flawless and confident and edged with a sincerity that couldn't be faked. He believed in what he was doing. Maybe he wasn't just "settling" as she'd basically accused him of doing.

His injured hand was on the podium, the slanted surface putting it out of sight of anyone except those who knew him well. Would these people be surprised to know that he had donned board shorts and carried a surfboard into the water?

Probably. Because right now he looked like the consummate executive. Confident, unruffled and perfectly groomed, his dark hair swept back from his forehead, not a strand out of place.

But they didn't know him as she did.

And Addy liked that. Liked seeing a side of him that no one else would or could.

She found herself staring, and was pretty sure an army of women in the audience also had a speculative eye on him. He was sexy. And unattached.

That made her come back to earth with a bump. Yes, she might know things about him that other people didn't, but it didn't make a difference. She had no claim on him, nor did she want one.

Even if a certain little someone might be lurking unseen who did have a claim on him.

She banished the thought as quickly as it appeared.

So, if one of these wealthy patrons wanted to take him home for the evening, she wouldn't care?

She would. She'd want to scratch the woman's eyes out. And that drove her crazy with irritation.

Whatever this little crush thing she had going on, it needed to be over and done with pronto. Because, if against all odds she did wind up pregnant, she was setting herself up for a very big fall. One that would hurt more than anything Leo had ever done to her.

I'm not having any more children.

Wasn't that what he'd said?

Garret ended his speech and a round of applause followed as he signaled the auction was set to begin. Addy found herself shaky and nervous, for more reasons than just holding up auction items.

But there was a lot riding on this event, so she needed to put aside her problems and pull herself together. A lot of kids like Matthew would get a chance to have an accurate diagnosis thanks to new modern equipment. They deserved it. And Matthew's family couldn't afford to pay for those kinds of things; they could barely afford to put food on the table. But this crowd could.

She willed the bidding to be fierce and competitive as the auctioneer worked his way through the first cabana: tools and DIY items. The big-ticket item in that lot was a flatbed trailer perfect for hauling everything from lawn equipment to camping supplies. It went for over a thousand dollars.

Addy hadn't had a chance to look through the bid

book, which listed each item and gave a suggested retail price. Maybe she should have.

Bidding was closed on the first cabana and moved to the second, which was housewares. Bidding went quickly on that one and then they were on Addy's turf. She got into place and waited for the auctioneer to name the first item—a set of gardening tools—lifting each item as it was named until the gavel came down with the words "*Sold* to—" and the bidder's number was entered into the record.

There were thirty articles ranging from snorkeling equipment to a long board, which was beautifully hand-crafted and had an estimated bidding price of twelve hundred dollars. She wouldn't have minded owning that board herself, but it was probably against the rules to bid on something in her own group. Using the carry straps that were included with the board, she put the webbed bands over her shoulder and demonstrated how to transport it, unable to resist running her fingers across the highly polished surface. She probably looked ridiculous carrying it around in her dress, but it didn't matter. She caught Garret's eye from where he stood to the side of the cabanas. He gave her a smile and a nod that turned something in her tummy all liquid.

She blinked back to what she was doing as the bidding continued to climb. She couldn't very well demonstrate how to stand on it because she could damage the fins on the hard floor, so she had to suffice with just moving around with it. The winning bid was almost seventeen hundred dollars. The board was worth every penny of that. With a sigh, she propped it back against the fake palm tree, allowing her fingers to trail across the warm surface one final time before moving on to the last item.

When her section was finished, she was able to slide

once again into the background. Garret met her at the edge of the crowd. "Good job out there. That was a beautiful board."

"Thanks. It looks like it's going well. And, yes, that board was the most beautiful thing I've ever seen."

"I can think of something even more gorgeous."

When she jerked to look at him, his gaze was fixed on the auctioneer.

Ha! Had she actually thought he was talking about her?

Dream on, Addy. There are all kinds of beautiful people and items in this room.

"Any idea how much the auction has brought in so far?"

"There's no official tally right now, and people can give a monetary donation without actually bidding on anything. But since it's more exciting to dress up and come to the auction than to just mail in a check, there'll be a time for that. The auctioneer will call out different amounts and the attendees will raise their paddles, committing to give that amount. It's almost as exciting as the bidding itself. And the whole event is a good way to get the hospital's name out there."

"I can't believe I've never come to one of these before. I like it. And it's good to see the generosity of people in the community. It looks like they really love Miami's Grace."

"South Beach has always supported the hospital. We couldn't do what we do without them."

Garret went with her to wait in line for a plate of finger food, ignoring her protest that the guests should go first. "Most of them already have their plates, if you look around the room. When they're not bidding, they're eating, so it's fine."

They got their tidbits and Addy got another pomegranate citrus drink, and then they found a place to sit in the vendors' area, where most of the auction items had come from. So far none of the donated items had gone without some kind of bid, so the product vendors would go back to their places of business empty-handed, a very good thing for both the hospital and the companies who made the donations.

"You said you don't have a tally right now, but how much does the hospital normally get from the auctions? I haven't paid attention, although I know I should have."

"A hundred thousand wouldn't be out of the ordinary."

"Out of the ordinary. I'd say that was extraordinary. Does the hospital already have plans for the money?"

He dropped his damaged hand below the table and picked up a finger sandwich, giving it a dubious look before taking a bite.

Addy laughed. "It's cucumber. I've heard they're pretty much standard fare at these swanky affairs."

"I thought you hadn't been to one of these before."

"Not to the hospital's, but I do put on a dress every once in a while. Just not very often."

His lips twisted to the side. "I'm not sure that longboard would have brought in as much as it did without you serving as its backdrop."

"I don't know about that—it was worth all of that and probably more." She decided to change the subject before she started thinking funny thoughts again. "So the money brought in will go for…"

"We have a wish list by price. It's in the auction pamphlet. It helps people know where their bidding dollars are going. It works very well."

"I can see how it would." She hadn't looked beyond the

cover of the pamphlet, since it had been hard to get past the picture of her pearls. "Do you like giving speeches?"

"Not particularly, but I do what needs to be done."

"Yes, and you do it very well. So well that I think I owe you an apology."

This time he turned to face her, sitting back in his seat. "For what?"

"For trying to convince you that you should teach, that you could still do something useful in the medical world. I was wrong. Not that you couldn't teach or do any number of things. But I'm coming to realize that this *is* useful. I just never realized how much so."

"Forgiven. And maybe you were right on some level. Maybe taking this job was a cop-out. But there really are a lot of things that need to be done to keep the hospital running smoothly. And I'll never perform surgery again, no matter how much use I regain of my hand."

"No, but you're so gifted—" She stopped herself. "And there I go again. Sorry."

Two more cabanas had closed out bidding.

The jewelry cabana was next and she suddenly stood. "Do you mind if I go outside for some air?"

She didn't really want to see the pearls or hear the bidding on them. She wasn't attached to them, and, right now, all they brought back were bad memories. Memories much better forgotten.

"Of course. Everything okay?"

"Yes. I just don't want to be here for this part. I know it's stupid. It's just—"

"Not stupid at all. If you want some company, I won't be missed for a minute or two."

She didn't answer—because she wasn't sure how she felt about being around him right now—so she just let him decide for himself. He ended up following her out and they soon found themselves across the street on the sidewalk, leaning against the rail, the scent of the ocean carried in on a gentle breeze.

"I love that smell. Have never gotten tired of it."

"The fragrance of seaweed?"

"Funny. No. The salt. The smell of damp earth and clean air that comes with living near the water."

He smiled, turning around and bracing his elbows on the low wall. "I will admit that, as crowded as it is in South Beach, there are times like this, when you get the impression that life isn't moving as fast as it is in places like New York. There's time to sit back and enjoy the beauty, even on a night as busy as this one."

"And days when you can just take your surfboard out and make any day into one of those quiet reflective times."

"Yes, there is that."

"Do you miss New York? I've never been there, so I have no idea what it's like outside of television shows." Was she curious about whether he might go back there someday? Especially with what he'd said about not putting flowers on his daughter's grave.

"Some parts, but not much. I miss seeing the seasons change. I miss sometimes feeling like you have a bubble around you—that despite the thousands of people passing by, you live in this isolated little spot where no one enters unless you invite them in. South Beach is friendly. And sometimes there aren't boundaries."

She gulped. Sometimes there weren't boundaries in more ways than one. She forced herself to keep talking, as if there weren't this little pain inside that just kept getting bigger and bigger.

"I never thought of it that way, but, yes, you're right. People socialize here in a casual, carefree way."

"I was surprised to find out that South Beach isn't always just about the beach. Or the ocean, although that's a big draw. I actually do like it here."

"Enough to stay here for the rest of your life?" Oh, Lord, why had she just asked that?

"I think so. The jury is still out on that."

That little pain widened, radiating from her heart out to the surrounding areas.

"I can't imagine the hospital without you."

"I can't imagine it without you either." His words were so soft that she had to tilt her head to capture them all. His arm looped around her waist for several seconds, and that ache inside went from uncomfortable to giddy. "Addy, I shouldn't even ask this, but will you meet me after this is all over with?"

Was he asking her to—?

This was the moment of truth. She was pretty sure she knew what was behind that request. She'd be pretty devastated, actually, if she was wrong. And despite everything, there was an answering need inside herself.

"Yes," she breathed.

It was as if all that fear and those countless admonitions this evening had never happened. She wanted to be with this man, wanted the auction to be done and on her way. But of course it wasn't.

She leaned her head against his jacket, reveling in the weight of his arm around her waist, the heady masculine scent that drifted up on ocean currents, the way his breath ruffled across her hair.

This was why it was so hard to resist him. Why she didn't want to resist him.

The moment grew longer and longer, until she felt his

lips brush the top of her head. "We'd better go back in before we're missed."

She was pretty sure she wouldn't be missed at all, but she knew he still had some things he needed to do before they could go.

Once inside, she forced her eyes to stay focused up front, even as she sensed Garret's impatience beside her.

She understood it completely—felt the exact same way.

"They're motioning for me up front. I'll be back in a minute." He curved his index finger around hers and squeezed. "Do not go anywhere."

"I won't." There was no way she was leaving now. She wanted to be here when he came back, wanted to go wherever he wanted to take her.

He gave his closing remarks, thanking everyone for coming and promising they would post the totals for the auction on the hospital's website.

"Enjoy your night. There is still plenty of food left and the bar will remain open for a while longer. When you're ready, you can turn in your bid cards and collect your items. For those things which are too large to carry or won't fit in your vehicle, we have asked a shipping company to set up a booth in the lobby. They can help you arrange transportation. Thank you again for coming. Miami's Grace Hospital is grateful to each of you."

He left the dais to applause, striding through the crowd, stopping to shake hands here and there and smile as people talked to him. He never gave the impression he was in a hurry, gave his undivided attention to each person that crossed his path, but with each step he managed to take, he was keenly aware of where she was.

His trajectory told her that, because he never wavered or veered off course.

All she could do was stand there, a sick sense of anticipation building in her belly. Because once he arrived and they were on their way, things were going to be off the charts.

And she was terrified of what that might mean.

CHAPTER TEN

ALTHOUGH GARRET'S APARTMENT was in a nice area of town, it was sparsely furnished. None of that mattered right now. All she cared about were the long, slow kisses that he was planting on her mouth.

They'd made it through the door, and then he'd backed her up against a nearby wall, tossing his keys onto a side table.

Then he'd kissed her.

Was still kissing her, hands pressed on the wall on either side of her head. He was leaning in. Taking his time, unlike at her place when everything had seemed so frantic and desperate.

Garret had voted for his place.

And she had readily agreed. She needed to be somewhere where she could remove herself from reality—needed to find out what, if anything, she meant to him. In case the unthinkable was actually true.

He eased her a couple of inches away from the wall and his hands went to the back of her dress. He found the zipper and she could feel the wrist of his damaged hand pressing the fabric at her nape as the other hand slid the tab slowly down, all the way past her butt.

When he let go, the fabric fell away, pooling on the floor around her feet.

She didn't care. Didn't want to pick it up, too entranced by the continued short touches of mouth to mouth. She squirmed, trying to deepen the pressure, but it didn't work. "Shh, I want to enjoy it this time."

She smiled against his lips. "Are you saying you didn't last time?" He followed her words with kisses, teasing her mercilessly.

"I enjoyed it very much. But I wanted more. I still do." His teeth nipped at her jawline. "Now step out of your shoes. One at a time."

He backed up a pace and watched as she used one shoe to loosen the other along the back. Then she let it drop on the floor. The other shoe came off just as easily.

She was barefoot before him, and, boy, did he seem to tower over her. "Do you need help with your tie?"

"I need help. But not with that." A quick flash of his teeth as he reached up with one hand and loosened the knot, slipping a finger under the tab until it hung free.

How had he tied it in the first place? She'd thought maybe he'd used a clip-on, but she should have known he wouldn't take the easy way out.

"Now the buttons." She moistened her lips and waited to see if he would do her bidding.

He did, undoing three.

She shook her head. "More." Then she noticed his sleeves. Buttoned with jeweled cuff links. She reached forward to touch one of them. "How?"

"I had the sleeves custom made just wide enough that I can slide my hand through it. My dry cleaner takes the cuff links out and puts them back once the shirt is laundered."

"You must really trust your cleaner."

"I do." As he'd talked, he'd been slowly undoing the

buttons of his shirt all the way down to the cummerbund. "Now your turn."

"Uh...you have more clothes than I do. It's still your turn."

He reached behind him and ripped the Velcro that held the black satin band, letting it drop to the floor. "Now you."

Well, since she was standing there in just a lacy one-piece bodyshaper—one that had boasted no panty lines— that was going to be hard. "Still you."

His rough laugh made her tummy ripple with need. "You can't blame a guy for trying." He pulled his shirt out of his dress trousers and finished undoing the buttons, letting it hang open. Then, when she shook her head, he slid it off his shoulders and let it drop to the floor.

His chest was now bare, just the slightest dusting of hair in the middle—a dark shadow that trailed down his flat torso and disappeared behind his waistband. All things she hadn't been able to notice the last time because of the rush.

"Yes. I like that."

"Are we even now?"

In answer, she slid the straps of her undergarment down her arms, letting them hang loose as she peeled a little bit of the bodice down. Just enough to entice him. She hoped. She'd never been the best at doing a sexy striptease designed to drive men wild.

At least, she had never gotten the hang of it with Leo, who wanted an elaborate show, but did very little in return. But Garret made her want to be sexy. Made her want to do a little give and take.

"You're killing me, honey."

"Shoes and socks?"

It was working. He did seem to like it.

He toed out of his shoes and reached down to undo his socks, tucking them into his black patent leathers.

"Okay, now—"

"Pants." She grinned a challenge at him.

"Don't make me come over there, Addy."

"Or what?"

God, her body was responding to all of this verbal foreplay, nipples pressing hard against the fabric of her shaper, a familiar tingling starting up in other places. She was ready for him to grab her up and get this show on the road.

He took a step closer, and her fingers reached for the straps on the last thing she was wearing. Okay, if he wanted to play hardball, she could definitely match him play for play. She tugged at it, suddenly wishing she'd worn tiny underwear instead, because she remembered just how snug this thing had been when she'd put it on. But she did it, stepping out of it with a triumphal glance at him, only to freeze in place.

His face had gone completely still and he swallowed hard. "You are so…lovely."

Lovely. That was good, right? Then why the hesitation before the word had come out?

"T-trousers?"

Where had that stutter come from?

Garret frowned. "What's wrong?"

"Just having a moment of insecurity, that's all." Her throat worked as she struggled to swallow back a rush of tears. She was too afraid to tell him the whole truth, because she herself didn't yet know.

Then he was there, grabbing her up in an embrace that was as tight as his earlier kisses had been tender. There was no mistaking his erection pressed hard into her thigh. "Don't. No insecurity. Feel what you do to me."

He cupped her face and tilted her head to look at him. "There are so many adjectives I could have chosen. Beautiful. Gorgeous. Sexy. *Hot.* There's one for the books. And they all would have been true. Every single one."

Her body went slack with relief. She had no idea why she'd suddenly felt as if she wasn't good enough. Maybe wondering how she compared to the mother of his child. Wondered how he would react if she too became the mother of his child. But his quick move to allay her fears had done just that, more than making up for her silly fears. He made her feel beautiful and all the other adjectives he'd mentioned.

"Just love me, Garret. That's all I need right now."

"Gladly."

With that, he swept her up in his arms and headed back to a different area of the apartment, past a living room and a leather couch. Down a hallway with two closed doors. He opened the first one and revealed a huge bed with four pine columns that ended just above the mattress. A bed that had no history with her, none at all. It was a blank slate. And she couldn't wait to put some writing on that slate.

He laid her down. Pulled his wallet from his back pocket and finished stripping the rest of the way. This time she didn't have to help. Maybe her zipper had smoothed the way for him. He seemed more secure himself this time. Whatever it was, she loved it.

Loved *hi*—

Her eyes slammed shut on the word before it fully formed.

No. Not right now. She could dissect feelings and possibilities later, but, for this moment in time, she just wanted to be with him.

She looked at him again. The thumb of his right hand was in the waistband of his briefs, his eyes on hers.

"Do it."

Then he was out of them, kicking them away and picking up his wallet again. For one infinitesimal second she wished he didn't have to use it. Wished they could just love each other without anything coming between them.

But they had to. If she wasn't pregnant already, she didn't want to become pregnant. Maybe, despite what he'd said in his office, he'd be able to go that route with someone else. Someday.

Why not with her?

Later, remember?

Unaware of her thoughts, he found a condom and laid it on a pillow near the headboard. She decided to make light of what, for her, was becoming a moment that was fraught with dangers she didn't want to face. "Just one?"

He smiled, coming onto the bed and pressing his body against hers, breasts flattening against his hard chest. She gloried in the feeling, reveled in not spoiling this moment with her hopes and fears.

"Don't worry—I have more where that came from." He rested his pelvis against hers. "And more where *that* came from."

Then his mouth was back on hers and he was kissing her as if he couldn't get enough, right hand exploring her, running over her breasts, down her rib cage, cupping her hip.

"Use the other one."

He came up. Looked down at her face. "Excuse me?"

Terrified he was going to be angry with her, but needing this so very much, she licked her lips. "Use your other hand. I want to feel it on me."

His eyes hardened slightly, and he acted as if he was going to get up. To run. "I can't."

Before he could go anywhere, she caught the wrist of his damaged hand and held on tight. "Use it, Garret. Please."

She lifted it to her chest, just above her breasts, and dragged the curled fingers against her skin. "Can they feel? Do they have sensation?"

"Yes." The word was rough-edged and seemed to be hauled up from some dark pit within him. This was a critical moment. He would either reject this…reject her, or he would open himself up and allow her to take everything. In the same way she was willing to give everything.

She touched her breast with it, using her own hands to guide him over the nipple. The sensation hit her hard and she arched, moaning.

"God, Addy. What are you doing to me?" Then he pulled his hand free from her grip.

Just when she thought she might have ruined everything, he took up where she left off, allowing his ruined digits to slide against her. He didn't cup anything or try to grasp, just let her skin provide tactile stimulation. The idea that she might be the first person to ask this of him was heady and it brought her to the very edge of the world.

If he could handle this, surely he'd be able to handle anything else she might throw at him.

His eyes slid closed as he continued to explore, and she hoped it felt as good to him as it did to her. She wanted this man. Wanted everything he had to give. When his fingers brushed over the curls at the apex of her thighs his eyelids jerked apart. "I don't think I can wait."

"Then don't. Don't." She reached around and grabbed the condom off the pillow and tore into it. Then she handed him the contents and held his damaged hand where it had stopped, keeping it there as he used his other hand to roll the latex sheath over his hard flesh.

She slowly spread her legs and slid his fingers a little lower. She bit her lip, breath coming in short bursts as she drew him closer and closer. "Feel it, Garret. Feel—" She exploded in a rush, pressing his hand hard against her as the contractions raged inside her.

Then he was right there, thrusting hard and fast, groaning against her throat as he went off a few seconds later; he kept pumping until he was spent, pace gradually slowing, while he pressed tiny kisses against her jaw, her cheek, her mouth. And then it was over, his body melting into hers, puffs of air sliding over her ear.

"Hell, Addy. Holy hell."

"Are you okay?" She tipped her head back so she could look in his face, worried about the tone of his voice.

"Okay? *Okay?*" He gave a laugh that lit her soul and turned her world upside down. "I don't think I'll ever be okay again."

He kissed her chin. "And I mean that in the best way possible. I have never felt like that in my life."

If he could just hold on to that thought.

She pulled in a huge lungful of air and released it as a wave of happiness spilled over her. "There are lots of ways to rehab that hand. I have a few more tricks up my sleeve."

"A few? I'm afraid to even imagine." He wrapped an arm around her back and rolled so he was on bottom and she was on top. "I don't want to squash you."

"You weren't. But I like the way you think."

And with that, she covered his mouth with hers and kissed him all over again.

* * *

Five tests were lined up on her bathroom counter.

Five reminders that the happiness of one night might not look the same two days later.

And it didn't. Not at all.

Addy huddled beneath the bubbles in her tub and trembled, her mind frantically working through all kinds of scenarios. Maybe he would be thrilled—would leap from his chair and kiss her senseless, tell her that he loved her as much as she loved him.

Because, yes, she did love him. Had realized it while they were making love. She'd tried to blot it out, to pretend it wasn't real, but the sensation hadn't faded away the next day. It had been there when she'd woken up to the smell of bacon and eggs—the very meal she'd tried to fix him all those weeks ago. In fact, she'd come out of the bedroom wearing one of his button-down shirts, saying she hoped he didn't mind. His answer had sent a shiver through her. A very different shiver than what she was now experiencing.

"Mind?" he'd said with a slow smile. "I don't know. What would you do if I said yes, that I minded very much?"

A weird giddy sound had broken loose from her throat and wrapped around her. "Well, I guess I'd just have to take it off, then. Very slowly."

The wordplay had soon turned into another kind of play altogether. And she'd hoped... So hoped...

But he'd never said the words. And she'd tried to not care.

Until today.

She lifted a palmful of suds, and with a quick puff from her lungs sent them up into the air. What was once a single cohesive mass broke into distinct sections, which floated in different directions. Some popped and disappeared forever. Some joined with other bubbles. But the original unit was gone forever.

Kind of like Humpty Dumpty. Once broken, he could never be made whole again.

Was that what would happen to her and Garret? Not that they could even be considered a unit. Not yet. Maybe not ever.

Her eyes went back to the counter. Would her news shatter any possibility of a future with him?

But if he cared about her, would those tests matter that much? Maybe it would precipitate something good, rather than the disaster she was imagining.

She twisted her hair and clipped it higher so she could lie against the smooth surface at the back of the tub. Her hands dipped beneath the surface and skimmed over her stomach.

Pregnant.

But how?

It had to have been from that first time they were together. Maybe the condom was old. Maybe they'd just been careless at some point—or maybe it had simply failed. It happened. You heard stories about things like this all the time. Right?

Those plastic strips caught her eye again. Five tests said that she was now one of those statistics.

And she was happy. Scared, but, oh, so happy. God, she shouldn't be. She should be upset and angry and confused.

But she saw everything with a clarity that had been lacking before. She wanted this baby. Had wanted a child for a very long time, even when her ex-husband hadn't. The fact that it was Garret's and not Leo's? Even better. At least it belonged to a man she respected. A man who'd already had a child and had loved that child deeply. He was made to be a father, no matter what his response to this particular pregnancy might be.

I'm not having any more children.

Not ever?

No.

That conversation burned across her memory banks, searing everything in its path. He might not have planned— or even wanted—to have any more kids, but fate was taking that decision out of his hands.

Surely he would love the child, once he found out about it.

Wouldn't he?

The shaking that had subsided a minute ago started up all over again.

She had to tell him. It would be wrong to withhold this kind of information. He had a right to know. And a right to choose what to do with the information.

She wrapped her arms around her midsection as if already protecting the tiny life that was just taking root inside her.

One thing was certain. His reaction would go one of two ways and it would determine the course of their future interactions—or lack thereof.

Either he was going to welcome the news—even if he was initially dismayed or fearful. Or—and this was the possibility that had woken her in a cold sweat for the last two nights. Or Garret was going to run for the hills as fast as he possibly could.

CHAPTER ELEVEN

GARRET SCANNED THE READOUT, trying to decipher what he was looking at, but he was unable to concentrate on much of anything right now.

It had been two days since he'd kissed Addy goodbye in front of her house after taking her home. He had no more answers today than he'd had after seeing her standing there in his white dress shirt. There had been turmoil then. There was turmoil now.

It was as if he'd been shot through the heart, something changing inside him.

But what?

He wasn't sure. And wasn't sure he really wanted to know. He'd vowed to give himself one more day and then track her down long enough to talk. No easy feat.

She seemed to be avoiding him as much as he was evading her.

And the spikes for those two days...

As bad or worse than they'd been that day he called her into his office. The day she dropped those pearls, setting a big machine into motion.

He didn't know what had made him look at the staff hours' readout. But he had. Maybe to see if their night together had had as profound an effect on her as it had on him.

From what he could see, it had. Only he wasn't sure what it meant.

She was back to keeping killer hours. In the days since they'd spent the night together, she'd put in five hours of overtime. It was a lot.

He could understand staying to finish up a case, but this was more than that.

Something was seriously bothering her. Or worrying her.

Well, she wasn't the only one. He was worried too. Only he wasn't sure what to do about it.

Talk to her?

And say what? "Listen, Addy, about that night…"

That was where his ability to reason fell apart. His brain cells had evidently developed a serious leak when it came to figuring things out.

Sitting back in his chair, he put his hands on the desk and stared at his damaged one. His injury was what came of getting his priorities in the wrong place. He couldn't afford to do that again—to bury his pain in his work.

What did Addy have to bury?

He had no idea, but one of them needed to drum up the courage to break the ice and start figuring this thing out.

He stood to do just that, only to stop in his tracks when a knock sounded at his door.

Surely not.

But maybe…

"Come in." He frowned at how eager those words sounded. Hell, it might not even be Addy.

He needed to slow down and think through anything he might say, if it was her. Preferably *before* he gave voice to it.

His intuition proved correct when Addy's head peeked around the corner. "Do you have a minute?"

"I was just coming to find you, actually."

"You were?" She entered the room, her face paler than he ever remembered seeing it.

Was she ill?

"Yes. Have a seat, please." He stood. "Are you okay?"

"I think so. I'm not really sure."

A rush of concern went through him. "What's going on?"

She didn't sit, as he'd asked. And something about the way she stood there made an alarm go off in his head. He decided to stay on his feet as well, just in case he needed to catch her. She looked ready to break apart at any second.

"I have something to tell you."

"Okay." He suddenly wasn't so sure he wanted to hear it, but those brain cells still weren't working at a hundred percent.

Instead of answering, Addy dropped some kind of white plastic object onto the center of his desk. It bounced a time or two then came to a stop in front of him.

He frowned at it for several seconds. Then a frisson of fear went up his spine as he recognized it. Evidently a few of those cells were still functioning. And now he wished they weren't.

"What is this?" The rough, hoarse quality of his voice gave away his thoughts. He didn't let his eyes focus on the test, kept them purposely averted to a spot just beside it, where the exercise balls lay.

Something about the disparity between those two things struck him as hilarious, in a way that was anything but funny.

There was only one reason for her to have brought that in his office.

He swallowed. No. There was no way. It had to be a

mistake. Still he kept his gaze away from it as if looking at it might somehow make it coil up and strike. Hell, he'd been worried about her working too hard, when in reality he should have been worried about—

She didn't answer for several long seconds.

"Garret, I am so sorry." Her hand reached out as if she might touch him, but then changed her mind. Maybe because he hadn't made any effort to meet her halfway.

Halfway to where?

The test stick had landed upside down, but to turn it over seemed beyond his abilities. Doing so might mean the very thing he'd vowed to avoid had managed to track him down. And he wasn't sure he could hold himself together if that happened.

A million flashes of firsts shot through his skull, each more painful than the last: Leticia's birth, her first baby tooth, her first steps, her first day of school—and the last breath she ever took.

Hot daggers assaulted the backs of his eyes and he struggled to make his tongue form words.

"We used—" His voice cracked and he had to start over. "We used protection."

"I know we did." A gaze awash with compassion met his.

"Then—how?"

"I don't know. Any number of things can go wrong."

Go wrong. That was an understatement.

He finally reached for the stick and flipped it, even though he already knew what he'd find. And there it was. A pink plus sign.

Why was it that those commercials always showed everyone giddy with happiness and excitement? He had been too, at one time.

But not now. It was as if he were trapped in a surreal world where things never quite worked out as they should. Where no one was giddy or happy.

Where there was nothing left to do but drop flowers onto a headstone. And he hadn't even been able to do that.

"You're pregnant."

"Yes."

He didn't ask if it was his. His brain might be screaming at him to find a way to escape, but his heart knew better than to listen to it.

She'd come here to—

Actually, he wasn't quite sure *why* she was there.

"What do you want me to do?"

That seemed to confuse her for a second or two. Then she stood a little straighter. "I'd like to know how you feel about it."

How he felt about it? He was pretty sure she wouldn't like his answer to that. So he rephrased and tossed the query right back to her.

"Maybe I should ask you that question, since you're suddenly putting in a lot of overtime again."

Her mouth opened. And closed, teeth coming down on her bottom lip. Then she tipped her head to one side and stared at him. "That's all you have to say? That I'm working too much overtime?"

"Can you take another test?"

"I've taken five. They're all identical. Do you want me to pull them out and show you? This is real, Garret. I have no reason to make something like this up."

"I didn't say you made it up." It had to have been from that time at her house, because they had only been at his house a couple of days ago, not long enough to register on a test.

"Did you know this was a possibility when you came to the auction? When you let me take you home afterward?"

She averted her eyes, and he knew. Before she even spoke the words. "Yes. I knew."

She sank into the chair he'd offered her moments earlier.

"And you said nothing." He swallowed. "That whole time."

Maybe she had. She'd whispered something in her sleep at his house. Something he hadn't caught, but she'd seemed distressed, stirring until he pulled her back against him.

Hell, how had this even happened? He'd lost one child already. Wasn't that enough for one lifetime? Surely she didn't expect him to take on another one. He couldn't. He even remembered saying that to her, sometime after that first night they'd spent together.

And still she was here. Wanting some kind of answer. One he didn't think he could give her.

His gaze went to her midsection and then slid back up to her face.

Just two days ago, he'd been envisioning spending more time with her. Had even started thinking about the future.

But now that future would include a crying infant, a toddler's tendency to get into everything in sight—and the worst thing of all: a small human who would capture his heart.

And he'd worry—every second—about the millions of things that could go wrong. Just like Addy's comment about that condom.

Any number of things can go wrong.

His stomach churned up bile that frothed and burned inside him.

She slid a hand on his desk, her palm up. "You're right. I suspected I might be pregnant and didn't say anything. I should have, and I'm sorry. I didn't want to face the possibility."

Any number of things can go wrong.

Those damned words wouldn't stop pounding in his head. They just kept looping around over and over and over, reminding him of the reasons he didn't want to father another child.

"I can't do this, Addy. Any of it."

She sat there for a second and stared at him as if waiting for him to say something else. Anything else. But he was completely blank. Completely empty. Except for that single drumming phrase that wouldn't let up.

She withdrew her hand and let it fall into her lap. Up went her chin. "Then don't. Don't do this. Don't do anything."

With that, she got to her feet, drew her lanyard over her head and dropped it on his desk.

Something about that registered in the back of his head, but he couldn't quite make sense of it. He couldn't make sense of anything.

"Goodbye, Garret."

He didn't move. Didn't argue with her. Just let her slowly climb to her feet and walk toward the door. And then she was through it, shutting it behind her. Only then did the words finally slow to a stop.

Any number of things can go wrong.

Garret was pretty sure something had just gone very wrong. And he had no idea how to make it right. Or if he should even try.

CHAPTER TWELVE

DAMN GARRET STAPLETON for making her care. Why hadn't he walked away after that first kiss on the beach?

Why hadn't she?

She didn't know. What she did know was that the night of the auction, after Garret had given his last speech and had headed her way, something profound had happened inside her. Something that had nothing to do with the new life she carried.

He was charming and sexy, and had a heart as big as the whole state of Florida. Only that heart had no room in it for a child. His child. He'd said so himself.

And that hurt more than she'd believed possible.

The baby she'd never dreamed she'd have was suddenly a very real possibility. And she was already in love with him or her. If she had to raise the child to adulthood on her own, then so be it.

Except she didn't want that. She wanted the entire glorious dream, not just part of it. And that included Garret.

Oh, he'd tried to call her after she'd walked out of his office. Three times, actually, over the last two weeks.

She had finally attempted to call the hospital yesterday afternoon on the off chance that he'd changed his mind, but when she'd asked to speak with him, she'd been told he was out of town.

A shiver had gone through her. "Do you know where he went?"

"New York City. He's not sure when he'll be back."

Or if.

The operator hadn't exactly said it, but it seemed to hang in the air.

Had he actually left permanently?

The pain in her heart threatened to overwhelm her.

She'd made a huge mistake by not telling him at the auction that her period was late. But she'd told herself that it was probably all a big mistake. That the timing was just off due to stress.

Only it hadn't been stress, and when she'd dropped that test stick on his desk, she might as well have dropped an anvil on his head. Maybe she had. She just hadn't been able to think of a better way to present it. All options seemed to lead to the same disastrous end.

And now he might be gone forever.

She'd quit *her* job over it, hadn't she? Was it so surprising that he might choose to do the same?

No, it wasn't. She could imagine him wanting to get as far away from the problem as possible. Just as her hurt and anger had driven her to walk out of his office.

Except Addy didn't see the baby as a problem. Not anymore. She'd come to see it as a blessing.

The fact that Garret didn't view the situation through the same lens had nothing to do with her.

She'd just have to learn to live with it. Somehow.

Until then, she could try taking the advice she'd given Garret all those weeks ago. She could try doing a little surf therapy. And hope that it really could work miracles.

Garret stood over his daughter's grave, unsure and alone. He could turn and walk away, and go back to life the way it was. Life before Addy's revelation. Or he could make a change. Turn a corner.

Except he couldn't see what lay around that corner. And that was where the fear came from. If he could see the future, it would make his decision a whole lot easier.

Only he wasn't a prophet. And neither was Addy.

What if she decided she couldn't raise a child on her own and did something about it?

His gut twisted. Was that what he wanted?

No. It wasn't. But was that really fair to her? He didn't want any part of what she'd told him, but he expected her to figure it out and make the best of it. While he turned a blind eye to everything and pretended it didn't exist.

Only it did.

He knelt beside the granite marker, laying what he'd brought to the side. He then touched the name engraved in the stone with the tip of his finger.

"Sorry I haven't been here in a while, sweetheart."

A while? That was an understatement.

He dusted a blade of grass off the stone. He'd needed to come here. Had needed to think.

He picked up his offering and laid it in front of the headstone. Daisies. Leticia's favorite flower.

And his too.

"I'm not sure what I should do. Or if I should do anything."

His head had been filled with nothing but Addy for the last two weeks. With the terrible sadness he'd seen in her expression when she took off her lanyard and placed it on his desk. He hadn't realized the significance of that act at first. He'd been too hung up on that pink symbol on the pregnancy test to care about anything else. Until the door had closed and he'd realized she'd just quit.

He'd quickly stuck the test strip in his desk and done his best to forget about it.

Only he hadn't been able to. Every time he'd opened that drawer, it had stared up at him in accusation. She'd trusted him enough to tell him she was pregnant, and he'd thrown it back in her face. And now as he sat in the spot where his life had changed forever, he wondered if he'd been the biggest fool on the planet.

Oh, he had been. Of that there was no doubt.

"Oh, Letty. You wouldn't be very happy with me right now."

He glanced at his ruined hand, lips twisting at what he'd done to himself all those years ago. What he was doing to himself all over again. What he was doing to Addy.

Addy.

He stared at the stone, a thought coming to him. He'd just thought about making a change and turning a corner. Except the fear of what might lie around that corner was keeping him from moving forward.

He forced himself to stop and look at the corner, to envision what might be waiting for him around that bend in the road.

Oh, hell. He swallowed as a realization pushed up from somewhere deep inside him.

It was Addy. She was what was around the corner. She and that tiny creature she carried inside her.

Wasn't knowing that enough? Did other people gain any more insight into their future than what he'd been given?

He didn't think so.

If he chose not to turn that corner, one thing was certain. He was going to lose her forever. Lose a chance at happiness. Was he willing to pay that kind of price to protect himself from pain? Wouldn't doing that just cause a completely different kind of pain?

He loved her. With all his heart. On some level he'd realized that back at the hospital and had tried to call her, even though he hadn't been sure what he was going to say. But she'd evidently not been ready to talk to him. Maybe she'd never be ready.

He'd never know if he didn't try.

But first, he needed to finally close the door on his past. A past he couldn't change, but one he could hopefully learn from.

"I think I know what I need to do." He scooted the daisies closer to the stone. "If things work out the way I hope they will, I might not be back for a while, but you'll have flowers on every birthday. I promise."

He kissed his fingers and touched them to her name. "You're going to be a big sister. God, I hope I do you proud as her father."

A rush of moisture blurred the writing. "Until next time, baby. I love you."

With that, he stood, praying that somehow Addy was still waiting. Just around that corner.

He sat on the beach for the third day in a row, his board beside him. He had no idea if she would even come, but he could hope. The hospital said she'd called once while he was in New York, but that she hadn't tried again.

He'd left her a voice mail on his way back from the airport asking her to meet him at their spot. He could only hope it wasn't too late.

If she didn't show up soon, he wasn't sure what he was going to do. Her house was empty, a For Sale sign planted in the yard.

That worried him.

The sun was hot and a trickle of sweat ran down his temple. He lifted his forearm to swipe it away. She evidently wasn't coming today either.

Just as he started to get up, he spied a familiar movement off in the distance. A flash of red. A gentle sway of hips. A surfboard held to her side.

A dream?

The vision kept coming, and he swallowed when he realized she was very real. She wore the same red bikini she'd worn the first time they came here.

She stopped in front of him and dropped her board, fin-side up, on the sand. "You're dry. You haven't been in yet?" There was no smile on her face. No clue as to what she was thinking.

"I was getting ready to leave, actually."

A frown formed. "I thought you asked me to meet you here at three."

"That was two days ago."

"And you're still here?"

A ghost of a grin found its way to his mouth. "Maybe I should have camped out." The smile disappeared. "I thought you weren't coming."

"I was in court finalizing my divorce when your call came in."

"And yesterday?"

"Doctor's appointment. Right at three." The words had a wary sound to them.

What kind of appointment? A trickle of fear slid across his heart. "Is everything—?"

"Yes. Still pregnant. Sorry."

Reaching up, he gripped her hand. "I'm glad." He patted his towel. "Can you sit down? I have a few things I want to say, starting with I'm sorry."

There was a momentary hesitation and then she eased down beside him.

"Sorry?"

"Yes. For all of it." He gazed out toward the sea. "I was shocked. And frankly terrified. I never expected to become a father again."

"I know. I was pretty shocked and terrified too at the way things happened. Only I can't run away from the reality of what's happening inside of me, like you can. Like you *did*." She stared at the sand. "You hurt me."

"I know. And I'm sorry. I went to visit Leticia's grave."

She looked up. "That's why you went to New York?"

"Yes. I needed to make peace with my past, and wanted time to work through some things about myself." He took her hand again, grateful when she didn't jerk away from him. "I also took her some flowers. Someone I care about very much made me realize how important that is."

"Oh, Garret." Moisture appeared in her eyes. "I'm so glad."

He threaded his fingers through hers. "I told her she's going to be a big sister. And that I would bring him or her to visit."

She didn't say anything for several long seconds and a different kind of agony went through him. Then her fingers tightened around his, squeezing as if she needed something to hang on to.

"Does this mean that you want to be a part of the baby's life?"

"I want more than that, Addy. I want to be a part of your life. If you'll let me." He lifted her hand and kissed it. "I love you. More than you can know. Can you forgive me for taking off like I did when you told me?"

"But you didn't. You sat right there in your office and barely moved. Barely looked at me."

"It may have seemed that way, but inside my head, I was running. The second I said 'I can't do this,' I was out of there." He covered their joined hands with his damaged one. "And now I'm done running."

She shifted her body toward him. "You need to be sure. Very sure. I don't want someone who will be there for a while and then start drifting away when things get hard. Or a crisis happens. I've done that once. I won't settle for it a second time. And I don't want that for our child."

"I'm very sure. I want to spend the rest of my life with you. I'm even thinking of weaning away from some of my administrative duties and moving back toward medicine itself."

"You are?" There was no mistaking the shock on her face.

"I've been researching diagnosticians in the field of neurology. It's actually a thing."

"That's wonderful."

"You're the one who made me think it was possible." A thought came to him. "Your house is up for sale."

"Yes. I've made peace with my past too. And I'm getting rid of the parts that no longer fit."

His heart chilled. Was he one of those parts? "I need to know how you feel about me."

"Isn't it obvious?"

"Maybe to you, but not to me."

She let go of his good hand, fingers curling around his damaged one. She held it tight. "I love you, Garret Stapleton. I think I have since that first day on the beach—when you tried the pop up, even though it hurt this hand so badly. And you kept on trying. You didn't give up. After

I realized I was pregnant, I hoped and prayed that you wouldn't give up on me either. On us."

"Never." A stream of pure hope rushed over him, peeling away the fear and doubt. "And then there were three."

She smiled. "Unless there are four."

"Four?"

Before the panicked thought could fully take root, she shook her head. "I'm kidding. I just wanted to make sure you were serious about the not running part."

"I am not going anywhere."

"Even though this has all happened as quickly as it has?"

He smiled. "Well, you took the quick route with your last marriage and I took the slow route, and neither of those worked. Maybe it wasn't a matter of timing. Maybe it was a matter of finding the right person at the right time."

"That means you're willing to give us a try? All of us?" She slid closer, linking her arm with his.

"You coaxed me into the water. And onto a surfboard. I think after those two things, this 'rest of our lives' gig might just be a piece of cake."

She tilted her head to look at him. "Garret, I think, just this once, you might be right."

EPILOGUE

THIS LIFE WAS a piece of cake. Literally.

She blew out the single white candle and made a wish. Except all her wishes had already come true. So she had to settle for a silly one about her baby taking after his handsome daddy. The sonogram had revealed their child was going to be a boy.

And he was all alone in there, much to Garret's disappointment. He had whispered late one night as he'd held her that maybe they should have a second one. She was fine with that, but she would really rather they had them one at a time.

He came up behind her and curved his hands around her midsection. Eight months along and she felt huge and unwieldy, but Garret made her feel beautiful, even when her feet swelled and she had to fan herself against the South Beach heat and humidity.

"I have a present for you."

She leaned her head against his chest, reveling in the fact that this man was hers and hers alone. "You smell good."

He chuckled. "That doesn't track with what I just said. At all."

"It tracks in my head—that's all that matters."

He kissed her temple, then took her by the hand.

"Come on. I've been keeping this a secret for far too long, and, let me tell you, it hasn't been easy."

"A secret?"

"Yep."

He led her to the spare bedroom that would soon be the baby's nursery. Garret had been in there for a long time yesterday painting and getting things ready.

Or so he'd said.

Addy was happier than she'd believed possible.

"What is it?"

"Open the door and see."

Giving him a puzzled glance, she turned the knob and pushed on the door. At first all she saw were the same furnishings and ocean motifs that Garret had worked so hard on. Then, against the wall, she spied a large curved board. A surfboard.

No. Not just a surfboard—a *long*board.

Her breath caught in her lungs. "I know this board."

Making her way toward it, she ran her fingers down the warm glossy wood and closed her eyes, trying to remember where...

It came to her in a flash.

"The auction. This is the board from the beach cabana."

"I hoped you'd recognize it."

"I remember wanting that board." She turned toward him. "But how? I was there when the bidding was going on. I saw the man with the paddle."

"He's a hospital employee. I asked him to bid on it for me."

"You bought this for me? All the way back then?"

He stood in front of her and cupped her face in his hands. "I knew I loved you all the way back then. I just had to grow into it."

"Grow into it. I like that." There was no hint of Garret

giving up or backing out. He'd told the truth. He was done running. And so was she.

She looked wistfully at the board and gave a huge sigh. "I wish I could use it, but I'd have to do a backstroke to get it to go anywhere. And I'm afraid my pop up might turn into a pop *out*. And I don't think South Beach is quite ready to see me give birth on the beach."

"I know of a doctor who would be nearby to assist."

Garret was still the hospital administrator. For now. But he'd kept his promise to himself. He was doing some consulting on the side, and, a year from now, he was going to be employed by the hospital as its very first neurological diagnostician, working with a team of other neurologists.

She was ecstatic, even as Garret remained cautiously optimistic. But she loved that about him.

"I happen to know that doctor. And he's excellent at a lot of things. But I would rather have this baby in the comfort of the hospital. *Our* hospital."

She twined her arms around her husband's neck and lifted her face for a kiss. It lingered, and then deepened until Garret finally pulled away with a shaky laugh. "I do not want to be the cause of that baby coming before he's ready."

Arching, she pressed her hands against the small of her back. "But what if I'm ready?"

He gently turned her so that she was facing away from him and massaged the area he knew bothered her, his right hand cupping her hip and using his thumb to apply pressure to her sore muscles.

"Mmm…that feels so good."

"Come to bed, Addy, where I can make you feel even better." The murmured words were said in that sexy baritone that made her knees knock. He wasn't talking about sex. Or even about making out. He really did just want to make her feel better, and if that wasn't love, she didn't know what was.

"Cake first?"

"Of course. What was I thinking?"

Giving the board one last look, she linked arms with her husband and closed the door, heading into a future that promised to be filled with plenty of surf therapy, a little bit of cake and a whole lot of love.

* * * * *

FRIEND, FLING, FOREVER?

JANICE LYNN

MILLS & BOON

To Samantha Thompson,
who puts together the best fundraisers ever!
Thanks for your big heart and all you do for others.

CHAPTER ONE

"Buy me at the charity auction."

Nurse Kami Clark didn't look up from the computer screen where she keyed in vital signs on the patient in bay two of the Knoxville General Hospital's emergency department.

Doing her best not to let her eyes veer in Dr. Gabriel Nelson's direction, she made a nurse's note on the normal results. "Not happening."

Wearing his favorite blue scrubs, Gabe moved into her peripheral vision. She didn't have to look to know the color paled in comparison to the brilliant hue of his eyes.

"You know you want me, Kam. Here's your chance."

"Right," she snorted, keeping her voice flippant despite how his accusation almost sent her into a choking fit. "Keep dreaming, lover boy."

Most straight women did want Gabe. Not that he typically encouraged their desire. He didn't have to. Not with his looks, personality, and quick intelligence. The fact he was a successful emergency-room physician didn't hurt. Women flocked to him.

But not Kami.

Oh, she thought he was all that and more. The man had the biggest heart of anyone she knew and seemed to always be able to make her laugh. But she knew better than to get caught up in his revolving-door love life that left a long line of broken hearts. She was immune to his love-'em-and-leave-'em charms. Mostly.

"More like I'm trying to escape a nightmare in the making." He gave a frustrated sigh that was almost believable as he plopped down into the chair next to hers. "Debbie is planning to buy my date."

Ah. Debbie. The latest ex-girlfriend who didn't want to admit it was over and had been finished for a month or so.

No wonder Gabe was in such a tizzy. Debbie had stuck like glue even after he'd told her point-blank on several occasions that their relationship was finished. The poor woman must be hoping to rekindle a spark. Good luck with that.

Gabe never dated the same woman for more than a couple of months and never went back to the same one. Not once. He was a move-on-and-never-look-back kind of guy.

"You have to rescue me."

"Says who? You got yourself into this mess," she reminded him, fighting back a small smile at her friend's overly dramatic tone. She could almost buy into his angst. "It's only right for you to face the consequences."

"I was roped into this charity fund-raiser and you know it. Not only do you know it—" he leaned close enough so that his words were just for her "—you're the one who convinced me to say yes."

"I meant the Debbie mess, not the auction," she clarified, fighting the urge to look his way. Better not to look into Gabe's eyes when he was trying to convince you to do something. Staring into those dazzling blues got women into trouble. Immune or not, she wasn't taking any chances.

"Besides," Kami continued, "even if you had to spend

a *week* with your beautiful and persistent ex, if it raised money to help Beverly's family and others like her, then so be it."

Anything any of them could do to raise money for their coworker's seriously ill infant daughter needed to be done. Although their medical insurance was covering many of the expenses, there were still co-pays and deductibles. Not to mention Beverly had been out of work since giving birth, as had her husband, most of it as unpaid leave of absence. Even after Lindsey got her heart transplant, months would pass prior to Beverly leaving her baby's side to return to work. Their friend had enough worries without having to be concerned about how she and her husband were going to pay their bills.

"Easy for you to say," Gabe pointed out. "You aren't on the auction block."

Yeah, as one of the fund-raiser's organizers she'd dodged that bullet.

"I'll be working the night of the auction, but not by being auctioned." Thank goodness. Kami would have been a statue. Not her scene at all.

"Not the same," he pointed out.

"You love the attention and you know it," she accused, closing out the patient's chart. Fun-loving Gabe would work the stage and have a blast.

She glanced at him for the first time since he'd barged into the nurses' station located across from the patient bays.

Her incorrigible playboy friend actually looked a little frazzled.

"Fortunately for you, it's not a week, just one night where you have to show Debbie—I mean, whoever wins your date—a good time."

Okay, that was bad but she couldn't resist teasing

him. It was so rare to see him off his game. Actually, she couldn't recall having ever seen him off his game. Not during any crisis that came through the ER doors. Given he was such a goofball at times, Gabe was one coolheaded dude.

Plus, she wasn't buying his woe-is-me-buy-my-date-package-so-Debbie-can't act.

"You're real funny, Kam."

"Come on. That was a good one." Kami had thought so. He didn't look convinced. "I'm sure you'll manage one night with Debbie if needed."

After all, he dealt with situations and people a lot more intense than the Z-list television actress he'd been involved with still obsessing over him. Debbie might be crazy over Gabe, but the woman didn't have any real psychiatric problems.

"And risk encouraging her nonstop calls and texts continuing?" He winced. "Thanks anyway."

Kami raked her gaze over his six-foot frame. "You're not *that* bad, Gabe." She patted his hand as if reassuring a small child. "There will be other bidders." Faking a look of uncertainty, she shrugged. "Well, hopefully."

One side of his mouth cocked upward. "Gee, thanks for the compliment, *friend*."

"Anytime," she assured him, her lips twitching. "What are friends for?"

Eyes sparkling, he gave a pointed look. "To rescue each other when one's relentless ex plans to buy her way back into your social life."

He had a point.

If Kami believed he was in real need, she'd probably empty her house-deposit fund to bail out his butt. Good thing he wasn't because she'd been hoarding every spare penny for years, had a hefty down payment saved, and would hate to have to start over to make her dream of owning a home come true just as she finally had enough saved to actually start looking for the perfect house.

"Just because Debbie plans to bid doesn't mean she'd be the winner," she said on a more serious note. "Stop worrying."

He didn't look assured. "Debbie doesn't like to lose."

Kami gave a semi-shrug. "Who does?"

He raked his fingers through his hair. "Come on, Kam. Place the winning bid and I'll show you the night of a lifetime." He waggled his brows. "We'd have fun."

Kami laughed. As if. "You must have me mixed up with one of the other women running around the hospital who actually wants you to show them a 'night of a lifetime.' I've better things to do than mess with the likes of you."

Looking as if she'd said exactly what he'd expected her to say, he chuckled. "Or maybe I want you to buy my bid because I know I can ask this huge favor and not worry about you freaking out down the road when I break things off."

Yeah, there was that. She wouldn't freak out over a man. Never had. Never would. She'd watched her mother do that one time too many.

This time it was she who gave the pointed look.

"If I ever gave you the privilege of dating me—" she stared straight into his blue eyes, held her chin a little higher than normal "—who says it would be *you* to break things off?"

Although she adored his friendship, his arrogance irked. Then again, was it arrogance if it was true he'd been the one to end every relationship he'd had during the time he and Kami had worked together? Probably his whole life?

Gabe chuckled, then surprised her by tweaking his finger across the tip of her nose. "You might be right, Kam. Only a fool would break things off with you. Speaking of which, how is Baxter?"

Ha. Talk about turning the table.

"Our breakup was a mutual decision," she reminded him, not that she hadn't already told Gabe as much a dozen times previously. "We aren't talking much these days, but he's fine as far as I know."

Just as she was. Baxter had been sweet, only she'd realized continuing their relationship was pointless. When he kissed her, she felt nothing. No sparks. No butterflies. Nothing.

Kami wasn't so delusional she thought someone would come along, sweep her off her feet, and give her a fairy-tale romance. But she wasn't going to settle for *nothing*, either.

Good friendship and sparks—it could happen.

Not that it had, but she was only twenty-seven. There was plenty of time for someone special to come into her life.

And, if not, she'd rather be alone than like her mother and with the wrong man over and over.

"Keep telling yourself that he's fine. Dude was devastated last week when I bumped into him."

Baxter hadn't been devastated. When she'd broached the subject of their relationship not working, he'd seemed relieved. Obviously, he hadn't felt any sparks, either. On paper they were a good match. In reality, there had been little chemistry beyond their initial attraction.

"When did you run into my ex?" Baxter, an accountant for a law firm, and the usually laid-back man in front of her didn't exactly move in the same social circles.

"At the gym."

Kami's jaw dropped. "Baxter was at the gym?"

She shook her head to clear her hearing because she couldn't have heard correctly. Not once during the time she'd known Baxter had he ever gone to the gym. To her knowledge, he'd not even had a membership.

"Pumping the iron in hopes of winning you back." Gabe's eyes twinkled with mischief. "Too bad you aren't up for grabs at the auction 'cause he could buy a night to remind you of all you're missing out on. You, him, Debbie and me could go on a double date and reminisce about the good ole days."

Kami rolled her eyes.

"Baxter is a great guy," she defended the man she'd dated for over six months. He truly was. He'd been steady, quiet, dependable. She'd wanted to feel something, had tried to convince herself she did because he'd make a good husband and father someday, but *nada*.

"Just not the guy for you?"

"Exactly. Now, was there a reason you interrupted my work other than to whine about Debbie?"

"As if she isn't enough of a reason." He gave an overly dramatic sigh that should have put him up for an award or two. "I can't believe you're refusing to help, Kam. You know I'd do it for you."

"I wouldn't want you to." She curled her nose and shuddered at the mere thought. "Can you imagine the rumors that would start around the hospital?" She gave a horrified look. "Uh-uh. No way. I can, however, put out word you're hoping someone outbids Debbie at the auction. I'm sure there'll be a few takers."

He shook his head. "I'm disappointed in you, Kam. I was sure I could count on you to save me."

"You have the wrong girl, but no worries. You'll find someone over the next few weeks to outbid Debbie."

* * *

Gabe disagreed. He had the right girl. The perfect girl.

Kami wouldn't get happily-ever-after ideas. He always had fun when she was around. And, best of all, she already knew the real him. The him who had no intentions of settling down anytime in the near future.

But he changed the subject instead of pursuing the topic further. As she said, they had a few weeks before the fund-raiser. A lot could happen during that time.

Like his convincing Kami to buy him.

Not that he couldn't deal with Debbie. He'd just rather not have to.

She was great, but had gotten too clingy too fast and he'd started feeling claustrophobic in their relationship by the end of the first month. At the end of the second, he'd been done. Too bad Debbie hadn't been.

"How is Racine Mathers tonight?" he asked to change the subject.

Apparently, the fragile elderly woman had arrived by ambulance in hypercapnic respiratory failure earlier that day. Yet again. She'd been admitted to the medical floor, which neither Gabe nor Kami had anything to do with, but he knew Kami would have checked on the woman prior to clocking in for her shift. She cared about people and that big heart was one of the things he liked most about the perky little blonde who'd quickly become one of his closest friends.

At the mention of their patient, her green eyes filled with concern. "Her arterial blood gases are still jacked up. Her CO_2 level remains in the upper fifties."

"I was hoping once they got her on BiPAP her numbers would improve." He logged in to the computer, began scanning messages in his inbox.

"That makes two of us, but apparently she hasn't wanted to keep the mask on and the day-shift nurse caught her with it off several times."

He shook his head. "Racine knows better than that."

Kami nodded.

The woman did. This wasn't her first respiratory failure rodeo. Then again, Gabe suspected the elderly woman was tiring of her inability to breathe and the medical community's failure to do much more than Band-Aid her back together until the next episode.

"I'm going to swing by and see her. If I'm needed before I get back, page me."

She arched a brow. "You think I wouldn't?"

Gabe grinned. No, he never doubted that his favorite nurse would do the right thing and get him where he needed to be when he needed to be there. Kami was an excellent nurse. There was no one he'd rather spend his shift working with. Fortunately, their schedules were on the same rotation and he got to spend several nights a week in the emergency department with her.

Whether it was busy, slammed, or on the rare occasion slow, he was never bored. Not with Kami around to keep him entertained with her quick wit and sassy mouth.

Which was yet another reason she should be the one to rescue him from Debbie. Not only would Kami not get the wrong idea, but Gabe would truly enjoy their "date." Not that they'd ever gone anywhere just the two of them, but when the work gang gathered, he gravitated toward Kami and they almost always ended up paired off.

There was just something about her that made him feel good on the inside.

She needed to buy his auction package and he intended to make sure she did.

* * *

"That is the most exciting thing I've heard in weeks."

While dropping in a urinalysis order for bay one, Kami curled her nose at the woman who'd been her best friend since they'd bonded during nursing school. "You would say that."

Mindy gave her a *duh* look. "The man is gorgeous and I saw that once-over you gave him. I think you should go for it."

Kami shook her head. "You misunderstood. That once-over was a joke and Gabe doesn't want me to buy his date so we can go on a *real* date. He wants me to save him from having to go on a date with someone else. Either way, no, thank you."

Mindy leaned against the desk. "I'm just saying, the most eligible bachelor in the hospital asked you to buy him at the fund-raiser. I think you should see that as a sign and go for it."

Go for it? Her friend had lost her mind.

"A sign of what?"

Mindy waggled her brows. "Your good fortune. Do you know how many women would kill for Gorgeous Gabe to ask them to buy his date package?"

Kami made a bleh motion with her tongue. "They can have him. He's too stuck on himself for my taste."

Mindy didn't look convinced. "That's not how I see him."

Kami didn't, either. Not really. Gabe was gorgeous, but he didn't seem to get caught up in his looks other than that he took care of himself and worked out regularly. Nothing wrong with trying to stay healthy.

Gabe was the picture of good health.

Great health.

Health at its finest, even.

Yeah, yeah. The man was easy on the eyes. No big deal.

"He's got a big heart and you know it," Mindy continued, oblivious to Kami's wayward thoughts—thank goodness. The last thing she needed was Mindy pushing her toward doing something she knew better than to do. She might be immune, but you didn't rub your face in germs to tempt fate, either.

"He doesn't mind getting his hands dirty. He's the first to jump in and help when someone needs something. I've never known him to pull the doctor card." Mindy gave a pointed look. "I'd be hard-pressed to name someone, male or female, who didn't like him."

"Since you're a walking, talking advertisement of his virtues, you bid on him," Kami suggested and wondered at the slight twinge in her belly at the thought of her friend buying Gabe's date.

Her two friends getting together would be a good thing, right? Well, except that Gabe would eventually break Mindy's heart and then Kami would have to bust his chops for hurting her bestie. That was what the issue was. She didn't want to have to dislike him for breaking Mindy's heart.

But Mindy's eyes lit at Kami's suggestion and a smile slid onto her face. "I might do that."

Kami's brow shot up. Her mouth opened, but she didn't comment as Gabe came strolling back into the emergency department.

"What have I missed?"

"Not much. Been a slow one so far," Mindy told him, all smiles and looks of all sorts of possibilities.

"Bite your tongue," Kami and Gabe said at the same time.

"Listen at you two," Mindy said, giving Kami a mischievous glance that said maybe her friend hadn't really veered from her original mission after all. "So in sync."

"Not wanting you to jinx our evening is common sense. Nothing in sync about that," Kami corrected, hoping her friend caught her warning tone. "Now, Dr. Nelson." She turned her attention to Gabe, ignoring his curious looks between her and Mindy. "Bay one is a urinary tract infection. Onset earlier today. Her urinalysis results are in her chart. Bay two is a fever and sore throat. I've swabbed for strep, but the results are pending. Both are pleasant, stable, and accompanied by their significant other. You want me to go with you while you examine them?"

Bay one was given an antibiotic, a bladder antispasmodic, a handout on the preventions of UTIs, and was sent on her way. The woman in bay two, however, looked worse than she had a few minutes before when Kami had last checked.

Her temp was just over one hundred and three, her throat beet red, and her conjunctivae injected. The woman was also now complaining of a severe headache, which she hadn't mentioned during triage or when Kami had done her nursing assessment.

The woman shivered as if she were freezing and looked miserable.

"Can you get her a blanket or something?" her husband asked, looking frustrated that his wife was getting worse.

"She doesn't need to cover up," Kami reminded him. She'd intentionally not given the woman a blanket. She directed her next comment to her patient. "It'll hold heat to your body and you're already too warm. We have to get your fever under control before we can even consider giving a blanket or doing anything that might make you worse."

Wincing with discomfort, the woman tightened her arms around her body. "I'm so cold."

They had to get her fever down and stable. Once they did, then she could possibly have a lightweight blanket. Certainly not before.

"When did the headache start?" Kami asked.

"She had a headache when she got here. It's just gotten a lot worse," the husband clarified. "It wasn't bad enough to mention."

Apparently not even when Kami had directly asked about a headache. Ugh. She really didn't like when patients said something completely opposite when the doctor was present than what they'd told her during their assessment. It happened almost nightly.

Gabe ran through a quick examination of the woman. "Some swelling in the cervical nodes and neck stiffness. I want a blood count and a comprehensive metabolic panel on her STAT, and has that strep finished running?"

"Should be. I'll log in and check." Kami signed in on the in-bay computer and the test result was back. "She's negative for strep."

"Ache all over," the woman told them, her eyes squeezed tightly shut. "Cold."

Gabe gave some orders, which Kami turned to do, but stopped when the woman said, "I'm going to throw up." Then did exactly that.

Gabe was closer than Kami and got an emesis pan in front of Mrs. Arnold just in time.

"Give her an antiemetic IM now." He named the one he wanted given and the dosage. "Then let's get a saline lock on her."

Kami drew up the medication and injected the solution. The woman was shaking and looked much worse than she had when they'd entered the bay.

"Do something," the husband ordered, sounding worried, as he hovered next to his wife's bed, gripping the woman's pale hand.

Gabe sent Kami a concerned look. "Get phlebotomy to draw blood cultures times three and the previous labs I mentioned. It's off season, but run an influenza test, just in case. Let's get a CT of her head, too. I'm probably going to do a lumbar puncture."

He was thinking a possibility of meningitis. Rightly so, given how rapidly her status was changing.

"Let's put her in isolation. Just in case," Gabe continued in full doctor mode.

The husband was talking, too. Kami didn't want to ignore him, tried to answer his questions while she worked, but he continued to fret.

Gabe gave an order to get IV antibiotics started and told her which he wanted. Kami rushed around making things happen. Although she'd really not looked like more than a typical sore throat patient, Mrs. Arnold had gone downhill scarily fast. In case she continued on the decline, they needed to act fast to get an accurate diagnosis as quickly as possible.

Linda Arnold's blood count came back showing a significantly elevated white blood cell count with a bacterial shift. Her headache and neck pain had continued to increase and the woman refused to even attempt to move her neck. Her strep and influenza were negative.

Lumbar punctures weren't Gabe's favorite things to do as there was always risk, but his concerns over meningitis were too high not to test her spinal fluid. As soon as he had the CT scan results back, he'd pull the fluid so long as the scan didn't show any reason not to. He didn't want to risk brain herniation by not following protocol.

From all indications, the woman had meningitis. Gabe needed to know the exact culprit.

He cleared out two other patients who'd come into the emergency department. Then, protective personal equipment in place, he went back to Mrs. Arnold.

The woman was now going in and out of consciousness and didn't make a lot of sense when she was awake.

Also wearing appropriate personal protective equipment, Kami was at her bedside. She'd already gathered everything he'd need for a lumbar puncture. They needed to move fast.

Hopefully, the antibiotics infusing into her body via her IV line would be the right ones for whatever caused her infection, but if they weren't, waiting around to see could mean the difference between life and death.

That wasn't a chance he was willing to take.

"Dr. Nelson?" Mindy stopped him from entering the area where Mrs. Arnold was. "Dr. Reynolds just called with her CT results. He is concerned about meningitis and recommends proceeding with lumbar puncture."

This was the call Gabe had been waiting for giving him the safe go-ahead.

Checking to make sure his respiratory mask was secure, Gabe nodded, then entered the area where Mrs. Arnold was isolated.

From behind her clear plastic glasses, Kami's eyes were filled with worry when they met his.

"She has gaze palsy and mild extremity drift now," she told him. "I thought you'd prefer her husband not be in here for this as he was getting agitated. I sent him to the private counseling room to wait for you to talk to him after we get this done."

That was one of the things he loved about Kami. She was always one step ahead of him.

Except when it came to the auction.

On that one, he planned to outstep her. Not planned to—he *would* outstep her, because the more he thought about it, the more he wanted to go on that "date" with Kami.

CHAPTER TWO

"WHAT A NIGHT," Kami mused at the end of her twelve-hour shift that had turned into over fourteen. She couldn't wait to get home, shower, eat whatever she could find in the fridge, and crawl into bed to pass out until it was time to come back and do it all again for night two of her three in a row.

"You look tired."

She glanced toward Gabe. "You don't look like a bowl of cherries yourself."

He laughed. "Not sure if that was meant to be an insult or not, but I'll go on record saying I'm grateful I don't look like a bowl of cherries."

Kami shrugged. "Too bad. Cherries would be an improvement."

"A cherry fan?"

"They're my favorite," she admitted with a quick sideways glance toward him.

"You one of those talented people who can knot the stem with your tongue?" he teased.

Kami had very few silly talents, but tying a cherry stem into a knot was in her repertoire. Rather than admit as much to Gabe, she shrugged again.

"I'll never tell."

"Because you prefer to show me?" he joked, not looking tired at all despite the fact he had to be exhausted.

It really had been a long night.

"Okay." He gave a dramatic sigh. "I'm game. There's a pancake house a few blocks from here where you can get whipped cream and cherries."

She frowned. "You know this how?"

"A man has to know where he can get whipped cream and cherries twenty-four hours a day."

Kami scrunched her nose. "Ew. Spare me the details because I don't want to know."

Looking intrigued, he chuckled. "Your mind went to the gutter, Kam. I'm surprised, but I think I like it."

"Nothing to like about you grossing me out."

His brow arched. "My liking whipped cream and cherries on top of my pancakes grosses you out?"

She ran her gaze over his broad chest, down his flat abs that his scrubs failed to disguise. "Yeah, I can tell you regularly chow down on pancakes with whipped cream and cherries."

"You might be surprised."

Not really. She'd seen him put away a lot of food during their shift breaks. The man could eat. Not that it showed. Whether because of good genetics or his time spent in the gym, Gabe truly was the picture of good health.

"Doubtful," she tossed as she clocked out and grabbed her lunch bag. "Not much about you surprises me."

His brow rose. "Oh? You know me that well?"

"As well as I want to." She gave him a look that said she was well aware he had fallen into step beside her as she exited the emergency department. "Bye, Gabe."

"You have to eat, Kam. Let me take you to breakfast before I hit the gym."

Her brows knitted together. "You're going to the gym this morning after working over and having to be back here this evening?"

His eyebrows lifted. "Why wouldn't I?"

Kami stared at him as if he were the oddest anomaly. "Do you not need sleep?"

He grinned. "Not when I'm properly motivated."

"You that excited at the prospect of running into Baxter again?" She glanced at her watch. "You should hurry or you may miss him. Wouldn't want that to happen."

Gabe burst out laughing. "Okay, I'll take a hint and a rain check on the pancakes with whipped cream and cherries."

That evening, Kami glanced at her cell phone and winced. Her mother. Should she answer? Guilt hit her that she considered not doing so. Her mother knew it was time for her to be at work. If she was calling, something must be wrong, right?

"Hi, Mom. I'm about to clock in at work, so I can't talk but a second. What's up?"

"I'm headed out of town," her mother answered. Then a male voice spoke in the background and, muffling the phone, her mother said something back. Then she said into the phone, "Can you feed my cat while I'm gone?"

Why her mother had gotten the scruffy cat, Kami had no clue. Most days she couldn't take care of herself, much less a pet. But at least she'd not left without making arrangements for the stray she'd taken in. Then again, her mother should have been an expert at taking in strays.

Fortunately, her mother didn't make a habit of asking Kami to feed them. At least, not since Kami had moved out the moment she'd graduated from high school and escaped the constant chaos of Eugenia's life.

"I'll swing by in the morning and feed her." Then she couldn't hold back asking, "What's his name?"

"Bubbles. You know that."

"Not the cat. The guy."

"Oh." Her mother giggled and the person in the background said something else, which elicited another giggle. "Sammy. He's a drummer in a band and so good."

Her mother tended to be drawn to artistic types. Especially unemployed ones who needed a place to crash while they waited on their big break. Not that any of them ever stuck around long. They stayed. They used. They moved on. Another arrived to fill the vacancy. It was the story of Kami's childhood and was still ongoing. Would her mother never learn?

"Okay, Mom," she sighed, putting her lunch in the break-room refrigerator. "I'll feed Bubbles. Any idea when you'll be back?"

"A couple of days. I'll text to let you know for sure. Don't forget to love on Bubbles."

"Right." Because she wanted to stick around at her mother's apartment longer than she absolutely had to. Not. "Well, I'm at work, so I need to go. Bye, Mom. I'll feed Bubbles."

She'd probably love on the scrappy cat, too. Goodness knew that if her mother had a new man in her life, the cat would be ignored until his departure.

Kami had a lot of empathy for Bubbles.

"I was disappointed I didn't see Baxter this morning," Gabe teased as Kami came over to where he sat reviewing chart notes. Gabe loved his job, loved being a doctor, and loved knowing that, if the need arose, he could do everything humanly possible to save someone's life.

Knowing he'd see Kami made the prospect of going to work all the sweeter. He never knew what was going to come out of that sassy mouth of hers.

"Maybe he's already given up his exercise kick," Kami mused, not looking as if she cared one way or the other.

Actually, she looked distracted and he wondered who she'd been on the phone with earlier. He'd been coming back into the department from the NICU, where Beverly and her husband had been sitting with their baby. He couldn't imagine the stress they were going through as each day was a struggle for their tiny baby girl to live. He'd been thinking on the fund-raiser, hoping it raised enough money to cover the couple's out-of-pocket medical expenses, not to mention all their day-to-day expenses that still had to be paid despite their being at the hospital instead of their jobs. Whomever Kami had been on the phone with, it hadn't been a pleasant conversation.

"Doubtful." Gabe leaned back in his chair and eyed the petite blonde nurse standing a few feet away. Were there problems with the fund-raiser? Or had the call been personal? "My guess is he was already there and gone by the time I got there. He's determined to buff up for you."

"Yeah, yeah." She didn't sound impressed. "Someone should tell him I'm not into buff."

Gabe arched a brow. "I thought all women were into buff."

She rolled her eyes. "Men are into buff. Any intelligent woman would rather have a man of substance than bulgy muscles."

"Can't a man have both substance and muscles?"

Kami shrugged. "Apparently not."

"You're overlooking the obvious."

Her forehead scrunched. "What's that?"

He waggled his brows. "I'm substance *and* bulgy muscles."

Giving him a critical once-over, she seemed to be debating his claim. "You're not that gross. You don't have that no-neck, bulgy-muscles look I can't stand."

Gabe wasn't sure if she'd insulted or complimented him. "That means I don't count?"

"You don't count, anyway," she said flippantly, handing him a piece of paper she'd jotted patient vitals on.

Ignoring the paper, he asked, "Why's that?"

"We're talking muscles and *substance*, remember?" she said matter-of-factly and gestured to the paper she'd handed him.

Gabe laughed. "Right. I forgot. Disqualified on all counts."

"Exactly. Now, are you going to go see the poor lady in bay three? Her blood pressure is crazy high at two hundred and fifteen over one hundred and thirty-seven."

"Slave driver," he accused, glancing down at the numbers on the paper she'd handed him as he headed toward the bay. "But rightly so."

Connie Guffrey's EKG was normal, as were her cardiac enzymes. Fortunately, after Kami administered IV medication, her blood pressure decreased to closer to the normal range, but Gabe decided to admit her for overnight observation due to her having developed some shortness of breath and mild chest pain just prior to plans to discharge her home.

Kami agreed doing serial cardiac enzymes overnight was in Ms. Guffrey's best interest and arranged the transfer to the medical floor.

"Don't look now," Mindy advised, "but you know who

has been watching you all night. I think he really does want you to buy his date."

Kami immediately turned toward where she'd last seen Gabe. He was busy talking to a respiratory therapist who'd just administered a breathing treatment on an asthma patient.

"I told you not to look," Mindy reminded her.

"Doesn't matter that I looked because you're imagining things."

"Not hardly. And you know what?" Mindy looked absolutely smug. "He's not the only one who's been staring."

Realization dawning as to her friend's meaning, Kami frowned. "I have not been staring."

"Sure you haven't."

"The only time I've looked at the man is when we're discussing a patient or treating a patient." She scowled at her friend. "Don't you have something better to fill your time than making up stories?"

"You just looked at him, Kami."

She gave a *duh* look. "Because you told me not to."

"Exactly, and you immediately seized the excuse to look at him." Mindy bent forward and whispered, "I think you like him."

"Of course I like him. He's a nice guy who I work with. We're friends."

Mindy shook her head. "Not buying it. You should be more than friends."

Kami's gaze narrowed. "Says who?"

"Me." Mindy leaned against the raised desk area that provided a divider for the nurses from the examination bays. "Apparently he thinks so, too, or he wouldn't have asked you to buy his date."

"The reason he asked me to buy his date is because we're just friends and I wouldn't get the wrong idea."

"Which is?"

"That there could ever be something between him and me." Kami outright glared at her friend. "This isn't some television show where doctors fall for nurses and harbor secret feelings. This is reality and the reality is that he and I are just friends and that's all we want to be. Don't make this into something it's not."

"Maybe you should make it into something it's not."

"You sound like a broken record. Let it go," she ordered, then, frowning, added, "Besides, I thought you planned to bid on him."

Mindy crossed her arms, regarding Kami. "I should."

"Good. Buy him. He's taking his date to Gatlinburg for a fun-filled Saturday of visiting the aquarium, playing laser tag and putt-putt golf, riding go-karts, and topping the night off with a dinner show. You'd have a great time."

"I should hire you as my press agent. My bid might break records."

Kami jumped at Gabe's interruption. "I didn't hear you come up. I was…uh…telling Mindy she should bid on you."

"I heard." He grinned at Mindy. "She convince you?"

"I'm saving my pennies, Dr. Nelson."

He laughed. "Good to know."

Mindy looked back and forth between them, smiled as if she was in on a secret, and gave Kami a you-should-go-for-it look. "I hear the receptionist talking to someone. I'm off to see if it's a new patient and they're ready to be triaged."

Kami frowned at her retreating friend. She hadn't heard anyone registering. Her friend had purposely left her and Gabe alone. Mindy had a distinct lack of subtlety.

"Good to know that since you don't plan to buy my

package, you at least plan to save me by convincing others to bid."

"What are friends for?"

He met her gaze. "I've already answered that question."

"True." Still feeling irked at Mindy's comments, she gave him a tight smile. "And we've already established that I'm not bidding on you."

"I'd spot you the money. Imagine—you'd get a fun-filled day in beautiful Gatlinburg, my company, and you wouldn't even have to save your pennies."

"You're wasting your breath."

"Talking to you is never wasted breath."

"Don't try sweet-talking me, Gabe. I know you better than to buy into that garbage."

He held his hands up. "Hey, I was making a legitimate observation, not trying to woo you into bidding on me."

"Right."

He laughed. "Okay, you're right. I was trying to woo you into winning my bid. Can you blame me?"

She gave him a look she hoped said she sure could.

"Fine," he relented. "But I do enjoy our conversations, Kam. You make me smile."

He made her smile, too, but she wasn't convinced that was what he'd meant.

"How is Ms. Guffrey?" she asked to redirect the subject to work. "Any news of how her cardiac tests are holding?"

"She's stable. We're thinking she just panicked and that's where the new symptoms came in. I sure didn't want to send her home and her have an MI."

"Agreed. I'm glad she's doing okay."

He glanced at his watch. "Only another hour until the end of our shift. You want to go for pancakes with me?"

Surprised at his repeated offer from the day before, Kami frowned. "Why would I do that?"

"Because you didn't go yesterday and you have me curious."

"About?"

"You know what." He waggled his brows.

It took her only a second to realize what he referred to.

"Puh-leese. That's what this is about? You want to know how talented I am with my mouth?"

As the words came out of her mouth, Kami realized how her comment could be interpreted. Her cheeks flushed hot.

"That's not…" At his laughter, Kami's face burned even hotter. "You know what I meant, Gabriel Nelson, and what I didn't mean."

"Do I?"

She narrowed her eyes. "You know you do."

He crossed his arms and leaned against the desk. "Maybe, but saying I don't might be a lot more fun. Why are your cheeks so red, Kam?"

Deciding that ignoring him was the best approach, Kami grabbed a brochure and fanned her face. "It is hot in here, isn't it?"

Which was a joke if Kami ever heard one. The emergency department was notoriously cool—purposely so to help keep germs down.

But, for once, the area felt blazing.

"Not particularly." His grin was still in place. "Even better than you going for pancakes with whipped cream and cherries with me would be if you did that *and* went to work out with me. That would send Baxter the message that he was wasting his time, for sure."

"If I ate pancakes then tried to work out, I'd be sick, so, in that regard, you're right about sending a message."

He laughed. "We could have breakfast after we work out."

She looked at him as if he was crazy. "Again, wrong girl, Gabe. I'm not a gym rat and I'm not a girl who would work out on an empty stomach."

His gaze ran over her. "You look like you could be."

"Is that a compliment?"

One corner of his mouth slid upward. "It wasn't an insult."

Kami fought to keep heat from flooding her face again. "Either way, I'm not going to the gym."

"You don't want to see the new and improved Baxter?"

Not that she could go anyway since she had to go feed Bubbles, but Kami pointed out, "You don't even know he'll be there this morning."

"Then you do want to see him?" Gabe sounded surprised.

"No, I don't want to see Baxter. That's why I broke things off."

Gabe immediately seized on her comment. "I thought your relationship ended due to a mutual decision."

"It did. Mutual means I told him things weren't working and he agreed." She glared at Gabe. "Would you stop twisting what I'm saying?"

Feigning innocence, he put his hands up in front of him. "I'm doing nothing of the sort. I'm just trying to buy you breakfast. Quite friendly of me, I'd say."

"You just want to harass me into buying your bid," she countered, knowing it was true. Gabe was her friend, but he was a guy and guys had ulterior motives, right?

"Perhaps," he agreed. "But I was serious about buying you breakfast. We could discuss the fund-raiser."

"What about it?"

"I could help in ways besides the auction."

"Uh-uh." She shook her head. "You're not getting out of the auction, Gabe. We're auctioning off five men and five women and you're the big-ticket item."

Grinning, he asked, "You think so?"

Despite all her efforts to prevent the heat, her face went hot again.

"Women seem to think so." At his pleased look, she added, "Especially Debbie."

That ought to simmer his arrogance down. If not, the brilliant idea that hit her would.

"I'm thinking of asking if she'll use her television connections for local publicity to raise awareness of the fund-raiser."

Rather than look annoyed, he looked impressed. "That's brilliant. You want me to check with her?"

A bit floored he'd be willing since he was making such a big deal of the woman planning to buy his date, Kami nodded. Garnering as much free publicity as possible was important and she should have thought of Gabe's connection to the local television station sooner. "Would you?"

His eyes danced. "For you?"

"For Beverly and her baby," she corrected.

"If it would help Beverly's baby get a new heart, I'd talk to the devil himself."

Kami didn't recall Debbie being anywhere near that bad, but she'd only met the woman a couple of times when she'd shown up at the emergency department to bring Gabe a late dinner or a cup of his favorite coffee. On television, she smiled often as she made over homes in the Eastern Tennessee area and seemed nice enough.

"Great." Kami rubbed her palms together. "Encourage her to pay plenty when she wins that Gatlinburg get-away. Sounds like fun."

"Obviously not fun enough. I can't convince you to bid."

"Can I go without you?"

He gave an offended frown. "That appeals more than the total package?"

Rolling her eyes, she clicked her tongue. "You're hardly the total package, Gabe."

Later that morning, Kami hit the drive-through and ordered a coffee to keep her going long enough to get to her mother's when all she really wanted was to go home and crash.

Within a few minutes, she was sitting on her mother's sofa, Bubbles walking back and forth next to her while Kami stroked the cat from her head to the tip of her tail.

Silly cat. Often, Kami wondered if the cat was happier to see her during her short visits than her mother was. She glanced around the tiny, messy apartment. No family portraits lined the walls. No memorabilia from Kami's childhood. Instead, the walls were bare except for a Red Hot Chili Peppers poster. If there had been a photo, Kami wouldn't have expected it to be of herself, but of this latest guy.

Kami emptied the litter box, bagged her mother's overflowing trash, put in a fresh bag, and picked up the empty food containers and drink cans scattered around the apartment.

Making sure the cat had food and water, Kami grabbed the trash and headed out of the apartment to go home. Sleep had her name all over it.

Only, when she got back to her place and finally crawled into bed, sleep refused to make an appearance.

Perhaps she should have skipped the coffee. She didn't

need anything interfering with her rest prior to going into the third night of her three-in-a-row work schedule.

Especially not thoughts of her mother, a silly cat who was home alone, and Gabe.

Why was Gabe even on the list of things running through her mind?

He was a friend. Nothing more.

Ugh. Sleep was not happening.

She reached over and grabbed her phone off her night-stand. Ten a.m. Still early enough that if she dozed off she'd get plenty of rest before going back to work. Not that sleep seemed anywhere near.

Maybe she should get up for an hour, then try again later to go to sleep.

Sometimes after the first night of her three-in-a-row, she struggled to get to sleep the next morning, but never after the second or third nights.

Ugh.

Gripping her phone, she hit the text emblem, then Gabe's number from her contacts.

So, was he there?

Why she asked, she wasn't sure. She didn't care if Baxter had been at the gym or not. She just couldn't sleep. It made no sense, but deep down she knew talking with Gabe—even via text—would take her mind off her mother and off Bubbles, whom she'd considered packing up and bringing home with her. She might have, had her apartment not had a restriction against pets.

Who?

You know who.

Ah, the ex. He was there. Looking better every day.

Good for him.

There was a long enough pause that Kami wondered if Gabe was going to respond again.

Come on, Gabe. I need you to take my mind to a better place so I can close my eyes and stop my brain from racing because I feel sorry for a cat who has my mother as a caregiver.

Want me to take a picture for you next time I see him?

The idea of Gabe snapping a shot of Baxter working out had Kami laughing out loud.

People might get the wrong idea, think you had a man crush on him.

Yeah, well, I'm the kind of guy who would risk it to help a friend.

Good one. I'm still not bidding on you.

She lay back, head sinking into her pillow as she stared at her phone screen.

So you keep saying.

You think I will?

Hoping you will. Spoke to Debbie this morning. She's talking to her producer about the fund-raiser, see what they can come up with to help.

He'd already talked to his ex about the fund-raiser? Then again, Gabe had said he would and she'd never known him not to follow through on something he'd said he'd do.

Awesome. Hope it wasn't too painful. Thank you.

Thank you for all you're doing to help Beverly and her baby girl. If it wasn't for you and Mindy putting so much into this the fund-raiser wouldn't even be happening.

Ha, I'm not sacrificing nearly as much as you. She was only doing what she thought needed to be done to help with the overwhelming expenses that come with having a seriously ill baby. I'm not the one being auctioned off.

So you admit you feel badly for me?

That you're going to have women fighting over you with their wallets? Sure, I'm heartbroken. Poor, poor Gabe.

You're a funny girl, Kam.

She could picture his smile.

Something like that.

Why aren't you asleep? You were clamoring to get home to bed when I asked you to have pancakes with me.

Yeah, she had been. Too bad sleep continued to elude her.

I had errands to run. I may or may not have drunk coffee. Just saying.

It's not too late for those pancakes.

Sure it is. I'm in bed.

Nothing wrong with breakfast in bed. You want syrup or cherries and whipped cream? I recommend the cherries and whipped cream, but I admit I'm biased.

Kami stared at her phone screen and shook her head. The man was incorrigible.

Good thing she knew better than to take him seriously.

A smile on her face, she snuggled into her covers and began typing a response worthy of his outrageous suggestion.

CHAPTER THREE

G ABE STARED AT his phone. What was he doing?

Flirting with Kami, that was what. It didn't take a genius to figure that one out.

Question was, why?

He and Kami were friends. So why had he typed out the message and hit Send as if flirting with Kami were the most natural thing in the world?

They often bantered back and forth and he enjoyed their conversations a great deal. Talking with Kami was mentally stimulating. They'd texted before but always light or something about work.

This felt different, not quite all in fun and games.

How about both, Gabe? We can use the whipped cream and cherries for after the pancakes.

Gabe's eyes widened and he wondered if he'd fallen asleep while sitting on the sofa messaging with her. Not once during their friendly banter had Kami ever flirted. Usually she came back with something sassy to put him in his place.

Her comment had his throat tightening; had him swallowing to clear the knot that formed there; had him fighting to keep the image of Kami, cherries, and whipped cream out of his head.

Why did her comment have his heart picking up pace?

Have his breath hitching in his chest?

Have his… This was *Kami* texting him. His friend Kami. His coworker Kami. What was he thinking?

Obviously, he wasn't.

Because if he was he wouldn't be considering calling in a to-go order for pancakes with whipped cream and cherries.

His phone buzzed and he braced himself, drawing on all his willpower not to run out of the door to grab that order.

Only, can you just set them inside the front door? I'll let you know later what my company thinks of your thoughtfulness in delivering breakfast.

Her message dumped a mental bucketful of cold water over his being.

Sitting up straighter on the sofa, Gabe tensed. His teeth clenched and his heart pounded as he typed.

There's someone there? In bed with you?

Why did that bother him? She'd dated Baxter for months, had probably spent many mornings with the accountant. What did it matter who Kami spent her mornings with? It wasn't his business.

You didn't think I meant to share pancakes in bed with you, did you? Ew, Gabe. Get real.

Ah, there was the Kami he knew and expected. Still, for a minute she'd had him going.

Then again, the gutted feeling in his stomach that at this very moment Kami was in bed with some Joe Blow, well, he didn't like the thought at all.

Which didn't make sense. They were just friends, right?

"So, who is this mystery guy?"

Kami flinched. She'd hoped Gabe would have let her ridiculous attempt to cover her comment go. She'd been meaning to take him down a peg, have him backtracking, but he'd taken her comment seriously and clearly hadn't known what to say back.

To which she'd been flabbergasted with embarrassment and had done what needed to be done to ease the tension crackling over the phone.

She'd made up a boyfriend.

No big deal. Women had been doing it for centuries. Not that Kami ever had, or even fully understood why she had that morning. Not with Gabe. It wasn't as if it mattered what he thought.

"No one you know." She refused to look at him, just kept staring at the computer monitor.

"Does Baxter know about him?"

"Shh." Kami glanced around, hoping Mindy didn't overhear their conversation. The emergency department had been slow since they'd arrived, and her friend was chatting with a paramedic who'd brought in a non-emergent patient for direct admission just prior to shift change and had stuck around afterward.

"Your best friend doesn't know about a guy you're having sex with?" Gabe tsked, pulling up a chair next to hers.

"Would you keep it down, please?"

Gabe gave her a suspicious look. "What's wrong with this guy that you don't want anyone to know of his existence?"

"Nothing is wrong with him," she defended. There wouldn't be a thing wrong with him. If he actually existed, she thought. Too bad he didn't. She'd like to throw him in Gabe's face right about now.

"How long have you known him?"

She swiveled her chair to face him. "Since when do you have the right to question me on my love life?"

His expression didn't waver. "Since you invited me to breakfast in bed."

"I didn't invite you to breakfast in bed," she hissed, not bothering to hide her outraged horror at the mere idea.

"Technically, you did."

Technically?

Kami's temples throbbed as she thought back over their conversation. Technically. Ugh.

"This is the most ridiculous conversation I've ever had." She pushed back her chair, stood to walk away, but he grabbed her hand, his hold gentle but firm enough to stop her.

She glared at where he touched her. Anger. That was why her skin burned there.

"Be careful, Kami," he warned. "Don't jump into something so fast on the heels of your breakup with Baxter."

Kami didn't know whether to burst out laughing or to cry. That Gabe would say not to rush into a new relationship when he usually had a new girl on his arm the week following a breakup was comical. She and Baxter had called it quits five, no, six weeks ago. Had she been in bed with another man, she still would have logged more getting-over-it time than Gabe put in prior to jumping into another bed. She was sure of it.

Men were so hypocritical.

"Take note, Gabe." She pulled her hand free. "My love life is none of your business."

"I am one hundred percent positive I'd rather have been in on this conversation than the one I just had with Eddie Pruitt."

Ugh. Mindy would have to overhear that. No doubt her friend would jump to all sorts of wrong conclusions, but at the moment Kami just wanted away from Gabe. Far away.

"Then you're welcome to this conversation, because I'm done with it."

With that, she left Mindy and Gabe staring after her.

"You want to tell me what you said to my best friend that upset her?"

Gabe wasn't sure what he'd said that had put Kami on the defensive. He'd been concerned and her hackles had stood at full attention. Even if he had known why she'd gotten so irate, he doubted he'd discuss it with Mindy.

If Kami hadn't told her friend about this mystery guy, then Gabe wasn't going to be the one to spill the beans.

Mindy studied him a moment. Then her expression softened. "You trying to get her to buy your date again?"

"No." If Kami was involved with another man, she wouldn't be buying his date. Nor would he ask her to. That went beyond the call of friendship.

Only, something didn't feel right about the whole conversation.

Then it hit him.

"Excuse me, Mindy. Kami might have been done with our conversation, but I wasn't."

He found Kami restocking bay one despite the fact that the shelf wasn't low.

He wasted no time in asking, "If you were in bed with another man this morning, why were you texting me?"

Letting out an exasperated hiss, Kami turned toward him, pursed her lips, crossed her arms, and glared. "Fine. I wasn't in bed with another man."

He let that sink in, let the wave of emotions wash over him and sought to label the one beating him down.

Relief. Why was he relieved that she hadn't been in bed with someone?

Because they'd been flirting and he'd liked it?

"Why did you lead me to think you were?"

An annoyed sigh escaped her lips. "Because you shouldn't have said what you did about breakfast in bed."

Now she wasn't meeting his eyes, which made him all the more curious. "Why not?"

"Because you didn't mean it." She gave him a disgusted look. "No wonder women like Debbie don't let go if you make comments like those when you don't mean them."

"First off, I don't make comments like those to Debbie or any other woman. Second, who says I didn't mean my offer?"

She rolled her eyes upward. "Right."

"Right, what?"

Her hand went to her hip and she stared him down. "Right, you meant it when you offered to bring me breakfast in bed."

He had. It floored him as much as it did her.

He cocked a brow. "You're saying I didn't?"

Looking flustered, she huffed out, "Quit being ridiculous, Gabe. Of course you didn't."

He held her gaze, refusing to look away or back down. "Want to bet?"

"You'd lose," she returned.

The challenge in her eyes had Gabe knowing he'd do nothing of the sort.

"Guess we'll find out when I bring you breakfast in bed tomorrow, won't we?"

She let out a huff of air. "You aren't bringing me breakfast in bed tomorrow or any other day."

"You'll see. Tomorrow morning." He glanced at his watch, saw it was after midnight. "Technically, *this* morning. You're going to eat every bite and you're going to like it."

Annoyed at him and herself, Kami gawked at Gabe, not quite believing that she was arguing with him about breakfast in bed.

That he was arguing back.

Had they ever argued? Or raised their voices with each other?

Never.

That they were now, over breakfast in bed, was the most ludicrous thing she could imagine.

So ludicrous that, despite her tension of moments before, she burst out laughing.

His face tight, Gabe's gaze narrowed. "What's so funny?"

"You."

He frowned. "I see nothing funny about this."

"Really? You don't find the fact you just threatened to make me eat every bite of my breakfast and that I was going to like it hilarious?" Another round of laughter hit her and she grabbed her stomach. "Oh, Gabe, I thought you had a better sense of humor."

His expression easing, a smile twitched at his lips. "Okay, so maybe a little hilarious, but don't think that gets you out of breakfast. You are going to eat up. Mmm… good."

"Yeah, yeah," she mocked, grateful the tension inside her had dissipated. "Keep threatening me and I'm going to report you to my nearest supervisor."

"I am your nearest supervisor," he reminded her, his tone back to its usual teasing.

"There is that."

"Hey, you two, we have incoming." Mindy stuck her head into the bay. "Motor vehicle accident. One dead at scene, two critical on their way here."

Their slow night morphed into total chaos as at the same time as the first ambulance arrived, so did a private vehicle with an overdose victim requiring multiple doses of Narcan administration prior to them being able to revive the woman and transfer her to the ICU.

The night flew by with one patient after another. By the time she'd given her report to the day-shift nurse taking her place, Kami was exhausted.

She clocked out, visited with an even more exhausted-appearing Beverly in the NICU for a few minutes, stopped by to feed and water Bubbles, fought guilt over leaving her mother's cat home alone while she drove home, showered, and was about to crawl into her bed when she heard knocking.

"Who in the world?"

Glancing down at her shorts and well-worn Ed Sheeran T-shirt, Kami headed toward the apartment door. She wasn't wearing a bra, but she wasn't overly endowed and doubted anyone would be able to tell.

"Who is it?" she called through the door at the same

time as she stretched on her tiptoes to peek through the peephole.

Gabe!

Carrying bags displaying a local pancake house logo.

He hadn't.

He had.

"Delivery boy."

Heart pounding against her rib cage, she leaned her forehead against the door. Gabe was at her house. With breakfast.

Why?

Why was her pulse pounding in her ears?

"Wrong address. I didn't order anything," she called back.

What was he doing there? Why did she suddenly feel the need to go put on a bra after all? And a dozen other layers? Why was her heart racing as if something really good was happening?

"It's a special delivery."

"Sorry, I don't open my door for strangers."

"What's wrong, Kam? Someone in there with you?" he teased. "I could always leave the bags by the door."

Undoing the lock and dead bolt, she flung open the door. "That, Dr. Nelson, was a low blow."

He grinned. "You'd have done the same had the opportunity presented itself."

He had her there.

"Invite me in," he reminded her when she kept standing in the doorway, glaring at him.

"Because you're a creature of the night and can't enter unless invited in first?" She stepped aside, motioning for him to come in.

"Something like that," he tossed back, entering the apartment and glancing around. "Where do you want these?"

"Not in my bed." She closed the front door and followed him, not quite believing he was there, inside her home. With breakfast.

He laughed. "Ah, now come on. You're spoiling my fun."

"Right." She glanced around her mostly clean living room, thinking it wasn't in too bad shape for the end of three nights on at the hospital.

"How about you set them on the coffee table?" Then, thinking it might be easier, she suggested, "Or on the table over there?"

The apartment, although not really big, had an open floor plan so that the kitchen, dining area, and living room were all visible to each other. It was one of the features Kami had fallen in love with when she'd first walked into the place. That and its close vicinity to both the hospital and the university. She'd started out there with a roommate, but the woman had married and moved away several months ago. Kami had never bothered to replace her since she'd been mere months from reaching her house-down-payment goal and would hopefully be buying her first home soon.

Someday soon she would own her own home and no one would be able to take it away from her. A place where she'd never have to move from because it would be hers. A place where if she wanted to bring her mother's cat to her home, she could.

With her next paycheck, she'd hit the target she'd set for herself years ago and she'd start the search to make her homeowner dream a reality.

"Either way is fine," she rushed on.

"Let's do the coffee table." He set the bags down on the laminated wooden table. "Less formal."

Still way more formal than her bedroom.

Her cheeks heated at the thought.

She stopped moving. "Why are you here, Gabe?"

"I'd think that was obvious."

She arched her brows and waited.

"I promised you breakfast."

"Actually, you threatened breakfast in bed."

He picked the bags back off the coffee table. "Point me in the right direction."

Kami had thought her cheeks had been hot before, but the heat coming off them now could melt the polar ice caps.

"You goofball. I ought to take you up on that." She rolled her eyes, trying to ease the twirling in her stomach. "That would teach you."

At his mischievous look, she shook her head.

"Or, more likely, not teach you anything at all." She sighed. "You're not going in my bedroom, Gabe. Not now or ever."

"Now who's threatening who?" he teased, putting the bags back down and unpacking the plastic containers. "Jeez, Kam, you're grumpy in the mornings. Now I know why you work night shift."

Eyeing the numerous containers he was pulling from the bags, she asked, "How is it that you're so cheery when I know you were up all night?"

He waggled his brows. "What man isn't cheery when he's been up all night?"

Rather than respond, Kami gave in to the smell coming from her coffee table. "Why do you have three drinks?"

He pulled out a milk carton and a plastic orange-juice container from one of the bags.

"Five drinks?" she corrected.

"I wasn't sure what you'd want, so I got a variety of

choices. I aim to please, so I'll drink what you don't want."

"That was thoughtful of you."

He grinned. "I'm a thoughtful kind of guy."

Kami sank onto her sofa, suspiciously eyeing the man unpacking a third bag. "It's been my experience that when a man does something thoughtful he wants something in return."

He shot her a serious look. "Baxter has a lot to answer for."

Kami shook her head. "I wasn't referring to Baxter."

He continued unpacking plastic containers and setting them on her coffee table. "What was the guy's name before him? Kent or Kenny or something?"

Surprised that he recalled her previous boyfriend's name, Kami nodded. "Kent, but I really didn't mean him, specifically, either. Just was making a comment about men in general."

"I'm not like other guys."

"Sure you aren't," she said, although secretly she agreed. Gabe was unlike anyone she'd ever known. Although he never stuck around, just as her mother's numerous boyfriends hadn't, Gabe never made promises that he would. Plus, he was genuinely a likable person. She didn't recall liking any of the men her mother had brought in and out of their lives. "You delivered breakfast." She gave as mean a look as she could muster. "If you brought whipped cream and cherries, I'll know for sure you're up to no good."

Eyes sparkling with mischief, he popped the top off a plastic container. Sure enough, inside was a big dollop of thick whipped cream with six or seven long-stemmed cherries to the side.

Kami's breath sticking in her tight chest, she lifted her gaze to Gabe's. "Oh, my."

He laughed. "Am I in trouble?"

"I'm beginning to think you're always trouble," she mused, tempted to reach for a cherry. They really were her favorite, but no way would she stick one in her mouth while Gabe watched. Besides, as difficult as it was simply to breathe at the moment, she'd likely choke if she did.

"There goes my knight-in-shining-armor image."

"I've never thought you were a knight in shining armor," she scoffed.

"There is that." He placed the now empty and folded bags on the floor. "Which is one of the reasons I like you."

Ignoring his comment, she eyed the multiple containers as he popped off lids. "Which of those did you get for me?"

"The ones I knew you'd like."

She started to ask how he'd begin to know what she liked for breakfast, but asked instead, "What if I told you I didn't like pancakes?"

"I'd know you were lying." He scooted a plastic container toward her. "These are yours."

She eyed the contents. "Are those pecans?"

He nodded.

Rather than digging into the delicious-looking pancakes, she wrinkled her nose. "What if I told you I had a nut allergy?"

As if he knew she was purposely being ornery, his eyes twinkled. "I'd know you were lying," he repeated.

"Lots of people have nut allergies," she needlessly pointed out.

"But you don't." His smile said it all.

"How can you be so sure?"

He laughed, shaking his head at her obtuseness. "How

long have I worked with you, Kam? Nuts are your favorite snack. Pecans, almonds, walnuts, cashews. I've seen you eat them all and don't recall a single hive ever."

He had her there.

"But if you suddenly develop an itch, I promise to scratch it."

Um, no. Gabe would not be scratching her itch.

"I don't have a nut allergy," she conceded, wondering that he'd paid attention to what she ate for snacks. Who knew?

"Or an aversion to pancakes," he added in case she went back to that.

She sighed. "Do you really have to hear me say it?"

He nodded.

She glanced upward, as if asking for help in dealing with the likes of him. "Fine. I love pancakes. They're amazing. My favorite carbs. Especially hot pancakes, which these aren't going to be if you don't quit talking and let me eat."

He laughed and popped the lid on another container, revealing bacon and sausage links, and held the tray toward her. "Help yourself."

She shook her head, then reached for a tiny bottle of syrup, unscrewed the top, and poured a generous amount over the plastic tray of pecan pancakes. Taking a bite, she couldn't contain the pleasure her throat emitted at the fluffy cakes coated with sticky sweet syrup.

"Mmm...you're forgiven for being a pain. That's good."

"Apparently."

Kami opened the eyes she hadn't even been aware she'd closed, met his gaze, and smiled. "Don't go being all smug just because this is amazing."

"Would I do that?"

"In a heartbeat."

He laughed and, rather than sit on the sofa next to her, he sat on the floor.

"You could have sat up here. I wouldn't have bitten you."

"Which is why I chose the floor."

"Seriously, Gabe, you need to quit that." She took another bite, enjoyed every morsel as she chewed, then added, "Someday it's going to get you into trouble."

"Possibly," he agreed, munching on a piece of bacon. "But life sure is fun in the meantime."

Still working on her pancakes, Kami eyed him. "It must be good to be you."

In between bites of the omelet he'd ordered for himself, Gabe stared from across the coffee table. "Why's that?"

She waved her empty fork in the air. "Women just let you do whatever you want and you get away with it."

His brow arched. "You're referring to me bringing you breakfast and you letting me?"

When he put it like that...

"Don't make yourself sound normal and me sound like the psycho."

"You said it, not me."

She laughed.

"Okay, so this was nice." It only hurt a little to admit that. "But I didn't really expect you to show with breakfast. I'd actually forgotten you'd threatened to do so."

"Good to know I'm so easy to forget."

She doubted any woman in the history of the world had forgotten him. Take Debbie, for instance. Had Gabe showered her with such attention—more, since they'd actually been dating—no wonder the woman was so desperate to get him back. Giving up a man like Gabe couldn't be easy even when one knew it was inevitable.

"Had you shown up fifteen minutes later, you'd have been stuck eating this all by yourself. I was about to go to bed."

He nodded toward her clothes. "Like your pajamas."

She glanced down at her T-shirt and loose shorts. It could have been much worse. "You should catch me on a good morning."

"That an offer?"

Good grief. If Mindy ever heard him making such over-the-top comments, Kami would never convince her Gabe was just teasing.

She shook her head. "No, Gabe, that's not an offer. Quit saying such things."

Kami was right. Gabe did need to quit saying such things.

But teasing her, getting a rise out of her, sure did tempt him.

"Afraid you'll get weak and say yes?"

She arched a brow. "Are you saying a woman saying yes to you is a sign of weakness?"

Gabe chuckled. "Never."

"For the record, you're leaving that whipped cream and cherries for me to eat later, at my leisure, without you."

"If I say yes does that make me weak?"

She laughed. "I'd say it makes you a smart man for not coming between a woman and her dessert."

"Point taken."

They ate in silence for the next few minutes. Then Kami stood and stretched, drawing Gabe's gaze to the expanse of skin on display, making him realize that he'd never seen her legs before.

Not unless they were covered by scrubs. But that couldn't be right because he would have seen her at the Christmas party and she wouldn't have had on her nursing uniform then.

He racked his brain.

"A black pantsuit."

Her brows veed. "Huh?"

"It's what you were wearing at the Christmas party."

She stared blankly. "What does that have to do with anything?"

"I was looking at your legs, and—"

"Hold up. Why were you looking at my legs?"

"I was thinking that I had never seen you out of scrubs," he continued, ignoring her question. "But that isn't right because you weren't wearing scrubs at last year's Christmas party."

"Which doesn't explain why you were looking at my legs," she reminded him.

"You have great legs, Kam. You should show them off more."

"Oh, yeah. I'll just roll up in the emergency room wearing a miniskirt."

He waggled his brows. "I wouldn't complain."

"I'm sure you wouldn't." She snapped her fingers and waved them in front of her face. "Eyes up here, Gabe. Not on my legs."

"You're such a party pooper, Kam."

She laughed. "You're crazy and did you really just call me a party pooper?"

"If the shoe fits."

Shaking her head, Kami gathered her leftover pancakes and the trash, using the empty bags to store them. "You're lucky I'm not wearing shoes or I might be throwing them at you."

His gaze immediately fell to her bare feet. "Are those emojis on your toenails?"

Kami's gaze dropped to her toes and the most secretive smile he'd ever seen lit her face. "Smiley faces, Gabe. Those are smiley faces."

"Now you've gone and done it. I'm never going to be able to look at you the same."

Her gaze lifted. "Because I have painted toenails?"

"Legs that go on forever and smiley faces on your toes. A man could do worse."

"Just you forget you ever saw my legs or my smiley faces."

He stood and helped gather the remaining food and drinks. "Not going to happen."

"They're burned onto your retinas for life? Like tragic scars?"

He followed her into her kitchen, took in the brightly colored walls and multicolored dishes on the counters. What was it called? Festive ware? That didn't sound quite right. Fiesta ware. That was it.

The room fit the barefoot woman opening a cabinet and tossing trash into a hidden bin.

"There's enough left for me to have breakfast tomorrow," she mused when she put the leftovers in the fridge.

"Or I could just bring you breakfast again in the morning."

She spun toward him and pointed her finger. "No."

"Now that I've seen those toes, I'm not going to be able to stay away, Kam," he teased, enjoying the color that rose in her cheeks. "You had to have realized that when you opened the door bare-legged and laid-back sexy."

"Yeah. Yeah. I have that problem all the time." Her gaze hit the ceiling, then came back to his. "Don't fool yourself, Gabe. I opened the door because you had food. No other reason."

He laughed. "I won't ever have ego problems with you around to keep me grounded."

"You don't need me to fluff your ego," she said. "You have a whole slew of women for that without me joining the fan club."

Something about the way she said it struck Gabe. Not that he had a fan club or that many women fluffing his ego. He'd always been blessed with an abundance of dates, but he had never seen himself as she was making him out to be.

"But you are a fan, aren't you, Kam?" he asked, curious as to her answer.

"Your fan?" she asked, turning from the refrigerator and leaning against it to stare at him. Her eyes flashed with something he couldn't quite read. "Yeah, Gabe. I'm a total groupie. You know it."

Her tone and expression were flippant, but something sparked in those green depths that he couldn't quite read, as if maybe there was a spark of attraction there, too.

"But, seriously, breakfast was nice. You'll understand if I throw you out because I'm ready for bed." When he started to say something, she jabbed her finger in his direction. "Don't even go there. Not if you value your life."

Yeah, his former thoughts had been nothing short of ridiculous. Gabe laughed. "So what you're saying is breakfast in bed with you doesn't start or end in your bed?"

She bared her teeth in an exaggerated smile. "Exactly."

"Anyone ever told you that you're a party pooper?"

"A time or two," she admitted with a small laugh. "Now, time for you to go so I can get some beauty sleep."

"You don't need it."

Her brow arched. "Pardon?"

"Beauty sleep. You don't need it."

She didn't. There was something inherently attractive about her air-dried hair pulled back in a braid with a few escaped strands framing her face, her brightly scrubbed skin with its faint spattering of freckles across her nose, her loose T-shirt and shorts, and those long legs and happy toenails.

"Right," she scoffed at his beauty claim, shaking her head. "What was in that milk you drank, anyway?"

"Calcium and vitamin D."

"Hallucinogenics, too, perhaps?"

Perhaps, because, looking at Kami, he was definitely seeing things he hadn't in the past.

She really was beautiful. Funny, he'd never thought about that before. Sure, if asked, he'd have said she was an attractive woman, but he'd never really looked at her before. Not in that way.

Not as he was looking at her. Not with the idea that he'd like to run his hands over those legs and...

"It's the toenails. They've cast a spell on me."

Kami wiggled her toes. "Lay off the toenails, dude. They make me happy."

"Since you didn't seem to think the bare legs thing would jibe, I could put in a motion to allow open-toed shoes."

Kami shook her head. "Yep, that'll go over so much better than the bare legs. Nothing like exposed toes, sharp instruments, and bleeding patients."

"You have a point," he conceded. "Maybe we just need to spend more time together away from the hospital."

Her smile slipped and she stared at her feet. "You really shouldn't say things like that."

She kept reminding him of that.

At first, he'd agreed. But the more he teased her, the

more he wondered why he had to stop when their conversations usually made her smile and come right back at him. When she made him smile.

"Why shouldn't I say things like that?"

Seeming taken aback at his question, she pushed off from where she leaned against the countertop. "Because we both know you don't mean them."

She rubbed one foot across the other in what was likely a nervous gesture. The motion drew Gabe's attention, had him wanting to touch her there, kiss her there and work his way up.

"That's where you're wrong," he admitted to her and to himself. "I've had a great time. So much so, I want to do this again. Same time tomorrow morning?"

Her eyes widened. "No. Not tomorrow morning or the morning after that, either."

"Why not?"

She looked flustered, as if she wasn't sure what to say. "Because you being here is insane."

"What's insane about us having breakfast together?"

"We're not that good friends."

Did she not think so?

"We will be."

CHAPTER FOUR

GABE DIDN'T SHOW at Kami's house the following morning, but he did text a photo that made her burst out laughing and eased the tension she'd fought all night.

She texted him back.

That does it. You're officially a creeper.

Some things a woman just has to see to believe.

Some things a woman should never see.

Hey, you were the one who dated the guy.

Not for his gym skills.

Which leads me to wonder what skills you were dating him for. Do tell, Kam.

Never.

A girl who kisses and doesn't tell, eh?

You'll never know.

Keep flashing those smiley-face toenails my way and I'll prove you wrong.

Kami gripped her phone a little tighter as she reread his message. There went the butterflies in her belly again, so she reminded herself Gabe was just being Gabe and she shouldn't read anything into his comments.

She texted again.

Ha. Ha. I see you had your morning dose of calcium, vitamin D, and hallucinogenics.

A full glass. Want to meet me for breakfast?

Nope. I already ate.

Her heart wasn't racing because part of her wanted to say yes. Really, it wasn't.

A pity. What did you have?

Whipped cream and cherries.

Now, why had she gone and admitted that? She was as bad as him.

Forget the toenails. I want to see your knotted stems. Show me.

She shouldn't do it, but she was going to anyway.

Feeling completely giggly, she held out her phone toward the seven perfectly knotted cherry stems she'd left on a napkin because she'd not been able to bring herself to toss them. Silly. What was she planning? To save them as a keepsake?

A keepsake of what? Gabe bringing her breakfast? They were only friends. Had only ever been friends.

Would only ever be friends.

Yet, here she was sending a picture of her knotted cherry stems and grinning like a complete idiot.

Someday you're going to show me how you do that in person.

Keep dreaming.

I am. Of smiley toenails and talented tongues.

Pervert.

Leaning back against her kitchen countertop, she typed on.

Obviously you aren't working out nearly hard enough if you're able to keep up your end of this conversation.

Keeping things up has never been a problem for me. Nor working hard. I'm talented that way. Want me to show you?

Kami took a deep breath. She and Gabe had always gone back and forth at work, had occasionally texted each other funny little snippets, but this...this they'd never done.

This had blatant sexual overtones. It was a kind of sexual energy bouncing back and forth between them.

She didn't understand it, and the more she reminded

him he shouldn't say such things, the more determined he seemed to say them.

Then again, how could she fuss at him when she'd been the one to bring up the whipped cream and cherries?

Gabe was a gorgeous man, a successful doctor. He had beautiful, successful women chasing him. His last girlfriend was a local television celebrity, for goodness' sake. What was he doing carrying on this conversation with Kami as if their relationship were blossoming into something beyond friendship?

He was just playing with her. Nothing more.

Why, she didn't know, nor did it matter. What mattered was her keeping things in perspective. Otherwise, she might get caught up in their play and end up hurt. Hadn't she learned anything from her mother's many mistakes? From the constant whirlwind of men who'd come in and out of her mother's life?

Gabe didn't run into Kami's ex at the gym the following morning.

Usually he put in an hour or so on his days off work, but today he had an excess of energy he needed to burn and he was hitting it hard.

Probably hard enough that he'd be sore, but he didn't slow his pace on the rowing machine.

Not even when his phone buzzed, indicating he had a text message. Hoping he'd be pleasantly surprised, he glanced down at his smartwatch, saw the name, and kept right on rowing.

The number hadn't been a pleasant surprise.

Although he didn't want to deal with Debbie's incessant efforts to get back together—efforts that had intensified since he'd contacted her about the fund-raiser—she wasn't the source of his restlessness.

Kami was.

He liked her, had liked her from the moment they met when he'd joined the emergency department in Knoxville the year before. She was dependable, fun, had a quick wit, and a sharp mouth that didn't mind putting him in his place.

And often.

He'd always found working with her refreshing, had always found himself seeking her company at the hospital and at the occasional work get-togethers they'd both been at.

Obviously, none of these had involved cherries as he wouldn't have forgotten had she tied a knot in a cherry stem.

An image of a knotted stem between her full rosy lips had a fresh trickle of sweat running down his forehead.

Now, where had that come from?

He didn't think of her that way. Not that Kami wasn't an attractive woman. With her sandy hair, heart-shaped face, big green eyes, and full lips, she was. Gabe had just always preferred tall, curvy brunettes or willowy blondes to petite women with smart mouths.

Since he'd seen that picture of those seven cherry stems with their perfect knots, his thoughts of Kami had changed.

Or maybe it had been the legs that went on and on.

Or the bare feet with their happy toenails.

Or the way her eyes danced when she countered him tit for tat and never let him have the last word.

Or the little happy bop she sometimes did when she put him in his place.

Or the...

Slowing his pace, Gabe wiped the sweat off his brow

with the back of his hand and forced himself to begin cooling down.

He'd had enough for the morning. Time to go shower, eat, and not think about cherry stems, long legs, happy toes, or little dances anymore.

He liked their relationship, the camaraderie they shared at work. Why would he risk messing up a great working relationship? A great friendship? There were dozens of women to date, to fantasize about.

He wasn't willing to risk losing a friendship he valued.

Kami was off-limits as anything more than his friend, so maybe she was right to tell him he shouldn't say certain things and he needed to start heeding her advice.

Now, if he could only convince his body to go along.

"You didn't answer my text yesterday," Gabe accused the first moment he and Kami were alone during their next emergency-room shift together. He'd just finished suturing a fifteen-year-old kid who'd cut his hand on a broken glass and he'd followed her to the supply closet.

"I was busy." Rather than look at him, she kept gathering the supplies she'd come for.

Gabe frowned. "Too busy to answer my text?"

She glanced his way, arched her brow. "Did I answer your text?"

"No."

She gave a pointed look. "Then I was too busy to answer."

Right. Gabe studied her, taking note of the tension pouring off her. The unusual tension. Kami rolled with the punches. Nothing ever got to her too much. She was usually all smiles and sass. He knew he'd made the decision to back off from their flirting to preserve their friendship, but someone had put a bee in her bonnet.

Or had their flirting been the culprit and he'd not checked things soon enough? Regardless, he'd contacted her about business, not pleasure.

"Then you don't care that Debbie's producer wants to meet with us about the fund-raiser?"

Kami's dour expression took on new life, sparking her into her usual excitement. "That's awesome."

Glad to see the light back in her eyes, he wasn't quite ready to ignore her former cold shoulder. "But since you didn't answer my text, I wasn't sure when to tell her we could meet them."

Her eyes narrowed suspiciously. "We? Them?"

"Me, you, Debbie, her producer."

Her brows veed. "Why are you and Debbie going to be there? Couldn't I just meet with the producer?"

As if she didn't know. "You tell me, friend-who-refuses-to-bid-on-my-charity-date."

Okay, so he probably needed to quit with the poking comments, but he was irked that she'd ignored his message the day before and him for most of their shift thus far.

Kami's nose scrunched. "Oh."

"Yeah, oh," he agreed, then returned her sharp look. "Have I mentioned that you owe me?"

A tolerant smile twitched at her lips. "A few times."

"I'll expect you not to forget."

"I never forget when I owe someone something. You're doing this because you're a good man and want to help our coworker raise funds to help cover her baby's heart-transplant expenses. This has nothing to do with me, so I owe you nothing."

Her comment had put him in his place and he couldn't argue with her, not even teasingly.

"Way to make a guy feel bad." He hung his head in mock shame, then looked up and winked.

She smiled, this time for real, and the tension within Gabe eased.

"I was complimenting you," she pointed out. "Can I help it if you had a guilty conscience?"

Eyes locked with hers, he took a step toward her, stared down into her wide green eyes. "First compliment that ever left me feeling reprimanded."

"That's because you don't get reprimanded nearly often enough," she countered, her gaze dropping from his scrutiny and landing on his mouth.

She sucked in a tiny sharp breath, then glanced away to stare at something behind him. He wanted to touch her face, to brush his fingers over the stray hairs along her face that had escaped her clip, to place his thumb beneath her chin and lift her mouth.

To his.

Gabe swallowed. "You volunteering for the job? Because I'm willing."

Her gaze cut back to his. "Gabe, I can't do this."

"This?" he asked, knowing the gap between them had somehow shortened because he was so close she had to feel his breath against her face. He could feel hers; he wanted to feel more.

"You. Me. This."

She closed her eyes, but rather than take advantage of the moment, he waited.

"We can't do this. We'd regret it forever."

"What would we regret forever?" He knew what she meant, but asked anyway. He needed to hear her say it out loud. Maybe then it would drive the message home because what she'd closed her eyes to hide hadn't been regretting what they might do, but what they wouldn't.

"Oops." Mindy opened the tiny supply room's door and spotted them. "Sorry. I didn't realize you were in here. Together. Alone."

Kami's eyes had popped open, had filled with guilt and so much more he couldn't label. Gabe wanted to pull her close, tell her it was okay, that he was positive Mindy would celebrate if she'd actually seen anything physical happening.

Gabe had wanted something physical to happen. Had wanted to kiss her. Maybe he shouldn't have hesitated. Maybe he should have covered her mouth with his and settled his curiosity of what Kami's mouth would feel like.

But probably not.

Her hackles were back up and she refused to look at him.

"Very alone," Mindy continued, looking quite pleased at what she'd interrupted. "I can come back later."

"No. Don't do that. I'm finished here." Kami stepped back, bumping against a shelf, then blushing at having done so. "I have what I need."

"I'm sure you do," Mindy teased, looking back and forth between them with a smile.

Kami winced. "As for Dr. Nelson, he was telling me good news about promoting the fund-raiser. Great news about the fund-raiser," she corrected, sounding breathy. "You should ask him about it, since you're the event's cochair and are going to have to take my place on this one because I'm done."

With that, Kami rushed from the room.

"What did you do this time? And why do I have to keep asking you that?"

"Good question."

Mindy's hand went to her hip. "What's she done with?"

Gabe shrugged. He wasn't sure of the answer to that, either, but suspected she'd meant him and whatever was happening between them.

Mindy let out a long sigh and shook her head. "You convinced her to bid on you yet?"

He glanced toward his coworker. "You think I have a chance of changing her mind?"

Mindy shrugged. "I'd say you have a chance at anything you set your mind to, including my best friend buying that date package."

"I guess we'll see."

She sure didn't seem to have any problems pushing him away.

Or not answering his text.

Plus, the last thing he'd call the way his body had responded to her closeness, to her staring at his mouth, to the sparks that had been flying between them, was safe.

Unless playing with fire was safe, because he felt that hot under the collar.

"I'm sorry."

Not wanting to acknowledge Gabe, but knowing she should, Kami nodded and took another bite of the sandwich she'd packed for her after-midnight "lunch." They'd finally gotten a slow moment and she'd clocked out for her break.

Gabe had been tied up with discharging an asthma-attack patient who had settled down perfectly with a steroid injection and breathing treatment.

He sat down at the break table. "I don't want to lose your friendship, Kami."

"I feel the same," she admitted, wondering if it was already too late. She'd felt something in that room. Something that had been hinted at and building for days, maybe longer, but that she'd been able to tamp down.

Now she wasn't sure she was going to be able to safely tuck it back away. *It* being the chemistry she'd felt with Gabe as he'd zeroed in on her mouth.

She'd wanted him to kiss her.

To run his fingers through her hair and hold her to him and devour her mouth; to press his body to hers and… Ugh. Her brain had to quit going there.

"Good," he agreed. "As much as I love to tease you, I don't want to do anything that undermines our friendship."

Not sure what to say, she nodded again.

He sat next to her, quiet for a few moments. "Something's changed between us, hasn't it?"

She turned to him. "Do you really need to ask me that?"

He eyed her for long seconds before asking, "Are we going to be okay?"

Did he mean individually or together? Because for all her mind slips since their supply-room episode, she really couldn't see there ever being a "together" between them.

"We're going to be okay." They would be. He'd forget whatever this little blip of attraction was and move on to the next hottie who caught his eye. She'd go on being happy with her life, and if the right guy, a safe guy who wouldn't use her or leave her, came along, then she'd get involved again.

Baxter had been safe.

Now, where had that thought come from? Baxter didn't count. There had been no magic when Baxter had kissed her, touched her.

Gabe hadn't touched her or kissed her and yet the supply-room incident felt surreal.

"Well, as long as we're going to be okay. I really don't

want to lose you, Kam." With that, he reached over and patted her hand much as an adult might pat a child's hand, then pushed back his chair and left her to stare after him.

Nothing awkward about that conversation, she thought as he left the small break room. Nothing at all.

Maybe she needed to stay away from Gabe for a while. At least until she got her head wrapped around what had happened.

Almost happened.

Because nothing had happened.

She closed her eyes, recalling the moment. Nothing physical might have happened, but something had happened.

Something intense and she didn't like it.

Gabe was messing with her immune system.

Maybe she needed to avoid him and pray her mother hurried home so she'd get another inoculation of all the reasons why messing with a man like Gabe was nothing but heartache waiting to happen.

CHAPTER FIVE

KAMI SUCCESSFULLY AVOIDED Gabe for the rest of that shift and most of the next night's. Unfortunately, she couldn't completely avoid him as there were times patient care demanded their interaction.

She was polite. He was polite. Everything was awkward.

A heart-attack patient came in by ambulance and coded minutes after arrival.

Under any circumstances Kami hated working codes.

Not that the medical demands were more than other emergency situations she encountered, but because a code meant someone's life was on the line, and if the code team failed, that person was gone forever.

And everyone who knew and loved that person would forever be changed.

The current code she was working, happening right at the end of her night shift, was no different and she silently prayed for the man and his family.

Gabe was doing compressions on the man's chest, while she delivered breaths via an air bag.

A unit secretary recorded the events and Mindy readied the crash cart for Gabe's instructions to defibrillate the man in hopes of shocking his heart into beating again.

"On the count of three, all clear," Gabe instructed,

keeping the compressions going. "One. Two. Three. All clear."

Kami and Gabe both stepped back as Mindy pushed the button and the man's body jerked from the electrical impulse.

Nothing.

Putting his interlocked hands back on the man's chest, Gabe went back to compressions and Kami to delivering precious air, watching the rise and fall of his chest from each squeeze and relaxation of the bag.

When the defibrillator had reset, Mindy motioned that it was ready.

"On the count of three, again, all clear," Gabe ordered. "One. Two. Three. All clear."

The man's lifeless body jerked. A bleep appeared on the cardiac monitor then went back to nothing.

Kami expected Gabe to call the code.

But he just kept compressing the man's chest in rhythmic pushes as the rest of the team did their jobs.

Gabe had Mindy defibrillate the man again. Nothing.

Still, rather than call the code, Gabe went back to his compressions.

Wondering why he hadn't called an end, why they were still trying to revive the man when too long had passed, she studied Gabe in between keeping a close check on their patient in hopes of a miracle. What did Gabe know that made him keep this code going so much longer than was usual?

"Want to swap places?" she offered.

He had to be exhausted. CPR took great effort.

Not glancing up from the man's face, Gabe shook his head, called for the defibrillator yet again.

Kami's gaze met Mindy's; she saw the same questions in her eyes that she was sure were in her own. She shrugged and stepped back when Gabe called all clear.

Nothing.

None of the crew hesitated to jump back into their spots, but they all knew the code had failed and were also all wondering why it was continuing. Still, Gabe was in charge and it was his place to decide when to stop.

"Time?" he asked, his voice sounding slightly off to Kami, but maybe she'd imagined it.

The recorder told them how long they'd been doing CPR.

Gabe winced, gave one last chest compression with arms that seemed to buckle, then called the code and hung his head.

Kami had worked codes with Gabe in the past, but wasn't sure she'd ever paid attention to him immediately after a code came to an end, when the adrenaline rush subsided and that deep sense of failure set in.

At least, that was how she always felt when a code hadn't worked. Unfortunately, statistically, few codes were successful, but the few that were made going through the many failures worthwhile.

Was that how Gabe viewed codes, too? As emotionally, physically, and mentally exhausting, but worth it if you revived a single person?

She studied the fatigue etched on his handsome face, the way his head bowed forward ever so slightly, the way he slumped making him seem several inches shorter than his six-foot frame actually was.

He looked defeated.

Vulnerable.

Very unlike the man who was usually teasing her.

He looked unlike any Gabe she could recall ever having seen before.

Emotion pinched her insides, making her want to do something to put his usual smile back on his face, to put that mischievous twinkle back into his eyes. Which didn't go along at all with her goal to avoid him for a while. Still, a man had just died and Gabe looked wiped out.

Despite all her crazy emotions, he was her friend. She cared about him as a person. She couldn't just walk away.

"You okay?"

Briefly glancing her way, he didn't make eye contact, just nodded. "Fine."

He didn't look fine. His eyes were watery, red, and her insides twisted up even more.

She wasn't sure what she should do, but knew doing nothing wasn't an option. Not for her. Not when Gabe looked so devastated.

What she wanted to do was grab hold of his scrub top, drag him somewhere private and make him tell her what had upset him so about the code.

Other than the obvious, of course.

What right did she have to do that? None. They were friends, but she couldn't demand he tell her what had upset him. Not really.

Full of tension, she moved about the emergency bay, doing her job, while Gabe disappeared to go tell the family of the man's death.

That she didn't envy him.

Maybe that had been the issue. Maybe the deceased patient had been someone he knew, the family he was about to sit down with a family he was familiar with. If so, that couldn't be easy.

The rest of the night was busy and she never got a chance to corner Gabe.

Giving report to the arriving day-shift nurse, Kami

was glad to see the shift end. She clocked out, but before leaving searched out Gabe.

She'd seen him a few times after the code, but he'd been busy with patients. No smiles, no jokes, no silly puns, no waggles of his brows, no…

Kami shook her head to clear her thoughts. Suffice it to say, Gabe hadn't been himself.

It didn't take long to find him.

He sat in the small dictation room off the emergency room that served as an office for the emergency-room physicians on staff.

First making sure he wasn't in the midst of recording a chart note, Kami poked her head in. "Rough night, eh?"

Turning toward her, he nodded.

Something didn't feel right. Not about how he looked. Not about how her gut wrenched. Not about anything that had happened since that stupid code. Why did she want to wrap her arms around him and hold him until whatever was bothering him subsided?

Because he'd messed with her brain in that closet.

Before then, too.

"I'll show you my toes if you'll smile."

As she'd hoped, Gabe smiled. It wasn't much of a smile, but he did smile and the gesture did funny things to her insides.

"Okay, but remember you smiled for it," she warned, bending and untying her shoe.

His eyes gaining a little spark of light, Gabe laughed. "Keep your shoes on, Kam."

She put her hands on her hips and pretended to be miffed. "So much for you implementing an open-toed shoes policy."

"Not one of my better ideas."

"Perhaps not, but I was willing to do my part." When

he went quiet again, she couldn't stand it. "Want to go eat pancakes with me?"

Surprise lit his eyes. "You're kidding?"

Yes. She was. She did not invite men to breakfast. Especially men like Gabe, who went through women as if they were disposable.

Then again, she'd already eaten breakfast with Gabe once, so what would it hurt if they went to breakfast again?

As friends, of course. She had a cat to feed, but she'd go by to feed and love on Bubbles after breakfast.

"I'm hungry and I don't want to eat alone." Her stomach growled to confirm her comment.

At first she thought he was going to refuse, but, standing, he nodded. "Let me tell Dr. Williams I'm out of here."

Out of here with her.

Because she'd asked him and he'd said yes.

Which made her uncomfortable.

But not nearly as uncomfortable as his forlorn look had left her feeling.

A teasing, flirty Gabe was one thing. A lost-looking Gabe quite another and not one she could turn her back on without doing what she could to help him.

That was what friends did, right?

They said everyone had a doppelgänger. Gabe had just performed CPR compressions on a man who could have passed for his father.

His father on whom he'd been too young to perform CPR and had watched die, helpless to do anything other than cry and wait for the paramedics to arrive and do what he should have been able to do.

Logically, he knew he'd only been eight years old. A

kid. He'd known to call for an ambulance, but hadn't been able to do one other thing but sob while he watched his father take his last breath.

Even now the moment played through his mind as if it had just happened.

He wasn't dense enough not to have realized long ago that his drive to become an emergency-room doctor had been seeded in that experience. Nor was he foolish enough to think that had he been able to perform CPR he'd have likely made a difference in his father's outcome.

But he *might* have, and because he'd been a kid with no skills, he'd never know what might have been.

Roger Dillehay, the man Gabe had done a code on that night, had been his shot. He'd failed again.

Maybe that was a sign, an assurance that he'd done all that could medically be done and it still hadn't been enough to save the man who looked so much like his father.

That had his eight-year-old self had skills, then the outcome would have been the same and he'd still have grown up without his dad there to cheer him on, would still have had to listen to his mother's tears.

"In all the time I've known you, not once have I ever accused you of being quiet."

Gabe blinked at the woman sitting across the table from him. Her big green eyes held a softness he'd seen as she cared for her patients but of which he'd yet to be the recipient.

He'd never had a reason to be the object of her empathy.

Nor did he want it now.

She'd been avoiding him and he'd let her because he'd waffled back and forth between thinking he needed to step back rather than risk their friendship versus giving in to what he was feeling and kissing her until they were both breathless.

"I'm sorry, Kam." He raked his fingers through his hair. "I should have skipped breakfast. I'm not good company."

"Which is exactly why you shouldn't have. We're friends." Had she really put emphasis on that last word? "Something is bothering you and I want to help."

Kami was a fixer. She wanted to fix her patients and now she wanted to fix him. He didn't need to be fixed. He wasn't broken, just…

"Want to talk about it?"

"You were there."

"You're right. I was. You went above and beyond with that code."

Gabe gave a low snort. "Let it go for too long, you mean?"

Her brows veed in disapproval of his comment. "As long as you had medical reason to believe there was hope of resuscitating him, then you were right not to call the code."

"I'm not sure that was the case," he admitted, unable to look into her eyes for fear of what she might see in his. "It was more a matter of the code patient reminding me of someone I once knew."

Now, why had he admitted that? He didn't need to go spilling his sob story to Kami, didn't need the sympathy that people had always given to the little boy who'd been alone with his father and had watched him die of a heart attack.

He was a grown man and didn't need sympathy or anyone knowing his past.

He hadn't talked to anyone about his father in years. He sure didn't want to start back today.

Especially not with a woman who was already getting under his skin.

"Oh," Kami said, then reached across the table and touched his hand. "I'm sorry."

Kami's touch carried the intensity of a defibrillator machine, so much so that Gabe was surprised when his body didn't jerk from the electricity in her fingertips.

His heart certainly jump-started as if it had been struck by a bolt of lightning.

He stared at where her hand covered his. "It's no big deal."

"One of the things I've always admired about you is that you are bluntly honest," she said. "Now I know why you're usually truthful."

Gabe glanced up, met Kami's gaze in question.

"It's because everyone would know," she continued. "You're a terrible liar."

He'd been called worse. One corner of Gabe's mouth lifted. "You think?"

"After that big whopper you just told? I know."

Gabe gave an ironic chuckle. "You're right."

"You could've just said you didn't want to talk about it."

"Would you have let me get away with that?"

"Probably not," she admitted with a sheepish grin. "I know things have been strained between us lately, but I don't like seeing you without a smile on your face."

Her admission warmed Gabe's insides. "Why's that?"

"Because we're friends."

He'd had enough of his wallowing in the past and focused on the woman across the table.

"You're a good person to have as a friend, Kam." As if to prove his point, he shifted his hand, laced their fingers.

Holding Kami's hand felt right and did make him feel better.

"Who did he remind you of?"

Gabe winced. "It was a long time ago."

"Sounds like the beginning of an interesting story."

"It's not."

"I'll be the judge of that."

He frowned. "You're sure pushy, lady."

She arched a brow and gave a *duh* look. "You're just figuring that out?"

He gave a low laugh, then lowered his gaze. "If it's all the same, I'd rather not talk about it anymore."

"Okay." She squeezed his hand. "But know I'm here if you need me."

"Thank you, Kami. You really are a good friend."

Her expression tightened for a brief moment. Then she seemed to shake it and teased, "Don't think buttering me up is going to change my mind about bidding on you."

Giving her hand a little squeeze, he laughed. "Maybe if I'd been on my game I'd have taken advantage of the moment."

"Too bad you missed your chance." Her gaze dropped to their bound hands.

"I'm not so sure I have," Gabe said half under his breath as their waitress set their plates in front of them. A loaded omelet for Gabe and a stack of cinnamon pecan pancakes for Kami.

"Pardon?" she asked, freeing her hand to reach for her utensils.

"Missed my chance to butter you up, I said."

Before Kami had the chance to question Gabe, he reached across the table, took her knife, and slathered her pancake with butter.

She rolled her eyes.

"Now you can say I have literally buttered you up."

"My pancakes don't count."

As his comment hit Kami, she glanced up, met his gaze, saw that the mischievous twinkle was back.

"That an offer?"

"You know it isn't."

"Why do I know that?"

"Because we're friends. Nothing more."

"Who better to slather butter on each other with than a friend?"

"Maybe that's something you do with friends, but that's not the kind of friendship I usually have."

"So you don't rescue your friends from their exes and you don't slather them in butter. What else do you not do with your friends, Kam?"

Rather than answer, she dug into her pancakes, grateful for the delicious bursts of flavor that practically melted in her mouth.

"I think I ordered the wrong thing."

Kami glanced up at Gabe.

"You make that look as if it tastes amazing," he clarified.

"It does."

"Prove it."

Kami started to tell him to be quiet and eat his omelet, but instead forked up a generous bite of her pancakes and extended the fork to him.

His eyes locked with hers, Gabe's mouth closed around her fork, then slowly pulled back. After eating the bite, he nodded. "You're right. That is good. I'm going to have to do double time at the gym if I keep having breakfasts like these." He chuckled.

The sound warmed Kami's insides. She much pre-

ferred Gabe's smiles and laughter to the solemn man he'd
been after the code. Not that it would have been appropriate for him to be all smiles after someone had died,
just that she wanted him to bounce back into his normal
self and he hadn't.

That had gotten to her in places she didn't want him
or anyone to reach.

Good thing she knew his revolving-door history with
women or she might fall for his brilliant blues, quick intelligence, and smile that encompassed his entire face
because, as much as she'd like to think herself immune
to his charms, she was quickly realizing that her heart
had taken up a mind of its own and was feeling all kinds
of awareness it had never bothered to feel with Baxter.

Or anyone, for that matter.

Just Gabe.

CHAPTER SIX

"WHAT'S UP WITH you and Gorgeous Gabe?"

Kami frowned at Mindy. "What's that supposed to mean?"

"I've caught you looking at him more than a dozen times tonight, and don't think I've forgotten walking in on you two the other night."

Yeah, it was best her friend didn't find out she and Gabe had gone to breakfast that morning.

"So what?" She made light of the incident because she wasn't admitting to Mindy that something had shifted in her relationship with Gabe. Something had shifted? Something had been shifting for a while. The supply room had been a landslide. "I was getting supplies."

"And Gabe?" Mindy pushed. "What was he getting?"

Kami's face heated. "Not what you're implying."

"Not even a little smooch?"

"Get serious. He's not my type."

Much.

Well, not her brain's type. Her body and heart seemed to have come out of a lifetime of hibernation with a vengeance.

"Smart and sexy as all get-out?"

She couldn't deny her friend's claim. "A total playboy.

We both know he never stays in a relationship more than a couple of months."

Mindy shrugged. "Maybe he just sees no reason to keep a relationship going once he realizes things aren't going to work long term. Maybe he's just being efficient in searching for the right one rather than wasting time with women he's realized aren't for him."

"Or maybe he gets bored once the chase is over and can't commit."

"I doubt Gabe had to chase any of them."

Probably not, but her friend was missing the point.

"Okay, so maybe he gets bored once the shiny newness of the relationship is over."

Mindy shrugged. "I like my theory better."

"Because you're planning to bid on him and want to think the best of him?"

"I don't have to *want* to think the best of him. I *do* think that and so do you." Mindy's expression dared Kami to deny her claim. "He's a good guy."

Kami started to reply, but halted her words when Gabe came over to the nurses' station.

"Bay one is ready for discharge home."

Kami gave Mindy a warning look not to say anything inappropriate to Gabe, then said, "I'll get her IV taken out and get her discharged. Any scripts you need me to send?"

Gabe shook his head. "I'll get them in the computer record and send them. Thanks, though."

"I'd be happy to do that for you, Dr. Nelson," Mindy offered, a big smile on her face.

Looking a little uncertain at her overly bright expression, Gabe glanced back and forth between them.

"Uh, sure. Go ahead." He told her the scripts and to which pharmacy. "Thanks."

"Anything for you, Dr. Nelson."

Gabe looked confused and Kami rushed to discharge the patient rather than stick around for whatever else was said.

The best thing that could happen would be if Mindy did make a play for Gabe. Dating one of her friends would no doubt kill this unwanted awareness of him. Mindy was welcome to Gabe.

Kami had even encouraged her to bid on him, would even donate to the cause.

Only... No, she wasn't jealous at the thought of Mindy with Gabe.

She just didn't want her friend to get hurt when Gabe moved on to his next conquest.

Unless Mindy was right and Gabe just went through women so quickly because once he knew the relationship wasn't going to work out, he ended it, and moved on to someone who might.

That didn't make him sound like a player, but someone who was smart.

Gabe was smart and efficient. He was also a player. Wasn't he?

He'd had dozens of girlfriends during the short time Kami had known him.

She'd had two boyfriends during the same time.

Two boyfriends she'd known weren't her forever guys but she'd stuck around with longer than she should have. Why was that?

Because she didn't want to be like her mother, so she stayed to prove she could hold on to a man if she wanted to? Because they'd both been safe, hadn't made her heart step outside its comfort zone?

Ugh. She so wasn't going to psychoanalyze her motives in staying with Baxter or Kent.

Nor did it matter why Gabe went through women so

quickly, because Kami wasn't interested, regardless of the reasons for his revolving-door love life.

If Mindy believed her theory, then she could bid on his date, or, better yet, save her money and just ask Gabe out.

They could have breakfast together.

As a couple and not just as friends.

That would be wonderful.

Great.

Awesome.

So why did her blood turn a little green when she glanced back and saw Mindy and Gabe laughing?

"Debbie wants to meet with us tonight."

"Tonight?" Kami asked Gabe as she finished last-minute cleanup prior to shift change. "It's Friday night."

"You have other plans?"

"I'm off work. Of course I have plans." Not that she was admitting to Gabe that her evening plans consisted of vegging out in front of the television while she caught up on her favorite reality show. "Don't you?"

"Even if I did, I'd cancel them. The charity auction is just a few weeks away. Any promotion Debbie helps with is going to have to be put into motion quickly. If we wait, it might not happen."

Guilt hit. He was right. Still...

"It's a television station. They're used to reporting on things as they happen. Promoting a charity event to raise money to help a sick baby shouldn't be outside their capabilities."

"Does that mean you want me to have Debbie reschedule the meeting with her producer?"

If the producer couldn't meet at a later time, she'd feel horrible that the event might not reach its potential. Especially since she didn't have any grand plans.

"Did you check to see if Mindy could go?" After all, she'd implied he'd have to take her co-organizer. Had he forgotten?

A stubborn expression took hold, tightening his jaw. "No. Either you go or everything's off."

Kami frowned. "Fine. I'll put off my plans so we can meet with your ex and her boss."

He studied her a moment, then seemed to have a change of heart of his own. "If your plans are that big a deal, I can see if Mindy wants to go."

Kami bit the inside of her lip and tried not to look addled. Did he want to take Mindy instead? Was he hoping she'd say she wouldn't cancel her plans so he'd have an excuse to invite Mindy? Had their laughter earlier in the week been bonding toward a more personal relationship?

No, Gabe was a man who would ask a woman out if he wanted to ask. He wouldn't play games. If he wanted to take Mindy to dinner, he'd take her to dinner.

"Someone special?"

Kami arched her brow. "Who?"

"Whoever you have plans with."

"I didn't say I had plans with someone," she countered, refusing to slide back into that untruth.

"Baxter's workout program softening you up?"

"I don't have plans with Baxter, and if I did, it's not your business."

He looked duly reprimanded. "You're right. I shouldn't tease you."

"No, you shouldn't." Not that she minded his teasing. Not really. Just, she didn't want him to know that she had no plans for the first weekend she'd had off work in close to a month other than working on the fund-raiser.

"I'll pick you up at six."

"If you'll tell me where to meet you, I can drive myself," she countered.

"I'll see you at six," he repeated and walked away before she could pry more details from him.

What did one wear to a Friday night dinner meeting with a television show hostess, her producer, and a coworker who was just a friend but that your body had become painfully aware of in beyond friendship ways?

Especially when you didn't know where the meeting was being held?

Okay, so, logically, they'd meet at a nice restaurant.

She'd had no chance to find out the location so she could drive herself. Him picking her up from her house seemed too much as if they were a couple going on a double date.

Quit being ridiculous, she ordered herself. Friends picked each other up for meetings. It was no big deal.

Still, what was she going to wear?

She could text him, but stubbornly didn't, just studied the contents of her closet. Her gaze repeatedly settled on a blue dress that was the right mix of casual and dressy. No way did she want to feel overdressed for the meeting, but she also didn't want to feel frumpy while with Gabe's beautiful ex.

Debbie was a knockout.

Kami put her hand to her forehead. What was wrong with her? What Debbie looked like did not matter. Not in the slightest. She was not competing to take Debbie's former place in Gabe's life. Far from it.

Kami needed to get her butt into bed and get a few hours of sleep after being up all night. That was what she should be worrying about.

Not about what she was going to wear or how she was going to look in comparison to Gabe's ex.

On her best day she couldn't compete with the television personality and, seriously, she didn't want to. This was a business meeting to discuss advertising a charity event for a coworker's daughter. Nothing more. Nothing social. Nothing. Nothing. Nothing.

That evening, Kami was still telling herself that when Gabe drove them to an upscale restaurant and her nerves were getting the best of her.

She wasn't a nervous person. This was ridiculous.

Glancing his way didn't reassure her.

He was too good-looking for his own good in his dark trousers and blue button-down dress shirt with the sleeves rolled up to reveal a generous glimpse of his forearms.

His manly forearms. Strong and skilled. The urge to reach out and run her fingers over them hit her.

Yeah, that urge didn't help her nerves, either.

Obviously, tossing and turning in her bed half the day hadn't done a thing to rest her brain because she was delusional. Sleep deprivation had to be the cause of this insanity.

"You look great, by the way."

Gabe's compliment didn't lessen her unease but she murmured a thank you.

"I like your dress."

"Because my legs are showing?" Now, why had she asked that? Just because he'd made a big deal of her bare legs the morning he'd brought breakfast didn't mean she had to point out her exposed limbs.

Putting the car into Park, he glanced toward her, then lower, letting his gaze skim slowly down her body, going lower to inspect her legs. Then, lifting his gaze to hers, he shook his head. "Nope, that's not why I like your dress."

With that, he turned off the motor and got out of his car.

Still trying to figure out his comment, Kami was even more stunned when her car door opened and Gabe extended his hand.

"You didn't have to open my door."

"My mom taught me good manners."

"Good to know, but this isn't a date, so you don't have to do things like that."

His brow rose. "Treating a lady right doesn't just extend to the woman you're dating. Ask my mom."

Good thing one of their mothers had taught good behavior. Kami's sure hadn't. Nor had she come home yet. Poor Bubbles. Kami put her hand in his and got out of the car. She immediately pulled her hand away and straightened her dress.

After Gabe closed the passenger door, his hand settled low on her back and he guided her toward the restaurant entrance. Kami wanted to pull free, to push away his hand, but would doing so be making a big deal out of nothing?

His palm burning into her flesh through her dress material didn't feel like something that was nothing.

It felt so not nothing it was a little scary after all her nothing relationships.

"I still think we could have done this with a phone conversation," she mumbled, feeling more and more self-conscious as they made their way into the upscale restaurant.

"No doubt, and you're preaching to the choir." He pierced her with his blue gaze. "I'm not the one who insisted on a dinner meeting."

"Right." Guilt hit her. He probably didn't want to be here any more than she did. "Debbie seized the excuse to spend time with you."

He feigned surprise. "You think that's what this is?"

"I only know her through things you've said. What do you think this is?"

He sighed quite dramatically. "Foreplay for my charity auction date."

Despite her nerves, Kami laughed. "You're crazy."

"Apparently or I wouldn't be here."

She paused. "Thank you, Gabe. I'm not sure I've thanked you for setting this up, but I do appreciate it. I know Beverly appreciates everything being done to help ease the burden of Lindsey's expenses, too."

A genuine smile slashed across his face. "You're welcome, Kam, and so is she."

"Worth the sacrifice you're about to make?"

He grimaced. "Ask me again after dinner."

CHAPTER SEVEN

IF GABE WASN'T enjoying himself, he was putting on a good show.

However, his attention wasn't focused toward the model-perfect woman who left Kami in awe of her beauty, grace, and poise.

Gabe's focus was on Kami.

Overly so.

As in, if she didn't know better, she'd think she and Gabe were a couple. She knew better and her head was still spinning.

Was that what he was trying to make Debbie think?

His little smiles, winks, and frequent touches of her hand and arm were getting to her.

To the woman sitting across from them, too.

She'd gone from super friendly to regarding Kami with suspicion.

Not that she wasn't nice.

Kami believed the woman was inherently pleasant and that was part of her television viewer appeal. She had a wholesome goodness that shone as brightly as her beauty. Plus, intelligence glimmered in her big brown eyes.

The woman wasn't buying that Gabe would be interested in Kami. What sane man would be when Debbie wanted him?

Tall, willowy, blonde, smart, successful.

"Gabe says you work with him at the hospital?"

"I'm a nurse." Kami took a sip of her water. She'd ordered a glass of wine but had yet to take a sip. She needed all her wits for this meal and didn't want to risk lowering her inhibitions even the slightest bit.

Especially not when Gabe gave her a fond look and said, "My favorite nurse."

"Every female nurse is your favorite nurse," Kami countered, knocking her knee against his leg in hopes he'd take the hint and stop with the cheesy comments.

"You know there's no one like you," he came right back, his leg brushing against hers. Only, rather than a cut-it-out knock, the grazing of his leg against hers was more an awakening of her senses as the material of his pants teased her thigh.

"You mean someone who doesn't fall at your feet?"

"Something like that." Gabe's expression said Kami had fallen at his feet a time or two despite her denials.

She decided to ignore him and finish this meeting as quickly as possible before she made a complete fool of herself over Gabe's attention.

"We appreciate your offer to help with the Smiths' fund-raiser." There, see, that sounded competent. "As your show is about home improvements, I don't know a possible angle for us to promote the fund-raiser for Lindsey's medical expenses. What were you thinking?"

Eyeing Kami and Gabe closely, the woman slid into professional mode.

"That's where Jerry comes in." She turned to her producer and smiled.

The slightly overweight man's entire persona brightened.

In that moment, Kami realized the producer was totally besotted with the woman. As in, head over heels. He'd probably jumped at the offer when Debbie had requested he meet with them just so he'd have an excuse to spend time with her outside work.

"He's going to arrange a segment on our late-night news that will run over a few days. Then—" Debbie's smile conveyed real enthusiasm "—we're going to do a home improvement for your coworker."

"The baby needs a new heart, not updated curtains and carpet," Gabe pointed out.

Debbie tsked. "There's going to be medical equipment and such, so it'll be a renovation to make their transition from hospital to home easier."

"I don't know if Beverly and her husband want their home renovated, but it's a generous offer. Certainly, I'll discuss it with them," Kami assured them, thinking the new family might need a lot of things. She didn't know. "I'll admit I worry the added stress of a home remodel during all the craziness of Lindsey's medical issues isn't a good idea."

"Obviously you've not watched my show," Debbie scolded with a pout of her full pink lips. "There will be no lengthy remodel. We'll time the remodel for while the baby is having her heart transplant. Everything will be done and waiting on them when they bring Lindsey home from the hospital." She glanced at Jerry, excitement practically seeping from her barely existent pores. "It'll be an amazing show."

"It sounds wonderful," Kami admitted. "But they don't have the money for a remodel."

Debbie smiled again. "There's no cost to them. This is our pleasure. We'll just want to film their story, of course, and especially when they return to the home the first time after the remodel, and maybe a quick shot or two of them in their new, improved home."

"I don't even know if they own their home," Kami confessed. "They may rent... We should have had them here with us."

"I'm sure Gabe can arrange a meeting."

Of course he could.

But he immediately passed. "Kami is organizing the fund-raiser, not me."

"Gabe, darling, the remodel has nothing to do with the fund-raiser," Debbie corrected. "We'll do a news piece for that, something we'll refer back to in the episode for their home improvement."

"It's a great idea for a show and ratings." Kami could have bitten her tongue when the words came out of her mouth.

However, Debbie didn't look offended. Instead, she and her producer nodded. "It's a win-win all the way around. Your coworker gets a renovated, state-of-the-art home free of charge. We get a phenomenal episode. Right, Jerry?"

The man beamed at his hostess. "It's rather brilliant."

"I'll give your information to Beverly," Kami assured them. "Anything beyond that will be up to them. Our purpose is to generate awareness of the fund-raiser so we can raise as much as possible. Everything will need to be between you and Beverly and her husband directly."

"Sounds perfect. Now—" Debbie flashed a smile that truly was Hollywood-worthy "—let's set aside shoptalk and enjoy our meal."

Kami looked at Gabe, gave him a look that hopefully conveyed for him to get her out of there as quickly as possible, then said, "Let's."

The meal was delicious. The conversation not too horrible as Debbie came across as a genuine, albeit ambitious, person. Jerry was probably a killer businessman, but this softened whenever he looked at Debbie—which was all the time.

Something she seemed oblivious to as she zeroed in on Gabe.

Who in return zeroed in on Kami in a move to deflect Debbie's attention.

Kami was exhausted from it all.

"Are you two seeing each other?" Jerry asked after their entrées arrived.

"Yes," Gabe answered at the same time as Kami said, "No."

"I see," Debbie said.

Kami was glad the woman saw, because Kami didn't.

Ignoring the couple, Gabe asked, "What was breakfast this week?"

Kami glared at Gabe. What was he doing?

Actually, she knew what he was doing and that was what irritated her.

"A meal because I was hungry."

His gaze searched hers. "Both times?"

Kami's glare intensified. He was purposely trying to make them think breakfast had involved a lot more than food.

Gabe wanted Debbie to think they were a couple so it would deter her from bidding on him during the auction.

He didn't mind using Kami in the process.

"Sorry, Gabe. I shouldn't have used my status as your favorite nurse to get a free breakfast," she said in an overly sweet tone, all the while shooting mental daggers at him.

"True, but since you paid the second time, it all balanced out."

Ack. She should have known he'd point out that she'd paid when they'd gone to the restaurant on the morning of the code. Not that he'd liked it, but she'd insisted since she'd invited him. Eventually, after she'd snagged the ticket and refused to give it to him, he'd relented.

His expression was smug. "Guess that makes me your favorite doctor."

She rolled her eyes. "Don't count on it."

Debbie and Jerry watched them curiously and Kami became more and more self-conscious. This was ridiculous.

"Don't let Gabe fool you." She leaned toward Debbie. "He's not my type and I'm not his. We enjoy our friendship and being coworkers. This is all a game Gabe plays. Nothing more."

There. That should settle any doubts and teach him not to trifle with her.

But rather than look repentant, he put his fork down on the table and stared at her, a confused look on his handsome face. "Who says you're not my type?"

Kami turned toward him and willed him not to have this conversation in front of the couple. "I'm not."

"Says who?" he persisted, oblivious or not caring that she didn't want to continue.

"You've never dated anyone like me," she pointed out, very aware of their curious audience.

"That doesn't mean I wouldn't like to."

He was laying it on thick for Debbie's sake. Kami didn't like it.

Then again, who liked being used?

Besides her mother, who seemed a glutton for punishment, that was.

"Thank you so much for meeting with us about Lindsey's fund-raiser," she told Jerry and Debbie, ignoring Gabe's last comment. "I'll give Beverly your business card." Despite only having eaten about half her meal, Kami pushed her chair back. "Now, if you'll excuse me, I've recalled that I had other plans tonight that really can't wait, after all."

When Gabe went to rise, Kami shook her head. "You stay and enjoy your meal. I'll catch a taxi."

Gabe joined Kami on the sidewalk outside the restaurant. "You didn't really think I'd let you take a taxi home, did you?"

A crowd had gathered, waiting for their turn to be seated inside the restaurant, but Gabe had had no difficulty spotting where Kami stood near the curb.

"You didn't really think I'd let you get away with using me like you were, did you?" she hissed without looking his way.

That had Gabe pausing.

"I'm sorry if that's what you thought. Let me take you home."

"What I thought?" she scoffed. "You know you were acting as if we were an item to put on a show for your ex."

"Aren't we an item?"

Risking escalating her wrath, he put his hand on her lower back and guided her toward his car. Whether out of a desire to get away from the waiting restaurant patrons or as a testament to how upset she was, Kami let him.

"You know good and well we aren't," she insisted, turning on him as they stopped at the passenger side of his car.

"We have a good relationship, have been flirting with one another, have had breakfast twice this week, and dinner together tonight. It's not illogical of me to imply there's something between us when there is something between us."

"Friendship," she spit at him, her eyes a vivid green. "That's what's between us."

"Yes. We're friends."

"Nothing more." She opened the car door, slapped his hand when he tried to help, climbed inside, and slammed the door.

Gabe stared down at her through the passenger-door window.

Friends. Nothing more, she'd said.

They were friends.

He drove her home, contemplating the night and what she'd said. He had flirted with Kami heavily during the meal. Had he been doing so to deflect Debbie?

Flirting with Kami had felt right.

Not because Debbie had been there, but because he enjoyed the back-and-forth between them. Enjoyed the chemistry he felt when he was with her.

He pulled into Kami's apartment complex parking area and turned off the motor. "I'm sorry, Kam."

She stared straight ahead. "Because you know I'm right?"

"Because I don't want you upset with me."

She sighed, touched her temple. "What does it matter?"

"Because you really are my favorite nurse."

She closed her eyes. "Fine, but don't use me ever again."

"Okay."

Kami was obviously surprised at his quick acquiescence, judging by the way her gaze shot to him.

"I won't ask you to rescue me at the auction again, if that's what you want." He crossed his heart.

"You won't ask me to rescue you from a beautiful woman? Oh, thank you," she said with great sarcasm and an eye roll. "Thank goodness I won't have to go through that."

He didn't come back with anything, just got out of the car, went around and opened her door.

She got out without taking his offered hand. Stubborn woman.

Gabe stared after her as she headed toward her first-floor-apartment building entrance, watched her fumble with her keys, then unlock her front door.

She was going to go inside without saying another word. Life was too short to let her go that way. He knew that all too well.

He sprinted after her.

"Kami?" he said from right behind her as she pushed open her door.

Standing half in, half out of the apartment, she turned.

"Why are you so upset with me over this?"

Rather than answer, she looked away.

Needing to know, Gabe lifted her chin, trying to get her to meet his gaze.

Finally she looked up, staring for long moments with her big green eyes, then dropping her gaze to his mouth.

"I don't like you pretending we have a relationship that we don't. It's as confusing to me as it was to our dinner companions."

Gabe was confused, too. He'd admit that. How could he not when Kami staring at his mouth had his brain turned to mush?

Obviously that was the case.

Because Gabe gave in to what felt like the most compelling thing in the world, but might be his most foolish move ever if she never forgave him.

He leaned forward and pressed his mouth against Kami's warm, sweet lips.

At the contact, her eyes widened.

One light kiss became two.

Still, she didn't push him away, nor did she tell him to stop.

Instead, she searched his eyes as his mouth explored hers, tasted her, and grew hungry for more.

Lots more.

Gabe wasn't holding her. She could pull away at any time.

She wasn't.

Quite the opposite.

She was kissing him back.

Slowly at first, uncertain and unsure, then with a mounting urgency that fueled his own.

He moved forward, bringing them both inside the doorway, and closed the door behind him as he pulled Kami against him so he could kiss her more deeply.

Her fingers went into his hair and she pulled him closer, her body now flush with his.

Her amazing body that still wasn't close enough.

He brushed his hands over her back, lower, cupping her bottom. Lifting her against him, he kissed her deeper, his tongue making its way into her mouth.

A soft sound emitted from her throat. She shifted against him, her fingers massaging his scalp, pulling him toward her as the kiss went on and on. As their bodies melted together.

He wasn't sure how long they kissed, touched, how long their bodies pressed so tightly against each other, moving, feeling. He wasn't even sure which one of them pulled away.

It had to be Kami. Only a fool would stop kissing her.

Kami's kiss had been tender, passionate, hot.

Had demanded his all, that he hold nothing back, but give everything he was to her.

He wanted to kiss her again. To sweep her off her feet and carry her to her bedroom and kiss her all over until she cried out in release.

Until he felt her release. His release.

Nothing pretend about that or his body's very obvious reaction to their kiss.

But Kami's mind and body obviously weren't at the same place as his.

She pulled away and stared up at him with confusion shining in her eyes.

"Kami, I..." he began, not sure exactly how to explain to her since he didn't fully understand himself what had just happened between them, not wanting to say the wrong thing, but wondering if there even were right words he could tell her.

Shaking her head, she held up her hand and pushed against his chest. "How could you? You promised not to use me again."

"Use you?" he asked, puzzled by her accusation and still more than a little dazed by their kiss.

"As a substitute or just someone handy or whatever it was that possessed you just then."

"What possessed me just then," he admitted, "was you."

That was when it hit Gabe.

What probably should have hit him months ago. He'd sought out Kami's company, laughed with her, flirted with her. They were friends, but he wanted more.

Lots more.

He'd been wanting more for months. Why hadn't he seen his feelings for what they were?

Because she'd been in a relationship with Baxter.

When Kami had ended things with the accountant, Gabe's interest in anyone other than her had dissipated. He'd wanted Kami.

Correction—he wanted Kami, and now that he'd admitted that to himself, he wasn't sure he could go back to how things were. He didn't want to.

Kami looked thrown off kilter by his claim, her eyes narrowing. "I did no such thing."

He raked his fingers through his hair, over the spots on his head that still tingled from her touch, and fought the stunned feeling in his brain, his body. "I think you did."

She shook her head as if to deny his claim. "What are you talking about?"

"This." He leaned forward and pressed a gentle kiss to her parted lips again.

Immediately, she softened against him, kissing him back.

Sometimes words just didn't cover what needed to be conveyed.

"That is what I'm talking about," he whispered against her mouth. "What I want and what I hope you want, too. You say we're just friends, Kam. I think you're wrong. We're so much more than that. But if not, then you're the only friend I want to date, to spend time with, to have sex with, and those things I want more than you might believe."

CHAPTER EIGHT

DESPITE HER RACING THOUGHTS, Kami had finally settled into sleep and crashed for a good ten hours before rousing the next morning.

Upon waking, she assured herself the events of the night before had been a dream.

Reaching up to touch her lips, she knew better.

Gabe kissing her hadn't been a dream. It had been real.

Gabe had kissed her, had said he wanted to date her and have sex with her.

How crazy was that?

How crazy was his kiss?

A fervent, hungry kiss that was like the wildest spice she'd ever tasted. Something so good, so addictive you had to keep tasting even when it was setting your mouth afire.

Gabe's kisses had lit infernos, had melted her down to the core.

His had been the most amazing kiss of her life.

Comparing Gabe's kisses to Baxter's or Kent's or any of the men she'd dated was like comparing a firecracker to a stick of dynamite.

Being anywhere near something so explosive was dangerous.

Kami got out of bed, went about her normal day-off

routine, spent an hour at her mother's playing with Bubbles, then headed toward the hospital where the board had volunteered the use of a conference room to store the donated items that would be auctioned off at the fund-raiser.

Kami and a few others were inventorying everything, gathering the smaller items, and making up baskets to be auctioned.

Working on the fund-raiser would hopefully distract her from the night before.

Or not.

The first person she saw when she walked in was Gabe. Gabe in a blue T-shirt and jeans that outlined his body in an oh-so-yummy kind of way.

Or maybe it was his smile that was yummy.

He was laughing with Mindy and didn't look as if he'd given her a second thought since she'd thrown him out of her apartment.

Of course he hadn't. If he wanted, he could crook his finger and have any number of women running to do his bidding.

Something gripped her belly.

Good grief. She was not jealous. Not of Gabe crooking his finger and women doing his bidding. Not of Gabe laughing with Mindy. Not of Gabe or anything he did.

She had no claim.

Despite the fact they'd kissed and he'd destroyed her brain circuitry with the way his hard body had felt.

That hard body, she thought, not able to pull her gaze away from how his T-shirt stretched over his chest, his shoulders. Not too tight, not too loose. Just right.

Like what was beneath the material.

Heat flooded at the memory of running her hands over those shoulders, of pulling him toward her as he kissed her.

At how he'd leaned down to press one last kiss to her mouth, almost as if he'd had to have one last touch, told her to think about what he'd said, and then he'd left.

As if she'd needed him to tell her to think about what he'd said.

She'd thought of little else.

She was surprised she'd slept at all considering the emotional surge his lips against hers had caused.

A tsunami of adrenaline and emotions had flooded her senses and knocked out all common reason.

Getting all worked up over Gabe was a mistake.

He ate women's hearts for breakfast and yet they invited him back for lunch and dinner and said, "Here you go," handing their entire beings to him on a platter.

She didn't want Gabe gobbling her up, even if his kiss had been out of this world. She didn't want to be so desperate for a man that nothing else mattered. Hadn't she learned anything from her mother's mistakes?

He turned, met her gaze, then smiled. One of those smiles that was uniquely him and encompassed his whole face, lit up his eyes, and made the room brighter. Like the sun coming out from behind a cloudy sky.

Listen to her, thinking sappy thoughts.

Gabe was not a man she needed to have sappy thoughts about.

As if nothing monumental had happened the night before, he winked and went back to what he was doing.

Her heart took that moment to skip a beat.

Oh, good grief. If she weren't careful she'd be hand-feeding Gabe her heart for breakfast, too, and asking if he'd like the rest of her for lunch, dinner, and dessert.

No, no, no. She was not on the menu.

There were more than a dozen volunteers making inventory lists and baskets for the fund-raiser. Kami had

expected to spend the biggest portion of her day working on the project, but, thanks to everyone's enthusiastic efforts, they finished after only a couple of hours that
had felt more like fun than work—aided by the fact that
Gabe had been on his best behavior and kept everyone
smiling, her included despite all her attempts to avoid
and ignore him.

One by one the volunteers left.

All but Mindy, Gabe, and herself.

"You want to go to lunch?" Mindy invited Kami as
they put away the last of the baskets.

Thank goodness. Going to lunch with Mindy meant
no opportunity to be alone with Gabe. It would happen,
but she wasn't ready for that this afternoon. Not when
she felt so rattled from his kiss.

"Sure." She beamed at her best friend. "That would
be great."

Lunch with Mindy sounded like heaven and gave her
the perfect excuse not to stick around to talk to Gabe—
assuming that was why he had stayed until the end. No
doubt, despite his smiles and friendly behavior, he wanted
to reiterate that what had happened the night before meant
nothing, that he didn't look at dating and sex the same
way she did.

As if she needed him to tell her that.

It wasn't *her* bedroom door that was in a constant spin
from the women going in then being pushed out.

Gabe cleared his throat.

Mindy glanced his way, her brows lifted, and then
with a barely contained smile, she recanted. "Oh, wait.
Sorry, I can't go to lunch with you today. I forgot I'd
made other plans."

"Um…maybe we can get together tomorrow," Kami
suggested, not quite sure what Mindy had seen in Gabe's

face that had her changing her mind about lunch. Regardless, it didn't take a genius to know what had taken place.

Mindy's smile broke free as she said, "You should take my bestie to lunch, Dr. Nelson. She deserves it after all her fantastic work this morning."

"I could do that," he agreed, all innocent-looking.

Ha, neither of them were innocent. She was going to have to have a serious talk with Mindy. The last thing she needed was her friend playing matchmaker.

"I thought you might be able to." She gave him an approving look, then glanced toward Kami. "You have to go to lunch with Gabe. Otherwise, I'm going to feel guilty for bailing."

Rather than wait for Kami to answer, Mindy hugged her and promised she'd talk to her later.

"Go," she ordered, "have lunch with Gabe, and have fun."

When her friend was gone, the conference room seemed a lot smaller than it had when filled with Mindy and the dozen or so volunteers. Or maybe Gabe's presence just seemed that much larger than life when she was alone with him.

She'd been alone with him before. This was no big deal.

Just because he'd kissed her the night before didn't change anything.

Not really.

Just everything. Because before she hadn't known what all the fuss was about.

Looking at Gabe, she recanted. Well, yeah, she'd known he was a great guy and that women were crazy about him. It was just that she hadn't personally experienced that greatness on a physical level.

Gabe on a physical level changed things.

Changed her.

Changed how being alone with him made her feel.

How could it not when every cell in her body throbbed with awareness of him?

Snap out of it, Kami.

She glanced around the room at the baskets and items that filled the table and that were pushed up against the wall. "I need to lock up."

He moved closer. "Anything I can do to help?"

Disappear so I don't have to deal with this right now.

Ha. Somehow, even if she had spoken her thoughts, she didn't think he'd comply.

Forcing a smile, she shook her head. "Thanks, but this is it for today. Later, we'll finish putting together items donated between now and the fund-raiser and move all this stuff to the convention center the day of the event."

Gabe nodded, followed her out of the conference room, then stood beside her as she locked the exterior door. Pheromones exuded from his pores. Had to. How else could she be so aware of him?

They walked down the hospital hallway.

"I didn't realize you'd be here today." She glanced toward him, then quickly refocused on watching where she was walking. The last thing she needed was to trip over her own two feet in front of him.

"There was an open call for volunteers. I volunteered." He sounded nonchalant, as if it had been no big deal. Why wasn't she buying it?

"The more help, the better, right?" Kami smiled at a couple of nurses they passed in the hallway, then walked through the hospital door Gabe held open for her.

When they were headed toward the employee parking lot, he asked, "Can I take you to lunch, Kam?"

She supposed they needed to talk, to work past this

awkwardness, because she didn't like this new apprehension she felt being near him.

This underlying nervousness.

This awareness of just how hot he was. How was she ever going to look at him and not remember what his body had felt like pressed up against hers?

"Okay, so long as it's not something heavy." She imagined their conversation would be heavy enough when she told him that, although she hoped to date again soon, she didn't plan on him being the one she dated.

Or kissed.

Or pressed her body up against as if it were a contest to see just how much of her could be touching him.

Sure, he'd been a great kisser. Would be great at other things, too.

Of that, she had no doubt.

But she wasn't going to have sex with someone she didn't envision herself having a long-term relationship with. Someone who would be no different than one of the guys who came in and out of her mother's life. Gabe wasn't a long-term relationship kind of guy. She wasn't a quickie relationship kind of girl. Better to nip whatever this was in the bud.

"Dinner date?"

As she stepped off the sidewalk, she cut her eyes toward him. "What?"

His blue eyes stared straight into hers. "Not wanting to eat heavy with me because you have a dinner date?"

She'd let him think that there was someone else when he'd offered to bring breakfast, but she wanted to be honest. Their friendship was tense enough without throwing in deceit.

"You know Baxter and I broke up some time ago," she reminded him. "I've not been on a date since."

Her response put a pleased expression on his face.

"Not counting me."

"You don't count as a date," she corrected and took off toward her car.

Falling into step beside her, he pretended offense. "Says who?"

"Me."

"I want to count."

She frowned. "Because you kissed me and have decided you want to do more than that with me?"

"I find you attractive and want to have sex with you. Is that so terrible?" His expression was full of mischievousness, one that said if she was smart she'd want to kiss him, too.

She did want to kiss him, but wouldn't risk being just another woman who came in and out of his life. More than that, she wanted to protect their friendship. Gabe meant more to her than just a good-time romp in the sheets. She didn't want to lose the special bond they shared. Sex would change everything.

Giving him a look of challenge, she asked, "I don't know. You tell me. Is sex with you so terrible?"

"I've not had any complaints."

Kami wasn't sure whether to laugh or groan at the way his cocky grin slid into place. "I bet not."

Although the sparkle was still in his eyes, so was something more, something that hinted that, despite his teasing, Gabe cared about her response. "Because you enjoyed my kiss?"

She wasn't going there. Not in the hospital parking lot where anyone could overhear. "I didn't say I enjoyed your kiss."

Not looking one bit fazed, he grinned. "But you did."

"What makes you so sure?"

"You walked to my car rather than yours."

Kami blinked. He was right. She'd walked right past her car and gone to his. Heat flooded her face.

"That only means I planned to conserve gas by taking one vehicle instead of two." After all, she had planned to go to lunch so they could talk. "Not that I enjoyed you kissing me."

He opened the passenger door and she climbed into the car.

She glanced up at where he stood, his hand on the open door. The sun shone on him, making his eyes dance with light, making his hair glisten, and his skin glow. No woman in her right mind would have not enjoyed his kiss.

He was a kissing Adonis. Beautiful and talented.

He closed her door, came around and got into the driver seat.

She sighed. "You make me want to say just forget this."

He glanced her way. "Lunch, you mean?"

Although she wasn't sure she just meant lunch, she nodded.

"Because you want to go straight to your place and kiss me all over?"

Images of doing just that, of stripping his T-shirt off him and trailing kisses over his chest, his abs, filled her mind.

Yeah, so a part of her, a carnal, feminine part that probably had something to do with good old-fashioned nature at work, did want to go straight to her place and kiss him all over. Fortunately, she'd evolved enough to have the good sense not to give in to those urges.

Rolling her eyes, she shook her head. "Not what I meant and you know it."

"Sorry." But he didn't look repentant. Not with one

corner of his mouth crooked upward and his eyes searching hers for things she didn't want him to see. "Wishful thinking."

"Truly?" she asked, frustrated that he wasn't taking her seriously and that her good intentions seemed to have come to a screeching halt, because all she could do was look at his mouth and wonder if those lips had really felt as good as she remembered. "If I said yes, I want to go to my place and have sex, you'd drive us there and go at it? Just like that?"

"Sounds crude when you word it that way," he complained, his smile slipping. "But yes." His gaze locked with hers. "If you told me you wanted to have sex, we'd be having sex just as fast as I could get you somewhere alone. But make no mistake—there won't be anything quick about it when we do and it won't be just me enjoying every touch of our bodies."

She pressed her fingertips to her suddenly pounding temple and contemplated what he said.

Part of her said, yes, yes, she did want to forget lunch. Another part kept reminding her that any involvement with Gabe beyond friendship was emotional suicide.

They rode in silence, but it didn't matter. Gabe didn't go far from the hospital, and when he stopped the car, Kami looked at him in surprise.

She wasn't sure what she'd expected, but certainly not a trip to the park.

"I thought we were going to lunch."

Grinning, he looked quite proud of himself. "We are."

"At World's Fair Park?" Not that she'd expected anything fancy, but they were at a park, not a restaurant. Whether it was nerves or hunger, her stomach gnawed at her and she wanted food.

She'd not had much of an appetite and had only eaten a few bites of her breakfast. No wonder she was starved.

"There's a couple of vendor trucks not far from here."

"Vendor trucks?" Well, she had said she didn't want anything heavy. She guessed hot dogs and hamburgers fit the bill. Still, eating at the park didn't quite jibe with their previous conversation. If he was trying to seduce her, surely he'd have chosen somewhere more impressive?

"You want me to take you somewhere else?" he offered as they got out of the car.

She shook her head. "Since I'm in jeans, a T-shirt, and tennis shoes, this is fine. I'm just surprised. I didn't think about you bringing me to a park for lunch."

"Never say I'm predictable." Stepping beside her, he closed her car door before she could. "It's Saturday. There's always something going on at Performance Lawn on the weekends. I thought we could walk along the waterfront, eat, and just hang out and enjoy being outdoors. No pressure."

"No pressure?" She eyed him suspiciously.

"I'll be on my best behavior. Scout's honor." But rather than hold up a scout's sign, his fingers made a space travel television show character's instead.

"I don't think Scout was his name," she mused.

"Probably not, but, either way, let's relax and enjoy the beautiful weather and the fact that we aren't at the hospital or having to sleep away a stressful night."

Tempting. And it fit with why she'd agreed to lunch to begin with. Gabe was her friend. She wanted to maintain that friendship. Maintain it? She cherished his friendship.

"Say yes, Kami." His tone was low, his smile full of temptation, his eyes mesmerizing. "Play with me this afternoon. I'll deliver you safely back to your car whenever you say the word, I promise."

The twinkle in his eyes, so familiar, so warm, eased some of the tension that had been bubbling just beneath the surface all morning.

"Okay," she agreed and meant it. An afternoon playing in the park with Gabe. Wide open spaces. Lots of people around. Sounded safe enough.

Plus, the early spring sunshine and gentle breeze combination felt great. She'd always thought the park was beautiful and being outdoors really did feel awesome.

Already she could hear a great band playing, probably a local one, on the Performance Lawn and they were good. When she and Gabe reached the area, there was a small crowd spread out over the grass on blankets and some type of festival was going on.

A festival with food vendors.

Kami took a deep sniff of the afternoon air and her stomach rumbled in protest of how long it had been since she'd eaten. "Something smells good."

"I remember hearing about a Beer and Barbecue Festival this weekend. I think it was John from work telling me."

"Ah, now I know why you brought me here." She laughed. "Beer and barbecue."

"Not a beer and barbecue kind of girl?"

"Surely you know I'm a champagne and caviar kind of woman," she replied flippantly. She enjoyed a sip of celebratory champagne occasionally, but didn't recall having ever tried caviar. Wasn't really something on her bucket list to try, either. "But since we're here, I want to go find whatever smells so good and then find a place to sit and listen to the band while we eat. If that's okay with you?"

"Fine by me," he agreed, then, "Champagne and caviar, eh? I'll keep that in mind for future reference. For now, we'll make do with grabbing a bite of something here and listening to the band."

CHAPTER NINE

THE RELAXED ATMOSPHERE of the park and the gorgeous spring weather promised a perfect afternoon in spite of any lingering nerves Kami might have about their shared kiss.

At least, that had been Gabe's plan when he'd opted to go to the park. She'd been uptight from the moment she'd walked into the hospital and seen him. Not that he didn't understand, but rather than let her apprehension fester, he planned to knock it out of the ballpark. What better way to get her to relax than to take her to the park, surrounded by people, sunshine, and an overall air of well-being and happiness?

From a vendor he bought a small orange-and-white throw blanket emblazoned with the University of Tennessee's logo. From another, he got drinks and barbecue. Kami carried the blanket and spread it out on the grassy knoll, sat, then took the food and drinks from him while he joined her on the blanket.

They ate, chatted, then lay back on the blanket to listen to the band and soak up some vitamin D.

Gabe reached for Kami's hand, filled with pleasure when she didn't pull it free, but laced her fingers with his. It wasn't much, but holding her hand felt pivotal.

Her warm, small yet capable hand clasped within

his made his insides smile much brighter than the brilliant sunshine.

Yep, a perfect afternoon.

Which was why it made no sense for him to go and ruin it, but he opened his mouth and risked doing so anyway.

"The code the other night," he began.

Kami turned her head to look at him and he considered stopping, but pushed on anyway, because he needed to tell her. Perhaps it made no sense, but the thought that he'd kept that from her nagged at him and wouldn't let up.

"The man reminded me of my father."

Kami's eyes widened. "Oh, I'm sorry. That couldn't have been easy." She squeezed his fingers. "I've never heard you mention either of your parents before."

"Yeah, neither one of us talk about them much, do we?"

Kami's nose crinkled. "There's a reason for that on my part, but let's not talk about mine. Tell me about your parents."

"My mom is great, always showered me with love and attention, and you'd probably say she spoiled me rotten."

Smiling and looking a little wistful, Kami tsked. "The woman has a lot to answer for."

Gabe smiled. "She tried her best."

"And your dad?"

Gabe's lungs locked down, refusing to budge to pull in much-needed air. "He died."

"Oh, Gabe, I'm sorry. I didn't know."

"How could you? Like you said, I never talk about him."

"How long ago did he die?"

"I was eight."

Kami rolled onto her side to stare at him. "That's young."

He nodded.

"How did he die?"

"Heart attack."

"So working a code on a man who reminded you of your father…" Her eyes watered. "Oh, Gabe."

"I don't want your sympathy," he rushed out. "I just wanted you to know."

She stared at him a moment, then surprised him by lifting their interlocked hands to her mouth and pressing a soft kiss against his. "I'm glad you told me."

Feeling awkward and more exposed than he'd felt in years, Gabe nodded, then rolled back over to stare up at the sky. Next to him, Kami did the same.

He wasn't sure how long they lay listening to the music, lost in their own thoughts—probably about another thirty minutes—but when the band took a break, Kami sat up and stretched.

"I feel lazy, like I could doze off," she admitted, smiling sheepishly down at him. "I need to move or I might."

"You didn't sleep well last night?"

"I slept great," she countered.

Glad she wasn't dwelling on their earlier conversation, he laughed. "So much for thinking you might have lain awake thinking about me."

"I slept like a log." Although her cheeks were a little rosy, she didn't look repentant and fortunately her shoulders didn't tighten back up with tension.

He didn't like Kami tense. Not when their relationship had always been the opposite, when being together had always made the world a better place no matter what was going on around them.

"I'm never going to get a big ego while you're around, am I?" He picked up their trash.

"You don't need me to inflate your ego." Kami dusted off stray bits of grass and foliage and folded the throw blanket.

"A little ego boosting now and again wouldn't hurt, though."

Laughing, Kami followed him toward the trash bins. "I'll keep that in mind."

"You do that." After he'd tossed their trash, he brushed his hands over his jeans. "Want to walk the waterfront? We can drop the blanket off at the car."

"Sure."

They put the blanket in his car, then strolled along the waterfront.

At one point, they stopped to stare out at the water. Then Kami turned and looked up at the Sunsphere.

"She's beautiful, isn't she?"

Yes, she was, but he didn't mean the big gold structure she referred to.

Still looking at the woman rather than the twenty-six-story-high Sunsphere, Gabe shrugged. "It's made up of real gold, so I guess it would appeal."

She furrowed her brows. "What's that supposed to mean?"

He shrugged. "Women like jewelry, and since the Sunsphere's glass panels contain twenty-four-karat gold dust, you'd be more prone to appreciate it."

Giving him a look of pity, Kami shook her head. "That, my friend, might be the most sexist thing I've ever heard you say, and that's saying something."

He gave a *who, me?* look. "I meant no harm."

She held up her ringless fingers and wiggled them. "You shouldn't lump all women into the same category."

"Especially not present company," he added, grinning.

"Exactly." Because she did not want to be lumped in

with all the women he'd known. What all that meant, she wasn't sure, just that she knew she didn't want to be like the others.

"I'm not like other women," she said, to be sure there was no doubt.

"Amen."

Obviously surprised at his affirmation, she cut her gaze back to him. "What's that supposed to mean?"

"You're different."

Her eyes narrowed. "As in good different or as in weird different?"

"Definitely weird different," he assured her, grinning, but inside feeling a bit sober at just how true saying she was different was. He'd never told any woman about his father, had never wanted to. And, as vulnerable as it left him feeling, he was glad he'd told her.

Kami playfully slapped his arm. "Tell me why I'm here with you, again."

"Because you like me."

"Lord only knows why."

That she didn't deny his claim reverberated through him. Finally.

Smiling, Gabe gestured toward the golden globe in the sky. "You want to go up?"

She glanced up at the iconic gold ball that had been built for a World's Fair decades before. "Seriously, you'd want to do that?"

"It's one of the first things I did when I moved to Knoxville. Amazing views of the city and the mountains."

"I've never gone up," she mused, staring up at the Sunsphere with a bit of longing on her face.

"You've never gone to the observation deck?"

"I was supposed to once, on a school field trip…"

She paused, stared up at the golden globe with a glimmer of sadness in her eyes. "...but I ended up not being able to go."

"That settles it." He grabbed hold of her hand and was once again grateful that she didn't pull free. "We're going up."

Gabe was right. The views from the Sunsphere were spectacular. So was the man beside her.

When she let herself forget everything she knew about Gabe and allowed herself to glory in being the recipient of his attention and smile, it was easy to smile back, to give in to the chemistry between them.

When that little nagging voice reared its ugly head and reminded her of all the women Gabe had been through just during the time she'd known him, nervous energy boiled in her belly. They needed to establish that they were never going to be more than just friends, but she kept putting off the conversation.

She probably should've done that when he'd held her hand while lying on the blanket.

She'd been so relaxed, had been enjoying the music, the sunshine, the peacefulness of the afternoon so much that she hadn't pulled her hand away when he'd taken it.

Gabe's hand holding hers should have wrecked her peaceful feeling, but to her surprise, despite the electricity in his fingertips, it hadn't. Lying on that blanket next to him, eyes closed, the sun warming her face, lacing her hand with his had felt natural. Like just another part of what felt like a perfect afternoon, a happy afternoon.

Because she was happy.

Hanging out with Gabe at a city park made her happy. That he'd shared with her what had happened to his father made her happy, too. He'd been too hesitant, his voice too raw, for her to believe that it was something he'd talked about much in the past. That he'd shared that with her made the afternoon all the more special.

"Just think, if you bought my date, you and I could explore those mountains."

So much for her peaceful, happy feeling.

She cleared her throat. "You promised you weren't going to ask me to bid on you again."

"I didn't ask you to bid on me. I was just making an observation. While on the observation deck." He winked and gestured to where they were.

She rolled her eyes. "Ha ha. You're so clever."

He grinned. "It's about time you noticed."

Ignoring his comment, she didn't point out that she'd noticed a lot of things about him, and, instead, smiled. "Are these panels really made of gold?"

He chuckled. "That got your attention, eh?"

Apparently when Gabe had previously visited the Sunsphere, he'd done his research because he launched into the history of when the iconic structure had been built and why.

"You sound more like a tour guide than a doctor," she teased, impressed at his knowledge of the architectural wonder and the World's Fair that had prompted it.

"A man of many talents."

"So I'm learning."

"You've barely begun," he assured, wagging his brows.

She rolled her eyes. Again. "There's that ego."

"Waiting for you to pop it."

She shook her head. "Not this time."

"What? No denials about my talents?"

"Like you said," she conceded, "I barely know what your talents are, so denying them seems a bit foolish."

He studied her a moment, then, eyes twinkling, said, "We need to remedy that."

His gaze dropped to her lips and any lingering sensations of peace dissipated into awareness. Awareness of the very maleness of the man holding her hand, of how he was looking at her, of how her insides trembled at the brevity of his touch, of his words.

Stop this, Kami. Stop flirting with him. You're supposed to tell him that you can only be friends, nothing more. That's why you came to lunch. Not to have a mini-date.

Mini-date? This afternoon was better than her last dozen dates. More than that.

"How do you suggest we do that?" That wasn't what she was supposed to say. Nor was she supposed to be staring back at his mouth, at those wonderful lips that had caressed hers not even twenty-four hours ago.

"You need a crash course in my many talents."

She suspected the course would be fabulous, full of pleasure and good times. It was the crash that worried her. "Sounds dangerous."

"Don't like to live dangerously, Kam?"

"Nope. I'm a safety first kind of girl." Although, if that were true they wouldn't be having this conversation, nor would she still be staring at his mouth and wondering if it had felt as good against hers as she remembered.

"I can appreciate that about you."

"Good thing, because I don't plan to change for any man." She'd watched her mother do that to no avail whenever a new man popped into her life. No, thank you.

"That why your previous relationships haven't worked out?"

"Why's that?"

His gaze lifted to hers. "Your unwillingness to change?"

"Are you saying you change to make relationships work?" she challenged, not believing he did.

He considered her question. "That's a good question. My initial response would be yes, but the truth is, probably not."

Interesting that he'd given such a thoughtful answer.

"A person shouldn't change to make a relationship work." Which was why she needed to point out that she had no desire to join the ranks of his has-beens. No way would she and Gabe ever work. He was a pro with women at his command and she was an amateur with really high checklist standards. They were a recipe for disaster.

"Sure they should."

Surprised at his comment, she frowned. "You just admitted you hadn't changed for past relationships."

"You're right. I did." Holding her gaze, he took a deep breath and said, "Which is why those relationships are in the past. For a relationship to work, both parties have to care enough about the other to give and take, to change. Otherwise, the relationship is doomed before it's started."

That was a good lead in to why a relationship between them would never work. And why they should stop this before they irreparably damaged their friendship.

Yet, she didn't. Instead, she turned back to stare out at the mountains just beyond the city limits and let her mind wonder. *What if?*

She'd had such a great time with him today. Thrilled at the tingles his hand holding hers shot through her entire being.

What if they *could* have a relationship and still be friends afterward?

* * *

"Safe and sound, as promised," Gabe reminded her as he pulled into the empty parking place next to Kami's sedan.

"Thank you for a lovely afternoon."

"You're welcome. We'll have to do it again sometime." The sooner the better as far as Gabe was concerned. He'd truly enjoyed the day.

Silence hit them and then Kami reached for the car door handle.

"I'd like to see you again, Kami." Surely she knew that, but he didn't want there to be any doubt.

Grinning, she pointed a finger. "Lucky for you, you get to work with me three to four nights a week."

There she went popping his bubble again.

"Not what I meant."

Although her hand toyed with the door handle, she didn't make a run for it. "I enjoy our friendship."

So did he.

"You'd enjoy dating me more," he promised. He'd make sure of it.

Her lower lip disappeared into her mouth. "I—I don't know."

"I'm attracted to you and want us to explore what's happening between us."

She stared at where her fingers perched on the door handle. "Which is what exactly?"

"Something worth taking our time to figure out."

"I really don't think I need to be here for this," Kami insisted as she got out of Gabe's car the following afternoon and stared at the faded white-framed house where Beverly Smith and her husband lived.

Debbie was a fast worker. She'd arranged a meeting and insisted on Kami and Gabe attending as well. Or maybe she'd just requested Gabe and he'd embellished to say Kami had to be there, too. She'd tried to plead out, but he'd insisted that if he had to spend the afternoon with Debbie, then so did she.

"That's because you're heartless and have no qualms about throwing me to the wolves." Gabe came around to her side of the SUV and led her across the paved driveway.

"So dramatic. You really went into the wrong profession, Gabe. You'd have been great on prime-time television." Pausing on her way up the porch steps, she feigned a light-bulb moment. "Hey, I bet Debbie could introduce you to a few of her friends. You could be the latest and greatest thing since sliced bread."

"And deprive all our emergency-room patients of my tender, loving care?" He clicked his tongue. "No, thank you. Besides, you'd miss me."

"You have a point," Kami conceded, knocking on Beverly's front door. She gave Gabe a nervous look. "I hope this works out for Beverly. I can't imagine everything she and her family are going through right now. I'm going to feel terrible if it doesn't or adds to their stress."

"If Beverly and her husband don't want their story to be an episode of Debbie's show, then all they have to do is say no." Gabe touched her arm in what was meant to be a reassuring gesture.

Only his fingers against her bare arm added to the swirling in her belly.

She arched one brow. "Just like all you have to do is tell Debbie no?"

He chuckled. "Good point. Maybe we should bar the door and not let Debbie anywhere near the Smiths." Then his expression grew more serious. "But, really, whatever they decide is what they decide. Debbie can't force them to do anything they don't want to do."

"I know." She did know but felt protective, as if she'd be responsible since it was through her that the opportunity had presented itself.

The front door opened and a tired-looking twenty-five-year-old nurse and her husband of the same age stood on the other side.

"I wasn't sure if you'd both be here," Kami admitted to her friend, as they joined the couple on their sofa.

"My parents are with Lindsey while we're here," Beverly said, her face filled with guilt. "I wanted to meet at the hospital, but because of the show Debbie wants to do, she insisted upon meeting at the house. Leaving the hospital was hard, but...but Gregg says that we need to do this." She gave a little shrug. "I know he's right."

Lifting her hand to press a kiss there, her husband nodded. "If nothing else, you needed a few minutes away from the hospital, a shower in your own bathroom, a minute alone with your husband."

The two exchanged looks and, despite their horrid current circumstances, Kami felt a stab of envy.

That was how a relationship should be, she thought. Not the way her mother's relationships had been. Not the way her own relationships had been. But the deep abiding love that shone in the couple's eyes as they looked at each other, even while they dealt with great financial and emotional burdens with their new baby's health needs.

Debbie and her producer arrived moments later, along with a cameraman, who sat in a chair awaiting further instructions with his camera ready to go at a moment's notice.

Debbie asked Gabe's opinion several times and she

threw out comments left and right to her producer, but, other than a few smiles and polite pleasantries, she didn't have much to say to Kami.

Truly, Kami was unneeded. Other than answering a few questions about the event, she didn't say a word.

Jerry was pleasant enough, but, again, he only had eyes for his show's star.

Motioning to the cameraman, Debbie led the Smiths through a series of questions about their relationship, Beverly's pregnancy, when they first found out about Lindsey's heart problems, and what her status was now.

The cameraman moved about, getting different angles.

Her hand locked with her husband's, Beverly's shoulders slumped as she looked at the television producer. Her voice quavered as she said, "Do you know how difficult it is to pray for a heart for your baby, so your child can live, when it means someone else's baby has to die to give that heart?"

Kami's eyes watered at the implications of what her coworker said, at how heavy Beverly's heart ached for what her baby and family was going through, but also for what another family would have to go through for the Smiths to get their miracle.

Within minutes, Jerry presented the Smiths with a contract giving the television station the rights to the footage shot that day, permission to film their upcoming big moments, to have behind-the-scenes shots, and to completely renovate their home any way Debbie saw fit.

Neither of the Smiths looked nervous or hesitant.

No problem—Kami was nervous enough for them. "Are you sure?"

Without batting an eyelash, the Smiths both nodded.

"We talked about this before everyone arrived. Our biggest hope is that this will raise awareness of the need for organ donation. If us signing these—" Beverly gestured to the papers "—helps achieve that, helps one person sign their donor card, then it's worth sharing our story."

Her heart full of admiration for her coworker, Kami watched as the Smiths signed the contract.

Debbie made arrangements to meet with the couple at the hospital to film them with Lindsey. Then she, the Smiths, Jerry, and the cameraman went through the house.

Which left Kami and Gabe sitting in the living room. Alone.

Gabe's gaze met hers.

"They can always say no, you said," Kami mock whispered, but with a smile on her face and her eyes a bit watery.

"You think they should have?"

She shook her head. "How could I when their reasons for saying yes are so powerful?"

Gabe nodded. "If Debbie's cameraman is worth his paycheck, he got Beverly on film and they'll use that. If I wasn't already an organ donor, I would be after the emotion Beverly just poured into this room."

Feeling much better about the whole ordeal than when they'd arrived, she nodded. Maybe the story would help the Smiths and other families, too.

"You ready to leave?"

"Before we got here," she admitted, but was glad she'd come, was glad that she'd gotten to hug her friend, witness the love the couple shared, and was even more glad that she and Mindy had initiated the fund-raiser.

He grinned. "Me, too."

"Yeah, yeah. I saw you making googly eyes at Debbie," she teased.

"Any googly eyes I was making were meant for you, not her."

"Um…right." She was saved from having to comment further as the others rejoined them in the living room.

Kami hugged Beverly again, making her promise to call if there was anything she could do to help, even if it was just running errands or picking up something to bring up to the NICU as this was one of the few times Beverly had left the hospital since Lindsey's birth.

Within minutes, Kami was back in Gabe's car.

"You hungry?" he asked.

She was about to say no, but her belly growled, making any denial seem petty.

"Champagne and caviar?"

She smiled that he remembered her quip from the day before. "You planning to ply me with expensive food and drink?"

"Would it work?"

She shook her head.

"I didn't think so." He grinned. "How about we hit my favorite steak house instead? No caviar on the menu, but they have a wide variety of options and I've never been disappointed."

"Sounds good."

The steak house was good. Gabe ordered a cedar plank salmon and Kami ordered a shrimp pasta. Both were delicious.

"Only a few more weekends until the fund-raiser," Gabe mused. "Everything ready?"

Kami shrugged. "As ready as we can be. There are still some last-minute donations coming in, which is great. The more that come in, the better."

"Anything I can do to help?"

She gave him a pointed look. "Don't forget to show up the night of the fund-raiser."

He laughed. "As if I could."

Kami set her fork down next to her plate. "You know, I don't understand why you're so worried about Debbie. She's beautiful, talented, and successful. A guy could do a lot worse."

From across the table, he arched a brow. "Are you trying to sell me on my ex? I may not let you order dessert for such treachery."

Kami laughed. "You mean, like you trying to sell me on the new, improved Baxter?"

"Definitely not trying to sell you on him. Just trying to make sure you weren't interested in getting back together regardless of how buff he becomes."

She shook her head. "His physique had nothing to do with why he and I weren't working."

Eyeing her, he leaned back in his chair. "What were the reasons? Besides the fact that he wasn't me, of course."

"Of course," she agreed with a great deal of sarcasm, trying to decide if she really wanted to go there with Gabe, whose kiss made her feel everything Baxter's had lacked. "Let's just say our chemistry wasn't right."

Gabe studied her for a moment. Then to Kami's surprise, rather than push for her to elaborate, he accepted her answer.

"I'm glad."

"Because?"

"If you'd had the right chemistry with him, you wouldn't be here with me."

"This isn't a date," she pointed out.

"It doesn't make my comment any less true. If you and Baxter were still together, you wouldn't be with me regardless of how we labeled the meal."

She conceded his point. If she'd had the chemistry with Baxter that she felt with Gabe, she'd not have wanted to be with anyone but Baxter, would have wanted to spend all her spare moments, all her meals, with him. That wasn't the case.

Baxter had been ideal on paper, but in reality, not so much so. What he'd been was safe.

Gabe… Gabe was not safe, but that didn't seem to stop her silly mind from wondering *what if?* What if she gave in to the chemistry and told him she wanted him?

No matter what happened between them, friendship or something more, she would not make a fool of herself over him.

If, and that was a big if, something did happen between them, she'd not get attached and she'd be the one to walk away. She'd keep control.

She wouldn't chase him or hold on to unrequited feelings the way women tended to do where he was concerned.

She knew better.

Not that she planned on anything happening, but still…

Forcing herself not to stare at his mouth, she swallowed.

"Now, about dessert," she said, picking up the menu and studying it. "I'm more of a cake than a pie person, so if you're planning to share, I hope that's okay."

CHAPTER TEN

GABE HADN'T MEANT to share dessert with Kami, but watching her eat the sweets was more enjoyable than eating the carrot cake he'd ordered would have been. Not that she didn't let him have a bite here and there.

"This is really good."

"Better than your Death by Chocolate?"

Looking ecstatic, she nodded. "This could be Killed by Carrots."

Gabe laughed. "I don't think that's going to catch on."

"Probably not," she admitted, her lips wrapping around the fork, her eyes closing as she slowly pulled the fork out.

When she opened her eyes, realized he was watching her and that what she was doing was affecting him, she winced. "Sorry. I keep forgetting."

"Forgetting?"

"Nothing."

"You really think I'm going to let you get away with that?"

She shrugged. "You can only make me tell what I'm willing to."

He thought on her comment a moment. "The only thing you're willing to tell me is nothing?"

"Maybe."

"I never took you for a tease, Kami."

"Yeah, yeah. I've been teasing you for months. It's

what you and I do. What we've always done. It's safe and fun and, despite your momentary lapses, it's probably all there should be between us."

Elated at her "probably," Gabe studied her, trying to decipher if she was serious or testing him, wanting him to correct her.

"My momentary lapses? Are you saying you didn't have a lapse when you kissed me back?"

"Oh, I had a lapse, all right. A big one."

"Meaning you regret having kissed me back?"

As if she was trying to keep them from spilling her secrets, her lips pressed tightly together.

Gabe smiled. He couldn't help himself. She couldn't admit that she'd enjoyed their kiss, but she couldn't lie and say she regretted it, either.

Whatever her reasons were for not wanting to move into a more physical relationship, Kami wasn't immune to the chemistry between them. Not by a long shot.

"Okay, you refuse to tell me if you regret kissing me. I can live with that. But what I really want to know," he mused, picking up his fork and feeding her a piece of his carrot cake, "is when are you going to let me kiss you again?"

Kami choked on the cake. Coughing, she cleared her throat, took the glass of water Gabe offered, then coughed some more.

"Not exactly the reaction I was going for," he said wryly, his lips twitching.

"I imagine not." She took another drink of water and this time the cool liquid went down correctly. "Don't do that."

"Don't do what?"

"Say things that catch me off guard."

Gabe laughed. "That caught you off guard? You who always have a fast comeback for anything I say?"

"Yeah, well, I didn't just then."

"Apparently."

She put her water glass down and pushed what was left of both cakes toward him. "I'm finished. You eat the rest."

Gabe motioned for the waitress, asked for a box and the check.

"I can pay for mine."

"You could, but you're not," he corrected. When she went to argue, he reminded her, "It's my turn. You paid last time."

"Actually, Jerry paid last time."

"I imagine the television station reimbursed him." Gabe got the check from the waitress and paid while Kami boxed up her leftovers.

When they exited the restaurant, the sky was streaked with yellow, orange, and red hues as the sun made its final splash of the day.

"Wow. Beautiful sunset," Kami exclaimed as they made their way toward the car.

"It is. Seems a shame to call an end to such a great evening. You want to go downtown and throw back a few?"

She started to ask him to bring her home. He could see it on her face. But then she took on a determined look.

"Sure. Let's throw back a few," she surprised him by saying. Her eyes glittered with challenge. "Why not?"

Gabe hadn't thought she'd agree, but then, Kami had been surprising him from the moment they'd met. Everything about her kept him on his toes. He drove them downtown to a place he knew, then paid for a parking spot.

He took her hand and they walked to the club, found two vacant seats at the bar, then ordered drinks.

An hour later, they were both laughing at anything and everything.

Gabe wasn't drunk, but he was feeling good. Too good. Not because of alcohol, but because of the woman smiling and laughing with him.

Kami went to order another round, but Gabe shook his head. "No more for me. I've got to drive us home. You go ahead, though."

Her mouth made an O, and then she changed the order to one.

"You doing okay, still?"

Smiling, she nodded. "Since I never do this, surprisingly, yes. What about you? You come here often?"

He glanced around the club. "I've been here a few times."

"With Debbie?"

He frowned. "No."

"Some other woman?"

"Be careful, Kam," he teased, watching her closely. "You almost sound jealous."

She glanced away. "I'm not," she quickly denied, her voice not feisty. "I know you've been with lots of women. That's why you kiss like the devil."

"The devil, huh?" He laughed. "Since I think you're giving me a compliment, thank you."

"You're welcome." She half turned on her bar stool to watch as a dance instructor called for more to join in the fun. A country song was playing and there were a bunch of regulars line dancing and a few watching the instructor and doing their best to keep up. "I never could line dance. No rhythm and two left feet."

"I thought line dancing was for people who had two left feet and no rhythm?" he ragged.

She turned, stared him straight in the eyes, and challenged, "I suppose you're an expert?"

She was beautiful, Gabe thought. Absolutely beautiful. Her eyes sparkled, her chin jutted forward, and her lips parted just so. It was all he could do not to lean forward, cup her face, and take her sassy mouth for another "devilish" kiss.

"I've been known to scoot my boots a time or two," he said with an exaggerated drawl.

Leaning on her bar stool, she peered down, her gaze dropping to his shoes. "Too bad you aren't wearing boots. I'd make you put your feet where your mouth is."

Gabe's lips twitched. "Not having boots has never stopped me before."

Her brow arched. "Is that a backwoods way of asking me to dance?"

Grinning, he slid off his bar stool and held out his hand. "You want to dance, Kam? I promise not to step on your toes any fewer than a dozen times."

He wanted her in his arms, wanted to embrace every moment because life was short—just look at how young his father had died. It should be lived to its fullest. Still, he'd settle for whatever she'd give him until she realized they belonged together.

Like what his parents had. That was what he wanted, what he'd been searching for and never found. Looking into Kami's eyes, his chest inflating, Gabe couldn't help but smile as he thought, *Until now.*

Placing her hand in his, she laughed. "Oh, this is going to be good. Especially since if you're stepping on people's toes while line dancing, you're way worse than me."

Gabe wasn't way worse than Kami. Not that Kami had expected him to be. He was one of those guys who excelled at everything, so of course he line danced with ease, quickly picking up the routine for whatever tune played if it wasn't one he knew.

Kami, on the other hand, decided she was just going to go with it and not worry about her two left feet. She probably mis-stepped more than she grapevined or ball-changed, but she was having fun and was keeping time, mostly, with the other dancers.

Then again, it might be the alcohol making her think she wasn't doing too badly.

Either way, she was laughing, spinning, and having fun.

With Gabe.

In a completely different way than they'd ever spent time together before. She liked it.

A lot.

When the dance instructor announced she was taking a break, a slow number came on.

Kami started to head back toward where she and Gabe had been sitting at the bar, but he grabbed her hand and pulled her toward him.

"Not so fast, my little do-si-do. This might be my favorite song."

Putting her arms around his neck, she fell into rhythm with him. "Might be?"

He grinned. "Ask me when the music is finished."

"Deal." Kami rested her head against Gabe's chest, marveling at his heartbeat against her cheek, at his arms around her, his hands at her waist.

Why had she been fighting this? Pushing him away? This felt so good, so right.

Unbidden, she giggled.

"What's so funny?"

She smiled at him. "I feel like I'm in high school dancing with the cutest guy in school."

His eyes crinkled at the corners. "How'd you know I was the cutest guy in school?"

Kami laughed. "Just a hunch."

"I wasn't really, you know."

"Weren't what, the cutest guy in school?" She leaned her head back to look up at him. "I don't believe you."

"I wasn't," he admitted. "Tommy Smithson had all the girls after him. The rest of us guys were just there to collect his leftovers."

"Tommy must be amazing," she cooed, her fingers toying with the soft hair at his nape. "When's your class reunion? I want to meet him."

Gabe shook his head. "You think I'd risk introducing you to Tommy? No way. I'm already struggling to convince you to be more than my friend. You meet Tommy and I'm not even in the ballpark anymore."

"He's an athlete? No worries. I'm worse at sports than I am at dancing. Not my thing."

"For whatever it's worth, I think you're a wonderful dancer."

Her heart skipped a few beats at his compliment.

"Ha," she countered, her insides feeling warm and mushy. "You must have drunk more than you realized."

"Nope, but it might be that you fit into my arms so perfectly that I don't notice anything else. Not sure I'd care if you stomped my toes so long as I get to hold you."

She couldn't argue. She did fit into his arms perfectly.

At least, from her perspective it felt perfect. Just to be sure, she snuggled closer and laid her head back against his chest.

Yep, pretty perfect.

Gabe moved to the slow music, Kami in his arms, her head nestled beneath his chin, and decided that this really was his favorite song.

But then the next one came on and the next, and as

long as the music kept playing and he got to keep holding Kami, he'd keep on loving the songs.

Because he knew when the music stopped, he'd take her home, and he'd leave.

Not that he'd want to leave.

What he wanted was to make love to the sassy woman in his arms.

But he wouldn't.

Not tonight.

Not when she'd been drinking and might have regrets. As much as he wanted her, he didn't want her to think this was just physical, didn't want her to think he'd taken advantage of the first opportunity her guard was down.

He wanted more than just sex. Lots more.

So, he'd hold her, breathe in the sweet scent she attributed to soap, water, and lotion but that he was convinced was some aphrodisiac blend all her own, and he'd enjoy the moment.

In the moment, he was holding Kami.

And she was holding him back.

The line-dance instructor came back out and announced she'd be doing her last set of instructions for the night.

Full of enthusiasm, Kami jumped back in. Despite her fairly frequent incorrect moves, she seemed to be having a great time, which made Gabe happy.

Over the moon. Giddy drunk. But not nearly as giddy drunk as when he drove her home and walked her to her apartment and she kissed him.

He'd meant to just tell her good-night, but before he could say a thing, she'd stood on her tiptoes, wrapped her arms around him, and pressed her lips to his.

Fully, wholly, no holding back, hands in his hair, body grinding against his, enthusiastically kissed him.

His libido skyrocketed.

His willpower went to hell.

"Kami," he groaned, wondering how he was going to untangle himself when all he wanted was to lose himself in her arms and tell her all his crazy thoughts. "I have to stop."

"Why?" she breathed as she traced her mouth over his throat and spread her fingers over his back, holding him tightly to her. "I don't want you to stop."

"You're drunk."

"Not that drunk."

"Drunk enough."

Her hands slid down his back, pulled his shirt from his pants, and slid beneath the material.

Goose bumps prickled his skin.

Kami's fingers on his bare back undid him. His groin hardened. His jeans constricted to the point of pain.

Having to pull away from Kami caused pain, but he managed, instantly feeling defeat at the loss of contact.

"No," she told him, her green gaze locked with his and fire sparking to life. "You can't stop. Not now. Not when I want you."

Gabe groaned, then took a deep breath and cupped her face. "You have no idea what hearing you say you want me does to my insides."

"Apparently not what's happening to my insides," she complained. She moved against him, as if to show him.

"Worse."

"Impossible." She glared at him. "You're going to leave, aren't you?"

He nodded. "It's the right thing to do."

She let out a long sigh.

He was trying to do the right thing, but Kami wasn't making it easy. Not with her take-me eyes and pouty, kiss-me lips and with how she couldn't stand still, but instead swayed ever so slightly as if dancing to a song of seduction.

Gabe swallowed, fought for willpower. "What is it you think I should do right now, Kami?"

She stared at him a moment, then closed her eyes. "I think you should get back in your car and drive home. Alone. Without me. To a cold, lonely bed, knowing I would have rocked your world."

Knowing he was doing the right thing, Gabe leaned forward, kissed her forehead, then finished unlocking her apartment door and opening it for her to step inside. "For the record, you rock my world every single day."

With that, he picked her up, set her inside the apartment, reached around to make sure the lock would catch, then pulled the door closed.

With him locked on the outside of her apartment because, heaven help him, he was already questioning his decision to leave.

CHAPTER ELEVEN

"GO TO BREAKFAST with me?"

Having almost reached her car in the employee parking lot, Kami spun toward Gabe, not bothering to hide her surprise that he'd followed her out of the hospital and obviously jogged to catch her.

She'd seen him several times throughout the long night, had worked next to him, had talked to him in regard to patients, but she'd fought humiliation and felt the tension.

Not just on her part.

So his breakfast invitation truly did take her by complete surprise.

When she didn't immediately answer, he continued. "Your pick on where we go."

She bit the inside of her lower lip, then acquiesced. "Sure."

Why not? How much more could she embarrass herself than she had the other night?

"I tried calling yesterday. The day before, too," he said after they were settled in his car.

"I didn't feel like talking," she admitted, checking to make sure her seat belt was secure.

"What about now? You feel like talking about what happened the other night?"

"Nothing happened the other night," she reminded him, crossing her arms. Why had she agreed to this?

He shot a quick glance her way. "I wasn't sure how much you remembered. If perhaps that was why you weren't answering my calls."

"If you're implying something happened that I don't recall, I'm not buying it." She'd know if something more had happened between them. It hadn't.

"Sorry, that's not what I meant." He raked his fingers through his hair. "You're not upset with me because I left, are you?"

She wasn't. Much.

"I wanted to stay," he continued, staring straight ahead at the road. "But I didn't want you to have regrets, but now I think you do anyway."

She cut her gaze toward him, took in his profile, the tense way he gripped the steering wheel. Gabe didn't want her upset. He was trying to make things right between them.

She leaned back against the headrest and inhaled deeply. They were friends. Nothing had happened. This awkwardness was ridiculous.

She sighed. "I'm sorry I didn't answer your call or text. I needed some space."

"Understood." He glanced her way, then back at the road. "You still feel that way?"

"That I want space between us?" She shook her head, then admitted the truth. "I value our friendship, Gabe. I missed talking with you last night the way we usually do at work. I don't want to lose that. That's what scares me about what's happening between us."

"Me, too. I should have been more persistent in calling, should have pulled you aside last night to clear the

air, but I didn't want to put you on the spot or beg forgiveness at the hospital."

Beg forgiveness? Realization dawned. "You thought
I was mad at you? That's why you were standoffish last
night?"

His brow arched. "Weren't you?"

Only that he'd left her when she'd wanted him to stay.

"I was more upset with myself than you. I acted very
out of character on several counts. But it's okay, Gabe.
I understand."

He slowed the car at a traffic light, looked her way.
"Unbelievable. You thought I left because I didn't want
to have sex with you, didn't you?"

His eyes were so blue, so intense, it was like looking
up into the sky and losing one's self.

"I think you want to have sex with lots of women,"
she admitted, then sank her teeth into the soft flesh of
her lower lip.

"You make me sound like I've no scruples and have
sex with anyone."

"Don't you?"

"No." His answer was immediate and brooked no argument, almost as if he was offended that she'd thought
he might.

"If you want to have sex with lots of women, it's not
my business."

"I want to make it your business, Kam." He glanced
to make sure the red light hadn't changed back to green.

The light changed and Gabe accelerated the car, driving in silence until he pulled into a restaurant parking lot
and into an empty space near the entrance.

He didn't kill the engine, just turned to her and waited
for her to say something.

She'd known the conversation wasn't over. She'd been

able to feel the wheels turning inside his head as he drove them. She'd even known what he was going to say when he spoke next, so she'd prepared her answer in her mind.

She took a deep breath. "Despite what you might think from my behavior the other night, sex is a big deal to me."

"Sex is a big deal to me, too."

"No, it isn't," she countered. "You're casual about sex. I'm not."

"You're making assumptions about me that aren't true."

She turned in the seat, stared straight into his eyes, which shouldn't even be real they were so blue. "You've never had casual sex, Gabe?"

He didn't flinch but Kami read the truth on his face even before he said, "I didn't say that."

She reached for the passenger door handle so she could get out of his car. She'd gone from tense to her belly being in a tight wad to where she wasn't even sure she could eat. She should have asked him to take her back to her car.

"Sex between us wouldn't be casual, Kami. If you believe that, then you're fooling yourself and denying us both something that would be amazing."

"What's amazing is my friendship with you to begin with and why I want to hang on to that relationship when you're determined we completely destroy it."

"Is that what you believe would happen if we had sex? That we can't be friends and lovers? That's the real reason you won't have sex with me? Because of our friendship?"

"At the moment, I'm not sure we can be friends," she threw back.

"Then what's stopping you from closing your car door and asking me to drive us to my place right this very moment?"

Hand still on the handle, she glared at him. "What? So you can reject me again? I don't think so."

"Is that what this is about? I left because I didn't want to take advantage of you. Rather than see the truth, that I left because I care about you and want things to be right when we take that step, instead, all you see is that I left."

Kami's heart pounded in her chest. Her hands shook as she dropped them back into her lap.

"Take me home, Gabe."

"Fine." His movements full of frustration, he restarted the engine and backed out of the parking spot.

He drove in silence, pulling in at her apartment complex. When she went to get out, he gripped the steering wheel and leaned forward.

"I'm sorry, Kam."

"Me, too." She gave a resigned sigh, then a little shrug. "Because even though I asked you to take me home, well, my car is still at the hospital and, short of walking to work tonight, I'm going to need a lift back there."

"Oh! You're here!"

Startled by the woman stepping into the apartment, Kami glanced up from the worn sofa where she'd fallen asleep while petting Bubbles. The cat had apparently dozed off, too, and, yawning, stretched.

"Someone has to take care of your cat," Kami reminded her, sitting up on the sofa and staring at her, obviously shocked to see her mother.

"Hey, babe, where do you want me to put these?" A long-haired free-spirited man came into the apartment behind her mother carrying some grocery bags.

Ah, so that was why she was so startled at Kami being at her apartment. Eugenia had company.

Kami's mother glanced the man's way, then blushed. "In the kitchen is fine, Don."

Her mother didn't bother to introduce them. Why bother? None ever stuck around long.

The man nodded in her direction, then carried the bags to the small kitchen that was open to the living area and began unpacking the bags.

Don. Hadn't the guy her mother left with been named Sammy? Maybe Kami had misunderstood her. Then again, probably not.

"Hello, my Bubbles, did you miss Mommy?" her mother crooned to the cat as she picked her up and kissed her nose. The cat actually licked her mother's nose, so maybe the cat had missed her after all. "Mommy missed you, but it looks like Kami has taken care of you."

Had her mother thought she wouldn't? *She* wasn't the irresponsible one.

"You didn't mention you were going to be gone for so long," Kami said, watching as her mother continued to love on the feline.

It was more of a greeting than Kami had ever gotten, so maybe her mother really did care about the cat, just wasn't responsible enough to actually take care of the poor girl.

"I didn't know I was going to be," her mother admitted, then gave Kami a semi-annoyed look. "Was it that big a deal to stop by and feed Bubbles? I can find someone else next time if you're too busy to help your own mother with something as simple as feeding her cat."

Ugh. How had her mother turned things to make her feel guilty?

Kami sighed. "It was no problem."

"I didn't think so."

Don came back into the living area, stood quietly in the doorway and gave Kami's mother an expectant look.

Eugenia gave a nervous giggle, then said to Kami, "Then I guess you can be on your way since I'm back. Bye."

Kami's jaw dropped. Maybe not literally, but figuratively, it definitely fell. Just like that, her mother was kicking her out of her apartment. No *thank you*. No questions about Bubbles. No explanation of where she'd been, what she'd been doing, why she'd been gone longer than expected.

Then again, why was Kami surprised? Her mother had been pushing her aside for whatever man was in her life for years.

Kami worked her three on, had Friday and Saturday night off, then worked Sunday, Monday, Tuesday, and Wednesday nights.

She and Gabe hadn't found a happy medium.

They hadn't found a happy anything.

Because she wasn't happy at the way they were walking on eggshells, talking to each other without eye contact, and talking without saying anything at all beyond work.

"Bay two's CT scan shows a non-obstructing renal calculus in the right kidney."

Glancing up from where she stripped the bedding off in the next bay, Kami met the eyes of the man toward whom all her thoughts were directed.

"I'm going to print off some scripts," he continued, not meeting her gaze, "then discharge with instructions to see Urology tomorrow."

"Okay."

He stood watching her a moment, then left. Kami

quickly made up the bed with fresh sheets, wiped the countertops down with an antibacterial cleanser, then went to get the scripts and discharge orders from Gabe.

"Thanks," he said as he handed the scripts to her, their fingers touching. Her breath caught. His gaze jerked to hers as if he'd felt the jolt that shot through her at the contact.

Kami hesitated a few moments, wanting to say more, wanting him to say more, then berated herself for her idiocy.

She discharged the patient, then went back to do her nurse's note. Gabe still sat at the station, leaned back in a chair, with his eyes closed and a strained expression on his face.

Her heart squeezed. "You okay?"

He opened his eyes, nodded.

Again, she wanted to say more, but didn't know what. Maybe with time the tension between them would ease. Hopefully.

"I hate this."

Had he read her mind or what?

"Me, too," she admitted, sinking into the chair next to his.

Glancing around to make sure no one was close enough to overhear their conversation, he leaned close. "I miss you, Kami. I miss everything about you."

She bit her lower lip.

"I don't know what else to say. You know how I feel, what I want, that I don't like where things are between us. I'm trying to give you time and space to figure out we're worth taking a chance on." His gaze was intense. "I don't want to push you into something you don't want, but I don't understand why you refuse to give us a chance."

Oh, how easy it would be to give in, to tell him how

much she wanted him. To tell him how she dreamed of his kisses, of knowing what it felt like to wrap her legs around his waist and…

Stop it, Kami, she ordered herself. *Just stop it.*

"You and I want different things out of life."

Seeming to understand her turmoil, he still refused to back down. "Are you so sure about that? Because I'm not."

She found herself wanting to believe, wanting to forget a lifetime of lessons and just give in to her heart's desires.

"Need I remind you that you're the one who left me?"

"No, you've reminded me often enough." He held her gaze. "Invite me again, Kam, because I assure you I won't make that mistake a second time."

CHAPTER TWELVE

GABE'S CHALLENGE HAUNTED Kami for the remainder of her shift.

Even now as she gave report to the day-shift nurse taking her place, his voice echoed through her mind.

Inviting Gabe into her bed wouldn't change what would ultimately happen.

She couldn't fall into the same pit her mother willingly leaped into time and again. She was smarter than that.

Only, maybe she wasn't.

Because before she left the hospital, she yielded to her need to see Gabe and found him alone in the dictation room. When he looked up and her gaze met his, she saw the question in his eyes.

She didn't look away.

Couldn't look away.

She stared into his beautiful blue eyes and let herself be mesmerized, knowing she was about to change everything between them.

Who was she kidding? Everything was already changed between them. She might have been denying it, but they'd been in a relationship for weeks.

She was tired of denying that truth. Reality was, she was a woman. A woman with needs and wants and hopes and desires.

A woman who wanted Gabe more than she'd ever wanted anyone.

Scary, but also exciting.

Cocking her hip to the side, she gave what she hoped would pass for a seductive look.

"You're invited. Don't make the mistake of disappointing me a second time."

Gabe had been waiting for this moment for weeks. Longer. Now that he was here, in Kami's bedroom, he wasn't going to rush.

At least, he was going to do his best not to rush.

What he really wanted was to rip off her scrubs and taste every inch of her.

But part of him was enjoying letting her set the tone of what was happening.

Another part of him was still stunned that he was here, that Kami had invited him to her apartment, that she was taking this step. With him.

He wasn't a fool. He knew what being with her meant.

Finally, Kami realized how much she meant to him, was embracing what was between them.

Anticipation building, he'd followed her home from the hospital, parked next to her car, stood next to her while she unlocked her door, then followed her to her bedroom.

Calm, controlled, as if his insides weren't shaking in eagerness of finally making love to her.

Now he waited to see what was next with this lovely woman who monopolized his every thought.

Similar to his own bedroom designed for daytime sleeping, her window shades were drawn, leaving the room dark despite the morning sunshine.

Rather than raise the heavy shade, she flipped on a lamp, casting a low light around the room.

Pillows. Lots and lots of pillows registered first.

Then yellow. A pale yellow, the color of moonlight. And grays.

There was only one photo in the room and he didn't catch sight of who it was because the moment his gaze landed on it on the bedside table, she turned the frame face down.

"This wasn't preplanned, so I don't have protection." She shrugged a little self-consciously. "I am on the pill, though. I just kept taking it even after Baxter and I broke things off."

Gabe didn't like the thought of her with Baxter or any other man, but the past didn't matter. What mattered was that she was here, with him, and that she was finally accepting that they had a future together.

"I have protection."

She nodded, as if she'd thought he might.

Rather than say anything more, she lifted her hair from her nape. At first Gabe just stared, then realized she was waiting for him to undress her.

With hands that trembled from the significance of what was happening, he slowly pulled up her scrub top and the T-shirt beneath it, revealing her creamy flesh as he lifted the material over her head.

He intentionally kept his fingers from touching her skin, but did his best to take it slow, to savor every second of this moment he'd wanted for so long. One touch and he would be a goner.

He was already a goner.

Unable to resist, he slid his fingers inside her waistband and pulled down her scrub bottoms, placing a soft kiss on each thigh as he did so.

Her flesh goose bumped and her fingers went into his hair.

His knees almost buckled.

Yet he still had to pause, look up at her and ask, "You're sure this is what you want?"

"If you leave me now, I'll never forgive you." Kami wanted this.

Wanted him.

If he changed his mind, she really might curl up and cry.

She wanted her phenomenal sex experience even when she knew she'd pay the price later. She'd decided the price was worth what she'd get in return: Gabe. For however long they lasted, Gabe would be hers. Her friend and her lover.

"I'm not going anywhere," he assured her.

Kami trembled as his fingertips brushed over her skin. Wearing only her bra and matching panties, she stepped out of her scrub pants, waiting on his next touch.

She wasn't disappointed.

Gabe kissed her knees. Soft, delicate kisses. Then he stood and kissed her neck as his palms trailed down her shoulders, her arms.

Taking her hand, he stepped back and took her in. His eyes deepened to a dark blue as his gaze skimmed over her from head to toe.

"Mercy."

A smile spread across her face. She didn't have to ask if he liked what he saw. She saw it on his face, felt it in his touch, in his kiss, as he possessed her mouth in a blistering kiss. Gabe really did want her as much as she wanted him.

She wanted to touch him, to see him; her hands found

their way to his waistband and tugged his shirt free, but he stopped her by taking her hands into his.

"No." She pulled her hands free.

Surprise darkened his eyes.

"You aren't going to deny me touching you back," she told him, not willing to be a passive participant in what was happening. "I get to touch, too."

Rather than argue, he took her hands and placed them back at his waistband and helped her undress him. "I'm all yours."

She wished.

Which scared her.

But now wasn't the time for such thoughts. Now was time for enjoying the here and now because what was happening would be fleeting.

She planned to enjoy it.

Every touch of her hands over his body. Every touch of his hands over hers.

His lips, his mouth tasting.

Hers replying in kind.

"Gabe," she moaned as he pushed her back on the bed and tossed a half-dozen pillows to the floor.

He stared down at her as he donned protection, then joined her on the bed, his body poised over hers.

His eyes were dark, turbulent. "I've wanted this for so long."

"Me, too," she admitted, knowing the time for denials had long passed. "I want you, Gabe." She gripped his shoulders, lifted her hips to push against him, ready for everything his eyes, his body, promised. "I want you now."

"Kami," he groaned, shifting his hips to join their bodies.

She kept her eyes locked with his as he stretched her

body to accommodate him, as his hips rocked against her, creating a rhythm that melted her insides into a hot, quivery mess.

Until she exploded beneath him and had to hold on to keep from shattering into a million pieces.

Then he did it all over again.

Blown away, Kami stared at the ceiling, tracing patterns in the tiles as she caught her breath.

Ha. She'd never catch her breath. Not after what she'd just experienced.

She'd never be the same.

Not her body, her mind, or her heart.

She turned to look at Gabe, to see if he was as affected as she was. Instead, her gaze landed on the face-down photograph.

A photo of her and her mother that had been taken at her nursing school pinning.

A day on which she'd felt empowered because she'd checked off another important step in her life. Graduate from college with honors.

Her next big life goal had been to get her dream job. Most nights, she believed she'd checked that one off, too.

Up next was buy a house—a goal she'd been saving for from her very first paycheck.

Because, as much as she loved her, she didn't want to be like her mother.

She didn't want to get so caught up in a man to the exclusion of all else and make bad decision after bad decision.

Taking her hand into his, Gabe gave her a little squeeze, drawing her attention to where he lay next to her.

"You have to go."

Okay, so her voice had sounded strained, but surely

that could be chalked up to the vigorous activities she'd just engaged in.

With Gabe.

Sex with Gabe was a marathon. A marathon with orgasms around every bend. Who knew? Who knew her body could have such a meltdown of pleasure? Could shatter into a million pieces and yet still be whole?

She'd had sex with Baxter, with Kent. Pleasant enough, but no meltdowns. How did one live without meltdowns once one had experienced them?

How was she going to live without Gabe now that she'd experienced him?

"You want me to leave?" He rolled onto his side and stared at her. Confusion shone in his blue eyes. "Why?"

"Because *I* can't. *I* live here."

"I'm not leaving you, Kam. Not after what we just shared."

"This is my apartment," she reminded him, surprised that he wasn't leaping at the out she'd given him.

"You're overthinking, going back into that shell you hide behind. What we just shared was amazing. I know you felt it, too. So, again, I ask, why are you telling me to go?"

Kami closed her eyes. "Because you will leave, Gabe. It's what you do. What men do."

She waited, waited for him to say whatever he was going to say, but only silence met her ears. Slowly, she opened her eyes, looked into his.

His brows furrowed. "You dumped Baxter. I know you did. He told me himself one day at the gym."

He'd talked to Baxter about her at the gym?

"And that Kent guy, too," he continued. "I don't know about the men in your life beyond that, but I do know that the two guys you've dated since I've known you didn't leave you. You left them."

"What does that have to do with this?"

"Because this is about you. Not me. You're the one who always leaves in your relationships. The one telling me to leave now. Why is that?"

What he said hit her hard.

"What?" She scooted up in the bed and glared at him. "You want me to wait a couple of months? Wait until you get bored, then you'll leave? Is that it? You have to be the one to make that call?"

He stared at her as if she'd grown two heads, then calmly reminded her, "A very smart woman once pointed out to me that if she ever gave me a chance it wouldn't be me who left. Perhaps she's forgotten that, but I haven't."

How dared he quote her to herself?

"Yeah, well, she was bluffing because you were so full of yourself and needed to be taken down a peg or two."

He studied her. "Is that what this is about?"

"No," she denied, shaking her head and feeling very exposed. She flipped the comforter up, covering her vital parts, yet still felt vulnerable. Reaching over, she grabbed one of the few throw pillows still on the bed and hugged it to her.

"Then what?" he pushed.

Why couldn't he have just said okay and left? Why did he have to question everything? Make her question everything?

She didn't want to admit the truth.

She didn't like the truth, didn't like how naked she felt.

"I don't want to be like all the others, Gabe. Nor do I want to admit any of this to you." She hugged the pillow tighter to her chest. "If you leave me and I care, it makes me...weak."

He scooted up beside her, took her hand in his, and studied their interlocking fingers. "You're the strongest woman I know."

Fighting the emotions threatening to overwhelm her, she shook her head. "I'm not strong."

"Because you're with me?"

She didn't answer.

"Kam, I don't want to leave you. Not now or this afternoon or even tonight. But at some point, I will go home. What I don't want to happen is for you to question how I feel. Nothing has changed."

She scowled at him.

"Okay, so some things have changed. Obviously. But not how I feel about you."

"Which is what?"

She waited for him to answer, curious as to what he'd say. Would he feed her a bunch of crock?

"I care about you."

His voice was too sincere to be crock and she heard herself admit, "I care about you, too."

He lifted her hand, kissed it. "That's a pretty good start, I'd say."

Her insides trembled at what was happening between them. "A good start to what?"

"That's what time will tell us. For now, I'm not leaving because I plan to sleep with you in my arms and make love to you again this afternoon."

"You're quiet this morning."

Turning to look at Gabe in the driver seat of his car, Kami forced a smile. What could she say? Over the past twenty-four hours, the man had made her smile. A lot.

"You were there," she reminded him. "The ER was swamped last night."

Looking unfazed, he nodded. "It did get a bit crazy for a while. So crazy, in fact, that I failed to execute my plan to woo you into the supply room for a kiss or two."

Kami's eyes widened. She wouldn't have put up much resistance had he done any wooing. "There's always tonight."

He laughed. "Want to swing by and get breakfast before we go to your place? I don't think either one of us took time for a break and I can't have you weak from starvation."

She was hungry.

"Breakfast sounds great." An idea hit her. "Pancakes, please. Wherever you got those the morning you first showed at my place."

The corner of his mouth twitched. "Whipped cream and cherries?"

"That's the one."

"You going to show me?"

Although Gabe had no doubt that Kami knew exactly what he referred to, she played innocent. If you could call her toying with the long-stemmed cherry innocent.

"Show you what?"

"I think it's time."

She sighed, put the cherry in her mouth, then, a few seconds later, pulled a de-cherried knotted stem from between her lips.

Gabe grinned. "Such a talented tongue."

"You should know."

Oh, he knew.

"You might need to show me again."

She glanced down at the remaining cherry on her plate. "If you insist."

Eyes locked with hers, he laughed. "I didn't mean tying knots. Although that might be an interesting twist."

Her eyes widened. "Oh."

"Yeah, oh."

She pushed her plate away. "Think we can get an order of these to go?"

Gabe brushed stray hairs away from Kami's face. "I'm crazy about you."

Wondering where his comment had come from, Kami smiled up at him. "You are pretty crazy," she teased, turning her head to where her lips brushed against his fingers so she could press a kiss there. "For the record, I'm rather fond of you, too."

She'd expected him to grin or to say something silly back. He didn't, just stared down at her with a look in his eyes she couldn't quite read.

The longer he stared, the more unease filled her and she found herself babbling just to be saying something.

"I have an appointment with a Realtor next week." Now, why had she told him that?

"You moving?"

"Maybe." She shrugged. "I've been saving for a while so I could put a down payment on my own place and I've finally reached my minimum-down-payment goal. I'm not in a rush, but I don't want to miss it when the right place comes along. I'm meeting with the Realtor so she knows exactly what I'm looking for and can be on the lookout."

Propping himself on his elbow, Gabe regarded her. "What is it you're looking for, Kami?"

"In my dream world or what I'll most likely end up with?" She gave a little laugh. "I dream of a place of my own, not too far from the hospital, but far enough out that I can have a decent-sized yard. A yard with trees," she added. She'd never lived in a house with trees before. Just apartment complexes with a few decorative trees in front occasionally. "And I think I'd like a pet."

His brows rose. "A pet?"

She nodded. "I've never had a pet."

"Never?"

She shook her head. "We moved a lot while I was growing up. Most of the places we lived didn't allow pets, so it was easier not to have one, even when we lived at the few places where we could."

Odd that her mother had Bubbles now. Kami remembered many a time begging her mother to keep some stray she'd found and brought home. Her mother hadn't once even considered letting her, demanding Kami get rid of the animal and not dare bring it into their home.

"What about you? Did you have pets growing up?"

"A few. Dogs mostly, but a few cats along the way, too. My mother liked a full house."

"Sounds heavenly."

"It wasn't really. Mainly, she just liked a lot of things to keep her distracted from thinking about my father."

"She must have missed him a great deal."

Gabe sucked in a deep breath and waited so long to answer that Kami didn't think he was going to. Then he said, "She did. We both did. For years I had nightmares about him dying."

"Oh, Gabe."

"I watched him die, Kam." Gabe wondered why he was still talking, why he was admitting the horrible truth to her. "I watched him take that last breath and didn't do a thing."

"You were eight years old. What were you supposed to do?"

"Logically, I know you're right, but it took me a long time to accept that."

She hugged him. "I'm sorry, Gabe."

"It was a long time ago." So long ago, he wondered why he'd been thinking of his father so much over the past few weeks. Why he'd had to tell her that day at the park. Then again, after working the code the other day, no wonder thoughts of his father had haunted him.

"At least you were old enough to remember him."

What would she think if he admitted that he'd likely be better off if he'd been young enough not to recall? Gabe closed his eyes. No, not true. Because prior to the heart attack that had claimed his father's life, Gabe's memories of the man he'd helplessly watched die had all been good.

"What about you?" He changed the subject. "You talk about your mother, but never a word about dear old dad."

Kami snorted. "My father was just some guy who came in and out of my mother's life. Not anyone special or amazing. Just another in a long string of failed relationships."

"That's sad. Tell me she found happiness eventually."

"Oh, she finds happiness a lot. He just never sticks around."

Gabe rolled over, took Kami's hand into his, and stared up at the ceiling. "Guess that's why you're so adamant that men don't stick around even when you have no personal basis for thinking that way."

Kami pulled her hand free. "No personal basis for thinking that way? Did you not just hear everything I said? Every man who came into my mother's life used her, then left. That's a pretty strong personal basis for thinking that men don't stick around."

"Not all men are like that, Kami."

"I didn't say they were."

"I'm not like that."

Kami didn't comment. Next to her, Gabe sighed, then, after a brief silence, lifted her hand and pressed a kiss to her fingertips. "Good luck with the Realtor next week. If you want someone to go with you to look at houses, I'm your guy."

"Unless she just has something perfect, I won't start looking until after the fund-raiser."

"Makes sense." He closed his eyes; his breathing evened.

"Guess we'd better get a little shut-eye before having to be back at the hospital tonight." She leaned over, kissed his cheek. "Sweet dreams, Gabe."

"Unfortunately, I'm going to have to take a pass this morning," Kami told Gabe at shift change a few mornings later.

Gabe glanced up from the computer where he made notes regarding a patient, his expression concerned. "What's up?"

"My mother."

His eyes darkened. "Something wrong?"

Kami shrugged. Where did she begin to explain about her mother's frantic phone call? A call during which her mother had been crying so profusely she'd barely been able to understand her pleas for Kami to come to her apartment.

"Let me finish here and I'll go with you."

Kami shook her head. The last thing she wanted was for Gabe to meet her mother. Especially as her mother was already so upset. Kami hadn't asked over the phone, but past experience told her what the problem would be.

"Sorry, but now isn't the time for you to meet my mother." She gave a look she hoped conveyed she'd much rather spend the morning with him and didn't reveal that she didn't expect him to ever meet her mother. Her heart squeezed and she fought back the panic that rose in her chest, reminding herself that it was the call from her mother making her antsy, not Gabe. She forced a smile. "I'd say to call me when you wake up, but, truth is, who knows what time I'll even get to go to sleep?"

"Then you call me when you wake up. We'll go somewhere for dinner."

Leaning against the doorjamb of the small physician's area, she eyed him and smiled for real. "Sounds perfect."

When she got to her mother's, Kami found her mom was a bumbling mess, as was the apartment. How someone could accumulate so much trash in the short amount of time since Kami had cleaned the apartment, she couldn't fathom. The place was a wreck, stank of the stench of the cat litter box and old food.

Ugh.

"Where's Don?" she guessed. Although was it really a guess when she had years of experience of seeing her mother all to pieces over whichever guy had just walked out on her?

"Gone."

Kami sighed and stared at the woman who'd raised her; the woman who fell in love at the drop of a hat and left herself vulnerable to any Tom, Dick, or Harry. Or in this case, Don.

How was it her mother continued to put herself out there after all these years? Didn't she ever learn to protect her heart?

"He didn't deserve you," she offered, trying to comfort her mother. How did one comfort a woman who'd been through more men than stars in the sky? When none of them had ever stuck around and most had taken everything they could and then some from the pitiful woman hunched over on the sofa with her cat cradled in her arms?

Why did her mother keep diving into relationships with her heart wide open?

Amid another big tearful bout, her mother cried, "That doesn't stop me from giving my heart."

Frustrated at her mother's reaction to the man leaving when surely she'd expected it, Kami reminded her, "Mom, you hardly dated Don for any time at all."

"What does time have to do with anything? I loved him."

Hardly any time at all. That's how long you have been "dating" Gabe. What if it was her who'd been dumped? Would she feel any different than her mom?

Of course she would. Unlike her mother, she knew Gabe would leave. For some reason, her mother believed Don, and all the others, was actually going to stick around.

Kami sighed, moved closer. "I'm sorry. It's just that he didn't seem so different from any of the others."

Her mother blew her nose. "Maybe not to you."

True. To her, he hadn't.

"To me, he was the one."

"You think that with every man you date."

Her mother looked up at her with sad eyes. "Is it so wrong to believe that I'm lovable? That this man is finally the one who will love me back and won't do me wrong? Just because you've never been in love and don't know how it feels, don't you judge me."

Kami opened her mouth to correct her mother, to say she had been in love, that she *was* in love, then, stunned, bit her tongue, instead.

Shaken to her very core, she tried to comfort her mother the best she could.

Finally, her mother drifted off to sleep. Unable to walk away from the messy apartment, Kami emptied the litter box, picked up the trash, then sat in the chair opposite the sofa where her mother slept.

Bubbles jumped up into Kami's lap for some attention, purring in pleasure when she got it.

"I don't love him," Kami told the cat. "Well, as a friend, but I'm not in love with him."

Bubbles ignored her and circled back around for another head-to-tip-of-tail stroke.

"But if I'm not careful that's what's going to happen."

Her gaze focused on her pitiful mother, who had nothing in life because she'd given away what little she had to useless men.

For the rest of the morning, Kami's insides felt rattled.

That would be her. Someday soon. How much longer until Gabe lost interest? Until he moved on to someone new and left her brokenhearted like her mother?

Kami slept a little but was restless and finally got up to run errands and catch up on her laundry, all the while battling the demons in her head.

That night, when Gabe called, she apologized for not calling, begged off dinner, stating she'd not slept much and really just wanted to go to bed and catch up on her sleep.

When he called first thing the following morning, she declined breakfast under the guise that she'd fallen behind with her cleaning.

To keep her mind occupied, she pulled everything from her closet and began sorting through the items, culling out things she never wore and straightening favorites.

The knock at her apartment door startled her, but the person on the other side of the door wasn't really a surprise.

"Gabe," she said as she opened the door and stared at the smiling man. "What are you doing here?"

"Two sets of hands are better than one."

She eyed him suspiciously. "You're going to help me sort my closet?"

He gave a suspicious look of his own. "If that's what you're doing."

"See for yourself." Grateful she'd dug out a ton of stuff, she led him to her bedroom.

He eyed the stack of clothes on her bed, then turned to her with a dubious look. "Maybe I can give a thumbs up or thumbs down while you try those on."

Kami suppressed a laugh. "Sorry. You're too late. That's the bye-bye stack I'm donating to charity."

"Want me to load them into your car?"

She shrugged. "I can do it later."

"Or I could do it now and you wouldn't have to."

He had a point. "Fine."

While Gabe loaded the stack into her car, she stored the keep items back into her closet, and was waiting in the living room when he came back into the apartment.

"What next?"

She shook her head. "Nothing. I'll finish up later."

"I didn't mean to interfere with what you were doing. I wanted to help."

"You did. Thank you for carrying the load to my car."

He studied her a moment. "Everything okay?"

"Fine."

Not looking convinced, he eyed her. "That's what you said on the phone, too. So why don't I believe you?"

She shrugged but had to glance away.

He sighed. "You're never going to trust me, are you?"

She lifted her gaze to his. "What do you mean?"

"No matter how long we're together, you're always going to be waiting for me to leave just like all those guys did to your mom."

She shrugged. "It's what men do."

Staring at her for a long moment, he nodded. "I can't deny that it's what I've done in the past."

"And what you'll do in the future."

He didn't deny her claim, just sank onto the sofa and looked defeated.

"I knew something wasn't right when you canceled dinner. I thought something had happened at your mother's, so I stayed away last night. But it's just this same old thing, isn't it? You not trusting in me, in us."

She didn't answer. Something had happened at her mother's but she wasn't telling him that.

"Kami, the past couple of weeks have been wonderful."

They had.

"But, even after everything we've shared, you don't trust me any more than you did that first morning."

Going on the defensive, Kami lifted her chin. "Don't pretend you plan to stick around, Gabe. We both know that isn't your style."

He studied her. "Is that what you want me to say? That I'm never going to leave you? Would you believe me if I did tell you?"

Pain shot through her at what she saw in his eyes. This was it. What she'd been dreading.

She shook her head in denial.

"I didn't think so." He raked his fingers through his hair. "I care about you, Kami. If you haven't figured that out by now, then you're never going to."

Was this how he did it? Tried to convince women that it was their fault that he was leaving?

Heart breaking, she crossed her arms.

Face gaunt, he added, "I came here because I wanted to be with you. Too bad you can't believe that."

He got up and walked out of her apartment, quietly closing the door behind him.

CHAPTER THIRTEEN

"I HEARD A dirty rumor that you and Gabe had broken up."

Kami shrugged without looking at her best friend. She was at the hospital to work, not gossip about her nonexistent love life.

"This is the part where you tell me I shouldn't believe dirty rumors," her friend persisted.

"That particular rumor is true."

Mindy slapped her hand against her forehead. "What happened?"

"Nothing."

"Couples don't break up over nothing." Mindy frowned. "Did you have a fight?"

"Not really." How could she explain to Mindy what she didn't want to acknowledge? What was easier to ignore? "It was just time for us to end."

"Kami, you and Gabe are perfect together. Why would things ever end?"

"Because that's what he does."

Mindy looked taken aback. "He broke things off with you?"

"Yes. No. I think so." She thought back over their conversation for the millionth time. "He left. He hasn't called or texted." She shrugged and kept her voice monotone. "So, yeah, he broke things off."

"You don't sound too upset."

Was that what her friend thought? Tears didn't change anything. She would not cry at work. Would not break down. Would not carry on as her mother did.

She refused.

"I knew before we started that we weren't going to last."

"Because you wouldn't let it."

Mindy's staunch defense of Gabe irritated Kami.

"Why do you always take his side? You're supposed to be my friend."

Mindy put her hands on her hips. "I am. Which is why I'm pointing out that you refused to give this relationship a chance."

"Where have you been? I gave this relationship all I had to give."

"Not your heart."

"I gave him all I had to give," she repeated. "It's not my fault that all I had wasn't enough."

She spun to walk away and almost collided with Gabe. A red-faced Gabe.

"We need to talk."

"I can't. We're at work."

Gabe glanced at Mindy.

"I'll come get you if I need either of you," Mindy assured them.

His grasp on her arm firm, but not painful, Gabe marched Kami to the tiny dictation room and shut the door behind them.

"All you had wasn't enough? Seriously? That's what you think?"

"You shouldn't have been eavesdropping on my conversation."

"You shouldn't have been talking about me if you didn't want me to overhear."

"This is ridiculous. We have nothing to say to each other."

"Wrong." He put his hand on the door, preventing her from being able to open it. "We have a lot to say to each other. Perhaps this isn't the best place to say it, but hell if I'm going to just let you walk away without explaining your comment."

"I don't have to explain myself to you. I owe you nothing and you can't make me stay."

Her words hit their target and seemed to deflate him. His hand fell away from the door.

"You're right. I can't keep you here."

Kami reached for the door.

"But you're wrong, Kami."

She hesitated.

"All you had was enough. The problem was—*is*," he corrected, "that you never gave all you had. Not even close. Maybe it was me who wasn't enough."

The rest of the night passed in a blur. They had a couple of wrecks come in, several upper respiratory infections, an overdose, and a chest pain.

Kami worked side by side with Gabe, pretending that there was nothing between them.

Pretending that her heart wasn't breaking.

Pretending she hadn't lost something, *someone*, special.

"Oh, Kami! We got the call."

At Beverly's breathy, nervous tone, Kami didn't have to ask which call that was. A heart had been located for Lindsey.

Even as excitement filled her for her friend, she felt a stab of pain for the family who'd donated the heart.

"When?"

"The transplant team is prepping her for surgery now.

I'm so scared and can't believe this is happening," her co-worker gushed over the phone line. "Gregg and I wanted you to know that she's going into surgery."

Kami glanced at her fitness watch. She'd had a half-dozen things on her to-do list for the day, most of them picking up donations for the fund-raiser, but none of them mattered in light of what was happening in the Smiths' lives. She could pick up the items later.

"I'll be there."

"The surgery is going to take hours and hours. I don't expect you to sit here with us. I just wanted you to know Lindsey is getting a new heart. You did so much for my family and we love you."

Kami's chest squeezed. "I want to be there. See you soon."

Gabe winced when the first person he saw in the transplant family waiting room was Kami.

He should have known she'd be here.

Of course she would.

If Beverly had called him, she'd certainly called Kami.

He'd been out with friends on the lake when the call had come and, after they'd returned from their water-skiing trip, he'd showered, then headed to the hospital.

Several hours had passed, but Lindsey was still in surgery and would be for some time.

Kami averted her gaze.

Anger and frustration filled Gabe. Anger that she'd not given them a fair shot.

If she couldn't freely care for him, they were just wasting their time.

Ignoring Kami, he went to Beverly, hugged her, then shook Gregg's hand. He chatted with them for several minutes, then joined the others in the waiting game.

As luck would have it, the only empty chair in the small, crowded private waiting area was next to Kami.

He'd almost rather stand than take it, but to do so for who knew how long was ridiculous.

With a nod of acknowledgment her way, he sat and pulled out his phone, skimming through his text messages.

Five, then ten, then fifteen awkward minutes went by, during which he was acutely aware of how near she was, of how much he missed her.

But she'd made her choice. Her choice wasn't to open herself up to him, wasn't to give them a chance, to trust in what was between them.

Maybe he didn't even blame her. Lord knew he had enough issues of his own without digging into hers.

On the Friday night before the fund-raiser event, volunteers had worked hard finishing the baskets and organizing the donated items. As he'd promised, Gabe came, helped, and made several of them laugh when he finally got his ribbon to curl just right after several failed attempts.

Not that Kami laughed.

Or even looked his way, but he refused to let that dampen his spirit.

Over a week had passed since Lindsey's heart transplant. The first few days were the most critical, but Lindsey had gotten through them with flying colors. She still had a long road ahead, but the tiny baby was holding her own.

When they'd finished the last basket and had each auction item to be listed, labeled, and numbered, Kami thanked them all for their dedication to their friend and her family.

"Well, I don't know about everyone else, but I'm parched. Anyone up for drinks?"

Kami's gaze narrowed and he realized how she might take his comment. Too bad. He wasn't going to walk on eggshells just because she'd bailed on their relationship.

"Unwinding for a while before the big event sounds perfect." Mindy spoke up. "Hope that's okay with you, Kami, since you rode here with me. We won't stay late, I promise."

Kami looked as if she wanted to argue, but when all the other volunteers said they were going, she just nodded.

Gabe and Kami ended up next to each other in a large round booth with their friends bookending them on each side.

No one commented on the sitting order, but Gabe doubted it had been accidental. Although few of their friends had commented on their personal relationship, or recent lack thereof, they all knew something had transpired between him and Kami; knew and were obviously playing matchmaker by trying to throw them together.

Good luck with that.

Kami ordered water and Gabe ended up doing the same.

She didn't speak directly to him, but conversation was going on all around them.

The chatter was loud, fun and varied from the fundraiser to an upcoming marathon several of them were running. There were lots of laughs.

Except nothing felt right.

Not to Gabe.

He needed to forget her and move on. Fine, he could do that. He would do that.

He turned and started talking to Eddie, the paramedic

who'd volunteered with them, asking if he'd caught any of the Stanley Cup playoff game the night before.

Fortunately he had and they launched into a discussion regarding their winner predictions.

Saturday morning, the day of the fund-raiser dawned bright and early. Kami leaped out of bed and rushed about, getting her day started. It was going to be a long day, but a good one.

At least, she hoped so. What they had raised from selling raffle tickets and dinner tickets would more than pay for the few expenses for the event and would be a nice addition to the Smiths' funds. Hopefully, before the night was over the coffer would be overflowing and they wouldn't have to worry about how to pay the bills for months to come so they could focus on Lindsey.

Kami, Gabe, and a handful of other volunteers moved the baskets and donated items from the hospital conference room to the convention center where the event was being held.

When they got there, Mindy and other volunteers were setting up the tables.

"Here, let me get that for you," Gabe offered when Kami went for a particularly heavy basket.

"Thanks." She stepped aside and let him effortlessly grab the basket and head into the building.

She watched him go and was filled with such frustration she wanted to scream. Frustration at him. At herself. At the whole world.

Frustration that had interfered with her sleep and had her edgy as she'd dreamed of stomping his toes under the table and demanding he talk with her the night before. He'd totally humiliated her, turning his back to her and publicly shunning her in front of their friends.

Then today, he showed up and was all nice. What was with him, anyway?

Not that it mattered. It was just as well that he'd turned his back. Maybe their friends would take a hint and quit with the cupid.

When the fund-raiser was over and she didn't have that worry hanging over her, she'd go back to feeling like her old self. Not this uptight, frustrated, on-edge woman who couldn't stop overanalyzing everything that happened.

Sighing, she grabbed a lighter basket and followed him inside the hotel.

"Where do you want me to put this one?" he asked when she walked up beside where he stood in front of one of the display tables.

"All the items are numbered. We're going to auction them in numerical order to make it easier for the emcee and the recorders to keep up with what's what during the auction." She realized she hadn't really answered his question and he was still holding the basket.

"Here." She pointed to the right area on the display table. "It goes here."

Gabe set the basket in the appropriate spot, then turned back toward her. "Everything looks fantastic. You've done an amazing job."

"Mindy and the other volunteers have done most of the decorations and taken care of the food. I was in charge of donations and we won't really know until tonight how that went."

He gestured to the numerous items on display. "I'd say you did good."

"For the Smiths' sake, I sure hope so."

"Are they coming tonight?"

Look at them making small talk. Kami's heart hurt from the brevity of it. This was her friend whom she'd teased and laughed with on so many occasions, her lover who had wowed her time and again. Now carrying on a simple conversation that was nothing but a farce.

Not able to bring herself to look him in the eyes, she answered, "As long as there are no changes with Lindsey at the hospital, they plan to. She's doing great, but everything hinges on her, of course."

"Kami, where does this artwork go?" one of the volunteers asked, joining where they stood by the table.

"Somewhere around here is a display stand for that piece. We're going to put it at the end of one of the tables. It's the first item up for auction."

Gabe stuck his hands in his jeans pockets and shrugged. "Guess I'd better get back outside. There's still several things to be carried inside."

"I…uh… I'm going to help position the painting," Kami said needlessly since he hadn't waited on her response. He'd just walked away.

When they'd finished arranging everything on the tables and had double-checked to make sure everything was lined up numerically, Kami and her volunteers joined in on setting up the guest tables and their decorations.

When mid-afternoon rolled around, Kami glanced at her fitness watch and gave Gabe a pointed look.

"Don't you need to head home to shower? We need you looking good so you'll bring top dollar."

"You make him sound like a piece of prized meat," Mindy accused, having overheard Kami's comment.

"What about you?" he asked. "Won't you and Mindy need to be heading out to clean up, as well?"

"I'm heading out in the next five," Mindy said, then winced. "Except the band's not arrived yet to set up their equipment and I promised I'd wait around so they could."

"I'll wait until they get here," Kami offered. "I'm planning to stay until the rescue squad arrives anyway. They had some last-minute donations to be auctioned off tonight and I'll need to get them labeled and on the recorder's list."

Mindy offered to stay, but Kami declined. "Go," she ordered Mindy. "Just get back as soon as you can in case I'm still here."

Her friend gave her a quick hug and promised to do just that.

Kami turned to Gabe, who was still standing next to her. He looked so good her heart hurt.

"You should go, too," she told him, keeping her voice light. "It's going to be time to get started before you know it."

He hesitated, then nodded. "You're right. The night of the big auction."

"I really do appreciate all you've done."

His gaze met hers. He raked his fingers through his hair, took a step toward her. "Kami, I…"

She wasn't sure what he'd planned to say as at that moment a long-haired kid twirling a drumstick came walking into the ballroom and asked if this was the Smith party.

She stared up at Gabe, wondering what he'd been going to say, wondering what, if anything, words could change.

"Looks like the band is here." Not what he'd been going to say, but whatever had been on the tip of his tongue was gone. She could see it in the way his expression had hardened.

"Looks like it." She waved at the guy who'd been joined by a few others. "Over this way."

When she finished showing them where to set up, she glanced around the room and noted that Gabe had left.

Good. He had to be back soon.

So that he could be auctioned off to the highest bidder, because she'd asked him to.

Not just because of that, she assured herself. He wanted to help the Smiths.

She understood. She wanted this night to be all it could be, for as much money to be raised as possible to help the sweet family.

She'd hoped to make it home in time from the setup to leisurely get ready for the big event.

No such luck.

Still, she got a quick shower, styled her hair, and put on more makeup than she usually wore, so she figured she was doing well.

When she got to the convention center and saw Gabe already there, looking like a zillion dollars in his tuxedo, her breath caught. Right or wrong considering the state of their relationship, she wanted Gabe to think she looked good, too. For him to look at her and feel the same *vavoom* her lungs had undergone when she'd caught sight of him.

Was that why she'd donned a splashy short dress that showed off her legs? She'd be on her feet too long for heels, but her comfy sparkly slip-ons weren't bad. Either way, she was showing leg.

Gabe had said he liked her legs.

Only, when he turned her way, caught her watching him, his gaze didn't drop to her legs. His pale blue eyes locked with hers for a brief moment, and then he averted his gaze.

Because he was no longer interested in her legs. Or anything about her.

Kami couldn't avoid Gabe all night, and it wasn't long before she got drawn into a conversation with the volunteer running the sound system.

The volunteer he'd been talking to gushed for a few minutes, then was called over to double-check the equipment.

Which left Kami alone with Gabe.

He glanced around the room. "Everything looks great."

Ah, there went the small talk.

She responded with more small talk. "There have been dozens of volunteers. Everyone has worked hard."

"True, but without you and Mindy putting it together, I doubt tonight would be happening, so, again, great job."

"Sometimes it just takes someone getting a project started to have lots of volunteers jumping in. Certainly, this is one of those cases where we've been blessed by so many helping out from the hospital and from the community." A blonde in a flashy red dress stepped into Kami's periphery. "Speaking of volunteers from the community…"

Gabe turned, frowned a little. "Let me brace myself."

"I don't know why you say such things. She seems nice."

"She is."

Kami started to say more, but instead smiled as the television hostess descended upon them.

"Everything looks perfect," Debbie praised. "My cameraman and I are going to do a few commentary pieces as everyone arrives."

Kami nodded. "We really appreciate all you're doing to help the Smiths."

"When we run the piece on tonight's news, there should be more money raised via the online donation page. Especially with the shots we have of that adorable baby girl." Debbie gave a heartfelt sigh. "Seriously ill babies pull on people's heartstrings and make for great stories."

Kami would take the woman's word for it on the great story part as she didn't find anything great about her co-worker's baby having been born with a defective heart. Thank goodness a match had been found, the transplant had been a success so far, and Lindsey was getting stronger every day.

"If you'll excuse me, I need to make sure everything is going smoothly with the food preparation." Kami was pretty sure she had made the woman's night by leaving her and Gabe alone.

Good. More power to them. Kami didn't care.

Much.

Fortunately, everything was going smoothly. The volunteers from the rescue squad and the fire department were ready to serve the five hundred guests who'd bought meal tickets.

"Do you feel as crazy as I do?" Mindy gushed as she came up and hugged Kami.

"Crazier. Thanks for letting me sneak away long enough to get cleaned up."

"Cleaned up? Girl, you did more than that." Mindy gave her an up and down. "You look great."

Kami's cheeks heated at her friend's praise. "Thank you. I feel a lot more presentable than when I headed out of here earlier, for sure."

A feminine laugh rang across the room. Both Kami and Mindy turned toward where Debbie chatted with Gabe.

"Please tell me you're all dolled up for him."

"I wouldn't hold your breath."

Mindy eyed Debbie with Gabe, and her nose crinkled. "Surely, you aren't going to let her win him."

Kami fought to keep an I-don't-care expression. "It's an auction for a single day's date. What he does beyond that is up to him."

She eyed how the hostess brushed an imaginary speck off Gabe's tuxedo jacket. An excuse to touch him, no doubt.

She'd touched him, had her arms around those shoulders while he held her close when they'd danced, when they'd kissed, when they'd made love.

Mindy sighed. "Just seems such a shame for you to let this opportunity pass you by."

"What opportunity is that?"

"To win Gabe back."

"As if I'd buy a date to try to win him back," Kami scoffed. Buying a man was even worse than the things her mother did.

"Your loss." Looking disappointed, Mindy shrugged. "Maybe you'll get lucky and Debbie won't win him back, but I think you're a fool to risk it. That woman has talons she's dying to hook into him."

Kami's gaze cut to the couple. Despite his woe-is-me antics, Gabe didn't appear to be in any hurry to get away from his beautiful ex.

Quite the opposite.

No, she wasn't jealous. Kami rubbed her pounding temple. She wasn't jealous. Only…she averted her gaze from the couple and met Mindy's curious eyes. Rather than launch into another spiel about why she should bid on Gabe, Mindy just gave her a look of pity.

"What?"

Her friend sighed. "Whatever your reasons are for not hanging on to that man, I hope you don't live to regret that decision."

Glancing back toward where Debbie smiled up at Gabe, Kami agreed. Yeah, she hoped she didn't live to regret that decision, too, but for her long-term sanity and heart, she'd made the right choice.

Not that she'd really made the choice. He'd been the one to leave her apartment. He'd been the one to stop calling and texting. He'd been the one to step out of her life.

Why her friend acted as if it were all Kami's fault was beyond her. He'd left. Just as she'd always known he would. She'd let him, but he'd been the one to leave. End of story.

The dinner went off without a hitch and the band played while everyone ate. Both the food and the meal were a hit.

After the meal finished, the auctioneer relieved the band, taking command of the stage.

Time for the auction.

Prior to the date packages being auctioned off, the baskets and donations were being auctioned. One after another, prizes were sold.

Kami won a basket full of body, hair, and bath products donated by a local hair salon and felt quite proud of herself.

"Practicing?" a male voice whispered close to her ear.

Turning toward Gabe, she caught a whiff of his spicy

scent and fought inhaling and holding the scent of him inside her forever.

Her heart sped up at his nearness, at how his whisper in her ear toyed with her equilibrium. *He left you, remember?* her heart whispered. *Sure, you kind of pushed, but he left.*

Pulling herself together, she smiled. "You wish."

"I like that your sass is back."

She cut her gaze toward him, thinking a more handsome man had never lived. "It never left."

His dark brow rose. "Just wasn't pointed my way?" He scanned the room, spotted the television crew at a table near the front of the venue. "Pretty sure Debbie plans on picking out china with me in the near future."

"Poor Gabe. It's so hard to be you and have to fight off beautiful women."

Rather than smile back or make a quip, he turned, searched her eyes a moment, then said, "The only beautiful woman I'm interested in won't give me the time of day."

Kami's heart thundered in her chest. He shouldn't say such things, but her silly body responded full throttle that he had. Unbidden, her eyes closed. She wasn't sure she could deal with him making such comments, not when her heart ached so.

"Kami?"

Opening her eyes, she flashed her teeth at him in a semblance of a smile and glanced down at her fitness band. "It's almost eight."

Looking as if he'd seen more on her face than she'd have liked, he asked, "You going to bid?"

"Only in your dreams."

He studied her a moment, then softly said, "You'd be surprised what you do in my dreams."

Kami wanted to ask, wanted to know what he dreamed of her doing, but what would be the point? She was not going to act on anything Gabe said.

Been there, done that, and had a lost friendship and tearstained pillow to prove it.

CHAPTER FOURTEEN

THE NIGHT'S TAKE was going to be awesome even before Gabe's date came up for bid. Kami had been keeping a mental tally of what the different items and dates were going for and the Smiths must have been relieved.

She glanced toward the couple sitting at the front of the room. Despite the stress of the past few months, her friend was smiling and enjoying her evening with her husband.

That Lindsey was doing so well so quickly after her heart transplant went a long way in causing those smiles.

The emcee who was doubling as their auctioneer introduced the last package to be auctioned before Gabe's.

Gabe was next.

Kami's stomach knotted and she suddenly wished he'd never agreed to the auction, that she'd never asked him to take part in it.

Which was silly.

Several of the others had gone for four figures. His date would raise a nice amount for the Smiths.

She needed to shove aside her selfish thoughts. They'd had their time. He never went back to the same woman after he'd left her. He had left Kami. Sure, he'd given some spiel about her not opening herself up to him, not trusting him, but he'd been the one to walk.

She had opened herself up to him. She had. Only…

Her blood doing a jittery dance through her veins, Kami shook her head to clear her thoughts.

"Please tell me you're shaking your head in protest of what is about to happen."

Kami looked at Mindy. "What's that?"

"You blowing what might be your last chance with Gabe."

"He left me. That was our last chance."

"Seriously? Is that pride speaking, Kami? Because I don't understand how you could just let him leave without putting up a fight to hang on to him."

"Isn't that what started all of this? Him asking me to bid on him tonight to keep one of his exes from trying to hang on?"

"Are you really so blind?" Mindy asked, shaking her head. "Did you ever stop to think that it's not Debbie buying his date that ever concerned him? That it's wanting you to buy his date that's important to him? That all of this has been about you from the very beginning? Not his ex or any other woman."

No, Kami hadn't considered that. Nor did she believe it.

Gabe hadn't teased her about buying his date package because he'd been interested in her and wanted her to bid on him. He hadn't.

The current auction ended and the emcee told the crowd about Gabe's Gatlinburg Getaway.

The bid started at a thousand dollars and quickly rose five hundred dollars at a time as Debbie immediately countered every bid anyone else made.

The others being auctioned off had smiled and flirted with the crowd, encouraging more bidders. Kami had thought Gabe would work the stage, too, but he wasn't.

Then again, Gabe didn't need to do anything but stand and smile at the crowd.

It was good to be Gabe. To have women wanting you to the point of them thinking nothing of emptying their wallets for the opportunity to spend time with you.

Then again, she supposed it was the way of the world. Men emptied their wallets to impress women by taking them to fancy restaurants and driving fancier cars. Women emptied their wallets to buy the latest fashions and to try to preserve their youth.

Her mother had emptied her already rather pitiful wallet anytime a new guy came along, that was for sure. Even if it meant not being able to pay the rent or buy groceries.

How many times had they been kicked out of their home because they couldn't pay the rent—all down to her mother's foolish heart?

"Bid," Mindy stage-whispered.

Kami frowned. "Mind your own business."

"You're my best friend. Your happiness is my business. Fight for him. Let him know he matters, that your relationship matters, and that you want to date him."

"You have this all wrong, you know," she corrected her friend, her gaze going back and forth between the current bidders. "He doesn't really want to date me. He just wants…" Kami paused. What did Gabe want? To have sex with her again? Why? He could have sex anytime he wanted it. The room full of rabid wallet-wielding women was testament to that.

Mindy gave her a *duh* look. "Then why aren't you bidding?"

Kami's eyes widened. "You want me to have sex with him, knowing it won't last? That he's left me once and will leave me again? Knowing if I do this, he'll only end up hurting me? How is it that we're friends when you give such bad advice?"

Her heart was pounding so loudly it must be drowning out the emcee. She had life goals, and getting used by a man, even a man as fabulous as Gabe, wasn't on the list.

Only, what if he really had left because of her? Because she'd constantly been waiting for the ax to fall? What if she'd pushed him into doing exactly what she'd feared most?

She had done that.

"Bid, Kami. Do it now."

"Are you crazy? Or just deaf? The bid is way out of my budget." Financially and emotionally.

"He's worth it and you know it," Mindy prompted. "Bid now before it's too late. Blame me, if you must, but *bid*."

The stage lighting prevented Gabe from seeing where the bids were coming from, but it didn't matter. Debbie wasn't going to let anyone else win him. Even if a miracle happened and Kami had considered bidding, the bid was too high.

Who would have thought a day with him would go for so much?

Especially when he couldn't get the woman he'd wanted to spend that day with to admit she wanted him, to open her heart and trust in what was between them.

He'd thought… Never mind what he'd thought, what he'd wanted. It no longer mattered.

Kami wasn't willing to risk anything for their relationship. Instead, she'd kept up her defenses and in the end that had suffocated what was happening between them.

Perhaps he shouldn't have expected more. What made

him think he deserved more in life? That he should get to have what few attained?

Love.

It was what his parents had had prior to his father's death. What he'd wanted with Kami, but that kind of relationship took two working at it.

"Going once," the auctioneer said, working the crowd. "Going twice... Wait—we have a new bidder!"

Gabe couldn't see where the new bid had come from, but his belly did a flip-flop because he instinctively knew who the bidder was.

The crazy thumping in his chest told him.

Kami had just bid on his date package. Why would she do that? Guilt? Pity?

He didn't want either.

Well, hell, this was unexpected and left him not quite sure what to think.

"Yes!" Mindy squealed in Kami's ear and did a happy dance next to her. "Yes. Yes. Yes."

Kami ignored her friend's antics and kept her gaze trained on Gabe.

Because if she looked away she might wonder why she'd just raised her number and bid on his Gatlinburg Getaway.

She'd just bid a lot of money. So much, her stomach hurt.

Of course Debbie immediately countered her bid, looking around the room to try to spot who her new competition was. She looked bored, annoyed, but resilient. She planned to take Gabe's date package home.

She planned to take Gabe home.

"You in?"

Swallowing the lump in her throat, Kami nodded to

the auction volunteer who'd taken her initial bid and was waiting on her answer.

The man called her bid and the auctioneer ate it up that there was a new battle on.

Ha. Not much of a battle, she thought, as Debbie seemed to grow tired of the back-and-forth and raised the bid by a whopping four-figure amount.

Kami bit into her lower lip. What was she doing? Why?

"I'll toss in a few hundred," Mindy offered. "Bid again. Don't lose Gabe. This is important. You know it is."

Kami hadn't really seen this auction as winning or losing Gabe.

But suddenly it did feel that way.

That if she didn't win this bid she'd be losing him forever. That she'd never get another chance to show him he was important to her, that he mattered, that she regretted letting him walk away.

She had to risk this, had to put herself out there and bid. She didn't have time to analyze or to figure it out. The auctioneer was calling for another bid.

She couldn't.

But she had to.

Kami nodded to the volunteer and he called out to the auctioneer.

Again, Debbie turned to search the crowd and countered Kami's bid by going up another four figures.

Kami gulped. This was getting serious.

Getting?

It had been serious for a while now. They were talking figures that equaled long periods of work time for her to earn. *Long* periods.

Which was why raising her number and saying the

exact amount in her house down-payment fund would be absolutely crazy.

Her down payment that she'd been building for years in order to buy the house which was the next big item on her life list.

Her down payment that would give her the security of knowing she owned her home and that she'd never be homeless again.

Her down payment that proved she wasn't like her mother, that she didn't throw away everything she had on a man.

If she bid on Gabe, she'd literally be throwing away everything she had on a man.

But the bid was for a good cause, right? She remembered the emotion in Beverly's voice when she'd talked about why they'd agreed to the television bit.

What was making a down payment on a house compared to helping pay for the medical expenses of a precious baby?

Or bidding on the only man to ever make your belly do somersaults because you didn't want him to go on a date with his ex?

Or anyone else.

Ever.

Just you.

Or bidding because you had to prove to him that you did trust in him, in what was happening between you. What had happened between you.

Bidding on Gabe and emptying her savings would be something her mother would do.

It would be stupid in so many ways.

It would be the antithesis of everything Kami had always held important.

So her next move made no sense.

She raised her number and kept it held high as she quoted the amount in her down-payment fund.

"What?" Mindy gasped from beside her, reaching out to take hold of her arm, trying to pull it back down.

The bid taker repeated the amount to be sure he'd heard her correctly.

Number still held high despite Mindy's tugging on her arm, Kami nodded and repeated the amount.

Looking impressed, the bid taker called out her new bid to the emcee.

This time Debbie's gaze collided with Kami's and she stared at her for what felt like an eternity but could only have been a few seconds.

Myriad emotions shot toward her like daggers meant to knock her off her feet, no doubt.

No matter. Not Debbie, nor any other woman, could have Gabe without a fight. Without Kami telling him, showing him, how much he meant to her. If he couldn't forgive her stupidity, then she only had herself to blame.

But until she'd tried, she wouldn't give up.

Hand high with her number on display, Kami held her breath, waiting to see what the television hostess would do. Gabe had said she didn't like to lose.

One penny higher bid and she'd have Gabe.

His date package, at any rate. Because even if the woman bid higher, Kami had gone all in. All she had for Gabe—her heart and very being, her dreams, her future.

As they eyeballed each other, Kami was positive the woman knew she'd put all her cards on the table.

When the emcee pushed for a higher bid, the television hostess surprised the entire room, especially Kami, by shaking her head and saying, "I'm done. He's hers."

"Sold! To the pretty woman in the blue dress," the

emcee announced, eliciting a loud round of applause from everyone in the room save three people.

Debbie, Kami, and Gabe.

She'd just bought a day in Gatlinburg. With Gabe.

By using her house-deposit fund.

By proving that she was her mother's daughter and the acorn didn't fall far from the tree no matter how many times she'd sworn she'd never be like her mother.

She'd lost her mind.

But maybe, just maybe, she hadn't lost Gabe, a small voice whispered.

Gabe watched as a shell-shocked Kami was pushed toward the stage by well-wishers giving her high fives and hugs. The emcee held out his hand and escorted her up the couple of steps onto the stage.

"Little lady," the emcee said into his microphone, "make sure this fella gives you your money's worth."

"Oh, I intend to," she assured him, garnering a few laughs from the crowd, as the emcee escorted her over to where Gabe stood.

Trying to make sense of the fact that Kami had just bid on him—had won his bid—Gabe bent, kissed her cheek, then clasped her hand.

She didn't look directly at him, just nervously faced the crowd and gave a thumbs-up with her free hand. The event photographer moved around them, snapping pictures.

Gabe felt dazed, and not from the flashes of light.

The emcee called for all ten couples to come back onto the stage for photos.

While they were waiting for the others to join them on stage, Gabe took advantage of the moment to lean down and ask, "What changed your mind?"

"I… You're my friend. I couldn't not rescue you."

"Pricey rescue."

Not meeting his eyes, she nodded. "Guess I'll be staying in my apartment longer than I once thought."

What?

"You used your house savings to bid on me?" Gabe must have misunderstood.

Only he hadn't. Then again, hadn't he thought earlier that the bid had already escalated far beyond Kami's price range, even if she'd wanted to bid? Never in a million years would he have guessed she would use her savings. For him.

Her face was pale, but she nodded, confirming what he'd guessed.

"Why?" When she didn't look at him, he touched her face, turning her toward him. "Tell me why, Kami."

"We're being watched," she reminded him through clenched teeth. "Smile, Gabe."

She was right. He'd forgotten where they were, that they were literally on stage being photographed at an event that was important to the Smiths.

He smiled as several photos were taken, then escorted Kami off the stage. As soon as they were out of the spotlight, he turned her to him.

"Why, Kami?"

One blue-spaghetti-strap-covered shoulder lifted. "It was for a good cause."

He'd wanted her to bid on him, had secretly craved her taking that step and admitting she wasn't ready for them to end, that she didn't want him with another woman, not even for a second or for charity. But he hadn't meant for it to cost her so much.

It had cost her so much.

It had cost her everything. He knew how important

buying a house was to her, how long she'd been working toward that goal. Why would she throw her deposit fund away on him?

The only possible reason hit Gabe and he stared down at her in wonder.

No way could he let her give up her savings. "I'll pay for your bid."

Not quite meeting his gaze, she shook her head. "I placed the bid. Not you. Besides, I wanted to help Beverly and her family."

Gabe considered her a moment, trying to decipher if helping their coworker had actually been what had motivated her outrageous bid rather than how he'd taken her bid.

"Don't look now," she warned, "but we're about to be accosted. Will she hurt me?"

"You were the one saying how nice she was," he reminded her, squeezing her hand.

"That was before I snatched you away from her. Now I'm just plain scared."

Both Kami and Gabe had pasted-on smiles as they greeted Debbie and Jerry.

"I knew it," Jerry announced, sticking his hand out toward Gabe. "Congrats."

Staring at Kami, Gabe fought with the realization that she hadn't pulled her hand away from his even after they'd been out of the limelight, that she'd given up something she'd worked hard for to win him, something she held dear that gave her a sense of security. She'd gone out on a limb, for him.

Whether she'd realized it or not, Kami had made a monumental decision regarding their relationship.

Mainly, that they had one at all, and that it was worth

sacrificing for, fighting for, changing for, that it was worth trusting in.

Which left him feeling exactly what?

Kami stared at the television producer, a bit baffled. She'd won Gabe's date package. Nothing more. Surely the man's enthusiastic pumping of Gabe's hand was overkill?

"I knew there was no point in raising my bid once I realized you were the new bidder," Debbie admitted while the men were distracted.

"I couldn't have gone any higher," Kami confessed, although she wasn't sure why she was making her confession.

"I knew you were all in," Debbie admitted, "that I could win if I raised the bid."

Kami regarded the woman. "Why didn't you?"

"Because once you were all in there was no way I could win what I was really after." The woman shrugged, gave a self-derisive smile, then surprised Kami with a hug. "Congrats. May you hold on to him longer than I did. Something tells me you will."

"I, uh… Okay. Thanks," Kami blustered, wondering if she should check herself for knife wounds or maybe even claw marks. Was Debbie really so nice that she'd just conceded and congratulated Kami on her win?

The next hour passed in a blur. A blur where Gabe didn't leave her side as the emcee brought the event to a close and a loud round of applause went up at the large amount that had been raised by the event.

"Need me to stay to help clean up this place?"

In a bit of shell shock at everything that had happened and not knowing exactly what would happen next, what she needed to do next to make sure Gabe knew how she felt, Kami shook her head at his offer. "No, a group from the medical floor agreed to break down the decorations and pack them in boxes to be donated. The hotel will do any cleanup beyond that."

His expression unreadable, he asked, "Any reason you have to stay?"

Kami's gaze cut to where Mindy was giving instructions to the volunteers on what to put where and what to trash.

She caught her friend's eye, read Mindy's expression, which seemed to say, *Get out of here now 'cause I have this and I'm so happy for you.*

Kami's stomach twisted. Her friend might be happy for her, but Kami wasn't sure exactly what she'd gotten herself into.

Just what did buying Gabe's date package mean? Other than that she was financially broke and wouldn't be buying a home anytime in the next few years?

Could he forgive her for how she'd refused to trust in him? Refused to let her guard down?

Not that it had mattered. She'd fallen for him the same as if she'd dived in headfirst with all the enthusiasm her mother did time and again.

Fighting the nervous flutter in her belly, she forced a smile. "I can leave anytime you're ready."

Gabe regarded her for long moments. "Does that mean you're leaving with me?"

Why didn't he smile or say something to let her know where his thoughts were? Where his heart was?

Kami mentally took a deep breath, assured herself that she was not making the biggest mistake of her life, but she was all in now, so what did it matter?

Only everything. He meant everything.

Sure, she'd be fine if he walked away. She wouldn't wallow, or go into some deep pit of despair. She'd work and keep moving toward achieving her life goals, would save up another down payment.

But nothing would shine quite as bright without Gabe to share her life with.

She looked straight into his blue eyes and knew that she wasn't going down without a fight.

"Yes, I'm leaving with you. You're mine, remember? Bought and paid for."

Gabe's eyes darkened and one corner of his mouth slid upward. "Is this part of getting your money's worth?"

Finally, a smile.

That smile was priceless.

"Only if it's what you want, too. Like I've told you from the beginning, your only obligation to the winner is your date in Gatlinburg. Beyond that is up to you." Kami took his hand, clasped their fingers, and hoped her eyes told him everything she was feeling. Then she realized that hoping wasn't enough. She needed to tell him. "But, just so you know, I will spend every day between now and our 'date' making sure you know how important you are to me and that I don't intend to let you walk away from me ever again without doing everything I can to convince you to stay."

"Is that so?" His eyes danced with mischief as he reached out and caressed the side of her face.

"Everything in my arsenal," she assured him, turning her head to kiss the inside of his palm. "And I'm not above playing dirty if I have to."

Gabe's smile made everything else in the ballroom fade away, everything but him and the way he was looking at her, the way his hand cupped her face. He stared into her eyes with more emotion than she'd ever had directed her way.

Her heart squeezed in her chest, racing and slowing down in the same beat, making her head spin.

"As intrigued as I am by the thought of you playing dirty, I have to ask—what if I want a lot more than a date in Gatlinburg?"

Reaching up, she wrapped her arms around his neck. "Good, because otherwise I might have to ask for a refund."

"I've missed you, Kam."

Kami's cheek pressed against Gabe's chest as she listened to the beating of his heart. "Not as much as I've missed you."

"You going to tell me what happened tonight?"

Toying with the light spattering of hair on his chest, she considered his question.

Her gaze went to the photo on her nightstand. The photo she'd stuck inside a drawer after that first morning with Gabe and hadn't pulled out until after he'd walked out on her. Somehow, looking at the photo had been a balm to her achy heart, a reminder that Gabe had only done what she'd expected him to do.

What she'd pushed him to do.

"I decided I wanted to be more like her."

Gabe turned and looked at the photo. "Your mother? You look a lot like her."

Kami nodded. "I've spent my whole life doing everything I can not to be anything like her. It almost cost me you."

"What's so bad that you didn't want to be like her?"

"She loves with all her heart and that makes her an easy target to be taken advantage of."

"She's been taken advantage of a lot, I assume?"

"Time and again. My whole life I've been waiting for

her to finally learn, to finally realize, and not jump into love heart first. She never has. I thought that made her weak, foolish."

"Doesn't it?"

She rose up, propped herself on her elbow, and stared at him. "I thought so. Until I bid my entire house down payment at a charity auction."

"Let me at least halve the bid with you, Kam. Don't get me wrong. I appreciate what you did, what it meant, how it made me feel to know you'd do that for me, but I don't want being with me to cost you your dream."

She shook her head. "It didn't. That money bought me exactly what I need most. You."

He cupped her face, his thumb caressing her cheek. "Not just a Gatlinburg date?"

"As many dates as you'll have me."

He grinned. "Before this is all said and done, you're going to think you got a bargain."

She leaned down, kissed his lips. "I already do."

He wrapped his arms around her and hugged her close. "I'm never going to leave you."

"I know," she whispered back, knowing in her heart he spoke the truth. "Nor would I let you. Not ever again. Not now that you're bought and paid for."

He laughed. "I love you, Kam."

Her heart filled with joy, because Gabe wasn't just spouting off words. He meant what he was saying.

She knew because she recognized what she saw in his eyes, what she felt in his touch. It was what was in her own.

"I love you, too, Gabe."

EPILOGUE

"OKAY, GABE, YOU'RE freaking me out a little," Kami admitted, adjusting the blindfold he'd insisted upon putting on her prior to leaving her apartment.

"Oh, ye of little faith. Bear with me for a few more minutes."

"Yeah, yeah. Easy for you to say. You aren't the one being hauled around town blindfolded."

"You trust me, don't you?"

"With all my heart." She did. She and Gabe had been inseparable for the past six months and she was looking forward to their first Christmas together as a couple in just a few days.

"Good answer," he praised from the driver's seat of his car.

Not that she could see him thanks to the heavy blindfold.

"Honest answer. Are we there yet?" she asked, wondering where he was taking her. A show maybe? Or perhaps he'd rented them a cabin in Gatlinburg for the holidays? They'd had so much fun in the idealistic little town on their "date."

He'd certainly given her her money's worth a million times over. Every time she looked into his eyes and saw the love there, she thanked her lucky stars that he was hers.

"Has the car stopped moving?" he teased.

"No."

"Then we aren't there yet."

"Is this like a Christmas surprise?" she asked, hoping he'd give her a clue where they were going and why he was being so secretive about it.

"I'm not going to tell you, so it's pointless to try guessing."

Kami sat back in her seat and quietly contemplated the wonderful man she was so desperately in love with.

How could she ever have doubted him?

He'd loved her so fully, filled her heart so completely, she couldn't imagine not having his love or giving him hers.

"Hey, the car stopped moving," she said, realizing that he'd turned the engine off. "Does that mean I can take this off?" she asked, reaching for the blindfold.

"Not yet…" He pushed her hands away from the thick material. "…but soon. No peeking."

He got out of the car, then came around and opened her car door. A swoosh of cold winter air filled the car.

"Brr. I hope we're going somewhere warm," she told him as she took his hand and got out of the car. Letting him guide her, she took a few steps away from the car, then stood while he shut the door.

She wrapped her arms around herself, pulling her coat tight. "Gabe, I'm freezing."

She felt him move in front of her, undo the blindfold and remove it from her face. He stood right in front of her, his body inches from hers.

A goofy grin was on his face. A goofy grin that was full of excitement.

"What are you up to?" she asked, staring into his gorgeous blue eyes. She went to lean in for a kiss, but he stopped her by pulling back.

Her gaze went past him.

"Gabe?" She looked back at him. If anything, his grin had widened.

"Where are we?"

He gave an address.

"I mean, why are we here? Who lives here?"

"What do you think?"

She looked at the house beyond him. It was a beautiful home surrounded by trees and a big yard. "It's gorgeous, but… Gabe?"

"Do you want to go inside and get out of the cold?"

"Um…sure."

When they got to the front door, Gabe pulled a key from his coat pocket and unlocked the door.

"Whose house is this?" she asked again, stepping inside. Then she realized there was no furniture. "Gabe?"

"Come on. Let's look around." He grabbed her hand, guiding her through the house.

Kami took in the gorgeous staircase, the large open-plan living room with lots of windows, the oversized kitchen with granite countertops and solid wooden cabinets, the master suite bedroom-bath combo, three other bedrooms, and then back into the living area.

"Wow, it's a beautiful house, Gabe." Her gaze went past him to a package on the fireplace mantel. A package that hadn't been there earlier. Had it?

He turned, saw what she was looking at, and, grinning, picked up the present and handed it to her.

"This is for you."

"That's not fair. It's still a couple of days until Christmas and I didn't bring your present."

"You are my present. Christmas and every other day of the year."

Leaning forward, she plopped a kiss onto his lips. "Thank you." She glanced down at the box she held. "I can wait until Christmas if you want me to."

"Open the present, Kam."

She laughed. "Well, if you insist…"

Carefully tearing off the paper, she eyed the velvet box inside. The small square velvet box.

Her breath caught and she lifted her gaze to Gabe's. Joy shone there. Joy and excitement and anticipation and perhaps a bit of nervousness, too.

Hands trembling, she lifted the lid, then swallowed at the diamond ring glittering back at her.

Before she could say anything, Gabe took her hand and dropped to one knee.

"Gabe…" Her voice broke as she said his name.

"Marry me, Kam."

Not quite believing what was happening, she nodded. "Yes." Tears streamed down her face. "Yes. Oh, yes."

Smiling, he took the ring out of the box, took her hand and slid the diamond onto the third finger of her left hand.

Kissing her finger, he stood, then kissed her with so much love she thought she might faint from the enormity of it.

"The house is ours if you want it. I told the Realtor what I thought you'd want, what your likes and dislikes were, what the things you once told me you wanted in a home were. I've been looking for weeks. When I walked into this one, it felt like you, like coming home."

Kami stared at him in amazement at the lengths he'd gone to.

"I've talked to your mother. As soon as they're old enough, you get first pick of Bubbles's kittens."

Kami's eyes widened further. "She's going to let me have Sunshine?"

"The runty little yellow kitten you love all over every time we visit?"

Kami nodded.

"I think she's hoping you'll take that one. House, pet, me," he ticked off items, then grinned. "I'm hoping kids are somewhere on that list of yours, because this house is way too big for just the two of us, and someday, if we have a son, I'd like to name him after my dad."

Kids with Gabe. Only in her wildest dreams would she have ever dreamed any of this possible once upon a time.

"A son named after your father sounds perfect. I love you," she whispered.

"I know." One corner of his mouth hiked up. "Any woman who uses her life savings just to spend a day with me must be in love."

"Yeah, well, you make sure I get my money's worth," she teased, wrapping her arms around his neck and smiling at him with her heart in her eyes.

"Every single day for the rest of my life."

And he did.

* * * * *

MILLS & BOON

Coming next month

A SINGLE DAD TO HEAL HER HEART
Caroline Anderson's 100th book

'I can't offer you a relationship, not one I can do justice to, but I'm lonely, Livvy. I'm ridiculously busy, constantly surrounded by people, and I'm hardly ever alone, and yet I'm lonely. I miss the companionship of a woman, and I'd like to spend time with one who isn't either simply a colleague or my mother. A woman who can make me laugh again. I spend my days rushed off my feet, the rest of my time is dedicated to my children, and don't get me wrong, I love them desperately, but—I have no downtime, no me-time, no time to chill out and have a conversation about something that isn't medicine or hospital politics or whether the kids want dippy eggs or scrambled.'

His mouth kicked up in a wry smile, and he shrugged, just a subtle shift of his shoulders that was more revealing than even his words had been, and she forgot the coffee, forgot her foot and her common sense, and walked up to him, put her arms round him and hugged him.

'Scrambled, every time,' she said, her voice slightly choked, and it took a second, but then he laughed, his chest shaking under her ear, and he tilted her head back and kissed her. Just briefly, not long enough to cause trouble, just long enough to remind her of what he did to her, and then he rested his forehead against her and smiled.

'Me, too. Preferably with bacon and slices of cold tomato in a massive club sandwich washed down with a bucket of coffee.'

'Oh, yes! I haven't had one of those for ages!'

He laughed and let her go. 'I'll cook you brunch one day,' he said, and it sounded like a promise.

'Is that a promise?' she asked, just to be sure. 'Not that I'll hold you to it, and I'm not in a position to do a relationship justice either for various reasons—work, health…'

'Health?'

She shrugged, not yet ready to tell him, to throw *that* word into the middle of a casual conversation. 'Amongst other things, but—whatever you want from me, wherever you want to take this, I'm up for it.'

'Is that what you want from this? An ad hoc affair?'

She held his eyes, wondering if she dared, if she had the courage to tell him, to let him that close, to open herself to potential hurt. Because she'd have to, if this was going any further.

But there was nothing in his eyes except need and tenderness, and she knew he wouldn't hurt her. She nodded. 'Yes. Yes, it is, if that's what you want, too.'

His breath huffed out, a quiet, surprised sound, and something flared in his eyes. 'Oh, Livvy. Absolutely. As long as we're on the same page.'

'We're on the same page,' she said, and he nodded slowly and dipped his head, taking her mouth in a lingering, tender kiss. And then he straightened, just as it was hotting up, and stepped away with a wry smile.

Continue reading
A SINGLE DAD TO HEAL HER HEART
Caroline Anderson's 100th book

Available next month
www.millsandboon.co.uk

COMING SOON!

We really hope you enjoyed reading this book. If you're looking for more romance, be sure to head to the shops when new books are available on

Thursday 21st March

To see which titles are coming soon, please visit

millsandboon.co.uk/nextmonth